USA TODAY bestselling author **Katherine Garbera** writes emotional, sexy contemporary romances. An Amazon and iBooks bestselling author, she is also a two-time Maggie Award winner and has sold more than seven million copies of her books worldwide. She loves to hear from readers via her website, www.katherinegarbera.com

Charlene Sands is a *USA TODAY* bestselling author of more than forty romance novels. She writes sensual contemporary romances and stories of the Old West. When not writing, Charlene enjoys sunny Pacific beaches, great coffee, reading books from her favourite authors and spending time with her family. You can find her on Facebook and Twitter, write to her at PO Box 4883, West Hills, CA 91308, USA or sign up for her newsletter for fun blogs and ongoing contests at charlenesands.com

TEXAS-SIZED SCANDAL

KATHERINE GARBERA

STRANDED AND SEDUCED

CHARLENE SANDS

MILLS & BOON

First Published in Great Britain 2019
by Mills & Boon, an imprint of HarperCollinsPublishers,
1 London Bridge Street, London, SE1 9GF

Texas-Sized Scandal © 2019 Harlequin Books S.A.
Stranded and Seduced © 2019 Charlene Swink

Special thanks and acknowledgement are given to Katherine Garbera
for her contribution to the Texas Cattleman's Club: Houston series.

ISBN: 978-0-263-27191-1

0919

TEXAS-SIZED SCANDAL

KATHERINE GARBERA

This book is dedicated to Lenora Worth,
Julia Justiss and Eve Gaddy, my soul sisters.
Thanks for always listening and having my back
and giving me a safe place to share the ugly bits
of life and then helping me to see the silver lining.

Prologue

Sterling Perry has to be feeling pretty smug now that he has been released from jail on fraud charges. Damn. The evidence should have been enough to keep him in jail. Nothing is going as planned. Ever since Vincent— Well, that doesn't matter. No one has any idea who killed the man. I guess I'll just have to direct them toward a suspect.

Perry is the most logical choice. The hatred the thought of him stirs inside me makes me want to punch someone. But instead I just take a deep breath and fight to find the calm part of myself. The part that makes it easier for me to plot the demise of the men who have stolen everything from me.

It's not as if they are good men. They both have flaws, too many to name, and they've hurt many people along the way. Collateral damage like me. But not anymore.

Ryder Currin and Sterling Perry are doing a good job of torturing each other, which doesn't hurt the plans that have been put in motion. But it wouldn't hurt to get Sheriff Battle on the case. He's a bulldog and would help to add fire to the charges simmering around Sterling Perry.

That text was sent from Vincent on a Perry Holdings phone. Everyone knows that no one does anything at Perry Holdings without Sterling's approval. That should be enough to get the case focused back on Sterling.

Glancing down at the email that has just arrived, a feeling of self-satisfaction spreads throughout me. Ryder Currin has some employment issues. Interesting. It shouldn't be that hard to get the information into Sterling Perry's hands and then let him use his information to ruin Currin.

It's hard not to feel self-satisfied. So embezzling didn't work out. There are still a couple of irons in this fire. Both of them are going to pay for what they've done. No matter how long it takes.

One

Melinda Perry glanced at her phone as she put the last hot roller in her hair. She was trying to ween herself off her social media addiction. While she loved knowing exactly what her faves were doing, she had learned she functioned better with far less FOMO if she started her day with a mug of… She wanted to say hot lemon water, but she'd never been able to make herself acquire a taste for it. No matter how unhealthy it was, she always started her day with coffee, a teaspoon of hot cocoa mix and nonfat half-and-half.

She glanced at the clock on her vanity mirror; she was running ahead of schedule. "Okay, Jeeves, give me the latest society news from the *Houston Chronicle*," she said. She'd programmed her electronic assistant to answer to Jeeves because she thought it was funny to pretend she had a proper British butler and because it had been going off whenever the commercial for it had come on prior to that.

"Good morning, Mels. Here's today's headline— 'Heiress and philanthropist Melinda Perry is going hot and heavy with notorious playboy Slade Bartelli. Photos available on *Houston Chronicle* dot com.'"

"Okay, Jeeves, stop," she said, fumbling for her phone and opening the *Houston Chronicle* app. *Oh, no.* She didn't want to be on the society pages. She didn't want the world to know about her love affair with Slade.

Her family had been a hot mess for the last year and she had struggled to remain above it. Going about her business and acting as if everything were okay. Her father had been accused of running a Ponzi scheme, arrested and released from jail. Her sister was having a scandalous relationship with one of her father's most hated business rivals. And of course, she had started a romance with the son of notorious mobster Carlo Bartelli.

To be fair, Slade wasn't part of his father's crime syndicate and she had met him at a charitable committee meeting. He was an upstanding citizen but the media never seemed to care about that.

As soon as she opened the app, she saw a photo of herself and Slade embracing...okay, kissing. Hot and heavy kissing in one of the alcoves of the Houston Symphony at Jones Hall.

She felt panic rise inside of her and her pulse raced. She was hot and bothered not only from being exposed but from remembering that kiss. She had to end this. It was getting out of control. She was behaving in a way that didn't suit her at all. Sure, she was thirty-nine and, as her twin had pointed out, not getting any younger.

If not now, then when? That's what Angela had said when Melinda had shyly mentioned she was seeing someone different from her usual type of guy.

But this wasn't what Melinda had had in mind. She liked her charity work, her quiet life. Also, Angela had been very plain in her disapproval of Slade as a lover for Melinda. Not that she needed her twin's approval of the man she dated.

She heard the sound of Pixie, her miniature dachshund, barking and then her bedroom door opened and her sister Angela walked into the room. They lived in the same building and always nipped into each other's places. The design of the condo was an open concept on the main living level and then an upper-level loft that was the master bedroom, bathroom and a living/sitting room that Melinda used as a workout space.

"I thought you weren't sure that Slade was the right man for you. Didn't you say you wanted to be a mom? He's a legendary playboy, you know that, right?"

"No need to ask how you found out," she said. "I just didn't know if we were serious or not and I didn't want to make a big deal."

"That photo looked pretty serious to me," Angela said. She sat down on the tufted bench at the end of Melinda's bed.

Her sister had a thermal mug in her hand and looked fashionable as always. No matter how hard Melinda tried, she always felt like the serious, preppy twin. She knew that no one else would ever call her that, but she was the quieter twin, in fashion and in personality. If anyone should have been dating Slade, it was Angela.

"That picture... I had no idea anyone would see us, or I never would have kissed him like that," Melinda admitted.

"You're blushing! We're thirty-nine, Mels. It's time for you to stop blushing when you talk about sex."

"I wasn't talking about sex! Slade just makes me hot. It's not embarrassment, it's— Oh, never mind. What am I going to do?" she asked her sister.

"Do you like him?" Angela asked.

Like him?

She hadn't thought about it that way. He was so intense. She knew about his family's rumored mob connections, but when she was with him, he focused on her. He made her feel...like she was the only woman in the world. And the most passionate person he'd ever met. But honestly, she knew that was only because of him. Donald, her ex-boyfriend of eight years, always complained that she hadn't brought any va-va-voom, but with Slade that wasn't an issue.

"I know you don't approve of him. You've made that very clear and I'm not sure how I feel about him. He's on the art council, which is how we met."

"He's on the art council? I thought his family were all mobsters—which, by the way, concerns me."

"He's not a mobster, Angela. He is also the only grandson of Philomena Conti. So he's representing the family. I think Mrs. Conti had a hip replacement earlier this year, which is why he filled in at the meeting. We just hit it off. He likes art as much as I do. It was my description of a Van Dyck that made him notice me."

Angela stood up and walked over to her, putting her hands on Melinda's shoulders and making her face the mirror. She met her sister's gaze, avoiding looking at herself. She had the big rollers in because it made doing her hair easier, and she hadn't put on any makeup yet so her freckles were visible.

"Look at yourself," Angela said.

She glanced up at her own reflection. She always smiled at herself because that helped her start the day in a good mood. Angela smiled back at her as well.

"That man noticed you because of you," she said. "And it's about time that you found a man who can make you forget yourself at the opera."

Melinda sighed. She knew her sister was right. No matter what Slade made her feel, at the end of the day their lives simply didn't fit together. He was more Cristal champagne and parties at his penthouse and jetting off to Dubai than local artist openings.

"I know. Not the danger part—he's really not a bad man, Angela. But he's not for me either. Honestly, I sort of thought after we slept together, he'd move on to someone else," Melinda said. "But he hasn't. There's something between us that makes it hard to keep our hands off each other."

"Passion, Mels. Finally, you've found a guy who brings out the fire in you," Angela said. "But not a Bartelli. Find someone else."

Melinda shook her head. She didn't want the fire… Well, not all the time. Fire was dangerous. She knew that had led to trouble in her parents' relationship and she'd always striven to keep her life on an even keel.

But now she wasn't on an even keel. She was already really overdue for her period and she'd always been regular. Maybe she was having perimenopause. She had read an article that some women started to experience symptoms at her age.

She met her sister's eyes in the mirror and knew better than to bring up that subject again unless she'd taken a pregnancy test. As close as she and Angela were, there were some things that they both just kept to themselves and this was going to be one of them.

"If it were that easy, I would have done it a long time ago," she said at last. "I'm not sure where things are going with Slade, but we both know it's not going to last."

"Good," Angela said, giving her a breezy one-armed hug. "Are you okay?"

She wanted to nod but the hot rollers made her head feel heavy and awkward. "Of course. I'm always okay."

"Except I know that you're not. You said you wanted to be a mom…and suspected you were pregnant. Are you? Is he the father?" Angela asked.

She wasn't ready to talk about pregnancy. She hadn't even been to her doctor yet, even though she had bought more than a few over-the-counter tests. She hadn't gotten up the courage to take them yet. She might want to be a mom, but she had in her mind the way it should happen. She was a traditional kind of gal. She wanted Slade to fall in love with her—desperately in love—and propose marriage, to have a huge society wedding—where her father, sister and family weren't in the midst of a scandal—and then have a baby.

"I don't know if I'm pregnant," she said, dropping her gaze from Angela's in the mirror. She wasn't a big fan of lying to anyone, but she wasn't ready to deal with being pregnant while the *Chronicle* was running a photo of her and Slade kissing. "I mean, Slade Bartelli doesn't sound like the right kind of man for me, does he?"

Angela propped her hip on the edge of the vanity and looked pensively at Melinda's bedroom. For the first time, Melinda realized that her sister might be hiding something of her own. "Are you okay? How are your wedding plans coming along?" Angela had just announced her engagement to Ryder Currin.

"Yeah, I'm fine. Nice try, but we are talking about you," Angela said. "I don't know what to tell you. If you say Slade's a good guy… Well, I'm on your side. Just make sure you know what you're doing. While fire is good and I have always thought that's what you needed to shake you out of your routines and lists, it can also burn you. I don't want to see you hurt."

Melinda turned and hugged her sister, resting her head against her stomach. "I don't want you hurt either. Men are…way more complicated than they look on the surface."

Her sister laughed as she started taking out the hot rollers in Melinda's hair. "They are. Why can't they just be hot, right?"

"Yes. And sophisticated and like the things we like and then go away when we need to get back to real life."

Her sister laughed again. "If only we were in charge of the world."

"Someday," she said.

"Someday," Angela repeated quietly.

Angela left a few minutes later and Pixie came trotting into the room and plopped herself on her bed. Melinda leaned into the mirror to finish putting on her makeup and fixing her hair and then she got dressed for the day.

She took extra care to make sure her A-line skirt was

straight, and her blouse tucked in properly; she didn't like it when it was too loose around the waist. She tied the pussy bow at the neckline and then switched the contents of her handbag to the purse that perfectly matched her magenta skirt. She had a lot of work to do at her foundation and meetings this morning.

She put her sunglasses on the top of her head, patted Pixie's head as she walked out the front door, then took the elevator down to the lobby of her building. Downstairs, she was met by a barrage of flashbulbs.

Panicked, she ducked back onto the elevator. She went back to her condo, texted her assistant she'd be out this morning and then hit the treadmill. Walking always helped her figure things out. Things were definitely getting too complicated and now she knew she had to end things with Slade. No one had ever noticed when she kissed Donald.

Slade Bartelli tossed his phone on the passenger seat of his Ferrari Lusso as he backed out of his parking space at his downtown offices. He'd been trying to get in touch with Melinda since he'd gotten the news notification from the *Houston Chronicle*. And nothing. Total radio silence.

She wasn't a fan of too much PDA, which he admitted was cute and one of the reasons why he liked her. She dressed like a lady but kissed like…well, like his hottest, wettest dreams. She was different, and he liked that about her. But his gut—the same one that had always warned him when trouble was at the door during his childhood—was telling him that if he didn't talk to her, she was going to walk out of his life without a backward glance.

Part of him—the part that he was constantly fighting with—wanted to find the paparazzo who'd taken that photo and pound him. But he wasn't that kind of Bartelli. He was trying to be the man his nonna Conti had raised him to be. But there were times when he had to admit his dad's way was a lot more efficient.

He pulled up in front of Melinda's building, parking illegally out front because he knew the doorman would relish the chance to drive the Ferrari if the traffic cop came by. He saw the paparazzi as soon as he neared the building. They were snapping photos, calling his name, and he faced them with a snarl, ready to unleash hell or his version of it on them, until he heard the doorman calling his name.

Not Slade but Mr. Bartelli.

That's right. He was better than his mobster blood. But, he reminded himself, that didn't mean he was good enough for Melinda Perry. Despite the scandal that swirled around her family—he'd heard rumors that her father was implicated in a murder now—Melinda was always above it. She loved her family but she kept her distance. No one who looked at her would ever believe she was anything but good and kind. Things no one would ever say about him.

No matter that he had to remind himself of that several times a day.

"Johnny," he said, walking over to the doorman. "I'm here to see Ms. Perry. How long have they been here?"

"All day. I helped her sneak back onto the elevator. But they're persistent and won't leave."

"Have you called the cops?"

"Ms. Perry didn't want to. She said they're just doing their jobs."

Of course she did. She had a kind heart. "Let's get rid of them. I'll call the commissioner and take care of it. Also, will you keep an eye on my car? Move it if you need to."

"Yes, sir, Mr. Bartelli."

Slade walked into the lobby of Melinda's building and stood there for a moment, battling both sides of himself before he dialed his assistant and asked him to take care of the paparazzi.

"Yes, sir. Also, you had a call from your father. Not an emergency. He just wants to speak to you. And your grandmother expects you for dinner with Ms. Perry."

"Ignore my father. I'll take care of Nonna."

"Yes, sir."

He hung up with his assistant and immediately went to the elevator that led to Melinda's condo. He knew why everyone was interested in them as a couple. Because he was flashy and courted the media. It was the only way he knew to prove that he was aboveboard ever since he'd taken over running Conti Imports. He'd been under so much scrutiny that he'd hired a PR firm that had advised him to make sure everything he did was very public and had as much publicity as he could throw at it.

He'd never have guessed he'd like the attention as much as he did, but it suited him. He liked talking to the press; he didn't even mind it when they followed him around. But with Melinda, he knew that was just another mark against him. His dad was a rumored mob boss and Slade knew the old man had tried going clean a long time ago and he'd never been able to. That was another reason why Slade really liked working for his mom's side of the family.

His dad had one time said that once he took his job as a hit man, there was no turning back. And Slade never wanted to be on that path. As much as his gut always wanted him to take the easy way, he fought it and made sure he never did.

But Melinda messed up his gut. She had him so hot and horny he felt like he was eighteen and not almost forty. He hadn't been this turned on by a woman in a long time. But it was more than the sex that was fabulous. It was the way she poured herself into her passions like art and opera.

When he got off the elevator on the twenty-fourth floor and walked toward her condo, he hesitated. It would be better for her if he let her drift out of his life. He knew that media attention wasn't something she was going to enjoy. And he'd done a good job of keeping their relationship private. Until now, obviously. He had to admit that he'd done it not for her—well, not consciously for her—but more for himself. So much of his life was in the spotlight that it had been nice to have someone who was just his. No one knew about her, and he knew she liked it that way as well. Though she might say that his family name didn't matter to her, he knew it did.

Hell, he wasn't even sure that Nonna was going to approve of him and Melinda. And of all the people on the planet, she was the one who loved him the most and always thought he deserved the best.

He pushed the doorbell and heard Pixie barking in the condo, but there was no answer. He waited for a few minutes and then punched the doorbell again.

Pixie didn't bark this time, which made him suspect that Melinda was in there and didn't want to talk to him. He knocked on her door one last time. "It's me. Slade. Let me in, so we can sort this out."

He waited, not sure if she would open the door for him, and another minute passed before she finally did and he saw her standing there. Her long blond hair was pulled back in a high ponytail—the kind she favored—that accentuated her heart-shaped face. Her blue eyes were troubled, and she'd chewed off all the lipstick he was sure she'd put on that morning. She had on her workout gear, which showed off her athletic physique. Her skin appeared pale and she didn't smile when she saw him, which set warning bells off in his mind.

Melinda smiled at everyone. *Everyone.* The bellhop who opened her door, the barista who made her coffee, the doorman. She was one of the friendliest people he'd ever met. Now, though, she didn't step back to invite him inside.

"Are you okay?" he asked. He had no idea how to fix this. To be honest, he knew that she had liked their low-key relationship but this reaction... Was she embarrassed by him?

"I've had better days, but yes, I'm fine," she said, clearly lying to him as she had one arm wrapped around her stomach as if she were trying to hold herself together.

"I don't know how the media were alerted to our presence at the opera last night. I know my people didn't say anything," he said. "I've got a call into the police department to get rid of the paparazzi who are hanging out downstairs. We'll get on top of this and get it sorted out."

"Will we?" she asked. "Why?"

"Why? I thought we liked hanging out together," he said. "Isn't that reason enough? Why don't you let me come in and we can talk about it?"

She shook her head. "If you come in, we will probably do more than talk and I need to be clearheaded about this, Slade."

He smiled at the way she said it. "You are being clearheaded. I promise to be on my best behavior."

Melinda's building was sleek and modern, a tall high-rise made of glass and steel, but her condo was much like the woman herself, warm and welcoming. The entryway had an antique hall tree, on which she always kept a vase with fresh-cut flowers in it. Moving into the main open living space, he noted the two large couches as well as two armchairs, all in cordovan leather that he knew from experience were buttery soft and the most comfortable chairs he'd ever sat in.

Her coffee table was made of reclaimed wood, where she kept art books on her latest obsession. Right now, he knew she was researching Dalí for an exhibit the art council wanted to bring to Houston. But she also had a few magazines that she kept tucked in a basket on the lower shelf of the table. She'd even started storing the business magazines he liked to read there.

Her kitchen was demarked by a tall countertop with high-back stools. The cushions matched the colors of the large Cruz Ortiz painting that hung above her fireplace. The colors of the Ortiz painting were bright and reflected, in Melinda's words, the *vibrancy of Texas*.

She stood there between the living room and the kitchen, watching him with her eyes wide and troubled. He had done this to her. It hadn't been his intent, but he was bringing scandal to her door the way her father and her sister had. Something he'd promised himself he wouldn't do.

"I like it when you're at your best," she said, then shook her head. "See? No. You can't come in. I'm not me when you're around."

He didn't like the way she said that. As if he were a bad influence on her. "I think you're more yourself with me than you've ever been before."

Two

Melinda wished she'd left the door closed, but manners had forced her to open it and now the plan she'd hatched to break up with Slade and get back to her normal life wasn't going to be easy at all. He stood there, looking so hot, his square jaw with a little bit of stubble, his thick black hair curled a little on the top and his lips firm. And oh, her stars, she really wanted nothing more than to blurt out everything that had happened since Angela had left that morning. But she hadn't yet decided what she was going to do about anything.

"I'm actually glad you stopped by," she said. "Can I get you something to drink? Maybe some sweet tea or lemonade?"

"I'm fine. I'm more concerned that you haven't returned my texts or calls. What's up?"

"Oh, well, are you sure you don't want something to

drink? Even water?" she asked. She was stalling and though she normally prided herself on being brave and facing difficult situations, she was going to give herself a pass today. She really had more than one woman should have to deal with. An image of the seven— SEVEN—pregnancy tests she'd taken lined up on her bathroom counter flashed into her mind.

"I'm positive," he said. "What's going on, babe? I know you don't like the media spotlight, but it was one kiss and, honestly, the photo isn't that bad. Are you concerned that you might be linked to the rumors about your father? I know I'm probably the last man you want by your side while murder rumors are swirling."

The murder victim had been found at the Texas Cattleman's Club newest site in Houston, at her father's Perry Construction site, and the victim was Vincent Hamm, a Perry Holdings employee, and her father was on the short list of suspects.

She shrugged, searching for the words. She couldn't just blurt out that she liked to rise above scandal. That she expected more of herself and her family or that she didn't like for anyone to see her looking so...well, totally enthralled by him. Slade gave off that aura of danger and that was part of what drew her to him, but the truth was she didn't want the world—rather, her world, the Houston society circle she traveled in—to see that embrace and judge her.

"It's a lot of things. Frankly, I think we both know we aren't right for each other," she said. "I figured I was a novelty for you, and you'd get bored and break up with me before this."

"Yeah, well, I'm not bored. Are you?" he asked. His

tone was almost belligerent, but she could sense the vulnerability beneath it.

She'd learned that being Carlo Bartelli's son brought with it a lot of expectation of the kind of man Slade was. And he spent a lot of his time pretending not to be upset by being prejudged by his last name.

She chewed her lower lip before she realized what she was doing. She'd never be bored with Slade. He was exciting and everything that she'd always dreamed of finding in a man. But dreams weren't reality and she knew that better than most. She'd always wanted a picture-perfect family and hers was far from that.

"No, I'm not bored, but we really aren't cut out to be a couple. I mean, when I saw that photo I blushed remembering everything that followed. But you… What did you do?"

He came closer to her and she stepped back, which made him pause. She wasn't normally someone who backed down from anything, but honestly, she wasn't prepared to be in the middle of this kind of mess. It was one thing to stand on the sidelines and offer advice to Angela or sympathy to her father, but to have the papers talking about her? That wasn't in her plan. But heck, when had anything gone according to plan since Slade had come into her life?

"Are you afraid of me?"

"No, never," she admitted. "It's me. I have no self-control around you, Slade."

"From my point of view, that's a good thing," he said with that wicked smile of his that made her remember all the reasons why she'd kissed him at the opera the night before.

She felt the blush creeping up her neck and cheeks

and shook her head. She wished she could stop doing that, but she'd never been able to control it. "That's exactly what I'm talking about. The reason why we need to break up. I mean, is that too high school for us?"

"No," he said.

"No?" Which part was he saying *no* to? Did he think they should stop seeing each other? Or that the term *breakup* wasn't too high school? Why did she do that? She always asked complex questions because her mind was constantly running with a million thoughts.

"Both. We aren't breaking up and it's not too immature to say it. I'm not going to let one picture taken by some intruding paparazzo intrude on us."

She loved the way he sounded. So in control of his life and never letting the outside dictate who they were. But at the same time, she knew that it wasn't that simple. At the end of the day, rumors still abounded about him being a mobster, even though he had reassured her he wasn't part of his father's illegal operations.

And now there was an even bigger reason she needed to walk away from Slade. She was pregnant. All those home test kits had proven her suspicions.

From now on, she had to make all of her choices based on that. Before, it was okay for her to pretend that Slade was going to turn out to be one of the white knights she read about in her books. But real life told her that a man who lived as large as he did would never be happy with her quiet life.

She knew that.

She had to remember that.

She couldn't be tempted by the way he offered her everything she'd ever wanted.

She had to think of her baby.

"What are you thinking?" he asked. "You're looking at me with both longing and fear, and I'm not sure what to make of that."

She took a deep breath. "I'm thinking that as exciting as it is dating you, I know that there is no future in this. I think we should stop seeing each other."

"No."

She shook her head, not sure she'd heard him properly. She smiled and tried again. "I mean you and I really are two different types of people and it makes more sense for us to stop going out."

"No," he said again.

She took another deep breath. Sometimes people didn't take her seriously because she was soft-spoken and polite, and they took her ladylike manners and modest dress to mean she was a pushover. But Slade should know better. The fact that he didn't just cemented in her mind that they definitely weren't meant to be.

And he was making her lose her temper.

"You can say no as much as you want, but at the end of the day, my decision is final. I'm not going to go out with you anymore. I'm not going to be on the society pages kissing you. I know it seemed to you as if I were asking you what you thought, but I wasn't. I'm telling you. This is over."

This was worse than he'd thought, but he'd faced tougher situations. For a moment, Slade thought about just leaving. It was the lady's request, but he wasn't entirely sure that she wanted him gone. He had been walking a tightrope with Melinda since they'd met in a committee meeting.

He remembered that afternoon vividly. She'd been dressed very prim and proper, yet she'd made some hilarious comments under her breath to him while the meeting had been going on. Then apologized later because she'd said she was used to his nonna getting her sense of humor. She'd been such a contradiction that he couldn't help but want to learn more about her. So, he'd asked her out.

She'd said no.

He'd asked her out again, claiming he needed her help because he was representing the Conti family, and she immediately said yes. One thing had led to another and they'd wound up in bed. He couldn't regret any of it.

And he wasn't ready for it to end. If he believed that she was asking him to leave her alone because it was what she wanted, he'd do it in a heartbeat. But a big part of him thought it was due to the photo in the paper. She didn't like the limelight. She left that to her twin, Angela, and just kept to her quiet philanthropic work.

Her family had been one scandal after another lately and he knew that Melinda had been trying to rise above it while being supportive of everyone. Her twin was engaged to her daddy's business rival—Ryder Currin of Currin Oil—a man rumored to have had an affair with her mother years ago.

He knew he had to handle this delicately and if when he was done trying to convince her to give him another chance she still wanted him out of her life, he'd leave.

"I don't think you can just dictate things in our relationship," he said. "That's not really fair, is it? Is it because I'm a Bartelli?"

"Slade, you know I don't hold your family's reputation against you. You've assured me you have no part in that criminal world and I believe you," she said.

"Thank you for that," he said. He was always having to prove he wasn't a thug to most of the people he met. And as much as he was using the details of his life to make himself seem not good enough for her, he knew she'd jump to defend him.

"You don't have to thank me for that," she said, reaching out to gently squeeze his forearm. "You're a good man. Don't let anyone tell you otherwise."

"I won't," he said, taking her hand in his and running his thumb along the back of her knuckles. She shivered delicately.

"Is it because your family doesn't like me?"

"Seriously, if they ever met you, I'm sure you'd have them eating out of your hand in no time," she said. "You can be very charming when you want to be." She pulled her hand away from his. "I see what you're doing."

"What am I doing?"

"Trying to point out that there are a lot of good reasons for us to keep dating. But, Slade, you haven't taken into consideration that we are at our core very different people. I'm single, but there is a part of me that is always hoping that whomever I date will turn into Mr. Right-for-Me. I want the whole shebang—husband, family, big house in the suburbs—and when I'm being honest with myself, I can't see you as that guy to give them to me," she said.

He couldn't argue with that. "I'm not ever having kids, you know that. I don't want a child of mine to have to grow up like I did in the shadow of my father's reputation."

He'd told her that on the first night they'd gone out. They had stayed up until the early hours of morning, talking about life and family and just everything. He had been honest with her because she was Melinda and she was different from the other women he'd hooked up with. For one thing, she was his age and she didn't seem to be a part of the hook-up culture. He hadn't wanted to hurt her in the long run. He still didn't.

And when she framed her objection to their being a couple that way, it was hard for him to keep on with his plan to talk her into not dumping him.

"I get that. I know I'm not a family man," he said. "But I'm not ready to say goodbye, Melinda."

She tipped her head to the side, studying him for a long moment before she nodded. "I'm afraid if I don't end things now, I never will, and when you do walk away, I won't find the man I need who can give me what you are making me realize I want."

Her words just made this even harder. She wanted him to stay but to turn into the man she dreamed of. And if there had ever been a man who was made for Melinda, he was the polar opposite of that. He knew the gentlemanly thing to do would be to walk out that door and never see her again. She was too good, too honest for the likes of him. But as much as he wanted to believe he wasn't a Bartelli through and through, he knew he was.

And he wanted her for himself. All he'd have to do was pretend he'd reconsider, and she'd be his, but he wondered if he could live with himself if he did that. Nonna always said one white lie was all it took to start down the path to the gray area that his father operated in. One where crimes were framed in a way to make it seem as if there were no other option.

He had to find a way to convince her to give him another chance. Because he wasn't ready to let her go. Not yet.

Three

He knew that he needed to do something to win her back.

He had no regrets about the PDA at the opera the night before. He was never going to be able to keep his hands off her. She called to him like nothing else in his life ever had. It intrigued him and kept him coming back for more.

But she was still nibbling on her lower lip and looking over at him, her blue eyes full of regret, longing and resolve. That didn't bode well.

"I'm sorry about the press. I have my man on it and he's going to put a spin on it that's going to make this all seem like nothing but harmless fun," he said. "That's what you want, right?"

She blinked rapidly and shook her head. He tried to keep his mind on her emotional state, but she wore a pair of leggings that hugged her curves, revealing her belly button and midriff. His fingers tingled with the need to reach out and touch her, caress her.

When she was in his arms, none of the other stuff mattered. It didn't matter that he was the reason the social bloggers and society pages were following her. He was the scandal. Not Melinda. She had spent her entire life doing good deeds in her work as a philanthropist. He'd never met someone who always thought of others before themselves.

He did a lot of good work at Conti Enterprises but in his gut, he knew it was to prove he wasn't like his father. Somehow, he was pretty damn sure that tinged the good deeds.

Neither did his family name matter once he held her in his arms, nor the fact that they really were very different people. Only the attraction and the passion between them mattered. That and the fact that she liked walking on the wild side with him. He knew she wasn't used to dating a man like him. Sure, she'd dated wealthy bachelors but most of them had been doctors or lawyers. Not sons of dangerous gangsters.

Once again, he realized how much he hated that part of himself. He was constantly at war with that side of himself and it had cost him opportunities all of his life. He knew that one day it would cost him Melinda Perry as well.

But it wouldn't be today.

"Slade—"

"Don't. Don't do this. Give me a chance before you kick me to the curb," he said.

"I shouldn't…but I want to," she said, biting her lower lip again.

This time he groaned. He reached out and rubbed his thumb along her lower lip. She had the kind of mouth that always inspired wet dreams in him, even when he sat across the table from her at a charity meeting. He couldn't help it. She was so prim and proper when they were in public.

But in private…

She bit his thumb and then sucked it into her mouth. He put his hand on her waist—God, she was so soft—and then he drew her closer until her body was pressed against his. He ran one finger around the waistband of her leggings and then let his finger slowly move up her spine.

She shivered in his arms and arched her back, thrusting her pelvis against his. He rubbed his erection into the notch between her thighs as she parted her legs to accommodate his hard-on. She put one hand on his shoulder and tipped her head back. Their eyes met and he knew this would solve nothing.

He wanted to believe that a day spent burning up the sheets would make all their problems go away, but he knew it wouldn't. That this wasn't going to do anything but distract them for a little while.

And since he'd sort of gotten used to being a distraction for her while her father had been under suspicion of financial wrongdoing, it was a role he fell easily into. He liked it because this was the one time when it didn't matter that he was the son of a dangerous man—a reputed mobster who had a long list of crimes he was suspected of committing, though there had never been any witnesses to convict him.

Except Slade.

No. He wasn't going there now. He was holding this

gorgeous woman in his arms, and he planned to distract them both from the real world and their problems.

Cupping her butt, he lifted her off her feet and she wrapped her legs around his waist as he brought his mouth down on hers. That sexy mouth of hers melted under his and she pushed her fingers through his hair, holding him to her as she angled her head to deepen the kiss.

Her tongue rubbed over his and he sucked it deeper into his mouth as he moved toward the kitchen counter. It wasn't ideal, but it was the closest flat surface and he couldn't wait one more second. He set her down on the counter and stood between her spread legs. She didn't scoot back, still kept her ankles locked together, holding him with a grip that he knew he could break. But why would he want to?

He had everything that he'd always wanted right here in his arms. The publicity was a road bump, but they'd get past it and move on. They'd figure this out, but not right now. Right now, he had other things to focus on. Like the feel of her hand roaming down the front of his pants, cupping him and stroking his erection while she kissed the side of his neck.

"You like that, don't you?" she asked, her voice deeper than normal. A husky tone that sent shivers down his spine and made it damn near impossible for him to talk.

"Yeah."

She laughed at the way he grunted the word but then he took the hem of her sports bra in his hands and lifted it up over her head, tossing it aside. Her breasts were full and her nipples pert from being aroused. He reached down and cupped both breasts, rubbing his thumbs over her areolae until she was arching her back, thrusting her breasts toward him.

"You like that?" he asked her.

She just ran her finger around the tip of his erection until he was about to melt into a puddle at her feet. "Yeah."

He loved this. Loved the way she turned sex into fun. It wasn't a game of power with Melinda; it was always something they shared. Both of them enjoying every minute of it and neither one trying to manipulate the other.

Leaning down, he kissed the side of her neck, working his way lower. She smelled of her flowery perfume and the sweat from her workout, and it made him even harder. He loved that she always felt real to him. Not like she was trying to be someone else. Melinda was one of the few people he knew who was always just herself. She owned her life and that was a big turn-on.

He nibbled on her and held her at his mercy. Her nails dug into his shoulders and she leaned up, brushing against his chest. Her nipples were hard points—he glanced down to see them pushing against his chest. He shifted his shoulders, rubbing his chest over hers, and she leaned forward to bite his neck, her fingers going to his tie. She undid it and then moved slowly down the front of his shirt, undoing the buttons and pushing the fabric open until he had to let her go to get the shirt off.

He wore French cuffs because it was something that set him apart from his father, but right now he regretted it as he fumbled to get the cuff links off. Melinda brushed his fingers aside and took them off, putting them on the countertop behind her.

"I got you these, didn't I? I like them because they require a woman's touch," she said.

"Your touch…not any other woman's. Actually, every part of me requires your touch," he said.

She ran her finger down his chest, swirling her finger around his nipple before moving lower toward his belly button. "Every part? Not just this one?"

She reached below his belt and caressed his hard-on through the fabric of his pants.

"Every part," he said, but the words were raspy, and speech was quickly becoming harder for him. He just wanted to rip her clothes from her body and take her.

He always fought against his animal instincts with Melinda. He wanted to protect her from that darkness inside of him, yet she called to it. And sometimes her touch tamed it.

But not right now.

She enflamed him and it was only the sheer force of his will that kept him from acting like the animal he knew he was.

He slowly drew his hand down the side of her neck, taking his time to note all of the things about her that excited him. She had a scar on her upper arm that she admitted she'd gotten when she'd fallen out of her high school boyfriend's pick-up truck. He rubbed his finger over the crescent shape, watching goose bumps spread down her arm, and then her nipples tightened even more.

He ran his other hand down her shoulder blade to the line of her spine, slowly caressing her back. She rolled her back against his touch, her breasts brushing against his chest. Slowly he worked his way down her back, taking time to fondle the indentation of her waist and then moving lower until he reached the base of her spine.

He cupped her butt and drew her forward until he could rub his erection against the center of her. She dug her nails into his shoulders and arched against him as he palmed her buttocks. She moaned and rubbed herself against him.

He wrapped one arm around her waist and lifted her off the countertop. With the other hand, he shoved her leggings down. Once she realized what he was doing, she helped him, pushing the fabric down her legs until she was free. He stepped back and just looked at her, sitting naked on her kitchen counter and he almost came in his pants.

Her eyes drifted closed and he saw her chest expand as she inhaled. He reached up and cupped her breasts, running his fingers over her distended nipples. He loved the pink perkiness of them and the way they responded to his every touch. He rubbed his fingers back and forth over them until her head dropped back and her back arched. He needed to make every sexual experience they had top the last. With any other woman that might have been difficult, but not with Melinda.

"Slade, baby, do that again," she moaned as she tipped her head to the side, exposing her long neck. He couldn't resist leaning down to nip at it, sucking against the pulse that beat strongly there. Her hands fell to his shoulders, holding on to him for a brief moment, and then she moved her hands down his arms. He flexed his biceps, knowing how much that excited her.

No one had ever turned him on this quickly before. Somehow, she was a thirst that he couldn't quench and as much as he knew that made her dangerous, he couldn't resist her.

He liked that she couldn't resist him either. She arched against him as he leaned down and sucked one nipple into his mouth. He looked up at her, wanting to remember her like this—turned on, so full of need and want and knowing he was the only one who could satisfy her.

A few tendrils had escaped her ponytail, but he wanted to feel her hair against him, so he pulled the hair tie from it and she shook her head as her hair fell around her shoulders, curling just above her breasts. He buried his head in the soft strands and inhaled deeply.

He noticed her eyes were heavy lidded as her hips began moving against him. He felt himself straining against the zipper of his trousers and reached between them to pull the zipper down and free himself.

He fumbled in his pocket for the condom he had stuck in there before coming over. She took it from him and their eyes met. Something passed over her face and he started to ask her what it was, but then it was gone. She undid his belt and shoved his pants down his legs, along with his boxers. The elastic got caught on his erection and he stepped back to shove them down his legs, taking the condom from her and putting it on.

She looked like something from his hottest fantasies. There were moments when he wondered why it had taken him so long to find a woman like Melinda, but then he knew his younger self wouldn't have known how to handle her.

He leaned down and licked the valley between her breasts, imagining his erection sliding back and forth there. He bit carefully at her delicate skin, suckling at her so that he'd leave his mark.

"Enough foreplay. Take me, Slade," she said. "I need to forget everything except this for a little while."

Her words enflamed him because he wanted nothing more than to drive himself into her again and again. No woman had affected him the way she did. She seemed to accept him as the man he was. Son of a mobster and grandson of one of the richest, most prominent women in Houston. She seemed to understand that both parts of him made him the man he was.

She spread her thighs, leaning back on her elbows, beckoning him to her. He groaned at the sight of her. This was an image he hoped to carry in his mind for the rest of his days, even after this affair ended. He knew it would. He was poison to a good woman like Melinda, but not for the short term.

He stepped between her legs, cupped her buttocks and drew her closer to him. Rubbing the tip of his erection against her center, nestling it to the opening of her body. She shifted against him, wrapping her arms around his shoulders as he entered her. Just the smallest bit because he couldn't wait.

She reached between his legs and fondled his sac, cupping him in her hands, and he shuddered. "If you keep doing that, this is going to be a very short experience."

She squeezed him and sucked his lower lip into her mouth. "I don't mind."

He held her hips steady and entered her slowly until he was fully sheathed. Her eyes widened with each inch he gave her. She clutched at his hips as he started thrusting, holding him to her, eyes half-closed and her head tipped back.

He leaned down and caught one of her nipples in his teeth, scraping very gently. She started to tighten around him. Her hips moved faster, demanding more, but he kept the pace slow, steady. Wanting her to come before he did.

He suckled her nipple and rotated his hips to catch her pleasure point with each thrust and he felt her hands in his hair, clenching as she threw her head back and her climax ripped through her.

He varied his thrusts, finding a rhythm that would draw out the tension at the base of his spine. Something that would make his time in her body, wrapped in her silky limbs, last forever.

She scraped her nails down his back, clutched his buttocks and drew him in. Sensation feathered down his spine, his blood roared in his ears and everything in his world centered on Melinda.

He called her name as he came, collapsing against her chest. Her arms held him, one hand moving up and down his back, until his breathing steadied, and he shifted until he stood between her legs again. He looked down at her face and kissed her softly. He had no idea what he was going to do with Melinda. She wasn't the right woman for him, but he couldn't walk away.

He heard her doorbell ring and she looked at the two of them, still joined and naked.

"Who could that be?" she asked.

"I don't know," he answered. "Want me to handle it for you?"

She glanced at him as he stepped back and pulled

on his trousers. "No. I need to do this. Let's go and get dressed and I'll take care of it."

She picked up her phone from the table and glanced at the video app to see who was there. "It's my sister Esme."

He lifted her off the counter, caressing her as he did so, and she batted his hands away. "Not now."

"Give me a minute," she yelled at the closed front door as she dashed upstairs to her bedroom. He collected their clothes and followed her upstairs to her bedroom. When he entered, she was already twisting her hair back into a ponytail and wearing a flowery patterned wraparound dress that accentuated her curves.

"Hurry back," he said as she kissed him before running out of the room. He couldn't last long without her.

Four

Melinda dealt with her younger sister as quickly as she could. Esme had just stopped by to make sure she was okay after hearing she hadn't gone to work, but honestly, she wasn't. She wouldn't be until she was able to have a few minutes to herself to deal with the reality that she was facing. She knew it would be better once Slade was gone. He didn't want a child and she was thirty-nine and pregnant. She had no idea what she was going to do.

She walked into her bedroom and found Slade standing in the doorway to her bathroom.

Crud.

She'd completely spaced on the fact that the pregnancy tests were still lined up on the counter.

"So, this is why you are dumping me?" he asked, gesturing to the tests.

"No, maybe. I just know that you're not interested

in a family and unless all seven of those are defective, I'm definitely pregnant and it's your baby."

"This changes everything," he said.

"It most certainly doesn't," she said. "If you had felt differently, you would have already said so."

He shook his head. "No, I wouldn't have. We were talking possibilities. This is a reality. And there is no way I'm going to be that guy—the one who walks away from his kid. Oh, damn, this kid isn't going to have it easy."

She didn't know what Slade was referring to exactly, because he'd only once mentioned how hard his childhood was and somehow that was why he didn't want children. "Our child will be fine. We need to make choices that are best for the child, not what we want."

Because what she wanted was for Slade to suddenly confess he loved her and then demand a large fairy-tale wedding before she got too big for her dream dress. But that *was* a fairy tale and she knew it. Even if he did those things, she wouldn't be able to believe him. He'd been trying to talk her into continuing their affair, not starting a family.

"You're right. But everything we've seen with our work on the Coalition for Families shows that kids have a better quality of life when both parents are actively involved. We need to be making decisions together."

He had a point, but she wasn't ready to deal with this with him. Or anyone else. Her sister was still saying that Slade wasn't the right man for her. She'd had several concerned texts and emails from women and men on the various committees she served on, all warning her that Slade was bad news. And he was standing here looking panicked, yet trying to convince her that the child she carried should have both parents.

She just wasn't ready to deal with this. Not today.

Her phone started buzzing again, and she glanced down at it, shaking her head. Another media request for an interview. Slade came over and looked down at the phone.

"How many of these have you had today?"

"A million. That's an exaggeration, but it feels like that. I don't know what I'm going to do," she said. "I can't keep dodging them forever, and wearing a disguise every time I leave the house isn't going to work either. Eventually they're going to notice I'm pregnant and I don't know what to do."

Slade put his arm around her, and she let herself be pulled into his embrace, resting her head against his shoulder as he rubbed his hand down her back. His spicy aftershave made her pulse beat a little heavier, as did being held in his arms.

She wished she didn't react so quickly to him each time he touched her. It made it hard for her to keep her perspective and be sensible.

He tipped her head with his finger under her chin and then rubbed his thumb over her jawline, which sent a tingle of awareness through her body. She parted her lips and then licked them as they were suddenly dry.

He groaned, then leaned down to kiss her, his mouth moving over hers slowly and deliberately. She turned more fully into his embrace, going up on tiptoe and twining her arms behind his neck and holding on to him. He tasted so good and she closed her eyes, letting the worries of the day disappear and allowing herself to just be in the moment.

When she was in Slade's arms, nothing else seemed to matter, and though she knew she couldn't stay there, she wanted to. But that wasn't realistic.

She broke the kiss and stepped away from him. She didn't know what to say, but she felt lost and she hated that. She'd always had a plan for her life. Even when it didn't work out the way she wanted, she was able to take steps to course-correct and get back to where she wanted to be.

But this thing with Slade was different. The man he was in real life blurred with the fantasy man that a part of her had been waiting for all her life and that made it harder to be sensible. *Ugh.*

"I have a solution," he said. "And I think it's one you'll like, because it's respectable and it will give the media something to cover instead of your family's... troubles."

"What do you have in mind?" she asked. She wasn't going to pretend she didn't want to find a solution that would give her the best of both worlds, but she knew how the media could be and she wanted to maintain an image that was above reproach.

Something that Slade never had been, whether fair or not. He'd always had to work double-time to prove he wasn't in the mob.

"Let's get engaged."

Her heart fell to her stomach and she blinked, trying very hard to maintain a poker face. His suggestion was the one thing she'd secretly been dreaming of. How could he have known?

But she knew there had to be a catch because Slade wasn't the marrying kind. She looked at him, sure he'd lost his mind or that she'd heard him wrong. But he was smiling at her like he'd hung the moon.

Even as the words left his mouth, he was questioning himself. But his emotions were roiling inside of him like a hurricane brewing in the Gulf of Mexico and he felt like he was in a little dinghy, trying to ride out the storm. Pregnant? Holy hell, what were they going to do? He had never thought about being a father.

He tried to focus his thoughts. One thing at a time. Melinda was a respectable woman. She wouldn't embrace being single and pregnant until she had time to figure it out. Then it hit him. She tried to dump him after she found out she was having a baby. Did she think he'd be a horrible father? Was that why she was trying to walk away? She wasn't wrong, but damn that was a hit to his ego.

But temporarily engaged? Had he lost his ever-loving mind? Of course, Nonna would be thrilled. She adored Melinda. But if she found out Melinda was pregnant and he hadn't asked her to marry him, there would be hell to pay.

He wasn't the marrying kind. He had a lot of dark baggage inside of him. Still, what else could he do?

Panic washed over him like waves and he didn't like it. He hadn't allowed himself to be in a situation he couldn't control since he'd been fourteen. He was always in command of himself and the events around him.

Though nothing about this situation was normal.

He put his hands in the pockets of his trousers and stood there, trying to project a calm, in-control facade. But he was wigging out.

A baby?

A BABY!

He'd never wanted children, had always been careful until Melinda and now he was faced with a situation that he had to get out ahead of. He did it all the time at Conti Enterprises, he reminded himself. And he would use those same winning techniques here. The one area of his life that he had always had complete control over was his role as CEO at Conti. It was the one time when he walked into a room and people talked about his reputation as an executive and not a rumored mobster's son.

He could do this.

Melinda needed him to be that man. To show her that he wasn't going to cut and run. They'd do this together, he told himself, even though he felt a tingle of fear run down his spine. What did he know about staying in a relationship?

And raising a child?

What did he know about being a father?

His pulse raced faster and harder than it had the one time he'd been sitting in the back of his dad's car when his father had gone to "take care of some business." That night had changed Slade forever and he had never been able to look at his father the same way again. It had cemented in Slade's mind that the life his father lived wasn't for him.

This was another big change. The kind that he had to take seriously. His child... A Bartelli. He needed to ensure that the child was safe from rivals and from his father's gang.

An engagement—a temporary engagement— seemed to be the best solution.

He told her so.

He saw the expression that flashed on her face before she spoke. A combination of confusion and disappointment. "A temporary engagement? How is that a solution?"

"I know it sounds crazy but hear me out," he said. He'd always been famed for being quick on his feet, which was why he'd had so much success courting the media and driving the Conti business. Now he wasn't sure that winging it was the right thing to do. But there was no time for careful planning.

She shook her head. "I'm listening, Slade, but honestly, this is the craziest thing you've ever said to me."

"I agree," he admitted. "But this baby changes everything. You have enough to deal with already without having the media hounding you. I'm not throwing shade, but your family has been a hot mess lately. If we were engaged, our relationship will seem legit and it's a positive thing. It won't stop the speculation when you start showing a baby bump, but it will make it easier for me to be the point of contact. Trust me, I can frame it so they think we're head over heels for each other."

He knew he should throw out the word *love*, but he couldn't say that, not even to convince her. He didn't know if he loved her or if he would ever love her. Right now, he was focused on step one. Convince her to be his temporary fiancée and then they could move on to… Oh, my, the pregnancy.

For the first time, he looked at her belly and she seemed the exact same to him. He would never have guessed she was pregnant from looking at her, but he'd seen the tests; he knew she was. He also knew she had to be losing her shit over it. Neither of them had expected this.

He'd used condoms every time except that one night…when once hadn't been enough and he'd been too into her to even think of reaching for one.

He expected her to come with more excuses, more reasons this was not a viable plan. Instead, she surprised him.

"How would it work?" she asked, moving over to the padded bench at the end of her bed and sitting down delicately on it. She crossed her legs as she looked over at him and he had to take a moment to gather his thoughts because she looked so pretty and unconsciously sexy. He knew she was in her serious mode so he couldn't make a pass at her, but he wanted to.

"I'm thinking we both go to dinner at my grandmother's tonight. Nonna already told me to bring you, so she's expecting us. I ask you to marry me, you say yes and we make an announcement to the media tomorrow."

"Why are we doing it now?" she asked.

He smiled. She was working through questions that some of the more persistent reporters might level at them. He liked this about her. She was a rule follower by nature, but she wasn't used to dealing with a world that liked to dwell in the gray area. But the problems with her father were making her more aware of it. So she knew the speed bumps they'd encounter.

"The photo in the *Chronicle* forced our hand," he said without needing much time to think. "We wanted to keep our relationship secret for a bit longer, but now that the cat's out of the bag, so to speak, we decided to go public."

She stood up and walked over to the window that afforded her a view of downtown and stood there with the September sunlight cascading over her, making her blond hair seem even brighter and giving her an ethereal glow. She looked down at the city and he wished he knew what she was thinking.

If she said no to this, he was sort of out of options. He couldn't stand to walk away from her and he certainly couldn't leave her on her own. He didn't know what his father might do if he found out about the grandchild. Slade kept calm because he knew that he would do whatever he had to in order to protect Melinda and their baby and keep them safe from everything and everyone.

Especially his father.

"So, what do you say?" he asked.

Melinda needed a minute… Okay, she needed more like several days to process this. Temporarily engaged? That didn't sound like something she wanted…or was it? At least she'd have time to think and Slade would provide a barrier between herself and the media. He'd also provide an excuse to avoid her family…just until she got her bearings again.

But that didn't really seem fair. Of all the things that she'd thought she'd encounter this morning when she woke up, this wasn't it.

"Okay. If we do this, how would it work? I mean, would we be pretending for a few months? And then I'd say I was pregnant, and you don't want a family and we'd break it off?" she asked. She needed to know all the rules for this engagement. She had to have parameters because obviously when she just went with her instincts, things happened. Unexpected things like a baby.

She still wasn't completely comprehending the pregnancy. She just wasn't the kind of girl—woman, she supposed she should say—who things like this happened to. She was the sensible twin. The quiet twin. The prim and proper twin. The actually-contemplating-a-temporary-engagement twin.

Oh, my stars. How am I going to handle this?

"Why don't we play it by ear?"

She shook her head. "No can do, buster. I need to know what's what, so I don't start to fall for the lie. It's easy for you because you never wanted a wife or a child, but I kind of always wanted a kid and a husband. I just don't want to let myself fall for something that's not real. So, if we are going to do this, I want to know when it ends and how."

He didn't like that. She could tell by the brief tightening of his mouth and narrowing of his eyes, but he covered it quickly with a flashing smile. "Of course, my darling, whatever you want. We'll sort out how it'll work. We just need some time."

"Your *darling*?"

"Unless you hate it," he said. "I think some endearments might help sell the whole head-over-heels thing."

"I don't think we have to do that," she said quickly. The last thing she wanted was Slade pitying her and pretending to love her. And he hadn't mentioned anything permanent before this or called her by a pet name. "We're both of an age where people will think we did this deliberately, not that it was an accident. I think it's better to play it like two rational, mature people."

He moved closer and she backed up till she felt the

bed against the back of her knees. "Are you afraid of what will happen if we act like a couple in love?"

He stared at her with that intense gaze of his and she felt like he could see straight to her heart where her deepest fantasies resided. The fantasy of him turning into her white knight. That totally-improbable-but-also-sort-of-what-she'd-like fantasy. She wanted to look away, but she forced her gaze to hold his. "I've never been afraid of a man, Slade. I'm not going to start with you."

"Touché, darling. You are one tough cookie. That's why I have to constantly stay on my guard around you," he said.

"Stop flattering me. One of the things I liked about you was that you didn't treat me like everyone else does," she said, then realized she was saying too much. She didn't need to let him know that his seeing the real woman behind the preppy exterior had been part of why she'd let down her guard.

"Okay. How about this?" he said. "I'll go and leave you to your thoughts. I'll pick you up at seven for dinner with Nonna—unless you don't want to come?"

"I'll come. I'll see you at seven," she said.

"Text me if you make your decision. I want to talk to Nonna before anyone else knows," he said.

One of the many things that she liked about Slade was his closeness to his grandmother. It always made her wonder why he was so dead set against a relationship, given how tight the two of them were. "I will. I just need a little time to myself to sort this out. You arrived just after I'd taken the last test."

"I understand," he said, squeezing her shoulder. "Why did you get so many?"

She rolled her eyes to the side. "I wanted to be sure. You know they aren't totally accurate."

"I do know that," he said.

"Oh? Have you had a pregnancy scare before?" she asked.

"Not since I was twenty. After that one, I decided that I needed to be more careful," he admitted.

"I've never had one before this," she said.

He laughed but it was dry. "I guess that's one more thing that makes me different from the rest."

She knew he was referencing his rumored mob boss family ties and she couldn't help but get upset for him. She might not want to be temporarily engaged, but that had nothing to do with how others thought of him.

"What makes you different, Slade Bartelli, is that you are genuine and never put on airs the way so many other men I've met do. You're honest and true and you don't let anything stand in your way. I've never met a man like you."

He looked away from her and when he turned back, he nodded. "I don't know that I'm as good as you just made me sound, but you do make me want to be a better man."

"I can't imagine how you'd be better than you are now," she said. He was a good man because he was constantly weighing the consequences for every decision. She liked that about him, but that didn't mean she wanted to find herself trapped in a temporary engagement to him. She knew, though, that if he'd asked her, he'd already run some sort of calculation in his head and this was the best solution.

She wanted to believe that it was because he wanted to protect her, but a big part of her was afraid it had more to do with him. Slade had worked so hard to prove he was better than his gangster daddy; the last thing he'd want was a baby mama who was pushing forty.

Slade knew the battle he always waged within himself. He knew he was always one footfall away from stepping over the line and becoming Carlo's son. But he fought it. The thing was, when he was with Melinda it was easier. She made the battle raging inside of him not as intense, and he didn't want to let that go.

Of course, now that she was pregnant that changed things a bit. He was panicking and doing his usual bid to ignore it and it was almost working.

Or had been until she'd decided that defending him to himself was the thing to do. She had an innate goodness that he'd rarely encountered in anyone before, even his nonna. Philomena Conti was a very kind and nurturing woman, but she was also tough as nails, having to make some hard decisions running the Conti empire since her husband's premature death in Vietnam in the 70s. Slade had taken the helm on his twenty-eighth birthday.

Melinda seemed the type of woman who'd never had to make those choices or if she had made them, the impact hadn't tainted her.

She wasn't naive or anything like that. She could hold her own with anyone, but she did it in a way that made the person she was going toe-to-toe with wish they'd never upset her.

He needed to stop extolling her virtues. He needed to get out of her condo. Turning to the bedroom door, he threw over his shoulder, "I'll see you at seven."

"I might jot down a few ideas for how this temporary engagement will work and then text it over to you," she said, following him. "Will that be okay?"

No. He didn't want a bunch of rules he had to follow. He really didn't do well with that type of thing. But she'd said she needed it and he was trying to protect her, keep his grandmother happy and his father far away from her, so he was going to have to go along with her ideas. "Sure, that would be fine. Send it when you have it ready."

He walked out of her bedroom but when he got to the front door, she reached out and caught his hand, squeezing it. "We're going to figure this out and give this kid the best shot it has for a great life. I really believe in us."

"Great." He realized he sounded a bit sarcastic, which suited his mood that was quickly heading south. "Once we know what we're doing, I'm sure it will make us both feel more confident."

But he wasn't sure. He had come from a mob family, she had come from a broken family and her mom was rumored to have had an affair with another man. Both of them were almost forty and had spent the bulk of their lives alone. That had to mean something.

Or else it was just him going insane.

"Thanks for being so chill about this," she said. "And for giving me the space I need."

"Of course," he said, pulling her close and kissing her. But it was different now. His mind reeled with all the things that were implied in this embrace. She was carrying his baby, she wasn't his and for the first time that mattered to him.

He'd never been one of those guys who had to have a

woman committed to him, but thinking about Melinda walking away—which she might do—he felt a need to put on the charm and convince her to stay.

Maybe he should take her to bed. She never said no to him when they were intimate. He tried to deepen the kiss, angling his head to the side and sliding his hands down her back to cup her butt and pull her more fully against him, but she twisted her head away.

She turned back to face him, and their eyes met. "That's a surefire way to muddle my thinking."

"And a surefire way to cement mine," he said.

"This can't just be sex anymore. It's not just the two of us anymore," she said.

That's why he wanted sex. He needed it, so he could lie to himself and convince himself that nothing had changed between them. That once he walked out the door, things were going to stay okay. But he knew they wouldn't. Nothing was going to be like it was before.

It wasn't the first time his life had done one of these huge shifts and to be honest, he'd hated it last time, so he was pretty damned sure he wasn't going to love it now.

But this was Melinda and she deserved the best he had to give. Kissing her on her forehead, he let her go and stepped away. "You're right. I'll see you later."

He walked out her front door and down the hall toward the elevator, making sure he didn't hesitate until he was out of her sight. Then he paused. For the first time since he'd seen all those pregnancy tests on the bathroom counter, he allowed his emotions free rein. His hands shook and he had that nervous sensation in the pit of his stomach. A heady cocktail of both fear and excitement.

A baby.

His baby.

His and Melinda's.

He should take a page out of her planner and go make some notes on what to do, but he didn't need that. His list was pretty damn short. Make sure the kid was nothing like his dad.

Five

As soon as Slade was gone, Melinda called her sister. Her phone went to voice mail, which it did a lot lately. She was worried about Angela. It was hard being in love with a man their father hated. Ryder Currin. The man who many believed had had an affair with their mother and who had framed their father for embezzling. But Angela loved him, and as a woman who was pregnant with her lover's baby, Melinda got it. The heart didn't always follow the most well-laid plans.

She almost let herself be distracted by that. Almost let herself focus on her twin instead of the very big problem in front of her. It would be so much easier to try to deal with Angela's issues instead of her own.

Her phone pinged with a reminder and she glanced down to see she had forty minutes to get to the board meeting for Help Houston Read. It was a charity that she had cofounded with one of her sorority sisters almost ten years ago. They worked on making sure that every kid had a library of books at home. It was an idea they'd borrowed from Dolly Parton, who had started doing it in her home state of Tennessee.

She hurried into her bedroom, showered and changed back into her A-line skirt and blouse with the bow at the collar. She took her hair down from its ponytail and then fluffed it around her face before grabbing her catchall bag, a Louis Vuitton that had been her gift to herself when she'd started the foundation. She made sure she had her planner and notepad, ignored the pregnancy tests on the bathroom counter and walked out the door.

She took the elevator to the ground floor and walked quickly through the lobby. There were no photographers waiting and the doorman smiled at her as she approached.

"Mr. Bartelli took care of the scavengers, so it's all clear," Johnny said.

"Thank you for letting me know," she said, putting on her wide-frame cat's-eye sunglasses as she stepped out into the Houston sun. She kept her head held high and her posture straight as she walked to her car. It was a VW Passat because she liked small cars that weren't too ostentatious.

She made good time to her meeting and realized once she was seated in the conference room with a large glass of sweet tea in her tumbler that she'd almost forgotten about Slade, the engagement and the baby. Almost.

"Hiya, Melinda," Carly said, walking into the room with a smile on her face. Her sorority sister and co-founder was always someone she was happy to see. "I guess I don't need to ask if you had a good time at the opera last night."

"Girl, you don't even know the half of it," Melinda said. "I have no idea how that picture got into the *Chronicle*."

"He's big news for that page and you are seldom seen outside of charity events, so they probably felt like they got the scoop of a lifetime," Carly said.

"They did."

"How are you holding up? I know that kind of publicity isn't your thing."

"It's not, but I'm doing okay," she said. Then she remembered that Slade wanted them to be engaged. She hadn't decided yet, but she knew she should start laying the groundwork in case they did it. "We've been dating for a while."

"I suspected you had a new man but had no idea it was Slade Bartelli. That is one hot-looking man."

She blushed. He was a hot-looking man and she made no bones that she liked the way his ass looked in his custom-made tuxedo, but she also liked the way he made her feel like what she was saying was important. Whenever they were out together, she had never seen Slade looking at another woman or being distracted by his phone—which was saying something because his phone pinged constantly with updates, messages and media alerts. But when he was on a date with her, he made her his priority.

"He is," she said. "No denying it."

"But you're not usually the type to fall for a great pair of biceps. Remember Antonio? He tried for months to get you to go out with him," Carly said, sitting down across from her and taking her laptop from her bag.

Melinda already had her laptop set up and glanced down at the screen as a notification popped up in the right corner, letting her know that she had over a hundred new social media tags.

Ugh.

"Antonio was all smoke and mirrors. Sure, he looked hot but the man had never heard of Dalí. Let's face it, if you're on the art council, you should at least have heard the name before," Melinda said.

"Agreed. Not saying you should have hooked up with Antonio. I'm simply curious why Slade," Carly said.

"He's smart and funny and sexy. I mean, there is a part of me that knows there is a dark side to him, but when I'm with him, he seems…well, too good to be true," she admitted. She knew that no man was perfect and yet when she was with Slade, everything seemed ideal.

"How long have y'all been dating? You know how it is when a relationship is new," Carly said.

"Not too long. A little over six weeks," Melinda said. Her friend had a point. The relationship was new. She'd been trying to be her best self as Slade was probably doing as well.

"Wait until you hit your first road bump and see how he reacts," Carly said. "That will give you the measure of the man."

Carly had a point, which she allowed herself to think about as the rest of the committee slowly came into the conference room. The pregnancy should have ruffled

Slade. Shown her more of the real man behind the gentlemanly image he'd been portraying for her.

But it hadn't.

Other than his temporary engagement idea, but even that had been framed in a way to benefit her.

It made her wonder if he was hiding something.

Something dark and dangerous.

Something... Bartelli family–related.

Though Slade had always assured her he had no part in his father's business, there was an edge to the man who was her baby's father that she'd never allowed herself to dwell on. Perhaps it was time she did.

Slade was ready for the press conference to discuss his latest project. Conti Enterprises was a multinational business, the bulk of which was made up of shopping malls and a global shipping company. Their malls were the best and the most popular destinations around the world.

His assistant had texted him the talking points in the note function of his phone and Slade was ready to do this. He smiled and then jumped up and down a few times. Jumping helped quell his nervous energy. He had learned early on that when he was nervous, he looked like he was hiding something and the media always assumed it was something illegal.

He shook his head, put his shoulders back and reminded himself he was the biggest badass in Houston before going into the press conference. In the audience, he saw many familiar faces but also a few reporters he'd never seen before and one or two photographers he was sure were paparazzi.

He gave his prepared remarks, talking about an innovative new shipping design platform they'd be using going forward that would reduce their carbon footprint and create more jobs in areas that needed them. The project had been close to his heart for a while, so he was glad to see it finally fully operational.

"I'll be happy to take any questions now," he said.

"Are you and Melinda Perry a couple now?"

"I'd rather talk about the new shipping platform," he said.

"I have your press release and my society editor asked me to find out what's the deal with Melinda Perry. She's usually not in the news, and we know that her family has been at the center of some…let's say, interesting issues lately."

"Melinda and I serve together on a committee for the arts and we have been dating, but you know I don't really like to talk too much about my personal life."

"So I can confirm you are a couple?"

"Sure," he said, starting to feel a little hot under the collar as he wasn't 100 percent sure what Melinda wanted him to say. But he decided to just give them enough to hopefully make the story die down.

"Do you think you are more acceptable to her now that her father is out of jail but still under suspicion for murder?" another reporter asked.

"I'm willing to answer questions that are legit, but I won't trade in gossip. I've never been one to credit alleged accusations or anonymous tips. Melinda Perry is the most upright and honest woman I know," he said. "Melinda and I aren't our parents and neither of us should be in any way associated with any allegations against our fathers."

"Well, that's a nice thought but let's face it, she has

a lot of money at her disposal to do all of her charitable work and it had to come from somewhere. There's bound to be questions about—"

"Enough. If you ever met Melinda, you would know that she's not the type of person who would engage in any criminal activity. For years, I've lived under the cloud of being a Bartelli, so I know what it's like to be unfairly tainted by association. Melinda doesn't deserve this. And I'm done taking questions for today."

He turned and left the room, knowing he could have handled that last part better but really he'd almost lost his temper. He didn't mind getting the side-eye himself; he'd grown up being treated that way. He'd been the kid that most parents didn't want as a friend for their own child. He'd been denied several things before he made his own name for himself.

It hadn't been easy.

But Melinda shouldn't have to be the one to deal with that. He was tempted to go and see Sterling Perry and tell the man to step up and be the father that Melinda needed him to be, but Slade knew that men like Sterling put themselves first. There was a cloud of suspicion around him and he should be taking steps to make sure his children weren't painted with the same brush, but instead he was busy trying to blame his rival Ryder Currin in the media.

His assistant was waiting for him in the hallway.

"I'm sorry about that. I gave them the talking points and did reiterate that you'd only be taking questions about the new shipping information."

He nodded. "It's not your fault. You know how they can be. I need you to reach out to Melinda's assistant and get her schedule. I think there is a good chance that she's going to have more paparazzi on her tail than she expected," he said.

His assistant nodded and left, and Slade went into his office and fought the urge to put his fist through the wall. The timing of that kiss last night showing up in the paper couldn't have been worse for the two of them. Her family name was tarnished, and she had enough to deal with without having to answer questions about the two of them.

And the baby.

He couldn't forget the child that she was carrying. The one that he wasn't sure he wanted to raise but knew he had to protect. And it seemed as if it wasn't just the Bartelli side that threatened Melinda and their baby, but also the Perrys. He needed information and one of his old friends Will Brady had just settled down in Royal, so he might have some intel that could help Slade understand what was going on.

Will was a computer genius and occasionally Slade hired him to dig around on the internet and find information before he did business with someone he didn't know.

He texted Will and asked him to look into the Sterling Perry thing. Then resisted the urge to text Melinda. She said she'd get back to him if and when she'd made her decision and she'd always been a woman of her word.

But that didn't ease the feeling in his gut that something bad was about to happen. He thought about the message his assistant had given him from his dad earlier. Was his father the cause of the bad feeling? Or was it simply that for the first time in his life, he had to look out for someone else and he wasn't sure he could protect Melinda?

* * *

Melinda hit the mute button on her phone when her dad's number popped up. He was the last person she wanted to talk to. She'd been doing her best to be there for him and to help him through this trying time, but he hadn't approved of her and Slade being on the same committee and she was pretty sure he was about to issue some sort of autocratic decree regarding her and Slade. And as much as she always tried to frame her father's overbearing ways as the only way he knew how to love her, she wasn't in the mood to be placating.

The meeting had gone well but there had been paparazzi and gossip bloggers waiting when she'd exited, and it had taken all of her willpower to just smile and walk calmly around them and not run for her car like she wanted to.

She knew that Slade thought an engagement would be a nice barrier between her and the media, and she had to be honest and admit she was beginning to believe that it would work. With her dad just out of jail on the dropped embezzlement charges, and the rumors swirling that he might know more about the Vincent Hamm murder, and her own scandalous embrace captured at the opera, maybe an engagement would be just the thing to make them all lose interest.

"Ms. Perry, can you confirm that you are dating Slade Bartelli?"

She kept walking, tried to keep her shoulders straight and her head up. Her personal life was no one's business but her own. She hadn't used the media to build her business or her charities. She'd done it through hard work.

"Don't want to talk about that?" the guy said. "What

about the rumor that your father is a suspect in the Vincent Hamm murder? Want to discuss that?"

She took a deep breath. She knew that engaging the guy would be akin to trying to be reasonable with a quack on social media. Whatever she said or didn't say he was going to spin to fit his own narrative.

"You always were the boring Perry. Interesting that you are now the one in the spotlight. Some think it's because you're trying to cover for your father and the illegal activities of Slade Bartelli."

That hit a nerve. She lost her temper, turning on her heel to confront the portly man following so closely behind her. "I can see, sir, that you are a man with very little manners and probably even less brain, so I'm going to speak slowly and use small words, so you don't get confused. My father is a good man who hasn't done anything wrong. And Slade has spent his entire life being more transparent about every dealing he's ever had than most businesses you consider legitimate. You can make stuff up about them all day, but in the end, it will only prove that you're a complete moron. That's all I have to say."

She turned back around, hurried to her car, got inside and turned the air conditioner on full blast so that maybe it would cool her down. She put her sunglasses on and slowly drove out of the parking lot despite the fact that she wanted to speed away. She wanted to race out of Houston and keep driving north until she reached Oklahoma. Someplace where no one would know her and she could find some peace and quiet.

It was impossible to say that she needed time to think away from Slade when everyone she encountered kept bringing him up. She pulled into the CVS parking lot at the next block and drove around back and just parked the car. She put her head on the steering wheel and closed her eyes.

In all her days, she'd never expected her family name to be raked through the mud. She had also never thought that she'd be pregnant and having an affair with a bad boy…man. But Slade wasn't a bad man.

She wished there were some way she could be Slade's temporary fiancée and not fall in love with him. But she knew herself. She couldn't walk around telling people they were getting married and not fantasize about it.

In her mind, she easily pictured the wedding dress she'd choose—a simple Givenchy satin gown with a ballet neckline and fitted bodice with a flowing skirt. She could picture it in her mind and that was a mistake. *Temporary*, she reminded herself. That was all he'd offered her.

Something to get her through the odious reporters who wouldn't stop with their questions.

And unless she really did leave Texas, there was no way she was going to be able to distance herself from Slade. Normally she'd ask Angela for advice, but her sister wasn't returning her calls at the moment and her father… Well, he'd never been an advice giver.

This decision was going to be all on her.

And to be honest, she knew what she was going to do. Had known since the moment that he'd said those ridiculous sweet words. She was going to say yes and become Slade Bartelli's fiancée in the eyes of Houston and the world. Everyone would see a couple who cared deeply for each other and had decided to commit their lives to one another. She felt tears burn her eyes because it was the secret dream she'd always harbored. But maybe it was time to be realistic. Maybe this temporary thing with Slade was all she'd have when it came to men. But she would have a child.

A family of her own.

One where no one was demanding. She and the child would have each other. Already Melinda felt better. And Angela. The child would have a wonderful auntie too. And if sometimes Melinda wished that things had worked out differently, then she would keep that to herself. She lifted her head off the steering wheel, wiped her eyes and picked up her phone.

This was a business deal. A PR stunt to distract the society reporters and bloggers, and when the heat died down, they would go back to their normal lives. Slade had been honest about not wanting a family and she knew that at the end of the day, she'd be raising the child on her own.

She was okay with that.

Really, she was.

And maybe if she repeated it often enough to herself, she'd start to believe it.

Six

Dinner at Philomena Conti's house was something that Melinda always looked forward to. Given all the craziness in her life currently, she definitely needed it tonight. She and Slade had postponed the previous week. She just hadn't been ready to talk to anyone about the engagement until they'd had time to sort a few details out. It had been a week since the news of her and Slade had broken, and she was no closer to figuring out what to do next now than she had been then.

"Jeeves, play my soothing playlist."

"Playing your soothing playlist," the in-home automated assistant said.

Melinda went back to getting ready, thinking about Philomena. She had a joie de vivre that drew people to her. Over the years since they had started serving on the art council together, Melinda had found her to be almost a kindred spirit.

Philomena lived her life in a bolder way than Melinda did, but at their core, they both sought to help others and surrounded themselves with nice people. She'd debated a number of times about driving herself versus letting Slade pick her up and, in the end, since she'd decided to go ahead with the engagement, he would be driving her.

As she zipped herself into a simple navy sheath dress with ruffles at the shoulders, she realized that she wouldn't have that much longer before she might not be able to wear it. She had gone to Katy, a suburb of Houston, and its fabulous bookstore to pick up a few books on pregnancy and then, because she couldn't resist, had tossed a few romance novels into her basket as well. She wasn't one of those people who went into a bookstore and came out with one book. It was always an armful.

Glancing at her Cartier gold-and-steel watch, she knew she needed to keep moving and not stop and check out the books on her nightstand. She was already going to be at least ten minutes late, something her own grandmother had said was key to making a man understand how much time she'd put into getting ready for him. To be honest, she was usually ready on time and had to stall for ten minutes.

But today was different. And how! She went back to the vanity to put her long blond hair into a chignon and then touched up her makeup. She realized she was a little bit stressed and trying to look perfect.

But why?

This wasn't real. She had to remember that. Slade wanted them to get through these troubled waters before they talked about the future. But the baby and the media left them with no choice other than to be engaged. Right? But it was hard. Harder than she'd imagined.

"I can do this, can't I, Pixie?" she asked the dog, who came over and danced around her feet.

Melinda reached down and scooped her up. Pixie put her front paws on Melinda's chest, her tail wagging as Melinda petted her. She wished that the world were as easy to please as this little dog.

She kissed Pixie on the nose and then set her back on the floor. That was a nice break from her worrying, but now she was back to it.

She wanted any photos taken of the two of them to look real. The kind of image that would hang on the wall in a house in tony River Oaks. But that wasn't the endgame here. They were both trying to salvage a situation that was going from bad to worse with her reputation and Slade's always scandalous one.

She tried to just leave her appearance as it was, but she couldn't do it. Philomena would definitely know something was up if Melinda wasn't wearing her pearls and princess-cut diamond stud earrings. They were her formal wear go-tos, which her friend would know.

She was struggling with lying to Philomena and her sister. She didn't mind letting the society bloggers and reporters believe something that wasn't true, or even her father. But her twin? That was much harder. And while she and Angela didn't share every detail of their lives, this was a big rock. One of the things that if it were real, she'd be giddily over-sharing every detail with her sister.

Instead... Well, to be fair, Angela had been incommunicado all day, so that did make it easier to keep from having to tell her she was going to get engaged. That was sort of okay too, because Angela had had a lot of gossip swirling around her and Melinda was trying to distance herself from that.

She supposed tonight at Philomena's house would be the test if she could pull off the temporary engagement with sincerity. She'd never been a good poker player or actress. She could be cordial to strangers but her friends always knew where they stood with her. If they could convince Slade's grandmother they were the real deal, the rest of the world would be easy.

Sure, it would be. But one thing at a time. That was how she'd been successful at accomplishing as much as she had in her life.

When the doorbell rang, Pixie jumped up from her bed and started barking as she raced to the door. Melinda glanced at her watch; Slade was twenty minutes early. She was ready, and keeping him waiting today wasn't going to happen. She wanted to discuss the engagement and make it clear he couldn't live with her, as he'd suggested. She'd written down the things she needed to ensure didn't happen, so she wouldn't fall for the fairy tale.

Number one: no more sex.

Number two: no living together.

Number three: don't fall in love.

She took a deep breath. She wasn't going to mention number three to him. That one was for her eyes only. A reminder to not let herself believe the temporary fix.

No sex was going to be a hard sell for both of them. He turned her on, and she had gotten used to sleeping with him. But she wanted to come out of this thing between her and Slade with as much of her soul intact as she could. And she knew herself well enough to know that if she slept with him or lived with him, then it was going to be hard not to fall in love with him.

She walked through her condo slowly and glanced at the video monitor before opening the door. Slade looked so good in a dinner jacket and tie that her heart started racing. His dark hair was slicked back the way he styled it for formal events and he'd shaved—Philomena didn't care for stubble.

She took a deep breath to center herself before she opened the door. Pixie greeted him with some doggy kisses on his leg and Slade bent over to pet her before he came into the condo.

She took a few steps back, realizing how much taller he was than her. Normally she always had on heels and it wasn't often she stood this close to him in bare feet.

"I know I'm early but I figured we should have a game plan before we head to dinner," he said.

She just nodded as she realized that not falling for him was going to be a lot harder than she'd previously thought. Mainly because she already was halfway in love with him.

Slade had never struggled so much with any decision and he guessed that was one thing he could thank his father for. He'd always been very focused on not following in the old man's footsteps that most of his choices were easy. But this one… Well, it was like the past coming back to haunt him.

His parents had had a marriage of necessity. His mom had become pregnant with him and, bowing to the pressure of the Conti family, Carlo Bartelli had married his mother. But the marriage hadn't worked out and had led to some very unhappy decisions by both of his parents.

Right now, the back of his neck felt tight, and as much as he wanted to be the cool and suave man he liked to think he usually was, he'd never felt more out of his depth. The engagement was simply for her protection, he reminded himself. He'd promised himself to never marry and that promise wasn't one he was willing to break.

Even for Melinda.

She looked breathtakingly lovely as she stood there in her blue dress and bare feet. It was all he could do not to sweep her up in his arms and carry her to bed. But he knew that was a temporary distraction and not what was needed right now. He rubbed the back of his neck to get rid of the tension there, but it didn't help.

"Would you like something to drink?"

"Hard liquor might be nice, but I don't think Nonna would appreciate it," he said. "So I'm fine."

"She definitely wouldn't. Okay, so let's sit down and talk this out," she said, leading the way into her formal living room and taking a seat on the armchair, leaving the love seat for him.

The room was so feminine with delicate-looking furniture and more flowers and stripes than he had ever seen before. It was classy and elegant and a part of him always felt out of place here, as he knew he was neither of those things.

"First, thank you."

"You're welcome," he said, "but for what?"

"Trying to help me by suggesting we get engaged and then giving me time to think it over," she said, twisting her fingers together.

"It was the least I could do."

"It wasn't and I appreciate it. I've thought about your suggestion that we live together, and I must say I don't think that will work for me. I'm too used to being alone and I need this time to get ready for the baby," she said.

"Fair enough," he said, feeling a bit hurt, but he reminded himself that he didn't want to raise a child. "That's probably for the best, as I'll be a financial support for you and the child but not physically in your life."

Her mouth tightened but she nodded after a moment. "Right. So we should set an end date for this engagement. I'm thinking three months? That's enough time for the interest in me to die down and hopefully Daddy's mess will be sorted by then."

Three months. That was longer than any of his previous relationships, and yet with Melinda, it almost felt too short. Which meant it was perfect. "Why don't we reassess the situation then? If we need to keep it going, then we will. And it will be before Christmas, so that will give the society bloggers something else to write about."

"Okay." She bit her lower lip and turned her head away. "This next thing is… Well, it's awkward so I'm just going to say it. I think we should definitely try to keep it platonic from here on out."

Hell, no.

"I'm listening," he said instead.

"The thing is I don't know what my body is going to be doing… I haven't had a chance to read any of the books I picked up today," she said. "Plus, you and I should be focused on keeping up appearances when we're out at events but in our private lives, we should be trying to work out how our lives will be after the baby comes. I know you don't want to be a part of the child's life…so us hooking up is probably not a good idea."

He leaned back against the love seat and pretended to be considering her idea. And he was doing just that, but he was also trying to manage the realization that this pregnancy had changed everything. He couldn't end the relationship with Melinda the way he normally would have, letting it trickle off and then having one big explosive sexual encounter at the end before he walked away. Instead, he had to end it now and then pretend it wasn't over.

He was about to just walk away from everything when his phone vibrated in his pocket and he got a notification of a new post about himself and Melinda. He couldn't leave her to face this alone. It was the least he could do for her and for that child she was carrying.

He knew he had to do whatever he could to make them as safe as possible. If that meant agreeing to no sex, he'd do it. But he suspected she wouldn't find that any easier than he would. There was something between them that Slade hadn't experienced before. An attraction that made it impossible for them to stay apart.

"Okay," he finally said. "But if you change your mind, let me know."

She gave him one of those unexpected grins of hers that made his pulse race. "Honey, you'll be the first to know."

He laughed as she intended him to but inside, he was beginning to wonder if he'd made a huge mistake in ever asking her out. She'd been different and he'd thought that meant something exciting. But maybe it had been dangerous.

Nonna Conti was seventy-eight but looked more like she was fifty-eight. She had a trim figure that she kept by playing tennis three times a week, something Slade had confided she did as much for the gossip as the exercise. Her hair was a deep auburn color and always perfectly coiffed. She smiled warmly at Melinda as they entered her house and swept her up in a big hug.

The entry to the palatial neoclassical River Oaks mansion was all Ferrara marble. It was ivory and shot with gold and had a thick four-inch panel of dark brown marble that framed the entryway. Her designer had hung luxurious gold and white curtains in alternating panels along the wall that was framed with hand-carved molding. There was a thick carpet in the center that led to the sitting room.

The sitting room followed the same design but instead of the hanging panels, there were alternating mirrors, which made the room seem even larger and reminded Melinda of Versailles but not as gold.

After the day she'd had, she just let herself enjoy the hug and soak up the joy and affection from the older woman. Most days, Melinda didn't let herself dwell on the fact that she really missed her mom over the last ten years since she'd died, but today she had reached for the phone more than once to call her.

"It's so good to see you. You look cute as a button as always. I had Henri mix us up some gin and tonics and he's waiting in the sitting room with them," Philomena said, turning to greet her grandson.

Oh, it wasn't going to be as easy to hide the pregnancy as she'd wanted it to be. Obviously, she couldn't drink gin and tonic but Slade sort of indicated with his head for her to go ahead to the sitting room, which she did. She knew Henri, the butler, would be circumspect about her choice if she had a quiet word with him.

She heard Slade telling his grandmother about the opera as she rounded the corner and walked into the sitting room. They were the first of Philomena's guests to arrive, so the room was empty except for the butler, who wore a crisp white jacket and black trousers.

The bar was opulent like the rest of the room and Henri looked like he was a throwback to another age, standing there ready to serve the guests. At last year's Boots and Bangles charity gala, Philomena had asked Henri to volunteer to be one of the silent auction prizes and he'd agreed. She'd paid the fee for him to be someone's butler for the day, so he wasn't out his salary.

"Hello, Miss Melinda. We have your favorite tonight," he said, reaching for the pitcher as she walked over to him.

"Thanks so much, Henri, that means the world to me. But my stomach is acting up today—probably a few too many last night. Would you mind keeping mine just tonic but discreetly?" she asked.

"No problem, ma'am," he said with a wink as he reached to the second shelf of the bar cart and poured just tonic into her highball glass and added a twist of lime as a garnish.

"Thank you," she said, taking her drink from him and giving him a warm smile.

She moved away from the bar cart as Philomena and Slade entered the room. Henri poured them each a drink and then they joined her in one of the seating areas in the massive room. Slade took the spot next to her on one of the love seats and Philomena sat in what Melinda privately referred to as her throne chair. It was a high-backed padded chair upholstered in a deep purple brocade, which complemented the opulent marble, cream and gold room. It was higher than the other seats in the room and gave Philomena the air of holding court once she was perched there.

"Slade tells me the opera was excellent. I saw from the *Chronicle* that you two are getting on well," Philomena said.

Melinda felt herself blushing at that comment, but she wasn't embarrassed. They might be doing the temporary engagement thing but her feelings for Slade were real. "You knew we were seeing each other."

"I'd hoped you were. Now the world knows. Even though it did make things a bit awkward for the two of you," she admitted.

It had only been after Philomena had encouraged her to give her grandson a chance to prove he was more than the media made him out to be that Melinda had accepted her first date with him.

"Actually, Nonna, we are getting along so well that I asked Melinda to marry me and she said yes."

"You did what?"

"Nonna, I asked Melinda to marry me and she said yes."

"Philomena, is that okay?" Melinda asked. Given the mess that her family continued to be embroiled in lately, she wouldn't be surprised if the society matron wanted someone more respectable for her grandson.

"Oh, I adore you, Melinda, but my grandson had always said he was never getting married," Philomena said, looking over at Slade.

"Nonna, I might have felt that way before meeting Melinda. She's the kind of woman that makes a man realize what's important, so I asked her to marry me and she said yes. We'd like your blessing."

"You have it. Congratulations! Henri, champagne, please," Philomena said, but Henri had already started moving toward the butler's pantry and fully stocked bar. "Did he do something super romantic?"

Crappola. She hadn't thought about this and she should have. She was off her game and she blamed the pregnancy and the scandals that kept dogging her family. It seemed as if each time they got one thing sorted, something else popped up. She should have known people were going to ask about his proposal and they hadn't worked out anything. And let's face it, she couldn't say he saw all those pregnancy tests in the bathroom and said "Let's get temporarily engaged."

She glanced at Slade, who must have read the panic on her face because he reached over and took her hand in his. "Well, Nonna, if you must know, I took her to the place where we had our first kiss and then went down on one knee."

She felt her heart catch in her throat. That would have been a very romantic gesture. The kind of thing that she'd always dreamed of. But men who were "doing the right thing" for their girlfriend's reputation didn't make gestures like that.

"Well-done, *Tesoro.* I knew you had it in you," she said. "You just were waiting for the right woman to come along."

"I definitely was," he said, keeping hold of her hand.

"And the ring?" Philomena asked.

Melinda would have pulled her hand back if Slade hadn't been holding it but he rubbed his thumb over her knuckles, which sent a sensual shiver up her arm.

He might be Philomena's *Tesoro*—treasure—but right now she wasn't so sure.

"I was hoping to speak to you privately about that matter tonight," he said.

"After we have a toast and some more guests arrive," Philomena said with a twinkle in her eyes. "You've made me very happy tonight, *Tesoro*. You know, I may have pushed him to take my seat on the art council because I wanted him to meet you. I'm glad to see he picked up my hints. I knew you two would be perfect for each other."

What?

Now the temporary engagement made more sense, she thought, as she tugged her hand from his. Had he only asked her out to please his demanding grandmother? Was he protecting her from the bad press and helping to repair her reputation after the scandals that kept consuming the Perry family only to please his grandmother?

She was disappointed and mad at herself for letting him deceive her. But she knew the real blame lay with herself. She'd been the one making him into a better man than he was. He'd told her he didn't want a wife or child and she'd believed him, but secretly she hoped he'd change his mind. Now she had changed hers.

Seven

The dinner party was comprised of polite society members who, though they seemed curious about her and Slade, didn't ask them anything directly. The dining room was comprised of a long table that seated sixteen and a smaller round table that seated only eight. Philomena reserved the round table for herself and her specially invited guests. Slade and Philomena had disappeared for a few moments when the first guests arrived and when he came back, he tried to get a few minutes alone with Melinda, but she refused.

Instead, she pushed away all of the doubt and troubles of the day and socialized the way she'd been raised to. In fact, as the evening drew to a close with after-dinner drinks and a three-piece ensemble playing classical music, she thought she'd done a good job of camouflaging the fact that she was mad and hurt.

Finally, as the other guests started to leave, she faked a yawn and gave a tight smile to Slade. "It's getting kind of late. I think I'll get a taxi home."

"I'll take you," he said.

"You don't have to."

"Oh, I definitely do. I can tell you have something to say to me," he said, putting his hand on the small of her back to direct her toward his grandmother. While the gesture was one she normally liked, tonight she didn't. She was mad. Hurt that she'd never even had a thought that Philomena was setting them up. She was angry that she'd played an unwitting part in her scheme by getting pregnant.

She took quick steps to increase the distance between them, but he just kept up with her, curling his hand around her waist to stop her. She turned quickly to glare at him, but he just smiled at her and said quietly, "We have to keep up appearances."

She realized he was right. The last thing she wanted was to fuel more speculation about the two of them. It didn't matter if she was angry. Her number one goal now was to drop off the radar of the society bloggers. After that happened, she could deal with everything else.

"Sorry, darling," she said loud enough that others in the room could hear her. "I've got a wicked headache."

Then she leaned in, heard his quick intake of breath as she ran her fingers along the column of his neck in a caress she knew turned him on and then kissed him, quickly but deeply, before turning back toward Philomena.

She saw speculation in the other woman's eyes, but Melinda was done with the Conti-Bartelli clan tonight.

"Thank you for a wonderful dinner, Philomena. I loved it," she said, kissing the older woman on the cheek before she started to turn away.

"You're welcome, Melinda," Philomena said, catching her wrist before she could leave. "I'd love it if you could join me for lunch on Friday."

She started to say no, but Philomena lifted one eyebrow and Melinda realized this was a summons. "I'll have to check my schedule. If not Friday, perhaps Monday."

"That would be nice. I'll have Henri follow up with your assistant," she said. Then she pulled Melinda close and gave her a warm hug. "Congratulations again. I'm so glad you are going to be a part of the family."

She hugged Philomena back, a part of her dying inside that none of this was real. Had she made the decision to agree to this engagement too quickly? It was beginning to feel like she had.

"Me too," she said, turning away quickly so that Slade could say his goodbyes. She walked through the room saying goodbye to a few other friends.

Slade followed her through the house to the front door, his footsteps loud behind her as she walked. She took her purse from the antique sideboard where it was waiting for her. Henri was very good about anticipating any guests' needs.

As soon as they were outside, she glanced up at the September evening sky. God, the sky was big tonight. A half-moon shone down on them and stars and satellites twinkled in the night sky. She took a deep breath and felt some of her anger seep away.

"I'm sorry you had to hear about Nonna trying to set us up the way you did," he said once they were in the car and heading back toward downtown and her condo.

"It was a surprise," she admitted. "Are you planning to actually marry me?"

"No."

His answer was so quick and almost forceful. Well, there it was, she thought. Was he lying to everyone? Was that why a temporary engagement had come to his mind so quickly?

"Listen, let's talk about this at your place. There is a lot more to it than it probably seems to you and I can't explain while I'm driving," he said.

"Sure," she said, turning to stare out the window at the passing scenery. All her life she'd lost herself in books. Ignored some things in her family that were less than ideal because she created a world for herself that involved the stories she read. She admitted it had been very nice. And at the age of thirty-nine, she'd finally created a reality around her where she didn't have to escape into those fictional worlds as often as she'd used to. But this baby and this engagement—they were rocking her real world. Shaking her reality and making her realize that perhaps she hadn't come as far as she'd thought.

When Slade pulled into the guest parking lot, she was relieved because he didn't plan to stay overnight. But when they approached her building, there was a small gathering of paparazzi waiting. She almost wanted to groan, but Slade just pulled her close, wrapping his arm around her shoulders as he led her past them.

Which just confused her more.

He did care for her. He was probably the last man

who wanted to be close to the scandal that was surrounding her and her family at the moment, but he was
still here. Of course, he was very good at ignoring the
rumors and rising above them.

Though she had known that from the first time
they'd slept together, this kind of gesture wasn't what
anyone in the media would expect from him.

"Fellas," he said, nodding toward the paparazzi as
the doorman held open the door and they walked past.

No one would ever call him a genius, but he was definitely picking up what Melinda was putting down. She
looked pissed. The kind of pissed that was going to take
a lot more than a Conti heirloom ring and some smooth
talking to get around. He didn't blame her one bit. Her
life was a mess and he was the one at the center of it.

Though to be fair, her father was doing his part
as well. But her dad wasn't here. Slade was and he
needed to figure out how to make this right. If he were
a different man, he'd be doing everything he could to
marry her.

A part of him knew that if he could make the engagement real, if he'd marry her and raise the baby together, that would do it. But he couldn't. He had ghosts
in his past and that was saying something given that
everyone in Houston and probably beyond knew he
was the son of an alleged mobster. And Melinda deserved better.

She didn't offer him a drink when they entered her
condo, just walked into the living room and sat down
on the large armchair that faced the door. The windows behind her twinkled with the lights of downtown

Houston and he had a real impression of how much he was costing her.

Until this moment, it hadn't even occurred to him what the price would be to her if anyone found out they were dating. As she sat there, though, with what used to be her city behind her, it couldn't be clearer.

And he was worried about how he was going to get back into her good graces for the next three months. How was she going to cope with the rest of her life?

"I screwed up," he said. The words were raw and ripped from the most honest place in his soul. The one that knew that he was one step away from following in his criminal father's footsteps. The one that never used the word *alleged* to refer to his dad's activities. Sure, he could put on the polish and look like a Conti when required, but even Nonna knew that the reason Conti Enterprises had flourished under his leadership was that he was a Bartelli through and through. He was the kind of man who never took no for an answer and got what he wanted.

He wanted Melinda. On his terms.

And if he needed further proof that he wasn't the right sort of man to marry and settle down, he'd gotten it. He'd charmed and seduced her until she was in his bed and then the Bartelli luck had kicked in and made a shit hole of her life. He had no way to fix this.

The smart thing to do would be to walk out her front door and find some respectable guy to be the "father" of her kid. But even as the thought entered his mind, he felt a rage welling up inside of him. She belonged to him. The child was his.

He turned away and took several deep breaths. She

was her own woman. Not his. But damn. It was hard to accept that.

"You did screw up. But mainly I blame myself because I thought… I should have known better than to trust Philomena. I thought we were friends, but she has told me more than once that blood is thicker than water."

"I know she thinks of you as family—"

"Spare me. I found out the hard way that isn't the truth. And I'm really not in the mood to be placated," she said.

"Fair enough."

She bit her lower lip and looked away from him, staring past his shoulder as she blinked a few times, and he died a little inside because he knew she'd been hoping—maybe not believing, but hoping—that he'd turn out to be a stand-up guy.

"I'm so sorry," he said, quietly.

She nodded. "Of course. Now let's get all our cards on the table. You know where I stand. Pregnant, reputation in tatters. What about you? Temporarily engaged or really engaged to make your nonna happy? Wants a family, doesn't want a family?"

He hesitated. The truth was more complex than he wanted to share with her, but at this point, his only chance of salvaging any relationship with her was to come clean. But that part of himself… He had never wanted her to know about it.

But now it wasn't as if she could think any lower of him than she did at that moment.

He moved into the living room and sat down at the hassock by her feet and looked up at her.

"I guess I should start with Nonna. She wants me

to settle down with a woman who could be a partner to me. She wants great-grandchildren and to be honest, she adores you. She suggested I take her spot on the art council to meet you. But the truth is, once I met you, I couldn't help asking you out."

"Why?" she asked.

He had never been one of those men who could easily verbalize his feelings. That wasn't the kind of man he was; but as he looked at Melinda, he knew he had to give her something. She wasn't the kind of woman who did temporary. There was a reason she had never married and it wasn't because men hadn't asked her before. She was selective about who she let into her inner circle.

And she'd let him in.

"In that art council meeting, you were funny while the chair was speaking. All of those little comments under your breath. I was intrigued and then when you got up to talk about Salvador Dalí and why we should sponsor the exhibit..." He couldn't tell her he'd gotten turned on just hearing her passion for the artist. "I knew I wanted to go out with you."

"I turned you down," she reminded him.

"You did. But I haven't gotten to where I am in life by letting a setback affect me. I knew eventually you'd start seeing Slade and not just a Bartelli."

She leaned over, touching his hand. "You were never just a Bartelli to me. But tonight I realized you might have more of your father's traits than I had anticipated."

"Sarcasm really doesn't suit you," he said gently. "I've apologized."

"I know. I'm hurt... Look, maybe we shouldn't do this tonight," she said.

"I think we have to. Let's get it settled so that to-morrow we can start fresh."

She put her arms around her waist and shifted deeper into the chair. "Okay. Go on."

"So Nonna was satisfied and tonight when we told her about the engagement, she was over the moon, but our agreement hasn't changed," he said.

"Why not?"

He took a deep breath. This was harder than he thought it would be.

"Do you mind if I get a drink? This isn't going to be easy to talk about."

"Sure… Go ahead and help yourself."

He came back and instead of sitting down near her, he stood next to her chair facing the floor-to-ceiling windows that overlooked downtown Houston. She loved the view normally. Liked looking down at the city she loved and seeing it from up here. But as she glanced over at Slade, she didn't feel the same kind of peace or satisfaction she normally felt.

She was still mad, so she was trying not to let her-self empathize with him. He'd indicated whatever else he had to tell was going to be difficult to hear.

She shook her head.

She had known a tight ass and a pair of bedroom eyes would be her downfall, but she'd never realized how far she had to fall. But he was more than a hot bod to burn up the sheets with. She liked the way he listened to her when she talked about her projects and how he'd sometimes text her during the day when he saw something that he thought she'd like.

Last week, it had been a brown-eyed Susan flower

that had somehow grown up between the cracked sidewalk outside one of the Conti warehouses. Those gestures made it very difficult for her to see him as someone with a dark past.

She heard the rattle of the ice in his lowball glass as he took a sip of the whiskey he'd poured for himself. He wasn't a sophisticated drinker and even though her bar was fully stocked, he always went for Johnnie Walker.

"Okay. Say what you have to say," she said. A part of her wanted him out of the condo, so she could re-group and figure out what was next. Angela was used to dealing with scandal and a fiancé their father didn't like. Maybe she could help Melinda figure this out. But Ryder loved Angela… That was one thing Melinda couldn't say about Slade.

She couldn't just walk away from him, because the party tonight had been full of Houston society elite. Everyone had seen them together as a couple, which was what they'd wanted until she found out…what? That he'd used her? Well, get in line, right? Her dad had been doing it for years if rumors were to be believed. Using her good work to cover his own shady dealings.

She'd about had it with the men in her life.

"Um, it's not… That is to say—"

"Stop. Just say it. Does it have to do with your fa-ther? I know you're associated with the Bartelli… What do they call it? Syndicate? Mob? Gang?"

"He calls it the family," Slade said.

"The family," she repeated. That had to make it harder for Slade to walk away from. She glanced over at him, standing so alone and stiff and staring out the window.

Despite her anger, she did feel the stirring of sympathy for him. He had grown up in such an odd world. High-society half the time, street-level crime the other.

"Yeah, this might seem like more than you want to know, but I feel like you will just think I'm the biggest douchebag in the world unless you know the whole thing," he said on a heavy sigh as he moved over to the couch and sat down facing toward her.

He had his legs spread and put his forearms on both of his legs. He had left his tie and jacket on, so he still looked like the cover of a *GQ* magazine, but in his eyes, she saw the steel that made Slade the man he was today.

"I'm listening."

And she was. She'd heard the rumors about the Bartelli family, and she knew that despite the fact that everyone said "alleged," they were not a family to be crossed.

"My mom was a bit of a rebel to hear Nonna tell it and her father was very strict. So when Carlo Bartelli flirted with her, she went after him with everything she had. I guess he was dangerous, and she liked that for a while, but her goal had been to piss the old man off. So once her dad was paying attention again, she went back to her regular life and then found out she was pregnant with me."

Melinda had never in her life sympathized with another person as much as she did with Slade's mom in that moment. Though she'd been older and more mature and should have known better, she totally understood what it was like to fall under the spell of a Bartelli.

"But her old man wasn't about to let her have a kid without being married and I think that Nonno honestly thought that he'd be able to bring Carlo around to his way of thinking. Make him legit and part of the Conti family," Slade said.

But he hadn't. That had to have been hard on everyone. The Conti family was old money and had been a part of Houston society since the early 1900s.

"What happened?"

"They got married, got a nice house in River Oaks down the street from my grandparents and until I was eight, everyone thought that Carlo had turned over a new leaf. He worked for Conti Enterprises, he went to the social engagements with my mom and he was a pretty good dad to me. But then he was arrested, and the truth started trickling out. He had never let go of his old life and had been living two lives. Getting caught and having his lawyer get him off on the charges, while the *Houston Chronicle* society pages painted it all as a misunderstanding. You see, my grandmother had a lot of influence back in those days. But Mom knew the truth and my parents separated.

"My dad said there was no way he could get out of the Bartelli family. There just wasn't a way to separate it from the man he was. I thought that was just his weakness and told him so. But I was engaged when I was twenty-one, Melinda. And the Bartellis were at war with another gang and she… Well, she got caught in the middle and was used as a bargaining chip against me. She was okay physically but after that…she didn't want a relationship with me. And I promised myself I'd never put a woman in that position again."

Melinda hadn't realized he'd been engaged but honestly, she hadn't researched him at all. Just took him at face value. That was more her style. And her gut said

that his few sentences about what happened were the
cleaned-up version.

"Okay. So, we stick to our original plan?"

"Yes. I will protect you and our child forever, but I
can never marry you unless I want to give my father's
enemies someone to go after. We will be engaged for
three months and then reassess and keep pushing the
date back until we know the scandal has passed."

Eight

It wasn't as if anything he said surprised her. She knew he'd come from a tough background. To be perfectly honest, that was what had drawn her to him. He was polished at times, but there was always an edginess to him that drew her like a moth to a flame.

"I didn't know you'd been engaged," she said at last.

"Not many people did. I wasn't the CEO of Conti back then. I was just on the fringes of society, some punk kid that might be joining the Bartelli family business. And despite how everyone acted toward me tonight, it took a while for polite society to warm up to me being at events," he admitted.

"I can understand that. I mean, my family is part of the Texas Cattleman's Club in Royal and the new one opening here in Houston and it is hard to become a member. It wasn't that long ago when it was men only."

"I bet you didn't stand for that," he said with a wry smile.

"Not at all. But I was here in Houston and not really part of the group who was pushing for membership," she admitted. "What are we going to do?"

"Well, I told you we'll do the engagement for three months like we agreed and then hopefully media interest in you will have died down enough that you can get back to your old routine."

She shifted in the chair, wishing she'd worn pumps instead of sandals with an ankle strap so she could just kick them off, but she hadn't, so she crossed her legs and sat up straighter. "What about the baby?"

"I'll provide you with everything you need. Money, furniture… I'll even pay for the child's tuition to the best schools in Houston."

"Thanks, but I'm not asking about money," she said. "What about you? Will you be a part of the child's life?"

"No. I'm not role-model material," he said. He took another swallow of his whiskey, finishing it and leaning forward to place the glass on the coffee table.

"Why not? Do you really not like me?"

"Hell, woman, you know I like you. You wouldn't be pregnant if I didn't," he blurted.

But that bluster didn't really bother her. She knew he was being defensive, but for the life of her, she couldn't figure out why.

"So what is it, then?" she asked.

He tipped his head to the side, studying her for a moment. "Not even a rebuke for the way I spoke to you?"

"I know you well enough to tell when you're lashing out to hide something," she said.

"We do know each other fairly well now, don't we?"

She noticed he was still not answering her question. Interesting. They did know each other well. She'd thought they were falling in love. But Slade wasn't that kind of man, she guessed.

"I would have thought so, but then I learned tonight that we were set up by Philomena…"

Right now, she wanted to get to the bottom of why Slade didn't want to raise a child. He wasn't just averse to making a home and having a family, he was talking about no contact with the child at all.

Why?

"So back to the child…" she continued.

"Please. Will you let it go?" he asked. "Just for tonight."

There was something raw in the way he asked, and she found that she couldn't force anything else. Her mind was already full of everything that had gone on today and maybe it was time to just let the day end.

"Okay, but I'm going to want some answers eventually," she said.

"Fair enough," he said, standing up. "I guess I should be going…"

Of course, she wanted him to stay. She was tired and if she were being completely honest, more than a little scared about being a mom at forty. But there were too many dangers if she let him stay.

Tonight had made it clear how complicated this entire situation was. If there was ever a time when she needed a clear head, it was now. She couldn't afford to let herself get used to Slade. That meant sleeping with him wasn't going to happen.

Again.

"Yes, I think you should be," she said.

"Fair enough," he said, standing up, and she did the same. He came over to her and pulled her into his arms and she noticed how easy it was to rest her head on his chest right over his heart.

She heard the sound of it beating under her ear as he held her close, rubbing his hands up and down her back.

"I'm sorry for all of this," he said. "I think that just goes to show how stupid I can be at times."

She smiled because he couldn't see it. He always surprised her. He was so aware of his faults and never hesitated to try to make amends for them. It was why she didn't understand his reluctance to be a father to their child. Surely whatever was in his past, he could overcome it.

She tipped her head back to look up at him. Their eyes met and she saw the hunger and need in his gaze. It mirrored the feelings churning inside of her. She knew it would be smarter to send him away. But she also knew by the end of the year, Slade would be out of her life. The man she'd waited forever for was only here for a few more months.

Could she take what she wanted and still be whole when it ended?

Leaving was the last thing he wanted to do. He wanted to hold her. Just hold her and for a moment forget that he'd been born a Bartelli.

Forget that his uncles and extended goombahs weren't ever going to let a child of his walk away the way he had.

"Slade, I know what I said earlier but do you want to

stay the night?" she asked. Her voice was soft and entreating, and she put her hand on his face like she did sometimes. It always made it impossible for him to say no to her.

"I'd like nothing more," he admitted. "But you have to know—"

She put her fingers over his lips to stop the words that would have warned her about him and his family, and he let her because the last thing he wanted to do was tell her what a mess his family was.

"No more talking," she said. "We both know the facts but tonight is for us. Just you and me…and our new child."

He had to smile at the way she said it. He wasn't a man given to wishing, but at this moment, he longed to be anyone but Slade Bartelli. It didn't matter that he knew in his gut he never would have met her if he weren't himself.

He wrapped his arm around her waist, lifting her off her feet, and carried her toward the stairs that led to her bedroom. She wrapped her arm around his shoulders and put one hand on his chest as she loosened his tie. After this day, which had felt like a lifetime, he needed this. Needed her in a way that he never would want to admit to another soul, but she did something to him that went beyond sex.

Maybe that explained that feeling he'd had when Nonna had said what she had about pushing him to meet her. As if he needed an incentive other than Melinda to ask her out.

He kissed her then. He couldn't wait another moment because he felt like she was slipping away from him. That he'd lost his chance to keep her… Wait, he wasn't keeping her. This was just for tonight.

Her tongue rubbed over his and everything masculine inside of him went on red alert. He wanted to take her in the hallway up against the wall. Just take her hard and deep until there was no doubt that she was his. That she belonged to him…with him. No matter what logic said, his instincts demanded he make Melinda his.

Pixie danced around his feet as he entered Melinda's bedroom. The little dog stood on her back legs and he realized she might need to go out. Maybe they were never going to have sex again, he thought. Between the paparazzi, his family, her family and now her dog, it seemed as if the cards were stacked against them.

He set Melinda on her feet. A tendril of hair had escaped her updo and fell against the side of her face. He touched her cheek, brushing it back behind her ear. She was so beautiful that she took his breath away.

Pixie let out a small bark.

"Does she need to go out?" he asked.

"She should be okay," Melinda said. "Let me check."

Melinda opened the door that led to her outdoor balcony, which ran the length of her condo. She had a small grassy "lawn" area that she'd had installed just for her dog. Pixie didn't like the noise on the streets and the nervous dog would often start shaking.

He followed Melinda to the glass door. As soon as she opened it, the little dog darted out and the warm September air rushed into the room. Slade took off his tie and loosened his collar. He tossed his tie on the chair and then toed off his shoes and socks.

Melinda braced one hand on the doorjamb and bent

to undo the buckle at her ankle on her sandals. He hardened watching her body move, so graceful and elegant. When she glanced over at him, finding him watching her, there was a heat in her eyes. He groaned.

She always met him heat for heat. He had expected a shy woman in the bedroom given her propensity for manners and rules, but she knew what she wanted from a man and didn't hesitate to demand it. Something he appreciated in her.

There was a lot about Melinda that had kept him coming back to her bedroom. He'd never admit it out loud, but he regretted the baby she was carrying. That child was forcing him out of her life. Yet at the same time, he was intensely protective of that child. The baby that shouldn't have been because he'd made a vow to himself. Of course, he'd broken it. Did he need further proof that he was a Bartelli?

He had it. No more thinking. He wanted Melinda in his arms and underneath him. At least then he'd feel like he was giving her what she needed from him. And when he held her, he could pretend even for a few moments that she was his.

Really his.

She got her shoes off and stood there across from him, looking sexier than anyone he'd ever seen before. She wasn't even doing anything to tempt him, just being Melinda, and honestly that was all that it took. He walked toward her, catching her in his arms and pulling her more fully against him, so that they were pressed together from chest to pelvis. He kissed her slowly, thoroughly and very deeply. He caught her earlobe between his teeth.

"I need you now," he said.

* * *

"Here?" she asked, but it was what she wanted and needed as well. There was something about Slade that made her forget all her normal rules of behavior. He called to something wild inside of her.

The city of Houston was spread out behind them, but she wanted him. She walked over to the glass doors and glanced at her dog as she played in her yard area. Slade came up behind her and slowly drew the zipper down the side of her dress and she shivered as his finger brushed against her side.

"Right here," he said, as he lifted the back of her dress up until she felt the brush of his trousers against the back of her legs.

He reached down and traced the fabric of her thong, his finger running on the edge of her crack and making her hips arch instinctively.

She put one hand on the glass door in front of them, as she heard him lowering his zipper and then felt the heat of him against her. His erection rubbed against her backside as he held her to him with his hand on her stomach.

She arched back against him as he kissed the column of her neck and sucked against the point where it met her shoulder.

His hands moved along her stomach and lower, pushing her underwear down her body and she worked them down to her feet. She pushed her hips back as she stepped out of them, her backside rubbing against his erection. He groaned and clenched her waist.

He put his hands over hers on the glass, lacing their fingers together as she felt him thrusting against her. He shifted his hips back until the tip of his erection was at the entrance of her body. She bit her lower lip as he entered her slowly, her head falling back against his shoulder, turning until their lips met.

He sucked her tongue into his mouth as he drove deep inside her. She moaned, arching against him to take him deeper, and he held her tightly to him with his hand on her stomach as he drove himself in and out of her body.

She felt so close to coming but wanted to draw this out and make it last. But really, could anything with Slade Bartelli last? She knew it was fleeting. Full of more emotion than she'd ever experienced before and probably something she'd miss for the rest of life once he walked out of it.

Tears burned her eyes and she ripped her mouth from his, turning her head away from him. In the reflection of the glass, she caught a glimpse of him and was dazzled by the intensity in his gaze as he moved in and out of her body. When their eyes met, she saw so much in him that she wanted to see. Wanted to believe.

Before she could finish the thought, his hand on her stomach moved lower. He rubbed her clit just the way she liked it and she felt herself tightening around him and then her climax burst through her. Spots danced in front of her eyes and she closed them as he thrust harder and faster into her until he came, calling her name. His head was buried in her back between her shoulder blades and he held her so tightly. She wanted him to keep holding her this way. To never let her go. But that wasn't possible.

He turned her in his arms, putting his hand under her chin and tipping her head back. She felt the tears stir again, knew it was because the sex had been so good. She wanted to make herself believe that he was going to stay. That he was going to be her man not just for these few more weeks but forever.

He brushed the tears away with his thumbs.

"Aw, baby cakes, don't cry."

She nodded and put her face in his chest against the fabric of his shirt, but as he rubbed her back, the tears continued to fall. She had to start being real with herself about Slade Bartelli.

She loved him.

She had been pretending that wasn't the case for a while, but it was. And she wanted him to be her fiancé not to get the paparazzi off their tail but because he wanted to spend the rest of his life with her.

"Every time I try to make things better, I make them worse," he said, his voice full of something close to regret or maybe loathing.

"No. It's not you. You've always been honest with me," she admitted.

"Somehow that isn't making me feel any better," he said. "I hate seeing you like this."

She wanted to be able to laugh and flirt and somehow turn this entire thing around, but she couldn't. It wasn't in her at this moment. All she could do was muster a weak smile as Pixie came running back to the door and she stepped aside, her dress falling back into place as she let the dog back inside.

"Should I leave?" he asked. "Would that make this all better?"

She had no idea. "I am so lost right now, Slade. I can't tell if anything will help. I don't know what to do and for the first time in my life, I'm going to be responsible for another person…a child. I'm just losing it in a way that I never thought I would."

"You're not alone," he said. "I'm here."

"But you won't be for long."

"Can't we just take this as it comes? Live in the moment?"

She wanted to say no. But really, what options did she have? She loved this man and right now, she wasn't strong enough to tell him she wouldn't settle for the bread crumbs he offered her.

"Yes, let's try that."

He didn't look convinced but spent the rest of the evening doing everything to make her happy. He drew a bath for her, washed her hair and then read to her because he knew she liked the sound of his voice. And she tucked the memory away along with her sadness because she didn't want him to know that when he was sweet to her like this, it made her ache for what could have been.

Nine

Planning a big soiree to announce their engagement was the last thing that Melinda wanted to do. Oh, who was she kidding? It was the exact thing she wanted to do and had been secretly dreaming of for most of her adult life. But she also knew the bigger deal that was made out of the engagement, the harder it was going to be to move on when it was over. Slade had said they'd reassess after three months, but she had also heard the iron in his voice when he said he didn't want to get married.

She wasn't stupid. She knew that she had to keep her head about this, but she couldn't help looking down at the huge rock, the Conti family heirloom, that Slade had slipped on her finger after he'd made love to her last Wednesday night. It was a week later and he'd been good to his word, escorting her to functions and even setting up a romantic lunch with her so that the media would have some photos to run other than that scorching hot kiss they'd shared at the opera...the one that had outed them.

"Earth to Mels... Anyone home?" Angela asked as she handed her a coffee and sat down across from her at the party planners. This kind of engagement announcement party was going to require the big guns and since they were holding it on Saturday, it really didn't give her enough time to do it on her own. Her father hadn't been over the moon at the news, but he liked Slade so he'd offered to foot the bill, which had reassured Melinda that his money troubles were all speculation and rumor.

"I'm trying not to be jealous of the fact that Daddy is so happy about your engagement and is still trying to convince me to break things off with Ryder."

"How is everything going with Ryder?" Melinda asked. "I thought Daddy would soften toward him now that he's out of jail."

"You know Daddy. He's tried, but he really can't seem to stop hating on Ryder," Angela said. "But that's not what we are here today to talk about. How can I help?"

"I'm just trying to figure out how to get this all done," she said.

"You'll do it and it will be the event of the season," Angela said. "You're always good at making your dreams come true."

There was a note of melancholy in her sister's voice. Their father had yet to give his approval of Angela's engagement, even though Ryder was a successful businessman.

"I'm sorry," she said.

"It's not your fault. But if Daddy says one more thing about how Slade is the catch of the century, I might have to remind him Slade's family is a bit... shady."

Her father just said things like that in what Melinda could only guess was the hope that Angela would drop Ryder and find another man, a man that in his eyes was a better one. Though Slade had assured her that he wasn't part of the Bartelli business, it was hard to dodge these kinds of inferences. "He's not like that, Angela."

"I know," her sister said, putting her hand over Melinda's. "I'm sorry, it's just hard to see Dad talking about Slade like he's the perfect future son-in-law and treating Ryder like he's some kind of disease."

She squeezed her sister's hand. She had been so caught up in her own crazy life she hadn't really been there for Angela lately.

"I'm sorry. Slade's not perfect," Melinda said. "I wonder if Dad would come around if we had a double wedding."

"Double wedding?"

"Yes, you know like we used to play when we were little. Remember?" she asked. But even as the words were leaving Melinda's mouth, she wondered if she were going crazy. Ryder and Angela were in love—real love—and about to really get married. She and Slade had some crazy, sexy lust thing between them, a baby that neither of them planned for and a temporary engagement that he had no intention to fulfill.

"You're sweet, but I don't want to intrude on your special day...or mine," Angela said.

"Well, if you change your mind... I don't mind making this about us instead of me," Melinda said. "I'm really not much for the spotlight. And a double wedding might be the thing to change the attitude of the journalists covering Dad's…troubles."

Angela laughed. "It might. I'd only do it if he accepted Ryder and I really can't see that happening anytime soon."

"To be honest, I'm surprised he likes Slade as much as he does. I was worried our relationship might have a negative effect on his legal issues, but the truth is, Slade is so transparent, I think it's actually helping Dad."

"I agree. I mean, his family is shady, but I've been hard-pressed to find anyone who actually believes that Slade is in the business with them."

"Me too," she admitted. "And the Contis are above reproach."

"They are. I think that's what makes him palatable. What does he say about his father's business?" Angela asked.

Nothing. But she didn't want her sister to realize there were things that she hadn't been able to talk to her fiancé about. If Angela told her that Ryder kept things from her, she would caution her sister to push for answers. This was a mess. She put her head down, staring at the red lipstick stain on the lid of her to-go coffee cup.

"What is it?" Angela asked.

What is it? There was so much she wanted to share with Angela, but could she? Could she tell her everything and still carry on doing what she needed to? Absently, she toyed with the heirloom engagement ring on her left hand.

Melinda lifted her head and glanced around. They

were still waiting for the party planner to come in and talk to them about Saturday's big party. They were alone in the conference room with the party books spread out in front of them.

"I'm afraid once I tell you, you're going to realize that I'm in over my head."

"What are you talking about?" Angela asked. "What's going on?"

"Well… I'm pregnant," she said.

"Oh, yay! I'm going to be an auntie! You said you wanted to be a mom and now you're going to be," Angela said, hugging her. "I love this. I was starting to think our family was cursed but this baby seems like a blessing."

"It does," Melinda agreed. She could never think of her child as anything but a blessing. "Slade suggested marriage to keep the society bloggers from guessing that it was unplanned."

"That's not what I was expecting, but he's standing by you as he should. How do you feel about that?"

"I want to marry him and have that whole white-picket-fence life, you know me, but I want him to love me too. And Slade has some baggage that makes him think he can't do that."

"I thought he asked you to marry him. He is your fiancé, right?"

Melinda rubbed her thumb over the lipstick mark on the cup. Angela might as well know the entire truth. "Temporarily. He won't marry me or be a father to our child."

Angela knew a lot of things about her twin and the most important was that she'd never agree to a temporary engagement without a plan to make it permanent. Melinda was just doubting herself and since Angela was so happy and in love, she knew she could help Melinda see what she needed to do.

"What are we going to do? Can you change his mind?"

"I don't know. But I said yes because I hope so."

Angela shifted around in the chair and turned Melinda's to face her as well. She was going to be an auntie. She hugged her sister. "Congrats on the baby. Are you excited about it?"

"I am. I mean, there's so much other stuff that I'm dealing with but when I have a quiet moment, I just think about it. I had pretty much written off being a mom. I was in denial at first. I mean, how could I be pregnant at this age?"

"Forty is the new thirty. I read that someplace, so you know you can believe it."

"Ha. It doesn't feel like the new thirty," she said. When she'd been twenty-nine, she'd felt like she had total control over her life and at this moment, she felt like she was rolling and spinning in a million different directions. She had no idea how to control anything.

"I agree some days it's harder than others to believe that this might be the new thirty, but to be honest, I think I like the attitude it gives me. I mean, Dad and Ryder aren't exactly best buddies, and Dad is still convinced somehow Ryder had something to do with the investigation into him and these murder rumors that are swirling, but I keep hoping both of them will come around eventually. Remember how you had said that no man that we like is inappropriate?"

"I guess I was... I don't know what," Melinda said

with a laugh. When she'd been starting to fall for Slade and saw Angela falling for Ryder, she had felt like they could have everything they desired. But it had gotten complicated for both of them.

Angela hugged her close, understanding that Melinda was trying to use humor to mask her fears. "Something drew you to Slade and him to you. And right now, he's saying that he doesn't want to raise a family—why did he ask you to marry him, then?"

Her sister flushed and then bit her lower lip, blinking several times. What the heck was going on with Melinda?

"He did it to protect me from the media. But he made it clear it's only temporary. We're going to distract them with the engagement and then reassess before Christmas."

That was crazy. There was no way a man who looked at her sister the way Slade did was ever going to let her go. No matter what Slade was telling himself.

"I think if he asked you to marry him to protect you, then he's not really thinking it's just for a short time. He has been single all these years," Angela said. "Something about you made him finally commit."

Melinda shook her head. "He doesn't want to disappoint his grandmother either, so I think the engagement is sort of a way to protect me, get the press off our backs and appease her."

"Do you even hear what you're saying? I can't for a moment imagine that Slade Bartelli would give in to that kind of pressure. If I had to guess, I'd say he wants you to force him to make the engagement a real one. Seems to me that he's done everything but say the words to show you that's what he wants."

"Angela, if you had to force Ryder to ask you to marry him, would you? Could you ever be happy, knowing that the only reason you were married was because you got pregnant? I want Slade to marry me because he wants to spend the rest of his life with me. Even when he was confronted with the fact that I knew he'd been influenced to ask me out, he still wouldn't say that he wanted me."

"No, I wouldn't want that," she said, hugging her sister again. This was one of those times when they needed their mom to give them advice, but it was only the two of them. "Oh, honey, I'm sorry. Are you sure?"

Melinda chewed her lower lip between her teeth and just shook her head. "No. There are times when I'm sure that Slade is the perfect man for me. But the truth is until he can come to me and say he wants this to be real, I'm not going to be able to believe it. I can't just act like it's real when it's not. I do feel bad about lying to Philomena. I mean, I'm wearing her great-grandmother's ring and I love it. I want to think it will always be on my hand, but it won't be."

Angela had no real words to comfort her sister. Her own love life, while happy, was still not perfect because their father hadn't accepted Ryder, but hearing this pain in her sister's voice made her heart break. How could Slade do this to her sister?

"I'm going to talk to him."

"No. You're not. I will figure this out," Melinda said. "I appreciate that you would try to intervene for me, but this is my mess and I'm going to sort it out."

"I don't think you should refer to the father of your child as a mess," Angela said with a smile, trying to tease her sister back into a better a mood.

"I agree, but it's better than calling him an ass," Melinda said with a tiny smile.

"Even if that is what he is," Angela agreed.

"Who's an ass?" their father asked from the doorway. "I hope it's not me."

Angela saw the look on Melinda's face and realized her sister wasn't even close to being able to carry off a temporary engagement. Slade was asking the impossible.

"You can be, Daddy," Melinda said. "But today with both of your daughters engaged, I think we can agree that you're not."

Nothing made Sterling Perry happier than spending time with his children. Now that the fraud charges against him had been dropped, he was ready to get back to his normal life. Enough of being treated like a criminal.

He couldn't be happier that Melinda had finally found a man who could keep up with her and wasn't put off by the walls that his daughter tended to place around herself. Slade might not have been everyone's first choice for a son-in-law, but Sterling knew the man to be shrewd in business and damn hard to intimidate. He was the perfect match for Melinda.

He remembered his own engagement and how happy he'd been. That had been a long time ago. Before things had fallen apart. Jealousy and pride had driven a wedge between them that Sterling had never figured out how to fix. He knew he had his share of the blame and he hoped his daughters fared better in marriage than he had. But both of them seemed to be making choices... that were going to make their situations harder.

"What do you think of this?" Melinda asked, smiling over at him with her blue eyes so full of happiness that he couldn't help smiling back. He loved seeing that joy on her face. Slade did seem to genuinely care about his daughter and the man made her happy, what more could a father want?

"I'm sorry, Mels, I wasn't paying attention. What is this for again?" he asked.

She laughed. "It's for the table linens."

He shook his head. "Why don't I leave my credit card and let you two handle the rest of the details."

"Sounds good, since you've never really cared about these kinds of details," Angela said.

He wasn't sure if there was an edge to her tone or if he was imagining it because she knew he didn't like Ryder. He wanted his daughters to be happy, but Sterling could never trust Ryder.

He kissed both of his daughters on their foreheads and left them to sort out the party details. He gave his credit card information to the receptionist and then stepped out into the hot Houston afternoon. He glanced at his cell phone and saw that some of his longtime investors were still messaging him to be reassured that they hadn't been set up in a Ponzi scheme.

Damn that Ryder Currin. He had made it look like all of Sterling's legitimate investments were questionable. What would it take for Angela to be free of Ryder once and for all?

He walked to his car when the idea hit him. Perhaps Ryder needed a taste of his own medicine. If Ryder's precious Currin Oil were to be engulfed in a cloud of suspicion, maybe Angela would wake up and find herself a better man.

All it had taken for the investigation to be started into Sterlings's dealings was an anonymous tip. Something he had long suspected that Ryder Currin had a hand in. The more he thought about it, the angrier it made him. And while he knew he should be happy the charges were dropped, thanks to his lawyer son, Roarke, Sterling hadn't enjoyed having the negative publicity surround him and his company. The Perrys had been in Texas for a long time and had always been upstanding citizens.

He couldn't help but believe that Ryder was behind him being questioned in regard to Vincent Hamm's murder too.

Sterling had always been an Old Testament kind of man. Eye-for-an-eye sounded about right to him.

He couldn't make the call, but there was no reason one of his staff couldn't raise a legitimate concern.

He drove through the afternoon traffic and when he was back in his office, he called for one of his staffers.

He remembered the way that Angela had looked when he'd walked out of the party planner's office. She wasn't happy with him. She wanted him to accept the man she loved. But how could he? Ryder was everything he didn't want in his family.

He rubbed the back of his neck. Throwing a man's business into jeopardy… That wasn't his way. He didn't want to cost good men their jobs, only bring Ryder to the attention of law enforcement and cause him the same kind of problems that he'd created for Sterling. And maybe, please, God, Angela would come to her senses and leave Ryder.

"I heard some rather disturbing news today and it's the kind of thing that needs to be brought to the attention of the labor board. But because of my personal involvement I'd rather someone else handled it," Sterling said.

"What is it about?" his second assistant asked.

"It's about unfair labor practices at the Currin Oil refinery. Now, because of my daughter I wouldn't feel right about saying anything but we both know that labor practices aren't something we can look the other way on," Sterling said.

"I agree. Can you give me a few more details?" his assistant asked.

Sterling outlined the details of the complaint he wanted made against Currin Oil and his assistant looked properly shocked as he took notes, nodding and then reluctantly agreeing.

"I'll call from my office and make the anonymous tip to the labor line. I think you're doing the right thing here, Mr. Perry. Even if he is your daughter's fiancé. That kind of treatment of workers can't be tolerated."

"No, it can't," Sterling agreed as his assistant left his office. He had put up with a lot of crap over the last few weeks, but letting his daughter marry Currin wasn't something he would tolerate and he would do whatever he had to in order to protect her. For as long as he could remember, he'd hated Ryder Currin because he seemed to have some kind of spell over the women that Sterling loved. First, his wife, and now, one of his daughters.

He leaned back in his chair. "You're going down, Currin."

Ten

Ryder Currin was everything that Angela always wanted and never thought she'd have. The fact that he'd finally put a ring on her finger she thought would be the beginning to her happily-ever-after. But nothing ever went that easily for her. Her sister's comment about a double wedding and then bombshell of the truth behind her own engagement had left Angela with a few, well, concerns. Three days after she and her sister had been planning a reception for Melinda's engagement, she decided to go and talk to Ryder about finally setting a wedding date.

Ryder had asked her to marry him, but he'd been stonewalling her about setting a date and some of the things her father had said made her wonder if he was using her. She wished her dad and Ryder could find a way to get along.

If there was one thing that Angela Perry wasn't, it was a pushover. She strode into the offices of Currin Oil, well aware that the men she passed all stopped to watch her. She enjoyed it and had dressed specifically so she looked her best.

Ryder was on the phone when she walked in and the expression on his face had her stopping in her tracks. He was angry. Angrier than she'd ever seen him before and that was saying something.

He glanced up and his face softened for a moment as he motioned for her to come in and close the door behind her.

She did, but stayed next to the closed door. Whatever was going on with his business seemed like it was pretty intense. She wanted to get a wedding date on the calendar but even she could tell that maybe this wasn't the best time.

Still, she'd come this far, had given herself a pep talk and was determined to find out if she and Melinda were in the same boat. Was Ryder really going to marry her?

He slammed the phone down with more force than was necessary and she had to admit that was one thing she didn't like about her cell phone. There was no way to angrily punch the disconnect button that satisfied the way slamming down the handset on a landline did.

"Sorry, sweetheart. I didn't realize you'd be stopping by today," he said, standing up and coming over to give her a kiss. He took her hand and led her to the seating area in his office. "Can I get you a drink?"

"No, I'm good. Are you okay? You looked like you were ready to kill someone when I walked into the room," she said.

"Not kill, but I'm not in the best mood. Why did you stop by?" he asked.

She smiled weakly but he was watching her and now that she was here, she realized that coming by his office might not have been the best idea. But he'd been dodging talking about them and she needed some reassurance.

"I wanted to discuss the wedding plans. I thought it might take your mind off all that's been going on here. And really all I need your input on is the date. I can take care of the rest."

"Angela." He stood up and walked away, but in the way he said her name, she felt his frustration with her.

"What?" she asked, getting up to follow him. "You asked me to marry you and now you won't set a date or even talk about a possible date. Why is that? Do you really intend to marry me or was this all some kind of plot to get back at my dad?"

He turned to face her, and she saw that anger but also a little bit of what she thought might be hurt in his eyes. "If you think that, then why did you say yes?"

"I love you, Ryder, that's why I said yes. It's not like I'm playing a game with you. I just want to know that we are planning our wedding," she said.

"I get that, babe, but the truth is I can't right now. Someone has leveled accusations of employee mistreatment against the company. I'm trying to investigate that and see if there is any merit to the accusation, because until now I thought I ran a pretty clean company. And I'm pretty sure your father had something to do with the accusation."

She shook her head. "Listen, he might not like you, but he wouldn't stoop to sabotaging your business."

"You really think so? Because I'm pretty sure you thought I had something to do with the allegations against your father."

"I don't understand you two," she said. "And I never said that you had anything to do with that mess, which is all cleared up by the way so it's old news."

But it wasn't. Her father really did believe that Ryder had been the source of his legal troubles and it hadn't made it any easier to try to get him on board with accepting her fiancé. She had to do something. Right now. "We should elope. Just run away—"

"No. You're not listening to me. This isn't some accusation I can ignore and it will go away. This could cost me everything. I have to find out if there is any truth to the claims and then fix this. I can't run off and get married and pretend everything is okay, or that my daddy will swoop in and fix it. I'm the only one who can do this."

"You're being an ass and I don't like it. You know I don't wait for Dad to save me. I just was thinking that together as a team we would be able to fight this better. But if you want to do it on your own, then—"

She broke off and turned toward the door, but he caught her around the waist, pulling her back into his arms. He hugged her and put his head in the crook of her neck, kissing her. "I'm sorry. It's not you. It's my company. I've invested so much of my life in it and I hate that it's in jeopardy."

"Then let me help you," she said, turning in his arms and kissing him. If it was her father stirring up this trouble, then she would confront him and get to the bottom of it. Helping Ryder figure out what was going on was the least she could do.

Ryder did love her, and she was going to help him figure out this newest obstacle so they could move forward with their lives together.

Ryder had always had a hot temper and most of the time he could control it, but right now it seemed like everything was falling to pieces. He had the woman he loved in his arms, but he couldn't relax. He knew that her father hated him… Nothing new there. He had always been the kind of man that fathers didn't want their daughters dating. Except he was a successful oil tycoon now and not the wildcatter he'd once been. Even he had to admit he scarcely resembled the rough boy of his past.

But that didn't mean that life had suddenly gotten any easier for him. In fact, there were days when he wished he were still a wildcatter who settled things with his fists.

That didn't excuse his lashing out at Angela. It was simply that he couldn't plan for a future when his livelihood was being threatened. And he'd just heard that one of his executives, Willem Inwood, had some questionable practices with the employees and was a terrible manager.

It could all be allegations, but the call he'd just ended made it seem like there was more than a little truth to them. Angela wanted to help, but how could she? And he didn't want to lose her. He needed her by his side.

"We are stronger as a couple," he admitted, lifting her up in his arms, and she wrapped her legs around his hips as their lips met. Damn, it would be easy to distract her and himself with sex, but his office door was unlocked and one of his assistants was coming to talk about Inwood.

"I'm sorry for how I was. I'm just in a piss-poor mood," he said, carrying her back over to the sofa and sitting down with her on his lap. "Seeing you has made my day better."

"Good, I'm glad to hear that," she said, wrapping her arms around him. "But I can do more than help you feel better. Want me to go do some investigating into the allegations?"

He took a deep breath and then nodded. He was too used to going it alone because for most of his life, the only one he had counted on was himself. But Angela was here, and she wanted to help. "I'm not sure you'll get any further than I did with the complaints officer. He said the tip was anonymous and it was only when he started talking to my employees that he found the accusation had any substance."

"Which employees? I don't think my father could get to them," she said. "The last person your employees would speak to is him."

"I agree, but he might have overheard some grumblings and called the tip in. But he isn't the source of the problems," Ryder admitted. As much as he wanted to blame Sterling, it seemed that one of his executives was at the root of the issue. Which pissed him off. He trusted his employees. When he hired someone to work at Currin Oil he always thought of them as part of his extended family. Now he wondered if that was a mistake.

There was a knock on his office door and Angela shifted off his lap to sit on the couch as he went to open the door. His assistant was standing there with her tablet in one hand and a stack of files tucked into the curve of her arm.

"I have all the files and there is definitely some cause for alarm—" She stopped talking when she noticed Angela.

"It's okay, Mary. Angela is going to try to help us out here. She has some connections at town hall and so she'll be asking some questions to help us get to the bottom of this."

"Great. I think we're going to need all the help we can get. I can't find Willem. It's almost as if he's just disappeared. I don't want to get the police involved unless we have to. But he might have skipped town."

Well, that looked damned suspicious. He would have liked it better if Willem had come in and denied everything. Or the man could admit to it, then Ryder would know what he was dealing with. Instead, the guy seemed to have taken the coward's way out. "Okay. I have a guy who does investigations for the firm. I'll ask him to try to track down Willem. In the meantime, tell me what you have on the complaints."

"Who is Willem?" Angela asked him.

"Willem Inwood," Ryder said, wrapping his arm around her as she came over to the conference table where Mary had spread out the employee files.

"That name sounds familiar. Have I met him at one of your functions?" she asked.

"I don't think so," Ryder said. "Do you know him from somewhere else?"

"I might. It's like a name from a long time ago," she said. "I'll figure it out. I don't think Daddy knows him but maybe he does."

"I hope not because that would feed into my suspicions of corporate sabotage," he replied. "But I'm sure you'll figure out how you know the name."

"I don't know that I should be looking at any employee files. Can you give me some information about the complaints? Then I'll go and see what kind of information I can dig up," she said.

Mary handed her a copy of the formal complaint, which Angela read. "Okay, let me see what I can find out."

"Thanks, babe," Ryder said, walking her to his office door and stepping out into the hallway with her. It was clear and he pulled her into his arms, kissing her again. "I am sorry about earlier. You mean the world to me, and once I get this sorted, we can start planning the wedding of your dreams."

"I want it to be the wedding of *our* dreams," she said, going up on tiptoe and kissing him before she turned and walked away.

All of his dreams were just to have the woman he loved by his side.

Melinda decided she'd had enough of everything and everyone and a trip to the Red Door Salon was what she needed to get herself back on track. She texted Angela to see if she wanted to meet her for an afternoon at the spa.

Angela had one more thing to do but she'd meet her around three o'clock.

Melinda decided to go early and get her hair trimmed.

Melinda's assistant was waiting for her when she came into her office at the foundation she cofounded with her sorority sister. She handed Pixie to Alfie. "I booked her a grooming appointment. Do you mind running her over?"

"Not at all," he replied. He handed her a stack of messages. "As you can see, we've had a few more media requests. Have you and Slade set a wedding date?" Alfie asked. "I'm thinking that would appease them for now."

A wedding date? For their big day? No, they hadn't set one and she knew they never would and that was kind of what pushed her over the edge. How was she supposed to do this? No one wanted to spend his or her entire life in one big lie…or rather, she didn't. She was really upset that Slade had put her in this position. Sure, she understood… No, actually she didn't understand why he couldn't just marry her.

Other than the fact that no matter how he tried to frame it, he didn't love her. And he didn't want to spend the rest of his life with her.

"I don't have a date, Alfie. But for now, tell them we're planning a big engagement party for Saturday the twenty-first. We will be inviting a limited number of social bloggers and reporters," she said. "And if you don't mind, make a list of those bloggers who you think will treat us kindly and not like some kind of salacious episode of a reality TV show."

"I'll do that. Come on, Miss Pixie," Alfie said, tapping his leg, and the dachshund followed him out of her office.

Alfie closed the door behind him, and Melinda walked over to her desk and sat on the edge of it. Right now, she had been running from fire to fire and trying to stay ahead of the blaze, but it wasn't working. She needed to dig a trench like those firefighters did when a blaze was out of control…or call in reinforcements. The only problem was she had no reinforcements.

Angela had said she needed to listen to her own advice when it came to Slade, and Melinda realized that she was afraid to do that. Afraid to admit that after all these years of waiting for Mr. Right, she'd made Slade into something he wasn't.

He had completely rocked her world and what they had together in bed was like nothing she'd ever imagined. She'd definitely believed sex was overrated until she'd done it with him. But there was more to relationships than sex.

Slade looked good in a tux and in a pair of faded jeans, but clothes didn't always make the man. She knew that. So was she seeing something in Slade that wasn't there?

Was she being naive because a part of her acknowledged that if she were ever going to settle down, this was definitely the time to do it?

Or was it that positive pregnancy test that had her convinced they had to be in love?

She'd had feelings for Slade for a while now. She'd been afraid to admit them because he clearly wasn't looking for marriage with her or, to be fair, with any woman.

And the baby… She touched her stomach not because she felt maternal but because she felt like she might be sick. She wasn't ready for a child. She still felt as lost and confused about her personal life now as she had at twenty-one.

She had no idea what she was going to do. She hated this feeling and she knew there was no list she could make or plans she could set in motion that would allay this fear. It stemmed from so deep inside of her that she knew it was time to just face it. Sometimes owning a fear would make it into something she could conquer. She'd done it one other time. When she'd turned thirty and realized that she was going to be on her own after she'd broken up with her boyfriend at the time, Wendall.

"This is the same thing," she muttered to herself. "Just say it out loud. Own it."

Own it.

"I'm not lovable. I have too many edges and rules that I surround myself with. No man can fit into the mold I've created. And Slade isn't going to wake up and realize he loves me."

Her voice cracked a little on the last note. "But I still love him."

There.

She'd said it.

She owned it.

"I love him, but he doesn't love me. Okay. But I can't stop loving him."

Oh, man, she was losing it. But there it was. That was the truth. Regardless of what happened with their engagement, she was probably going to love Slade for the rest of her life. And she had to find a way to live with that. A way to explain that to their child.

The child she wasn't even sure that Slade would be a father to. And that hurt her. That he wouldn't want to share a life with her and their baby. But that had nothing to do with her. And she had to figure out how to forge a life without him. Unless she could find out what his fear was…

Was it possible that she'd be able to help him see the other side? See that together they would be better?

Eleven

Back at her condo after the spa that afternoon, Melinda took Pixie out on the balcony and stood at the railing looking down at the city. Up here, it seemed so much easier to make decisions than it did when she was sitting next to her sister or when she was with Slade. The truth was that Angela had been right. If she was in love with Slade, she would figure out a way to make him be a part of her life now and forever.

The thing was she didn't want to manipulate him into loving her and committing to her. She didn't want to pressure him into staying in a relationship that would feel like a trap to him.

He'd shared the story of his parents' marriage and she'd seen firsthand her own parents' happy marriage break down. She certainly didn't want to end up like that. She knew from her own experience that having two parents who felt trapped wasn't necessarily better than just having one. Or she thought it wouldn't be. She had no idea what it would be like to grow up having only one parent. She'd lost her mom ten years ago and that had been hard enough. What would her child face if only she raised it?

Pixie barked and ran back into the condo, and Melinda followed her. She'd given Slade a key, but he had yet to use it without texting her first to let her know he was coming over. They had debated moving in together because they both knew that some of the more mean-spirited social bloggers had commented on the fact that the only time they were together was to hook up.

But Melinda had never let anyone push her into doing anything in her life and wasn't about to start now. Which was another argument for not doing the things that would make Slade feel like he had to stay engaged to her, that he had to marry her.

She wouldn't be able to handle the guilt that went along with that. The fact was she wanted this to sort itself out. But she'd never been able to leave things be. Her father liked to say that everything happened in its own time, but she had always been too impatient to wait.

She wanted things to happen in Melinda's time. When she wanted it, not when it was right.

"Hello," she heard Slade call out. "Where's your mistress, Pix?"

"I'm here. Just enjoying the sun and the peace up here," she called back. "I have some sweet tea out here if you're thirsty. There's also beer in the fridge."

"Sweet tea sounds perfect," he said as he came onto the balcony. He pulled her into his arms and leaned in to kiss her, but his mouth skimmed along her cheek. It felt different now that she'd acknowledged that she loved him. She still got that rush that she always did when she saw him but she knew that once the media stopped bothering her, he'd leave. And that hurt. This was exactly what she'd been trying to avoid.

"I noticed that one of the bloggers that has been watching you has a drone so we might not be alone."

She literally started shaking with outrage. Why did anyone believe they had the right to spy on her? She could understand their curiosity about her relationship…but a drone? That was too much. "They're going too far."

"I agree," he said, stepping back and rubbing his hands up and down her bare arms. "But I wanted you to know."

"I'm going to call the building managers. Surely there's some sort of legal reason why they can't fly it over the condos," Melinda said.

"I think we need to give the media something to print. Let's face it, we've been pretty low-key for the last week or so," he said.

She nodded. Giving them something to talk about was the entire reason they had gotten engaged. Her doubts had made her reluctant to walk around, letting anyone see the two of them together. She knew it was going to be much harder—much more humiliating—when they ended things if there were all those pictures of them being all lovey-dovey.

The knot in the pit of her stomach intensified and she honestly felt like she might throw up. She thought she could control it and then realized she couldn't. She tried to walk all ladylike into her living room and then as soon as she was inside bolted for the bathroom. She heard Slade behind her. The heels on his dress shoes echoed behind her on the marble floor and she knew he was saying something, but she was so focused on not throwing up until she was in the bathroom she couldn't comprehend or respond.

She got into the bathroom just in time. She heard Slade behind her as she finished throwing up. He handed her a towel to wipe her mouth and then a cup of water to rinse with. Then he pulled her into his arms and held her to him. Just a hug that offered comfort and she started crying. There was no reason for the tears, except she wasn't holding things together the way she usually could.

This entire situation was insane. Not what she had planned for herself or her unborn child or Slade.

She always had a plan and things usually worked out the way she planned them, but this time they weren't. She had no idea how to get back on track and it seemed the more she tried, the harder it was.

He held the back of her head, lightly massaging her scalp, and she just closed her eyes and pretended she hadn't just gotten sick or cried in his arms. Finally, she felt slightly better and stepped back.

"I'm sorry about that."

"Don't be. You're pregnant and life is a bit stressful right now. Do you feel up to a walk around downtown? Just something for the paparazzi to snap some pictures of and then we can come home, and I'll make dinner for you."

"You can cook?" she asked.

"Yes, and I'm pretty damned good at it. What do you say?"

She nodded. "That sounds good to me. I'll go get changed. I guess you'll need to change as well."

"I will. I'm glad I had some of my clothes sent over here."

"Me too," she said, thinking of his clothes in the master bedroom closet and in a drawer she'd emptied for him. Though last night she'd realized that wasn't helping her keep their lives separate.

A romantic walk… Not his smartest idea given that he should be trying to put some distance between him and Melinda. But here he was. Pixie didn't seem that happy about it either. She was on a leash and her little jeweled collar sparkled in the sunlight. Everyone who walked past them smiled at the cute dachshund and when they glanced up and saw him and Melinda holding hands and looking to the world like lovers who had the world on a string, they smiled at them as well.

Only, he felt the way that Melinda's hand tightened in his each time that happened. He knew this kind of outward deception wasn't her thing. He didn't need to be a mind reader to know that the further they got into the engagement, the harder it was going to be for her to pull off a breakup.

If he were a different man, he'd make the temporary promise he had made her into a real one. And he wasn't going to lie to himself, he'd thought about it more than once. But then he'd see one of his uncles at a distance or another news alert about the Bartelli family and he knew that he had to stay resolute.

He wasn't about to put any child of Melinda's through what he had gone through as a child. He had clawed his way out of the Bartelli family, but it would be impossible to protect a child of his from them. He knew from his own behavior as a teenager that rebellion was a big part of why he had to keep his distance from the child.

It would have probably been better if he had never gone out with her. But he couldn't undo the past and he had always used his mistakes to get stronger.

They stopped at a nearby café, needing a drink from the heat. After they were seated in a dog-friendly section, Pixie drank water from a collapsible bowl that Melinda had pulled from her bag and then she curled up on the scarf that Melinda laid down for her.

"What are you thinking about?" she asked, after the waitress took their drink orders. "You looked so fierce I think the waitress was afraid to ask what you wanted to drink."

He tried to smile but that was gone. They were in the relative privacy of the café and he didn't have to keep up the sappy so-in-love vibe he'd had going on the street. "Nothing."

"I can tell it was something," she said.

He just shrugged. He wasn't obliged to share everything with Melinda.

"Listen, if you want me to keep doing this, then you need to be honest with me. We can't be lying in public and in private... Well, maybe you can, but I can't. I won't. So either you level with me or I'm out of here."

He had seen her worked up before and, no lie, it did turn him on to see her passionate but not like this. She was angry and hurt and he was to blame. How many times did he need to see proof that he was the completely wrong man for her?

"You're Slade Bartelli," a tall man in a Stetson and

a serious expression said as he came over to their table.
Pixie got up and danced over toward the man, who bent
down and petted her. Not so fierce when he smiled at
the little dog.

Melinda glanced up at the man, who looked like he
didn't like Slade very much. Slade stood up and held
out his hand.

"I am. This is Melinda Perry," he said. "And you
are?"

"Nathan Battle, the sheriff of Royal, Texas." He
turned to Melinda. "Ma'am. Are you related to Sterling Perry?"

"He's my father," she said.

He tipped his hat toward her and continued to stand,
as did Slade, and the sheriff turned his attention back
toward Slade.

"Your father's activities are starting to encroach on
several of the more prominent citizens of Royal and I
don't like that much," Nathan said.

"I'm sorry to hear that, sir," Slade said. "I have nothing to do with my father's business. In fact, I'm the
CEO of Conti Enterprises. I'd offer to have a word with
him, but he doesn't listen to anyone."

"Would you sit down, Sheriff?" Melinda asked.

"I can't, ma'am. I'm in town on business and thought
I'd kill two birds with one stone."

"What is the other business that brings you to Houston?" Melinda asked, afraid that it might have something to do with the grisly murder of the man found
on her father's construction site at the new Texas Cattleman's Club.

"I'm investigating the Vincent Hamm murder. So
far I haven't been able to get much information from

Detective Zoe Warren, who is in charge of the Houston investigation, so I've come to do some of my own digging."

"Isn't it a Houston case?" Melinda asked, wondering why the Royal sheriff was investigating. Was there more to the case than just murder? Did it somehow tie to Royal?

"It is, but Hamm was from Royal and a family friend. I've promised his father I'd find out what happened. You know a text was sent from Vincent's Perry Holdings phone—after he was dead."

"Who would do such a thing?" Melinda asked. "That's horrible."

"It's awful," Slade added. "Some people will do anything to cover their tracks."

"Yes, they will," the sheriff said. "Well, I'll leave you two to your drinks. If you think of anything that could help with my investigation, give me a call."

He handed them his card and then walked away. Slade watched him leave before finally sitting back down. He looked at the card for a moment before tucking it into the inside pocket of his jacket.

Slade Bartelli hadn't been exactly what Nathan had been expecting. He had a firm handshake and he'd been respectful and forthright with him. Nathan rubbed the back of his neck as he headed to the Houston Police Department. He was frustrated by the lack of suspects in Vincent Hamm's murder.

He knew he'd stopped and warned Bartelli because of that. He normally wasn't the kind of sheriff who threatened men like Slade—a billionaire entrepreneur and not a street thug. He waited for Detective Zoe War-ren and decided he was ready to be back in Royal.

He liked being on his own turf. He missed his wife, Amanda, and the diner she ran back in Royal and the coffee that she always had waiting for him when he stopped by. He didn't relish going back to Royal with-out some answers for Vincent's family. They were all beside themselves, and he admitted to himself that that was one thing he really hated about his job. Talking to the victims' families. Especially when he knew them as well as he did the Hamms.

"Sheriff Battle, what can I do for you?" Zoe asked as she met him in the waiting area.

"Just following up to see where you stand on the Hamm investigation," he said.

"Come back to my desk and I'll update you," she said. "I have to be honest. We don't have much to go on."

He followed her through the precinct to her desk and he realized he started to relax being in the familiar environment. He liked cops and he felt most at home when he was surrounded by them.

"As you know, I've had Sterling Perry in for ques-tioning. The man was cagey and not very cooperative. Could be because he's been under investigation since the first time I talked to him." She shrugged. "But he didn't add anything new. Neither did Liam Mor-row, who, along with the construction crew, found the body. And none of Hamm's colleagues have anything to add either."

"Hmm, I don't like that. Someone has to know something," Nathan said.

"I agree. I'm shaking some trees… I was hoping that

since you were here, maybe you'd heard something in Royal?" she said with a question in her voice.

"Nothing yet. But I'll keep poking around and let you know what I find," he said.

"Good. I'll keep you in the loop if I get any breaks on this case," she said. "I know this one is personal for you. That always makes me more determined to solve it."

"I doubt you are ever not determined," he said, standing up.

"Very true," she admitted with a smile.

He shook her hand before leaving the station. When he got out on the street, he took a moment to think about the suspects. Hell, there weren't any. But Sterling Perry being cagey… That bothered him. He would put out a few feelers and see what else he could find out about Perry and his business.

Melinda watched Slade as he sat back down. He was on edge and looked like he wanted to punch someone. It was the first time she'd seen him like this. She could tell he didn't like being treated like a criminal when he wasn't one.

She didn't like it either. Slade was a good man. The man she loved. How dare that sheriff stop and talk to him like that.

"I cannot tell you how many times I've had that conversation with law enforcement," he said.

"I can't believe it," she said, realizing that there was a lot more to Slade's life than she had glimpsed. "I mean, your dad of course has a reputation, but you've never done anything outside the law. Is this what you are afraid of if we got married?"

He looked at her, his dark gaze a cocktail of emotions that she had a hard time reading. Anger and remorse and something else she couldn't identify.

"Hell, Mels, of course, I don't want you subject to anything like that. I hate that he felt justified in coming up to talk to me when I was with you. I'm not a criminal. I have lived my life above reproach…but this kind of thing isn't going to just disappear."

"It isn't," she said, her heart aching at the thought of Slade spending the rest of his life alone and isolated from her and their child to protect them. It was an honorable sentiment, but he shouldn't be alone. He didn't have to be. "I can handle that, Slade. I'm not as frail as you might think I am."

"I know that, woman. That doesn't mean I want you to have to fight the battle that comes with my last name," he said.

"You're not asking me to, I'm asking you to let me," she said. "Do you understand? For me, this is something that I can't just ignore. I care deeply about you. I can't stand the thought that anyone feels as if they can question you about your father's crimes."

He nodded, leaned over and kissed her so softly and sweetly that the love she was trying desperately not to confess almost spilled out.

"I'm sorry you had to see it," he said, as he lifted his head. "I have to remember that neither of us is responsible for our family's actions."

"That's okay," she said. "You're not your father."

"No, I'm not," he said. "Neither are you."

She sat back from him and narrowed her eyes, not sure why he would bring up her father. "What are you saying?"

"Just that you must endure some questions about your father. That's pretty tough to ignore."

"Not for me," she said. "The rumors aren't true. You must know that."

He shrugged. "I'm used to dealing with people whispering behind my back. You might have to get used to that on your own, even without adding the Bartelli name to the mix."

"What are you saying?"

"That people think your father had something to do with Vincent Hamm's murder," he said.

"If that were true, I think Sheriff Battle would have brought it up," she said, wondering where he was leading with all of this. "But he didn't. Don't try to paint my father with the same brush as yours."

"I'm not painting him with anything. I'm simply saying your father has rumors swirling all around him."

She shook her head, trying not to let her anger get the better of her, but the more he talked, the worse he was making it. "We were talking about you, Slade. Not my dad. Who, by the way, is nothing like your father."

"Well, that has yet to be seen," Slade said.

"Why would you say such a thing?" she asked, angry and hurt that he'd even think her father would be part of anything illegal, especially murder. She stood up and grabbed her purse and Pixie's leash, glaring down at him.

"How dare you, Slade Bartelli."

He stopped her by grabbing her arm gently. Her handbag hit him in the arm but he ignored it. He couldn't let her walk away like this. Not now. He pulled her into his arms when he noticed some of the other patrons looking at them, and kissed her gently, but she turned her head. She was ticked at him and fair enough.

"People are watching," he said, under his breath.

She looked at him with such disdain that he knew his solution was going to kill whatever had been simmering between them. She was something he was afraid to keep for himself, and he was doing what he always did when he had someone in his life who cared. Driving them away.

"Let's finish our drinks so we can both leave together," he said.

"Let's go. I can't do this right now," she said.

"All right, let's go," he said loudly, linking their hands together and leading her and Pixie out to the street. Wanting to get inside and find privacy, he decided not to walk back to her condo. Instead, he hailed a taxi.

He wrapped his arm around her shoulder and held her close to his body and he was pretty sure he was the only one who knew that she pinched him on his side when he did it, but she smiled up at him at the same time.

He simply smiled back and as soon as they were at her building, he got out and held the door for her as she scooped up Pixie. He put his hand on the small of her back as he guided her toward her building. A flurry of paparazzi was waiting at the entrance, snapping pictures and yelling questions. This was crazy. How had he ever thought his plan was going to help? But he'd had no other idea how to protect her and he hadn't been ready to stay goodbye. He still wasn't. But was he holding on for himself only?

He knew that this was harder for Melinda than she'd

ever admit. A clean break would have been better. He should have said he didn't want to be a father and just walked away. Better to let her think he was an ass than to break her heart.

As soon as they were across the lobby and in the private elevator bank, she stepped away from him.

"You don't have to come up."

"I do. We're not done with this," he said. Granted, his father had a much longer history of criminal activity than any Perry did. But her father had been making some interesting choices of late, so Slade's comment wasn't completely out of line. She had to know what people were saying. In fact, she probably did but she didn't want to hear it from him.

"I'm done. I can't believe you accused my father of murder. I've defended you more times than I care to admit, and everyone knows your family is organized crime. And I've taken your word that you're not involved," she said, jamming the call button for the elevator with more force than was necessary.

"Yes, you have. With good reason," he added. "When have I lied to you?" It bothered him that everyone judged him to be like his father without knowing him, but he couldn't say something... Hell, he knew he'd lashed out because that damned sheriff had made him remember he wasn't good enough for Melinda. It wasn't like that would be the last time in his life when a law enforcement official would question him, even though he had never done a single damned thing that was against the law. "Even when lying would have benefited me, I've always been honest with you."

She sighed. "I know. I know, Slade. God, I'm sorry, it's just that your question hit a little too close to home.

And I'm tired of pretending. I…" She hesitated, as if she didn't want to finish her thought, then finally said, "I like you, and I don't want to break up with you because you're afraid of commitment."

"I wish it were just that. But it's more. My family isn't like yours. Mine is really involved in things that are illegal and it took a lot of struggling for me to break free from them. I know if I claim you and the child as my own, my father isn't going to stay out of the child's life. We have to do it the way I described, or you're going—"

"Are you saying if it weren't for your father, you'd stay with me?" she asked.

He hesitated.

"No, you're not saying that. Is that the excuse you tell yourself to make it sound better?" she questioned. The elevator car arrived, and she set Pixie down, letting the dog walk on before her.

"It's not an excuse," he said, but as soon as he said it, he knew that it was. He didn't want to chance loving her. He'd seen what had happened with his parents' marriage. He knew that two people from such diverse backgrounds would have to struggle to make a situation like this one work.

He could handle her pissed off and mad at him, but hurt, broken—the way his mom had been after her divorce or the way his long-ago fiancée had been after they'd split up—no. He couldn't handle that. He needed to know that she was okay.

"You're right, Mels. But the truth is I can't handle being the man who disappoints you."

"You already are," she said.

"Not like I will," he admitted.

"Oh, Slade," she said, taking his hand.

And that was the moment when he should have walked away, but he let her lead him onto the elevator because he needed her more than he wanted to protect her.

Twelve

The next morning when she woke up, she found Slade sitting on the edge of the bed, head bowed as he looked down at his feet. His muscled back was strained and she saw the stress in him.

"Slade? Honey, what's the matter?" she asked.

He glanced over at her and smiled. "Morning, baby cakes. Nothing. Just a text from my dad."

"What does he want?"

"To see me," Slade said. "He sends me a text once a week, asking to see me."

"Why?"

"Because I haven't seen him or knowingly been in his company since I turned eighteen."

"Why not?"

"It's complicated," Slade said.

"I'm your pretend fiancée who is pregnant with your

baby that no one knows about, so I think I can handle complicated," she said.

He gave a laugh. "Yeah, I guess you can."

He turned and piled some pillows against the headboard and shifted around until he was lying against them. "I took Pixie out by the way."

"Thank you. Now you were saying about your father…" Somehow, she knew she had to get to the bottom of whatever it was that made him not want to be a family man. From her experience with her own family and from watching some of her friends marry and divorce, she knew that relationships were often influenced by the couple's own parents.

"You're not going to let this go, are you?" he asked.

She shook her head. "Nope. I have a vested interest in this, honey. Someday, our baby is going to ask me about his paternal grandfather, and I want to be able to answer honestly."

"This isn't going to make it easier," he said.

"Just tell me," she said, pulling the sheet up under her armpits and smiling over at him.

"Okay…so after my mom died, I lived with my grandparents and they had custody of me. It had been decided that it would be better for everyone if they continued raising me. It was a good life, but I was curious about my father. My memories of him had been tied to my childhood and my nonno hated my dad so I didn't know if that had colored my opinion of him," Slade said, not looking at her but looking at his own feet as he kept crossing and uncrossing his legs on the bed.

It was odd to her because Slade wasn't normally a nervous, fidgety person, but this story wasn't something easy for him to tell and it was over twenty years old.

"That makes sense. No matter how my parents fought, I am very glad that I got to know them both and that they were together for us," Melinda said. And she was. She wanted that for her child. She knew in her heart that she and Slade were very different people, but she also firmly believed that children needed to know both of their parents to be successful in life.

"Are you?" he asked gently, but the more she pushed him on this, the more defensive he felt. "I think that might be because you had them both. But if your father was like mine, you might not feel the same way."

"What are you trying to say?" she asked. "You know you're not anything like your own father."

"Am I?" he asked.

"Unless you've been lying to me and deceiving me since we started dating. Have you?"

He cursed and stood up, walking away from the bed and over to the glass doors that overlooked her balcony and then the city. She wondered what he saw. What was he trying not to tell her?

She got out of bed and put on her floral-print robe, belting it at the waist. Pixie trotted over to her and Melinda bent down to pet her and gave her a cuddle before walking over to where Slade stood. She put her hand on his back and leaned around, looking up at his face.

She remembered when they'd made love in her condo at the glass door. So much of her life was tied to his now. She knew she'd have a hard time separating from him when he walked away. But she also had no regrets. She might be confused about single parenthood and how her life was going to shake out, but she was also excited about entering this new phase of her life.

One she would never have had if not for Slade.

"Okay, so you're a teenager and rebellious and... you go see your dad?"

"Yeah," he said, putting his arm around her shoulder and hugging her to him. She wrapped her arm around his waist and put her other hand on his chest.

This confession haunted him probably the same way that the time she'd run away when she'd been in fifth grade had dogged her for a long time. She'd gone to keep her friend from being alone, but the repercussions had been a deterioration in her relationship with her mom, who thought she'd left because of the fighting at home.

"It's okay. Whatever you did," she said.

"It's not," he said. "I started sneaking out to see him and he's a really funny guy, smart and charming. I couldn't for the life of me figure out why my grandparents hated him or even why my mom left him. After about six weeks, he asked me if I wanted to go to work with him. See what my Bartelli family was like."

She had a sinking feeling in the pit of her stomach. She should stop him from telling her anything more, but at the same time she wanted to know exactly what had happened. She needed to see the entire picture, so she knew what she was fighting.

"I bet you were curious. You'd never met them, had you?"

"Not since Mom and I had left," he said. "I went with him and met my uncles and the rest of my goombahs."

"What's a *goombah*?" she asked.

"Well, in the Conti family, it means friends who are close like family. But for the Bartellis... Well, it's more like anyone associated with their crime family.

This thing I'm about to tell you, Melinda… I've never told anyone."

She nodded. "Your secret is safe with me."

And it was. She loved this man and would do whatever she had to protect him.

"Some of my uncles were like my dad. Funny, charming. But some of the others wanted me to prove myself. They thought I had no place in the Bartelli family. And my goombahs were even more adamant. So, Dad pulled me aside and said if I went on a job, proved myself, they'd leave me be and that would be the end of it."

"What kind of job?" she asked.

"I had no idea. I had been to work with Nonno and though I knew the rumors about the mob stuff, I still didn't really get what that meant. I mean, I had a vague idea from watching *The Godfather* and *Goodfellas* as a point of reference but that wasn't Houston. Wasn't my Italian American family, you know? God, saying this out loud makes me realize how naive I was."

She hugged him. "You don't have to say anything else."

"Are you sure?" he asked.

"Yes. You're nothing like your father," she said. "You don't have to tell me about him and how it affected you for me to see that."

She watched his face and noticed the ways his eyes flickered away from her, as if he didn't want her to see the truth.

"Right?" she asked him.

He took a deep breath. "The truth is I liked being part of his crew. And though the…"

She didn't want to know if he'd killed someone or beat someone up... Did she? "Activity?" she supplied.

"Yes. Though the activity wasn't something I could stomach, I liked being part of the family. Having the other guys around me. It was hard to walk away from. Harder than I'd like to admit. And then because I had ridden with him for a few weeks, my uncles and cousins didn't want me to walk away."

"What did you do? Did you kill someone?"

"No. I'd never do that. In fact, that was why I left. Like I said, riding with the crew was fun. It was like having brothers and for the first time in my life, I wasn't getting the stink eye from others because I was a Bartelli. I was accepted just for who I was. My dad sent me on collection runs to pick up money and stuff like that. But on my last ride...things went south, and my cousin Pauley pulled his gun and shot two guys. I just stood there. I have to be honest, Melinda. I was freaking out. This guy had been laughing and joking with me seconds before.

"Pauley took one look at my face and knew that I wasn't going to be able to help him and told me to get out of there. I did. Ran straight back to my grandparents and I haven't spoken to my dad since."

He saw the horror on her face, and he didn't blame her at all. Eighteen had been a long time ago and he'd been young and stupid. But the worst part was believing he could walk away. That the weeks he'd spent running with the Bartelli family wouldn't have a lasting effect. Until he got engaged. Then he saw the truth. How some of his goombahs had never forgiven him for the way he left. And they never would.

"That's why I can't be the family man you want me to be," he said, quietly.

She shook her head. "I'm horrified that you had to go through that. That your father put you in that situation. I knew you wouldn't knowingly harm anyone."

He could hear her working her way through the story he'd just told her, and this was the thing about Melinda that always made him regret that he wasn't a better man. She was going to find a way to use that to make him stronger in her own eyes. He'd honestly never met anyone who was determined to see the best in people. But he knew he wasn't the best. He'd taken the easy way out too many times. Running back to Nonno where he'd known that his father wouldn't follow.

His grandparents had been disappointed, but they'd understood his need to see for himself the man his father was. His dad tried to talk to him, but Slade had refused. He didn't want any part of that life. His cousins had beat him up after school and threatened to kill him if he ratted out Pauley, which Slade had no intention of doing. He wanted nothing to do with the Bartelli family. But once he left to go to college in Austin, he called the tip line and reported the crime. He hadn't been able to live with the knowledge that he'd witnessed those deaths. It didn't matter that the men who'd been killed had been rough criminals.

"I could never hurt anyone," he agreed. "But that's what the Bartelli family does. And if I'm in our child's life, then you and our child will be targeted by the family. I have no way of protecting you." He'd just named his deepest, darkest fear out loud and to be honest, it sounded even worse now that he'd done that. He wanted to be the man who protected her, not the one who led her to a place she could never come back from.

"You have one," she said.

"What's that?" he asked. Melinda was smart; maybe she saw something he didn't.

"Go to your dad, tell him you want a new life with me and that he needs to ensure that his family knows you aren't going to ever be a part of it," she said.

"My dad… Why would he do that? He wouldn't lift a finger to help my fiancée."

"Did you ask him to?" she asked carefully.

"I sent word to him through one of my cousins," he said. He hadn't been able to ask his father; he'd been afraid he might say no. That had been the one thing that Slade had never been able to understand about himself. He wanted to hate his father but he'd never been able to. He still loved his dad. Still wanted him to be the kind of father who protected his kid… Damn, his own kid was going to feel the same way.

He didn't know how he was going to live with knowing he was hurting Melinda's child.

"I can only tell you that from what I've observed, some men mellow as they get older," she said, "and if he has a chance to see our child…maybe that will be enough."

He shook his head. "He's dead to me. I won't ask him for anything."

"You're being stubborn about this."

He was, but there were some things that he wouldn't back down on, and his father was one of them. He didn't know if it was pride or just resentment that his dad had failed him so massively when he'd been a teenager, but he wasn't going to ask him for anything. Not now. Not even for Melinda.

"Maybe, but this isn't something I'm willing to do," he said. "I don't expect you to understand. Despite his shady dealings, your father has always been a solid figure in your life."

She chewed her lower lip and put one hand on her hip. "I think you're being an ass about this. We could have everything. A real engagement and a real wedding. We could raise this baby together. I would do anything that I needed to in order to make that happen."

He knew she would. She'd been like that from the moment she found out about the baby. Or from the moment he'd found out. She'd looked at him with hope in her eyes and he'd panicked and done what he could to protect her. But he was being the man Melinda needed him to be and not himself.

Every time he'd stepped away from owning his actions, it had backfired. Much like this entire morning was. She wanted something from him because she thought if he did this—went to his dad and asked him for something—then everything was going to be fine.

But it wouldn't be. He was a man who'd spent all of his adult life on his own, not having anyone dependent on him, and that enabled him to make risky decisions in business. To have fun when he wanted to. And not hurt anyone else because of his family name.

"I wish it were that easy, Melinda. That you could wave your magic wand and I'd become the man you want me to be. I think you've been seeing me as someone else. Some kind of prince like those heroes in the books you like to read. But I'm not that guy."

She shook her head.

"You could be."

He didn't think it was possible to hurt like this, but he did. He was frozen with a desire to be that man she wanted at the same time he was facing the reality of who he was. He didn't want to disappoint her but if he weren't true to himself, what kind of man would he be?

He wasn't willing to risk it or try to find out.

"I'm not going to do it," he said. "I will not talk to my father. I can't be a family man, because it's not the life I chose. And we're not children, Melinda, so I know you can understand that."

She wasn't having it and he didn't blame her. But he had never felt anything like this fear he felt when he thought of her getting to know his Bartelli family. He knew how quickly they could turn from normal to criminal. In a blink of an eye. He didn't want her or any child of theirs near that kind of life. And if that meant he had to spend the rest of his life without her... then so be it.

He'd rather she be alive and safe than with him for a short time.

"You could if I meant more to you," she said.

"You know what you mean to me," he retorted. He was trying to be cool, but it was harder than he thought. He was putting her first. Why couldn't she see that and accept it and just let this lie?

"Do I?"

"Yes, you do and I'm not going to play this kind of game. One of the things I've always admired about you is how forthright you are. I've never had to pretend to be someone I'm not with you."

"Good thing," she said. "We know how much you have to be you."

She turned away and he realized that he needed to do something to salvage this. "I'm sorry."

She glanced back over at him, hope in her eyes, and he knew that unless he made a clean break, she was always going to be hoping he'd be that better man.

"Me too. I love you, Slade. I haven't wanted to say it until we sorted everything else out, but my feelings aren't going to change. I want you by my side when the child is born. I want to have a family with you. I can't keep lying about that. I think when I said yes to the charade, I figured you'd come around to making it real. Have you?"

Everything inside of him froze. She loved him. He had both wanted that and feared it from the moment he'd seen those pregnancy tests lined up on her bathroom counter. Melinda Perry was everything he never knew he wanted in a woman and nothing hurt him more than knowing if he tied his life to hers, she'd be bound by the same prejudice and gossip and rumors that had plagued him his entire life. And she deserved better.

This was his nightmare. She was asking him for something that he'd already promised himself he'd never take a chance on. "Melinda, didn't you hear what I said?"

"I did, but I thought if you knew how much I care about you…if you saw me taking a chance on us, then you'd be able to as well," she said. "Can you?"

Dammit.

He couldn't think of anything to say. He just stood

there, watching her, and he saw her hope die and finally she shook her head.

"I deserve a man who can stand by my side, and our child deserves a father who will be a part of its life. I understand your fears, but you were a boy, alone and unsure. Our child could have both of us. If not, it will have me, and I will never let anyone—including you—hurt him or her."

"I understand. I can't be that man."

"If you can't be the man I need you to be, then I guess this is it," she said.

He watched as she took his ring from her finger— the ring Nonna had given him to give to her—and she handed it to him. "I'm going to get in the shower and when I get out, I expect you to be gone."

She walked away from him and all he could do was watch her leave. He gathered his stuff and walked away.

Thirteen

Melinda hadn't been surprised when she came out of the bathroom and Slade was gone. What did surprise her was that he'd taken all of his stuff from her condo. It was as if he'd never been there except for the lingering scent of his deodorant, which he must have put on before leaving. Pixie was sitting on her pillow in the middle of a sunspot near the glass door, but Melinda couldn't get her normal joy from seeing her dachshund.

Instead, she sat at her vanity and avoided looking herself in the eyes. She felt like crying but was trying not to because she had meetings to get through and without a doubt, the paparazzi would still be dogging her all day. She leaned forward, putting her head in her hands. She felt a little sick to her stomach and wasn't sure if it was because she'd taken a gamble on love and lost or if it was the pregnancy.

She'd told herself and Slade she'd rather go it alone than with a man who didn't want to be with her, but she didn't want that. Sure, she could do it by herself but who wanted to do this alone. The nausea passed and she lifted her head. She wasn't about to be someone that others felt sorry for. So that meant getting dressed and acting like she was happy with the choices she'd made this morning.

But she wasn't.

After last night, she'd believed that Slade really cared about her, that he'd never let anyone hurt them. But now she knew he was afraid to be hurt. It was as if he thought that she would walk away when things got tough, like that fiancée who had left him.

But she had steel in her backbone. He should have known that by now.

"Play some music, Jeeves," she said to her in-home assistant.

The first song that came on was "Let's Stay Together" by Al Green. That oldie that she and Slade had danced to on their first date. He'd taken her to Galveston for a private dinner on the beach and then they'd danced under the stars.

Tears burned the back of her eyes.

"Skip this song, Jeeves, and play 'Shout Out to My Ex' by Little Mix instead."

The song switched and she forced herself to get up from the vanity stool and sing along with the song until she didn't feel like crying anymore. The music continued with more dance and party tunes as she finished getting ready for her day.

She went to work and sat in meetings and smiled at everyone she saw throughout the day and if she were honest, she thought she did a pretty good job of acting like everything was normal. Until Angela texted to invite her out to dinner at the Flying Saucer. She accepted, then realized that fooling her twin that she wasn't heartbroken was going to be a lot harder than fooling everyone else. She went home and changed into a pair of jeans that felt too constricting around the middle, even though her belly hadn't changed. So she switched for a long flowy dress and a cardigan because the air-conditioning was sometimes too cold for her and went to meet her twin.

Angela was already waiting for her when she got there and waved from her table toward the back of the restaurant. She heard the music from the bar as she moved past the tables and noticed a family sitting to her right. Unbidden, an image of herself and a child sitting together popped into her head. She smiled and realized that she was going to be fine without Slade. She'd miss him and there would be times when she'd feel his absence, but she knew she'd figure out a way to make being a single mom work for her.

Angela got up and hugged her and then slid back into the booth. "I didn't know what to order you to drink. I mean with the, uh, you know."

"I know. Sweet tea will be fine," Melinda said when the waitress came over. They both placed their order. Because they'd eaten here so often, they knew the menu by heart.

As soon as they were alone, Angela leaned forward. "How are you doing? Did you get Slade to commit?"

She shook her head. "I'm doing okay. No, I didn't get him to commit and I gave him an ultimatum…

You know, we might need to consider the reason I'm single is that I'm sort of an all-or-nothing kind of girl."

Angela squeezed her hand. "Nothing wrong with that. Is there anything I can do?"

"You've already done it," she said, looking around. Being alone, she knew, was going to be difficult until she could think about Slade and not feel like crying. She was grateful her sister had asked her to dinner. "I really needed this tonight. I've been fake smiling my way through the day and with you, I can just be me."

"You know it, girl," Angela said. "Want me to kick his ass for you?"

She smiled at her sister. "I love you, you know that, right?"

Her twin nodded. "Do I need to go and find Slade Bartelli?"

"No. But thank you for that. I'm pretty sure this was rough on him as well."

"Okay, then. He always struck me as smarter than that. Do you want to talk about it?" Angela asked.

They both sat back as the waitress delivered two French dip sandwiches and a hot pretzel on the side. Melinda broke off a piece of the pretzel before answering her sister.

"Not now," she said. "It's too fresh right now."

"Okay. Then if you don't mind, I could actually use your help," Angela said while they enjoyed their dinner.

She hoped her sister wouldn't ask her to help plan her and Ryder's wedding. But she would say yes if Angela did. "What with?"

"Do you know a Willem Inwood? The name sounds so familiar and I wondered if he was a family friend or maybe someone we went to school with?" Angela asked.

Relief flooded through her. Something that had nothing to do with weddings. Thank the stars. No one came to mind, so she shook her head. "The name sounds sort of familiar, but I can't place it. I'll look through my address book at home."

"Address book?"

"Yes. I mean, I digitized everything but kept all my old paper books. One of them has Mom's handwriting in it and I couldn't part with that," Melinda said.

"Of course not, and it makes total sense that you'd have your hard copies. Don't want to take a chance on losing anything important, right?"

"Exactly."

They chatted and Melinda even laughed a bit with her sister before going home and it was only when she was back in her bedroom, after putting Pixie out and getting ready for bed, that she realized she was lying to herself about being okay with the breakup. She missed Slade and could only hope that in time the pain would lessen.

Angela called Ryder to see if he'd be coming over later, but he sounded frustrated with his Currin Oil employee relations investigation and she just gave him her best and hung up. She wished there were something she could do to help him fix this problem. Some way to figure out where Willem Inwood was. That would give Ryder a chance to actually get some decent answers.

Seeing her sister tonight and the way she was heartbroken over Slade, Angela knew she didn't want to let that happen to her and Ryder. She knew that Melinda was strong and that little baby she was carrying was going to be the most spoiled child on the planet if Angela had anything to say about it. But for right now, her sister was going to have to go it alone and figure out what kind of life she was going to make for herself and the baby.

She tossed her keys on her hall table and poured herself a glass of wine before going to sit on the couch.

Willem Inwood.

She wanted to help find this man so that she could maybe prove her father had nothing to do with the problems Ryder was going through. She wanted both men to get along and not be at each other's throats all the time. It would be hard to be happily married if her father and husband were always trying to implicate each other in crimes.

But she couldn't place the name Willem Inwood. Maybe Tatiana would know the man. She looked at the clock and seeing it was only a bit past ten o'clock, knew her best friend would still be awake. She and Tatiana Havery had usually hung out more often than they had in the last few weeks due to their busy schedules. It was time for a catch-up.

She would have invited Tatiana to dinner tonight but she knew her sister might want some one-on-one time.

She hit the button to call Tatiana.

"Hey, girl," Tatiana said. "How's things in lovey-dovey central?"

"Hey. They're good," she said, afraid to let on that she was feeling more and more out of control with Ryder while he was dealing with the business mess. That things were good, they were still committed but he was keeping her at arm's length.

"Glad to hear it. So, what are you two up to to-night?"

"Oh, Ryder's working. I just had dinner with Mels and now I'm back home," she said. She injected a note of happiness into her voice.

"How's your sister? I've seen way more of her on the society page and on the internet than Melinda usually likes," Tatiana said.

"Oh, she's struggling but she's managing it," she said, knowing that Melinda wouldn't want Tatiana to know everything that was going on with Slade.

"Not surprised. You Perrys always do," Tatiana said.

"Actually, I was calling because of Ryder's work," Angela said, taking a sip of her wine as she curled her legs underneath her.

"I don't know much about oil refineries."

"Ha. Me either. The thing is that Ryder is having some employee issues and he mentioned one of his managers—Willem Inwood. That name sounds so familiar, but I can't place it. Do you know him?"

"No. I don't know him. The name's not ringing any bells," Tatiana said. "How are the wedding plans coming?"

Angela sighed. Maybe she was just imagining she'd heard of Inwood because she wanted a quick resolution to Ryder's problems and to prove her dad had nothing to do with it. "We haven't had much of a chance to do much with Ryder's work situation. We've sort of put it on hold while he deals with some work issues."

"Your dad must love that," Tatiana said. "Or has he come around to liking your fiancé?"

"He hasn't. You don't think my dad would make a labor complaint against Ryder's company, do you?" she asked her friend. "I know he really felt like Ryder had some part in that financial investigation he was under."

"I don't know what your dad would do. But those two men don't get along. Maybe you should take this time while he's working so much to think about whether you two can make this work," Tatiana said.

No. She didn't want to take a break from Ryder or their wedding. She loved him.

"Just think about it," Tatiana said. "I'd hate to see you get hurt."

"Okay," she said, ending the call a few minutes later.

She put her phone and her wine down on the table and walked to the window. She loved Ryder and she wasn't about to leave him. Was she? Was that the only way to give them some peace? Tatiana wasn't wrong when she said that her father and Ryder were never going to get along and she was tired of always being in the middle.

But leaving the man she loved wasn't a solution.

Angela's phone vibrated. Melinda had sent her a thank-you text with a funny gif of two spinsters sitting on a beach, talking about the good life and she sent back the laughing emoji, but she didn't want to be sitting on that beach with her twin. She wanted Ryder by her side. And maybe if she could find this Willem Inwood, she could talk to him and figure out if he knew her dad. Maybe if she could find a way to bridge the distance between the two men, she'd finally be able to enjoy being in love with the man of her dreams.

Two days later, Melinda was still faking it like a champ at work and with her social engagements. Slade hadn't called and she didn't expect him to. Alfie had glanced at her ring finger and lack of engagement ring and raised one eyebrow in question, but she'd just shaken her head and he'd let it lie. Late in the afternoon of the second day, she had a call from Henri, Philomena Conti's butler, asking if she had time to stop by for drinks with Mrs. Conti.

Melinda wanted to say no, not sure she was ready to talk to Slade's grandmother, but she knew that she'd just be putting off the inevitable. She needed to start getting closure with all of the people who connected her to Slade Bartelli. She had already decided to step down from the art council because she didn't want to accidentally run into him again. She would still fund the arts and had reached out to the Houston Museum of Fine Arts to see if they had any room on their board for her.

"Alfie, I'm going to be leaving in a few minutes. Do you mind letting the building security team know, so they can make sure no one is waiting for me?" she asked.

"Not a problem, boss lady. My boyfriend and I are having a few friends over for dinner tonight and we'd love it if you'd come and join us."

"Oh, Alfie, thank you for the invite. I'd love to come over. Text me the time and what I can bring," she said, hugging her assistant.

This was good. She needed to be making more after-hours plans. Last night she'd spent sitting in front of the TV, watching *Pride and Prejudice* and eating a huge bag of potato chips. She really couldn't do that again. The pregnancy book she'd been reading warned that eating for two was an urban myth.

She grabbed her bag and straightened the jacket

on her Chanel suit as she walked out of her office. She smiled at Alfie and reminded herself how lucky she'd been to build a life where she was surrounded by people who genuinely cared for her. She knew she was going to need those friends in the coming months.

She drove to Philomena's house and tried not to think about the last time she'd been there. Their lunch plans had fallen through and this was the first occasion she'd been back. So many emotions. She'd been excited and nervous to start the charade of being Slade's fiancée and then had found out he'd been pushed to meet her. That should have been a red flag, but she hadn't seen it that way. Not after he'd pulled her into his arms. But that was sex. And she was old enough to understand that sex didn't equal emotions.

She sighed as she pulled into the circle drive and got out of her car. Henri answered the door and led her into the sitting room, where Philomena was waiting for her.

"Thank you, Melinda, for dropping by on such short notice," Philomena said, standing up to give Melinda a hug and then stepping back and sitting in her armchair again. "What would you like to drink?"

"Just some ice water," Melinda said. "The heat today is intense."

"It is," Philomena agreed, gesturing for Melinda to take a seat, and when she did, she noticed the ring box on the table next to the older woman.

"I guess Slade has told you we aren't engaged anymore," Melinda said.

"He did," she said. "He told me he couldn't be the man you wanted him to be."

She sighed. Her stomach hurt a bit, probably from

the tension of having to make this sound palatable to his sweet grandmother. "Slade is…"

She had no idea how to say this and her stomach was starting to knot and hurt really bad. She put her hand over it and leaned forward, realizing that this was more than tension. The pain was intensifying and shooting through her. She moaned.

"Are you okay? You look really pale," Philomena said.

"My stomach," Melinda muttered, holding her hand over her belly and praying that there wasn't something wrong with the baby. She couldn't help herself; she started crying.

"Henri," Philomena called out to her butler, who appeared at the doorway. "Get the car. We need to take Melinda to the emergency room." Then she directed her calm eyes to Melinda. "It will be okay," she said.

"It might not be," Melinda said. She'd always been worried that her age could be a factor in the pregnancy. "I'm so sorry, Philomena."

"Darling girl, you're not the first person to get sick in my home," she said. "And you mean more to me than any of them."

"You're very sweet, but Slade and I were lying to you. I need you to know that we didn't mean any harm." She could hardly speak. The pain was sharp now and she had to breathe heavily through it.

She didn't want to lose her baby, she realized. She had just started getting used to the idea of being a mother. She wanted this child.

"I know it was meant to be a temporary engagement," Philomena said. "Slade told me when he brought the ring back. He also told me that you objected to it, but he'd insisted and that the reason you broke it off was his fault."

She shouldn't have been surprised Slade had taken all of the blame. He was always trying to protect her. "There's more to it than that. We—" She groaned as another sharp pain ripped through her. "I think I need to go. My stomach…"

She stood up and she stumbled, almost falling, but Philomena was there to hold her. "Henri. We need to get Melinda to the hospital now."

Philomena held her hand as Henri rushed them to the hospital. Philomena took care of everything and stayed by Melinda's side, only stepping outside the cubicle when the nurse came, and Melinda felt alone and scared.

She told the nurse that she was pregnant and was having stomach pains, and she couldn't stop crying and feeling so very alone.

"Want me to get your grandma back in here?" the nurse asked.

"She's not my family," Melinda said, realizing how sad that made her. "Will you ask her to text my sister and Slade?"

"I will," the nurse said. "The doctor will be in here in a moment."

The nurse walked away and Melinda lay there on the hospital bed, staring at the ceiling and praying for her baby. She felt the tears streaming down her face. She felt scared and alone, and as much as she told herself not to, she wished Slade were here with her.

Fourteen

Nonna's call had come just as Slade was finishing up a meeting with his father. His head pounded and his heart raced when he heard Melinda was in the hospital. He wasted no time, turning from his father and running for the door. He'd had a lot of time to think about everything that Melinda had said, and living without her even for a few days had left him questioning his choices. He couldn't bear the thought of losing her now.

"I have to go, Dad. Something's wrong with Melinda."

"I'll drive," his father said, coming up behind him. "Do you remember when your mom cut her hand with that knife when you were about seven?"

He nodded. Why was his dad bringing that up now?

"I freaked out and barely was able to get us to the emergency room for them to take care of it. When the woman you love is in pain, it messes with your head."

"Yeah, it does," he said to his father. And to be honest, Slade was panicking. He wasn't sure how he thought that loving Melinda and living apart from her was going to work out, but he knew now that he wanted to be by her side and that he'd never again let anything keep them apart.

In their hours-long conversation, his father had reassured him that he didn't have to worry about the family coming after him. But the most startling thing his father told him was that he'd been working with local law enforcement for the last few years, trying to go clean. And he'd spent that time hoping that he'd be able to rebuild his relationship with Slade.

The sense of relief that had flooded him drove home how big of a weight the worry of bringing Melinda and their baby into a world where his father was still a crime boss had been on him. He'd always thought that he was cool with the rumors and whispered comments behind his back or at the very least, that he'd learned to deal with them, but he knew now he hadn't been.

His dad was changing, trying hard to make a new life for himself, and he hoped to forge a relationship with him. Slade knew he could change too.

Be the man that Melinda needed him to be.

It wasn't going to be easy, but she was worth the effort. He was going to have to work hard to convince her to give him another chance. To show her that he wanted her as his wife because, as his father had said, loving a woman wasn't easy but it was the best damned thing a man could experience.

He wanted that. He wanted to raise his child with Melinda, not watch from the distance. He could protect them. He deserved the happy family and the life he could have with Melinda. The one that he'd always been afraid to let himself want.

Carlo dropped him off at the entrance to the emergency room and Slade ran into the waiting area. Nonna and Henri were sitting off to one side. He went to see his grandmother. "Where's Melinda? Any word?"

"Room three," Nonna said, shaking her head. "I've got a call into the head of the hospital board to see if he can get her seen sooner."

"Thanks, Nonna," he said, rushing to room three. He opened the door and stepped inside and his heart broke.

Melinda looked so small, lying on the hospital bed. Her head was back and tears were rolling down her face. Had she lost the baby?

"Baby cakes, I'm here," he said.

He took her hand in his and when she looked up at him, he knew that he'd never leave her again. He couldn't. They belonged together.

"I'm sorry. I love you and I want to be the man you deserve," he said.

"You might not need to be," she said on a sob. "I don't know what's going on but I'm having horrible stomach pain. I think something's wrong with our baby."

"Don't worry. I'm here with you and I've got you," he told her. "Whatever it is, we'll face it together."

The doctor and nurse came back in and examined Melinda. All Slade could do was stand by her side, holding her hand because when he'd dropped it and moved away, she reached out to him. He tried to project a calm appearance but inside he was freaking out. This baby that he'd been unsure of was the reason why he'd been able to finally figure out what was important in his life.

And he realized that he didn't want anything to happen to Melinda or the child. He needed them both. They were the grounding he'd been so afraid to find. He thought they would tie him to a future that would be complicated and hard, but he realized now that without Melinda by his side nothing else mattered.

He looked up as the doctor spoke. "I'm going to have some tests run, but there is no bleeding, so I think your baby is okay. The pain could be from bloating or gas. Once I have the results of your tests, I'll be able to confirm it."

The doctor left and the nurse had Melinda transferred to a wheelchair and took her for the tests. He walked beside her, holding her hand tightly, squeezing it gently.

"If you want to go into the waiting room," the nurse said to him, "I'll come and get you when she's back."

He nodded and followed them out to the hallway, just watching as Melinda was wheeled away. He'd never felt like someone was his world before this moment. Had never allowed himself to care this deeply for another person or to hope that one day he'd have a family of his own. And he was so close to having it; he didn't want to lose it now. Slade was alone in the hallway when someone touched his shoulder. He glanced around to see his father standing there.

"I know we have a long way to go, son," Carlo said. "But I wanted you to know that I'm here. You are the only family that matters to me. Philomena is waiting to talk to you, and I think Melinda's family is here, so I'll go out the back, but I needed to see you."

"Thanks, Dad," Slade said. He and his father still had a ways to go before they would have a real relationship, but they were working on it. Slade hugged his father and then he left, going down the hallway away from the waiting room.

Slade stepped into the waiting room where Angela had joined Nonna. They both looked over at him expectantly.

"She's having some tests done, but the doctor thinks the baby's okay. We'll know more when she gets back. He said it could be gas. I'm praying that it is."

"We all are," Angela said. "Can we wait in her room? I want to see her when she gets back."

"The nurse said she'd come and get us," Slade said, sitting down in the chair and putting his head in his hands. He had never felt so powerless before. He didn't often pray; it wasn't something that made much sense to him since he was a man who made things happen by taking action. But in this moment, he reached out to God or the universe…anyone who was listening.

"Please protect my family," he said. Knowing in his heart that he needed them more than anything else.

As soon as Melinda was back in her cubicle in the emergency room, Angela rushed in to see her. Her twin hugged her and sat on the bed next to her. "Are you okay?"

"I think so. The doctor thinks it might be just regular stomach pain and nothing to do with the baby. We should know something soon. How embarrassing if it turns out to just be gas," Melinda said.

"Not embarrassing at all. It was probably stress. I hope that it is just that, so we don't have to worry anymore. Slade is beside himself. He wanted to come in, but then wasn't sure if you wanted to see him. I've never seen Slade Bartelli acting the way he is right now," Angela said.

"I know. I think he's worried about the baby." And her, Melinda wanted to add. But she needed to be cautious. She had promised herself to stop seeing Slade as she wanted him to be and to only see the man he really was.

His grandmother was out there, and she had to wonder if he was playing the concerned boyfriend for her. But the way he'd held her hand, the things he'd said to her before... Maybe it had been the pain making her see it in a different way, but she thought that Slade was being genuine. He'd never been one to pretend to feel something he didn't. It had only been her perception that she didn't trust.

"I think he's worried about you," Angela said. "I heard him talking to his grandmother and she was comforting him. Telling him that he'd have time to fix this."

"This?"

"Well, obviously I don't know what they were talking about, but I'm pretty sure she meant things with you. I had my doubts about him. He seemed like a bit of fun and you definitely were overdue for some fun, but now I think he might be the real deal, Mels."

She hoped her sister was right.

Angela stayed until the doctor came in and gave her the test results and the all clear. Her sister left to allow Melinda to get changed into her street clothes and to go fill the prescription the doctor gave her, but only after promising to send Slade in.

Melinda wanted to talk to him privately before she

went out to see Philomena. She hoped that none of the society bloggers had been alerted to her being at the hospital. She wasn't ready for all of Houston society to know that she was pregnant until she knew what was happening between her and Slade.

Someone knocked on the door and she called out for them to come in. It was Slade. He looked haggard, as if he'd been running his hands through his hair, but he smiled when he saw her.

"You're okay?" he asked.

"Yes. Just some stomach problems and the doctor has given me some medicine to take. He also wants me to try a bland diet for a few days to make sure that it's not serious. I'm supposed to go and see my doctor tomorrow."

"Thank God," he said. "I was so worried about you."

"I was worried too," she admitted. "So why are you here?"

"I guess that's a fair question," he said. "I want you to know that the last three days have been the longest of my life. I thought I was protecting you by leaving and for the first night while I drank a bottle of Jack in my den, I almost believed it. But the next morning I realized that you had been right when you said I wasn't eighteen anymore. I'd been afraid to reach out to my father because I knew that I had wanted that relationship to be something it couldn't be."

"Fair enough," she said. "Hopefully now you can resolve that."

She still wasn't sure why he was here. He'd been pretty adamant that he didn't want to be a family man.

"I already did. Once I realized that I needed you

back in my life, I realized I had to talk to Dad and let him know that I wanted no part of his life," Slade said.

"Good. What did he say?" she asked. Slade was always going to have a big gaping hole inside of him until he resolved his issues with his dad.

"He got it. We aren't totally there yet, but we're working toward it. He drove me here today."

"He did?" she asked, surprised.

"Yes. He said when the woman I loved was in danger, I shouldn't be driving," Slade said.

Love.

"You know you don't have to say you love me," she said. She wanted those words to be true, but she was afraid of them as well.

"I know I don't. You also know I don't lie, baby cakes. It might take you a while to believe them and that's okay," he said. "Because I'm not going anywhere. I'm going to stay by your side for the rest of our lives and tell you every day how much I love you."

He came over to her and took her hand in his, and then got down on his knee in front of her. "I know that I don't deserve you and for so long I was afraid I couldn't be the man you deserved, but I promise you that I will try to be. I love you, Melinda Perry. Please, will you consider marrying me? Not for the media or because your dad will likely kick my butt when he finds out you're pregnant, but because I love you and can't imagine my life without you by my side as my wife."

She looked down at him kneeling on the hospital floor and looking up at her with love in his eyes and hope on his face.

"Yes, Slade. Yes, I will," she said, tugging him to

his feet. And he pulled her into his arms, kissing her deeply.

She pulled back, smiling up at him. "This whole thing started with a kiss."

"Good. I like kissing you and we can do it often to remind us of how we got our start."

The engagement party at Philomena Conti's house on the last Saturday in September was spectacular and the society bloggers who were streaming live from the event were saying it was the party of the year. Angela stood in the corner, watching Melinda and Slade and feeling more than a tiny bit envious. Ryder had canceled on her at the last moment, so she was there alone. Her father was more than happy that she had come without Ryder and had told her more than once. But then her father was in a good mood and had maybe had one too many Lone Star beers. He was toasting Melinda, and Angela loved seeing her twin so happy.

She glowed with a look that Angela thought only someone in love had. Slade was completely doting on her twin, which both Melinda and Angela thought was funny. He had moved his office into Melinda's condo and had been working from home until the doctor gave her the all clear to go back to work.

"She looks happy," Tatiana said, coming over to Angela and handing her a glass of champagne.

"She does," Angela said.

"Soon that will be you," Tatiana said. "Where is your fiancé?"

She wasn't so sure. Ryder had been more distant than ever. "He had to work."

"He's been working a lot of hours lately. I hope you aren't marrying a workaholic."

"There are just a few things going on that are taking more attention than Ryder usually has to give them," she said.

"Probably for the best he isn't here, given how much your father and he don't get along," Tatiana said. "And this is Melinda's day."

"It is," she said, grateful when Melinda waved her over to her side. Lately, Tatiana hadn't seemed as supportive of her relationship with Ryder. She wondered if her best friend saw something that Angela herself was missing.

She hugged Melinda as soon as she got to her side.

"Where's Ryder?" Melinda asked.

"Oh, he couldn't be here. He had to work," Angela said.

"Dang it. I wanted to get a picture of the four of us together. Maybe we could have dinner next week. Just the four of us. Now that my engagement is for real, maybe we can seriously think about a double wedding," Melinda said.

"Let's have dinner and discuss it," Angela said. But with Ryder refusing to discuss a date, she doubted he was going to be all gung ho for a double wedding. She stayed for another hour and then made her excuses to head home.

When she got to her condo, Ryder was waiting in the living room for her. She was so happy to see him, she didn't think anything of it when he said, "Hey, sorry to do this today, but I think we need to talk."

"Okay," she said, sitting down beside him on the sofa. "How did you know when I'd be home?"

"Find My Friends app," he said.

"Oh. What's up? Melinda is crazy happy and in love with Slade. She brought up a double wedding—"

"Let me stop you there."

Her heart sunk and she felt a knot in the pit of her stomach. "Why?"

"Because I know that you're torn between me and your vengeful father. I can't ask you to choose between me and your family."

"But you're not asking me to do that," she said, her chest constricting. She didn't want to break up with him. She loved Ryder. And even though it wasn't easy to deal with her father, she still hoped someday her dad would come around and see Ryder the way she did.

"I know, but I can't bear to see you destroyed because of me. I love you too much, Angela. I think it's best if we end this now," he said, holding out his hand.

She blinked, trying not to cry. He couldn't really mean this. "We can make it work."

"Not without destroying your family and mine," he said. "I'm afraid my mind is made up."

She took the engagement ring off her finger and dropped it into the palm of his hand, starting to cry as he turned and walked out the door. As soon as it closed, she collapsed on the couch. Her heart was breaking in two. How was she going to live without the man she loved?

She missed her mom. She needed her mom. She would have called Melinda, but she didn't want to ruin her twin's day. She grabbed a tub of Blue Bell's Mardi Gras King Cake ice cream and opened up the digital file of her mom's memorial service. She sighed as, through her tears, she watched everyone celebrate her mom's life. In the video, Tatiana was by her side the entire time. She really was a good friend and Angela was lucky to have her. Melinda looked so lost and broken. Angela was glad her sister had found Slade Bartelli. His love had helped Melinda find new purpose.

She saw someone in the corner of the video frame. A young man. Who was that?

She rewound it and then hit Pause and gasped as she realized who it was.

Tatiana's half brother... Willem Inwood.

Tatiana hated him and his mother, but why wouldn't she have said that he was her brother when Angela had asked? Was it because she didn't want to bring up her family drama?

She thought about calling Ryder and telling him, but she didn't think she could bear to hear his voice.

Slade carried Melinda over the threshold into her bedroom later that evening. This had been the best day of her life. The one that she'd been secretly hoping for since Slade has asked her out that first time. She had been afraid to hope that a love like this would come into her life. The only wrinkle had been the fact that Angela's fiancé hadn't been there. She was so happy and in love, and for this one moment it seemed her entire family was in a good place.

She had her arms wrapped around Slade's shoulders and only had eyes for him. He put her on her feet next to the bed.

Leaning down, he kissed her so lovingly before he began undressing her. He traced a path down her body and around her breasts once she was naked. Then his fingers danced over her belly as he went down on his knees next to her and kissed her stomach. "Hello, baby. We can't wait to meet you."

She caught her breath, tangling her fingers in his hair. Slade, as always, once he committed himself to something or in this case, her, he was 100 percent on board.

"I love you, Slade."

"I love you too, baby cakes."

He lifted her off her feet, placed her in the center of the bed and made love to her. Then he held her in his arms as they planned for their future, and for the first time in her life, she felt like her real world and the world she was always making in her head were one.

Epilogue

*W*ell, that didn't go the way I'd hoped. Sterling hasn't been arrested for the murder and Angela and Ryder still care for each other. Perry is proud as punch that Melinda is getting married and giving him a grandchild.

Damn.

I hate this. Dreams of the man that I accidentally killed aren't making it any easier to move past the guilt. If the cops would just arrest and charge someone—preferably Sterling Perry—with the murder, maybe I could move on.

And then there's Melinda. Seeing her so happy and pregnant stirs so many emotions. It can't be jealousy because no one would ever be envious of a goody-goody like Melinda Perry.

But there's a part of me that is. What is it about the Perry family that they always get what they want, while *my own life keeps spiraling out of control? The plans that I have been working on for so long are slowly slipping out of my control.*

Maybe involving Willem was a mistake. But he was keen to make sure that Ryder Currin and Sterling Perry pay for what they have done to us. But he's never been smart. Not smart enough to do something simple without leaving his fingerprints all over it. But I'm not about to let Willem's screwup be the end of the road. Whatever it takes I will bring down Sterling Perry and Ryder Currin.

* * * * *

STRANDED
AND SEDUCED

CHARLENE SANDS

To my dear friends Mary and Richard.
Your friendship, love and support
mean so much.

Here's to more Palm Springs days
and happy times!

One

April always knew her luck would run out one day.

In a town the size of Boone Springs, she couldn't avoid River "Risk" Boone forever.

But she hadn't expected to see the tall, handsome Texan walk into her real estate agency that morning.

Her stomach in knots, she gazed at him from across her desk. He tipped his hat back, his eyes a mesmerizing dark brown, his skin still as bronzed as it had been in his rodeo days. Wearing crisp jeans and a tan button-down shirt, his business casual attire and good looks turned heads in the Texas town founded by his ancestors. He'd turned her head once, too, and that had been a big mistake.

"Hello, April."

The deep timbre of his voice, the way he drawled her name, gentle and sure, rang in her ears. On wobbly legs she rose from her desk. "Risk, w-what are you doing here?"

His brows arched as he looked her over from head to toe, a gleam in his eyes as if he was remembering the night they'd shared. Heat rose up her throat, and she was stunned Risk still had the ability to jumble her thoughts.

Clovie, her assistant and good friend, gave her a quizzical look from the desk adjacent to hers. Clovie knew something about her past history with him.

"I'm here on Boone business. I understand you've spoken with my brother Mason's secretary about the Canyon Lake property."

"Yes, that's correct. I answered some of her questions about the lodge. But that's as far as it went. I, uh, do we have an appointment?"

She knew darn well they didn't. And she also knew darn well she wasn't going to turn him away on some false premise that he needed to make one. She didn't know why she'd asked that question, other than a bad case of nerves. It's not as if she could ignore a member of the Boone family. The three Boone brothers were wealthy cattle ranchers and entrepreneurs. They owned much of the town.

"Never mind," she said. "If you have questions about Canyon Lake Lodge, I can help you."

He gave her a nod. "Apparently you did a great job talking up the lodge, because we're definitely interested in finding out more about—" Risk stopped speaking. Oh God, he'd noticed the pain in her eyes, the frown she couldn't conceal.

Two years ago, they'd spent one night together. She hadn't expected diamonds and flowers afterward, but she had expected him to be there when she woke up in the morning.

"Listen, is there someplace we can talk privately?" Risk asked after a long pause.

Clovie piped up instantly. "I've got the bank deposit ready, April. I was just leaving." She stood, gathering up a folder and hoisting her handbag over her shoulder. "I'll stop for lunch and see you in an hour or so."

"Okay."

Clovie dashed out quickly as both watched her leave and shut the door behind her.

"Ask and ye shall receive." April's sardonic tone shifted Risk's attention back to her. She was at a complete loss. Seeing him stirred up deep feelings of hurt and abandonment again. Mostly she hated that Risk Boone, the ex-rodeo champion, had treated her like one of his buckle bunnies when she'd believed they'd really connected that night in Houston. Though he'd once been her secret high school crush, the fantasy-come-true night they'd shared two years ago had turned into a bad memory.

"April, look, I'm here because you have the listing for Canyon Lake Lodge. I'm the new head of real estate acquisitions for Boone Inc. My brothers want to expand the business and like the idea of opening a lodge. I didn't make an appointment because I wasn't sure you'd see me. I owe you an apology."

"You were afraid I wouldn't want to see you?"

"Judging by the sound of your voice, I'm not far from the mark, am I?"

"Your apology is a little late in coming, wouldn't you say?" She folded her arms across her middle, not in a show of attitude but to help brace herself. "That was quite some time ago."

"I've been working out of town a lot these past few years. It's not an excuse, but simply the truth." He ran his hand through his hair. "Listen, I was in a bad place back then. I couldn't stay. Shannon really messed me up and, well, I wasn't ready for…you. I couldn't give anything back. I guess—no, I know—I ran scared. And I'm sorry."

I wasn't ready for…you.

Oh God, what a silly fool she'd been thinking that talking openly and sharing confidences and making love throughout the night would mean something, when all she'd been to him was a one-night stand.

She'd known about his two-year relationship with superstar actress Shannon Wilkes—the tabloids had made sure the entire country was well versed in the details of their relationship and scandalous breakup. Risk had been a rodeo celebrity at the top of his bronc-busting game, and Shannon had won a Golden Globe. They'd been paired as a super couple, until Risk took a bad fall from a bronc, injuring his shoulder and ending his rodeo career. Shortly after, Shannon broke up with him and immediately got involved with a top NFL quarterback, breaking Risk's heart and humiliating him in front of the entire country—the life he'd known all but gone. "Twice Dumped" had been the headline, showing side-by-side photos of him grounded by the stallion and an unflattering pose of him and Shannon.

If only April hadn't seen a recovering Risk guest hosting the Houston rodeo that day. If only she hadn't bumped into him later at the hotel bar. If only he hadn't been so vulnerable and open and kind to her that night, good sense might have prevailed. But they'd really connected that night, and his lovemaking led her to think impossible things.

But never in her wildest expectations had she thought he'd walk out on her the next morning without so much as an explanation, a note, a goodbye. It cheapened what might have been the best night of her life.

"Okay, I get it."

Risk exhaled, seeming relieved. "You accept my apology?"

If he'd come exclusively to apologize, it surely would've meant more. "Risk, why don't we just drop it and keep our personal lives out of this. Have a seat and we'll get down to the real reason you're here." She couldn't help the jab; he deserved it, and judging by the frown on his face, it hit the mark.

"Fine."

They both sat down, and she pulled the file for the list-ing. She had one month left on her contract with the owner, Mr. Hall, and selling the $5.3 million lodge would put her struggling agency in the black well into next year.

"Let's focus on the potential of the property," she said.

He nodded, and his gaze roamed over the office, lei-surely taking it all in. "But first let me say I like what you've done here. The place never looked this good when it was ole Perry Bueller's shop."

"Mr. Bueller was selling antiques. I had to modernize a bit, but I was hoping to keep some of the charm of the old place."

April had opened her own real estate agency in Boone Springs one year ago with goals to be the premiere high-end listing company in the county. She'd worked for three years in adjacent Willow County learning the ropes and getting her feet wet, but when Perry Bueller decided to re-tire and sell this storefront property in the heart of Boone Springs, April knew it was time to take action to realize her dream of living and working in her hometown. She'd scraped together the money and transformed his rustic an-tique store into a modern-day office.

A teardrop crystal chandelier hung from the center of the ceiling, beautiful mahogany bookcases hugged the walls and the computer-topped desks made of the finest polished cherrywood were all pieces generously gifted to her by Mr. Bueller, her late grandmother Beth's dear friend.

"You've done well for yourself, April."

She didn't take Risk's compliment lightly. April had worked hard, and it was nice to be recognized, but she had to keep it in perspective. She couldn't allow herself the lux-ury of liking Risk again, despite his long overdue apology or his Texas charm.

The last deal she'd worked on had fallen through at the

last minute. Six weeks of putting a deal together, all for naught. Her small agency couldn't take another hit like that, and she couldn't pass up the opportunity to sell the unoccupied lodge to the Boones. She had a mortgage to pay, a reputation to build and a desire so deep to make her dream a success, she wasn't about to let her feelings about Risk interfere with her goals. "T-thank you."

She gave Risk the file on Canyon Lake Lodge and pointed to the photos. "As you can see, it's a great piece of property."

"It's remote."

"I like to think of it as secluded, a perfect place for a getaway. The lodge is set back in the hills, miles away from traffic and the town. There's something for everyone, whether it's kicking back and relaxing or outdoor activities. The lake is amazing, and there could be horseback riding and fishing and boating. It's a perfect place for vacationers to experience nature."

"It gives *rustic* a whole new meaning. It's overgrown. Looks like it's falling apart."

She held her breath. "Looks can be deceiving."

"Or they can be dead-on."

"There's wiggle room for negotiation. And there's an intriguing story behind the lodge's history. I have the articles here." She reached into her drawer and came up with a manila folder with articles written about the lodge from sixty years prior. "You can read up on it. The research is fascinating. I have no doubt the lodge could be marketed in a very appealing way when the time comes to book guests."

She set the folder on the desk, and Risk flipped through the articles. "You've done your homework, haven't you?"

"I always do."

Risk looked up from the file just as she did, and their

eyes met. A sizzle worked its way down to her toes. She was close enough to breathe in his scent, to be reminded of her fantasy night with him.

"I'm impressed," he drawled in that special way he had.

She jerked back and fiddled with the papers on her desk.

"Mind if I take a better look at these articles?"

"No, of course not. Take them with you."

He rose, and she came around the desk to walk him to the door. When she was standing beside him, he filled her space, and she swallowed hard. "I'd better get back to work. If you have any further questions or would like to see the property, don't hesitate to call. The number is inside the folder."

"Give me a day or two. I'll definitely be in touch."

"Okay, sure."

"Oh, and April?"

She gazed into eyes that had softened on her. He seemed ready to say something but then shook his head. "Never mind."

She closed the door behind him and slumped in relief.

After two years, she'd finally spoken to Risk Boone again.

And because of a possible sale to Boone Inc., she had to hold back on the choice words she'd reserved just for him to hear.

Normally April didn't go out on a work night, but tonight was special. Tonight was her best friend's birthday, and she couldn't let the party go on without her. Jenna Mae turned the big three-oh today; it was monumental. So April donned her black party dress with silver rhinestone straps and met her friends for drinks at the Farmhouse Bar and Grill, a honky-tonk that was always bustling no matter the day of the week.

It was live band Thursday, and Jenna Mae kept glancing at the guitarist up on the platform stage. She was newly single after a disheartening breakup with a guy who didn't know the ass end of a donkey. Jenna was better off without him, and April and Clovie had let her know it. Because that's what friends did. When a storm was brewing, they got out their rain jackets and umbrellas and shielded each other as best they could.

April finished off her first mango margarita as all eight girls swarmed around Jenna Mae at their table near the long, handcrafted Farmhouse bar. They were already an hour into the celebration; gifts had been opened and funny birthday cards passed around.

"Yum, this is delicious," Jenna said, taking a big bite of her cupcake catered by Katie's Kupcakes. "Thanks for this, April. I'm glad you're here. Wouldn't be the same without you."

"I wouldn't have missed it, Jenna. You know that."

Jenna put her arm around April's shoulders. "I do know that. I'm just glad you moved back from Willow County when you did."

"Me, too."

"Are things getting any easier?" Jenna asked. "Sold any big-ass mansions lately?"

"I wish. Actually, I'm waiting to hear back on a potential huge deal. If I land it, it would keep the agency afloat into next year."

The waitress came by with another round of drinks. April wasn't a big drinker, but number two looked good, so she grabbed it up and took a sip.

"I hope it works out for you."

"I'm beginning to have my doubts," she mumbled. "My buyer was supposed to get back to me last week. And I haven't heard a word."

"Why not call and give him a nudge?"

"You won't believe who it is."

Jenna Mae grabbed her arm and pulled her away from the crowd. "Tell me." Jenna was on her third drink, which might just be her limit. She wobbled a little when she walked.

April spoke in Jenna's ear. "It's Risk Boone. If you can believe that."

Jenna knew all about her high school crush and fantasy night with Risk, and so it wasn't surprising that her mouth dropped open. *"No."*

"Yes. He was at the office last week. It was…awkward."

"I can imagine. Man, you crushed on him heavily in high school. You've always had a soft spot for that guy."

"Not anymore. Not after… Houston."

"Really? Because I didn't want to say anything, but he's sitting at the bar right now."

April couldn't believe it; now *her* mouth dropped open. And her heart sped up. She had her back to the bar, and she casually turned to look over her shoulder. Yep, there was Risk, sitting on a stool, flanked by two women, one on each side of him. They were leaning against the bar top, engaging him in conversation. Typical. Women swarmed around Risk like bees to honey. He'd been a big celebrity at one time. It was crazy to think she'd been one of his hangers-on a couple of years ago.

"Oh wow, I've never seen him in here before," Jenna said.

"No, neither have I," she muttered. "When we spoke, he made it seem like he hasn't been in Boone Springs much lately." And April wasn't a regular customer at the Farmhouse. She'd been too busy to go out during the week, and there was a diner closer to her office that delivered.

April was about to look away, a queasy feeling in the

pit of her stomach, only to discover that Risk didn't seem
to be listening to the women speaking in his ear. His eyes
were on her through the reflection in the wide rectangu-
lar mirror behind the bar. She was caught in his gaze, her
heart pumping hard. There was a moment of awareness,
pure and instinctual, that sparked in her veins.

His lips twitched upward. Was he smiling at her?

Oh boy. She stared another half a second then grabbed
Jenna's arm. "Let's get back to the table."

A few minutes later, April polished off the rest of her
drink as she chatted with her friends who were still seated
and not cutting loose on the dance floor. Her head was a
little fuzzy, she had a definite buzz going on, and the more
she thought about Risk Boone not giving her the courtesy
of a return call this week, the more it bugged her.

"I left him two voice mails about the lodge, and he never
got back to me," she told Clovie and Jenna. And now he
was sitting at the bar smugly, watching her every move.
How was she supposed to take that? "I'm gonna talk to him
now, whether he likes it or not," she said. As she began to
rise, two hands came down on her shoulders, pushing her
back down, Clovie from the right and Jenna from the left.

"Wait," Clovie said. "I know that look in your eyes,
April. You need to calm down. There's still hope for the
deal. You can simply, tactfully ask him what the delay is."

"Clovie's right," Jenna said. "You're a professional. Don't
blow it because you're ticked off."

April sighed and nodded, thinking it through. Risk was
a rich, handsome hunk, but he'd also been a jerk to her. Still
she couldn't let her personal feelings about Risk deter her
from her job. "Okay, you guys are right. I'll do that."

"And another thing you're going to do is put this on."
Jenna slid a diamond cluster ring off her right hand. "From
now on, you're engaged."

"I'm what?"

"You heard me, you're engaged to be married. It's just a form of insurance when dealing with Risk."

"I can't do that. That's your grandmother's ring."

"It's for a good cause. I know you'll take care with it."

"For heaven's sake, Jenna. I can certainly speak with the man—"

"Whoops, looks like he's heading this way." Jenna pushed the ring onto April's left ring finger. "Remember, you're a professional. *And you're engaged,*" she mouthed softly.

April's head swam, and the next thing she knew, she was standing up facing Risk wearing a ring on her left hand and all the other girls had vanished onto the dance floor.

"Evenin'," he said, the one word pronounced with enough charm to swallow her up. Suddenly, the ring on her finger didn't seem too over-the-top. There was something about Risk that was too darn attractive. Wearing this ring just might be a blessing in disguise. "Do you have a minute to talk?" he asked.

"I, uh, sure. Here?"

Music blasted from the live band, the drummer's rolling solo doing a number on her ears.

He shook his head. "It's too loud in here. Take a walk with me outside?"

She needed to hear what he had to say, and actually having some privacy would be better to discuss business. "I, uh, sure."

Risk led the way through the packed crowd and she followed behind him, bumping shoulders and ping-ponging through the patrons. A strong hand came out to take hers, and suddenly the bumping stopped, Risk forming a human barrier for her as he led her toward the door. As soon as she stepped foot outside, she shivered.

"Damn, it's cold out here," he said.

She couldn't disagree. She'd left her coat inside the Farmhouse, and not even the dizzying buzz from her second margarita warded off the winter chill.

"Let's go sit in my car—it'll be a lot warmer for you."

"Is it too cold to talk out here?" Her teeth clattered as she said the words.

"In the parking lot?" He smiled. "You tell me."

A blast of wind ruffled her curls, lifting them high in the air and chilling her to the bone. Goodness, she was being silly not wanting to be alone with Risk. She needed to make this deal, and not even having an unorthodox meeting in a client's car should deter her.

"C'mon, my car's over here." Risk took her arm, drawing her close to his body, and the heat radiating off him kept her a bit warmer as they walked to his SUV. He opened the door for her, and she climbed into the passenger seat. "Put this over you," he said, giving her the sheepskin jacket lying on his seat.

It did the trick immediately. The jacket was snug and warm around her shoulders and arms and was so long it partly covered her legs, too. "Thanks."

He closed the door and wound around to climb into the driver's seat.

And April found herself bundled up, sitting very close to Risk Boone, his male scent drifting her way, his presence filling the space inside the SUV.

"You look real pretty tonight, April." Risk blurted out the first thing he'd noticed about her tonight as he turned to face her.

Her chin went up. "Thank you."

"I didn't expect to see you tonight."

"No, I didn't expect to see you, either. But you promised

me a call that I never received. What happened? I guess I wasn't on your radar?"

Quite the contrary. After seeing April last week, he'd thought about her plenty.

He hadn't known her all that well in high school, but when he'd seen her that day in the rodeo stands in Houston, after his life had hit an all-time low, she'd been one friendly face, one person from home he could relate to, and finding her at the hotel bar later that night had been pure luck on his part. They'd sat and talked for hours, and then things had heated up really fast in his hotel room.

"Believe me, you've *been* on my radar."

Her head snapped up at that. Questions filled her eyes, and he wasn't going to answer any of them. "I'm sorry about not returning your voice mails, but I haven't had time to look at the articles about the lodge. The truth is, I was called out of town. A friend's mother was gravely ill, and she wanted to see me. I felt compelled to go. She was a wonderful, gentle woman that I really cared about."

"Cared? Did she pass on?"

He nodded. "Yes, I stayed in Atlanta for the funeral."

Sympathy touched April's eyes. "I'm sorry."

He kept it to himself that it had been Shannon Wilkes's mother who'd passed on. Shannon had been texting him for months, about her personal life being a hot mess, her career taking a bit of a hit and then her mother's illness. Risk had resolved things with Shannon a while back. Though the scars were still there, he'd realized she wasn't the right woman for him, yet he'd sympathized with Shannon over losing her mother. For the two years he'd dated Shannon, Mary had been like a mother to him, and they'd always gotten along. "Yeah, it was rough."

April gave him a sympathetic nod.

After he ran scared that night in Houston, he wouldn't

have blamed April if she refused to work with him. The
sale of the lodge was important to her, and he owed her a
fair shake, at the very least. "Do you have plans day after
tomorrow?" he asked her.

She looked at him skeptically. "Why?"

"Maybe we can drive out to the lodge and take a look
at it. I'll read the articles about the place tomorrow. Then
I can see for myself if it's doable."

April's eyes brightened. "Yes, I'd love for you to see the
lodge. I'll plan on it."

"Okay, good. I've kept you from your friends long
enough. Let me walk you back inside."

"No, that's not necessary." She handed him back his
coat. "Thanks anyway, but it's a short walk. See you Saturday."

She got out of his car, and he got out, too, and watched,
his instincts telling him not to let her walk through the
darkened parking lot by herself. And sure enough, when
April was less than twenty feet away, a drunken cowboy
approached her, blocking her passage, giving her grief and
making crude suggestions. Her voice rose as she told the
guy to back off, and then the cowboy began grabbing at
her. Risk moved fast and was there in seconds, shoving
the man's shoulders, pushing him out of the way before
he could lay a hand on April. "Buddy, get the hell outta
here or you're gonna be real sorry. Go sober up somewhere. Now."

The man eyed Risk with contempt. Risk would be all too
happy to nail the guy to the wall, but after a three-second
staring contest, the cowboy stalked off.

Risk turned to April. She was shivering, this time in
fear. He saw it in her eyes, too. "Are you okay?"

"I…will…be."

He wrapped his arms loosely around her shoulders,

bringing her into his warmth. "Come here a sec and calm down."

"Thank…you." She leaned against him, setting her head on his chest as if that's exactly what she'd needed. "That was scary."

"You handled yourself well." He'd heard the tone of her voice, the gruff way she tried to warn the guy off. "You know, the Southern in me would never let a woman walk through a parking lot without seeing her safely inside, but then again, the female revolution has changed all that. I never know what to do."

April pulled away from his chest to gaze up at him, the pretty blue of her eyes damn near mesmerizing. "You did good."

He smiled, and she smiled, too, and something clicked in that moment, a spark that he hadn't felt in a long time. He hadn't met a woman who interested him in months, and now, suddenly, he was thinking about April that way. "I did?"

She gazed at his mouth and nodded. Was it an invitation? In that one second, Risk's body twitched, and he tightened his hold on April. "You did," she whispered.

He laid his palm on her cheek and felt her softness, witnessed the sweet look she was giving him. "April," he said, right before leaning in to brush a soft kiss to her lips.

She moaned a little bit and gave in to the pleasure of his mouth. She tasted sweet and tangy, like a fruity drink, and he started remembering things about her that quickened his pulse.

Then out of the blue, April pulled away quickly, giving him a slight push on the chest. He backed off instantly. What in the world?

"Don't."

"*Don't?* April, did I read you wrong?"

"I've had too much to drink tonight and I do appreciate you protecting me from that drunk, but yes, you read me wrong."

She lifted up her left hand and wiggled her fingers right in front of his nose. "I'm engaged to be married, Risk."

Two

Normally Risk was good at reading women's signals but the other night at the Farmhouse, April had had him fooled. He could've sworn she wanted his attention. She'd looked at him, then at his mouth, as if she'd wanted to be kissed. Had it just been fear? Had she been grateful he'd come on the scene in the parking lot when he had?

April was a beautiful woman with sass and spunk.

And she was engaged to be married.

He'd remembered the chubby little girl she'd been, and when he'd met her again in Houston after he'd guest hosted the rodeo, her curvy body and pretty blue eyes had drawn him in.

"Risk, you're deep in thought this morning." Aunt Lottie poured him a cup of coffee and set the mug down on the kitchen table in front of him. Ever since his aunt had returned to Rising Springs Ranch, she'd doted on him and his two brothers, Mason and Lucas. Having an adventurous spirit, Aunt Lottie had been a world traveler always ping-ponging in and out of their lives, but after the death of their parents, she'd taken a more vital role with the family. And now was like a mother to him and his brothers.

Risk brought the mug to his mouth and sipped. "No one would ever call me a deep thinker."

Lottie took the chair adjacent to him, bringing her coffee to her lips and shaking her head. "You're a fine thinker, boy." Aunt Lottie was the first to come to a Boone's defense, unless of course they deserved a tongue-lashing, and then she'd be the first one to give it. "But something's bothering you. Your aunt knows you boys all too well."

"Nothing's bothering me, really. I'm just baffled about something."

About April. He'd been drawn to her the other night, the same way he'd been drawn to her in Houston. And that was precisely why he hadn't looked her up again. Why he hadn't pursued her after that night. It had been selfish of him, but he hadn't been in any shape to deal with a woman who wasn't a one-night-stand kind of girl. She'd been smart and sincere and compassionate. Once he figured that out, he'd run like hell. Not his finest moment.

"Care to tell me her name?" Aunt Lottie asked.

"Ha, nice try, Aunt Lottie. But it's all good." He winked and gave her his best smile.

"How's Drew doing these days?" he asked.

His aunt had an on-again, off-again relationship with Mason's future father-in-law, Drew MacDonald. It seemed the two of them never could get on the same page.

"I wouldn't know. He's barely talking to me."

"Oh yeah? Lovers' spat?"

Drew lived in the cottage on the Boone property. He was a recovering alcoholic, a good man who'd lost his wife some years ago. Maria had been Lottie's best friend, and now the two were playing a cat and mouse game of hearts.

"Hardly. We're barely friends anymore, Risk."

"Well, why don't you take some of those warm cranberry muffins you just baked and bring them to him as a peace offering?"

Aunt Lottie's blond brows lifted, and her eyes sparkled. She was a pretty sixtysomething woman who had a lot of love to give, and right now she was considering his suggestion. "You know, that's not a bad idea. And while I'm at it, I'll pack you a basket of muffins and some things for your trip."

"Thanks. It's a long drive out to Canyon Lake Lodge."

"Just give me a moment," his aunt said.

Minutes later, after finishing up his breakfast, he heard the front doorbell chime and the housekeeper answer it. He rose, taking the basket Aunt Lottie had made up, and walked out of the kitchen to the parlor where April Adams was waiting for him holding a brown briefcase. Those curly blond locks of hers flowed past her shoulders, and even the tan winter coat she wore over a pair of pants and a sweater couldn't hide her curvy body.

"Mornin', April. You're right on time," he said, coming into the room.

"I always try to be." She hoisted her chin up.

"I'll be right with you," he said.

He grabbed his sheepskin jacket, the one he'd lent April the other night, and showed her to the multicar garage attached to the house.

In the garage, he opened the passenger side door to his full-size SUV. He'd insisted he drive his car, and she was clearly not happy about it. April shot him a look and then climbed in. He waited while she buckled herself in and then handed her the basket.

"What's this?"

"My aunt Lottie made us a care package for the road."

"That's…very sweet of her."

"The Boones *are* nice people," he said.

Her eyes started to roll, and then she seemed to catch herself. Risk almost laughed out loud when her expression changed to an innocent smile. The trouble was he liked April Adams. Too damn much.

Risk started the engine and pulled out of the garage. There were gray skies overhead, and a light drizzle cascaded down from the clouds.

With any luck, they'd drive right out of the rain to better weather up ahead.

The rain came down steadily now, giving the windshield wipers a good workout. Of course, the weather had to be gloomy; it would make it that much harder for April to show off the grounds in a good light to Risk. But she didn't want to turn back. She couldn't trust that she'd get Risk back out to Canyon Lake Lodge any time soon.

She stared out the window, trying to think of ways to enhance her sales pitch. The lodge had been listed with her agency for five months, and she only had the listing for one more month. That gave her only weeks to find a buyer. The Boones' inquiry about the property had been the only real bite she'd gotten in all that time. She had to make this work, somehow. Risk hadn't been overly impressed with the photos of the lodge, and that parking lot kiss had only put a strain on their professional relationship.

"Cold?" he asked.

"A little."

He fiddled with a dashboard dial, and soon a flow of warm heat pushed out of the floor vents.

"Better?"

She nodded. "Yes, thank you. As long as it's not too hot for you?"

He gave her a sideways glance. "I'll let you know if it gets too hot."

Was that an innocent comment? She never knew with Risk. But she had to give him the benefit of the doubt, since he'd been put in his place the other night after she'd told him she was engaged.

Thank you again, Jenna Mae.

They drove a few more miles in silence, and then Risk gestured to the basket. "Since Aunt Lottie packed us up some food, why don't we have a muffin?"

"Sounds like a good idea." She lifted the basket onto her lap and then folded back the lid. "Oh wow. Your aunt Lottie sure knows how to make a care package."

"Why, what's she got in there?"

"Well, let's see. There's about eight muffins, a coffee thermos, protein bars and two apples."

A grumble rose from Risk's throat. "She still thinks we're twelve."

"It's sorta sweet that she cares so much."

April picked up a muffin, peeled back the cupcake paper, removing it entirely, and handed it over to Risk. It seemed an intimate gesture, but it was easier for him to eat that way. "Here you go."

"Thanks." A few bites later, the muffin was gone.

"Want another?"

He nodded. "One more will do. Make sure you have one, too."

"Oh, I intend to." April took a bite of her muffin. Warm and fresh, packed with cranberries, it was just the right amount of sweet and tart. "These are good."

"It's a family recipe. That coffee smells good."

"Want some?"

The wipers were at top speed now, and April hoped Risk wouldn't suggest they turn back.

"You first," he said. "Have some. It'll warm you up inside."

"Okay. Thanks."

She unscrewed the thermos and poured coffee into the cup. As she took a sip, the pungent aroma comforted her and made her smile. She handed the thermos over to Risk, and their fingers brushed again. "H-here you go." The contact wasn't lost on her. She quelled her racing heart and watched his throat work as he gulped down coffee.

Risk slid a glance to her left hand. "When's the wedding?"

Whoa. She wasn't really prepared to answer him. She'd hoped that wearing the ring was enough. Apparently she was wrong. "Uh, we haven't set the date yet."

"No?"

"No. A…a lot goes into planning a wedding, and my fiancé and I are very busy."

"Does he have a name?"

"Everyone has a name," she said rather evasively.

Risk scratched his chin. "So, you're not willing to tell me? He must not be—"

"He's amazing, okay? I met him when I was living in Willow County, and we're very happy."

"Bob? Bill? Toby? Or maybe it's more like Hector or Bubba?"

Bubba? Lordy. She folded her arms over her middle but still couldn't hold back a belly chuckle. "Risk, what are you doing?"

"Just making conversation. It's a long drive to the lodge. Especially with the rain slowing us down."

"Okay then, if you're so willing to talk, why don't you tell me about your love life?"

He grunted. "Or lack thereof."

She raised her brows. "That's hard to believe."

"Tell me about it. After what happened with Shannon,

I think I got gun-shy. No more permanent, all-in relationships for me."

"Are you saying you don't date anymore?"

He spared her a glance, his dark eyes meeting hers. "Now who's being nosy?"

"Okay, you're right. Forget I asked." It wasn't fair of her to ask such pointed questions of Risk when she'd barely given him the time of day about her fake engagement.

He was silent for a while. "The truth is, I haven't had a date in three months, maybe longer. I guess I lost count."

"I see. So, you must be really into your work, the way I am."

Risk's mouth twisted, and he gave his head a small, almost inconspicuous shake. "I'm trying to help out. The truth is…"

"What?" She gave him a pointed look.

"Nothin'."

She let it drop, because anybody with eyes in their head could tell that Risk wasn't the tycoon his brothers were. If he was, he wouldn't have become a rodeo rider.

"What did you think about the history of the lodge?" she asked, steering the conversation out of personal territory.

"Kinda crazy…neither one of them wanted to give in for the sake of success."

"So, you did read the articles."

"I surely did. That brother and sister team mixed as well as oil and water."

April nodded. "I don't have a brother or a sister, but I would think one of them could've given in rather than see the lodge fail."

"Yeah, those two were doomed from the get-go."

It was sort of like her and Risk. Doomed from the beginning.

Luckily, because of the ring on her finger, all she had to think about was convincing Risk that the lodge was worth the investment.

Halfway into the drive, Risk turned to April. "The storm's not really letting up. Let me know if you want to turn back."

"No," April said firmly. "I don't think we need to. We've come this far."

"Okay, fine by me." Risk didn't want to turn around, either. He wasn't opposed to driving in the rain, and he was sort of enjoying the adventure with her. He'd been in a rut lately, trying to figure out where he fit in the world.

He liked listening to April's melodic voice as she went into detail about JoAnna and Joseph Sutton, the twins who'd inherited the lodge some sixty years ago from their great-aunt. Her take on it was certainly more passionate and animated than any conversation they'd had before.

"JoAnna was a woman of the earth," she said, "a free spirit who wanted to use the lodge as refuge for the en-lightened of heart. She wanted bonfire parties and folksy dances, while Joseph was a hard-core outdoorsman who wanted to keep the rustic tone and promote it as a boating and fishing lodge."

"Must've made for some crazy interaction between the guests," he said. "Can you imagine the hunters and fish-erman going head to head with the vegetarians? I'm sure it wasn't pretty."

"It was a total failure. Finally, they sold the lodge to a recluse. He liked the fact that it was remote, off the beaten path."

"Is he the one selling the lodge?"

"No, he passed on. We'd be dealing with his grandson,

Michael Hall. I can't wait to show it to you. If we ever make it there."

"We will, trust me," Risk said, just as he hit a pothole in the road. The SUV bounded up in the air and landed with a huge muddy splash.

April gripped the handrail, color draining from her face. "You okay?"

She gave him an unsure nod.

He reached for her hand clutching the seat and gave it a slight squeeze. "We'll be fine. The SUV can take it."

She slid her hand from his and slunk back in her seat, warily folding her arms across her middle.

There wasn't much else he could say, so he shut his trap. It was better to forget the solid connection he'd felt when he grabbed her hand a few seconds ago. She was pretty and intelligent, and touching her quickened his pulse. For a man who hadn't had sex in a while, it was dangerous territory.

And he wasn't forgetting about that engagement ring on her finger. No, sir.

Rain pelted the windshield, and he concentrated on driving through the storm, the wipers giving him glimpses of what was ahead. He came to a low-lying bridge just around a curve in the road and slowed the car as the long wooden planks rattled under the tires. "It won't be long now," he told April and took a right-hand turn down a tree-lined road. April's face relaxed in relief.

A minute later, the road separated into a three-foot-wide ditch. "Holy crap." He swerved instantly, missing the biggest part of the gouge in the road, but luck wasn't with him. The car hit the very edge of the gap, and the front end plummeted into a gully of mud. He hinged his arm out to stop April's momentum, while her seat belt did the rest.

"You okay?" he asked her.

"Yeah, I think so." Color left her face. "W-what happened?"

"The rain washed away a good chunk of the road. It came up so fast, I couldn't see it, but I think we're on the edge of the ditch."

"Are we stuck?"

"Afraid so. The good news is GPS says the lodge is less than a mile away."

She sat silent for a few seconds. "And you can't get us out of the ditch?"

"Unfortunately, I left my superhero cape back at the ranch. We can't just sit here. We might sink farther into the ditch. Gather up your things, April."

He needed to make sure she was safe, and that meant high-tailing it to the lodge before the storm worsened. "We need to make a run for it. I'll get out first and help you. We'll call for help when we're safely at the lodge."

He gathered up a few essentials from the back of the SUV and dumped them into an old duffel bag he kept in the back. When he opened his door slightly, a wild gust of wind blew it open the rest of the way. He jumped down into a foot of mud, his boots catching the brunt of the ooze. Tossing the bag over his shoulder, he made his way around the back end of the SUV and opened the door for April. "Got what you need?"

She tucked her briefcase and her purse under her coat and nodded.

Risk reached for her, his hands firmly on her waist, and lifted her out of the car, holding on tight and twirling her around until they were clear of the ditch entirely before he set her down. "Ready to go?"

"I'm ready."

"Okay, let's get out of here." He took her hand and they trudged along the waterlogged road toward the lodge.

* * *

April had never been this soaked in her life. The mile sprint had her breathing heavily, but she was in good enough shape to keep up with Risk, who kept a tight grip on her hand. They hopped over potholes and dodged floating debris and then, finally, the sight of the lodge loomed like a big beautiful refuge. She hadn't been happier to see anything in her life.

Minutes later, they took the wide river-rock stairs together and landed under the protection of a covered veranda. Rain ceased to pelt them now, and the low veranda walls broke the wind gusts.

Risk stood by the double-door entry. "You have the key?"

Shaking from the cold, she opened the briefcase she'd kept as dry as possible and handed Risk the key. "H-here you go."

He opened the door and gestured for her to go inside. She'd been here twice before and remembered the layout. Risk followed directly behind her, a consoling presence after the ordeal they'd just been through. For a moment there, when the earth parted and the car careened into the ditch, she'd feared for her life. But Risk was there beside her, making her feel safe. Right now, it went a long way in reassuring her.

"Stay here while I check out the place and see if the power's on."

"It's supposed to be. Mr. Hall is keeping the electricity on through the sale."

Risk nodded and took off while she stood there, shivering. She scanned the interior of the main lobby. It had a floor-to-ceiling river-rock fireplace and settees positioned around the large room. Thick wood beams crisscrossed the tall ceilings, and black iron chandeliers hung from various points in the room. Though the room was cold, it was shelter from the raging storm outside.

"Looks like the storm knocked the power out," Risk said upon his return. "But there's some firewood here on the hearth, and I'm sure it's enough to keep us warm until the storm clears."

A puddle of water formed at her feet, droplets dripping from her clothes, her coat, her hair.

"I think that's a good idea."

"Give me a second to get a fire going."

While he was building a fire, she removed her coat and foraged inside her drenched handbag for her cell phone. Checking the screen, she wasn't surprised she had no service. Even on a good weather day, the cell service out here had been spotty. Now, it seemed nonexistent. She imagined the same was true of Risk's cell.

She walked over to the massive fireplace, where Risk was stacking logs. She found a magazine lying on one of the tables and rolled it up. "You can use this for kindling."

"That'll work."

She slapped it into his palm and shivered again. "I don't suppose you checked your phone yet."

"The minute we got inside. No service. You?" He tossed the kindling under the logs and lit it up.

"Same. Nothing."

Just then the kindling caught, and a small fire crackled and flamed. The burst of color also lent warmth, and she scooted closer to the new blaze.

Risk turned to her. "We should get out of our wet clothes. Get dry."

She blinked. She couldn't believe he'd suggested it. "How do you suppose we do that?"

"Peel 'em off."

"That's not what I meant. I don't have a change of clothes."

"Neither do I. But there's got to be towels or bedding or something we can wrap ourselves up in until our clothes dry out." He gave her an up and down glance. "Unless you want to shiver yourself into pneumonia."

Uh, no. She didn't want to do that, but she couldn't bring herself to say it. Risk caught her dumbfounded look and shook his head.

"April, you've got nothing to worry about with me. That ring on your finger might as well be a chastity belt. I'm only suggesting we don't catch our death of cold in these wet clothes. Should only take an hour or so to dry them."

She stared at the blaze burning bright orange, the glow rapidly growing. Risk was right, and boy, she hated to admit it, but the fire would dry out their clothes in no time. And that comment he made about her engagement ring hit home. She believed he'd be true to his word. "Okay. Let's see if we can find something to wrap up in. There's a master bedroom and a few other rooms on the ground level. I think Mr. Hall said he stays over once in a while."

"Sounds good to me." Risk walked over to where he'd dropped his duffel and came up with a utility lantern flashlight. He pulled the handle, and the light came on, flashing a halo over six feet of the room. "We'll use this only if we need to. Want to save the charge for tonight."

"Tonight?"

Risk turned to look her square in the eye. "The storm's going strong, and we're stuck. It's doubtful we'll get out of here today."

Thunder boomed, making her jump. She hadn't really thought that far ahead. "Won't someone come looking for us?"

Risk shrugged. "Don't know. Most around here must think this place is empty. No one's lived here for years, right?"

She nodded.

"And with the rain coming down in buckets and the car sunk in the mud…"

"Oh." A few seconds ticked by. "What about your family? Will they come looking?"

Risk smiled, his deadly dimples making an appearance. "My brothers know I'm smart enough to get out of the way of the storm. Wouldn't be the first time I didn't make it home at night."

April bit her lower lip. "I see. And your aunt?"

"Goes to bed kinda early. She probably figured I'd get in late."

That left Clovie. She was the only one April had told about this trip. And she wasn't due in the office until Monday afternoon.

It was her own fault for getting in this predicament. She should've postponed the meeting when the weather turned bad or at least asked Risk to turn back when the storm first hit. Now, she had to spend the night…with him. And soon they were going to get naked.

"Don't worry. We'll make do. We have some food, thanks to Aunt Lottie."

"You brought the basket?"

"Yep." He pointed to his duffel. "Now, let's go find us some warm things. Which way?"

She pointed to the passage to the left and then followed Risk down a murky hallway to a big double door. "This is the private master bedroom."

Risk opened the door, and they peered inside to a bedroom filled with just enough light to see a king-size bed made up with blankets and a quilt. They stepped into the room and began rummaging through a chest of drawers, and it was like finding a trove of precious treasures. They found extra blankets and sheets and candles. The furniture was large and sparse, made of solid wood. A fireplace sat against the far wall, and one big window faced out to angry gray clouds and pounding rain.

Risk grabbed two of the blankets and a big sheet. "This should do for now. You want to get out of your clothes in here? I'll get mine off in the lobby." He handed her the blanket, not really waiting for a reply, and walked out of the room.

She made quick work of peeling off her clothes, shoes first. She'd have to put her modesty on hold out of necessity. Just thinking about putting on dry, warm clothes again, undies included, made her heart sing.

She gathered up her clothes, wound herself up good and tight in the big blanket like a fruity roll up, and made her way to the lobby. Risk, casually wrapped in his blanket, had already set out a sheet for them to sit on between the two settees close to the fire. His clothes were laid out on his half of the hearth. She remembered he was a boxer kind of guy. Images popped into her head of that one night they'd had together. It had been pure magic, but that magic had vanished like a swift bird in flight the very next morning. No matter. She forced her gaze away from his clothes and proceeded to lay out her pants and top on the hearth. It was hard to be discreet with her undies no matter how she tried to conceal them, so she gave up and laid them out at the far end of the hearth. They'd be the first to dry anyway, comprised of far less material than her other clothes.

She took a seat facing the fire, allowing the warmth to seep into her skin. "Ah, this feels so good."

Risk gazed at her soaking up the heat and smiled. "Gotta admit this is a first for me."

"I'm afraid to ask."

"Being naked, enjoying a fire with a beautiful woman and not—"

"Don't say it, Risk." She shook her head. "Don't say it."

"And not having anything to offer but muffins and protein bars."

That was so *not* what he was going to say, but she smiled anyway. "Right now, a protein bar sounds pretty good."

His head snapped up. "Are you hungry?"

"I could eat."

"I'll get the food."

As he rose, the blanket around his shoulders slipped, exposing his granite chest and an incredible amount of sinewy muscles. Firelight glowed over his face and upper body, and she reacted with a sharp breath. It wasn't fair for a guy to look so darn good.

Luckily for her, she'd learned a hard lesson with him, so no amount of good looks could take away from what he'd done to her. He hadn't had the good grace to tell her face-to-face that he wasn't available in any way, and his abandonment had really hurt.

When she was six years old, her father had deserted her and her mother. That's when she'd begun eating heavily. Even though her rational brain knew Risk's actions were all on him, a part of her had reverted to that plump little girl who'd been abandoned by her father, the chubby girl who'd been invisible to most, as if people looked right past her, not really seeing her for the person she was.

But today, Risk was on his best behavior and he'd made her feel safe—as safe as a woman could feel, being naked under this blanket, having a meal with an equally naked-under-the-blanket guy, sitting by a luminous fire.

"Here you go," he said, bringing the food basket with him. "One protein bar coming up." He tossed it to her and as her arm came up to catch the bar, her blanket dipped, exposing her shoulders and, maybe, a teeny tiny bit of her cleavage.

Oh boy.

Risk's brows rose. He hadn't missed a thing.

A deep sigh escaped his lungs as he fell back against the base of the settee and bit into his protein bar. Still chewing, he glanced into the fire. "Maybe you should tell me all about this fiancé of yours."

Three

April's mouth gaped open. Risk's statement rubbed her the wrong way. What about his claims that her engagement ring was like a chastity belt? Was one glimpse at her bare shoulders enough to change his mind? If she wasn't so floored, her ego might have bumped up. "I have a better idea. Why don't you tell me all about Shannon Wilkes."

Risk stopped chewing and turned to her. "Why?"

"You seem so intent on my love life, but what about yours?"

"I don't usually talk about it."

"No kidding."

His mouth twisted at her sardonic tone. "My love life was plastered all over the tabloids. Couldn't pass a newsstand without seeing Shannon's face on the cover with her new guy."

"But that's not your story."

"Nobody wants to hear my story."

"I do."

He shook his head and stared into the flames again. "Why go there?"

"To help me understand what happened that night."

"Look, I blew it with you and I'm sorry. I was in a bad place."

"So you've said. What happened between you and Shannon?"

Risk remained silent. He finished his protein bar, his face turned to the flames rocketing like shooting stars in the massive fireplace. Safe from the storm outside and huddled in warmth, she could think of nothing she wanted to hear more than Risk's take on his life. At least she'd done one thing: diverted his attention from her made-up fiancé.

She, too, stared at the mesmerizing flames. It was peaceful and quiet sitting there together absorbing heat and trying to relax.

"There's nothing much to tell," Risk said, his voice low and deep. "She blindsided me, and it wasn't pretty."

Surprised that he'd said anything, April pursed her lips and listened.

"I met Shannon at a charity banquet to raise funds for children of military families. My brother Lucas was a Marine, and this was something near and dear to him. Shannon used her celebrity to persuade donors to help, and I was very impressed with her. She knew how to dazzle, and apparently, she dazzled me, too. I was all in with her, at the height of my game, winning rodeo after rodeo, and we were like some high-powered couple. Shannon seemed to bask in all that. But for me, I liked the challenge of the rodeo, of mastering something and being the best, but I didn't need or want all the added attention of dating an actress. We would argue about it. We'd be out somewhere together, and all of sudden there'd be a swarm of reporters snapping pictures, asking nosy questions. And then I'd find out it was all prearranged by Shannon's publicist."

"That wasn't the life you signed up for, was it?" April asked.

"I'm a Boone—a town was named for my family—but I never flaunted that or wanted to rub people's noses in it. And I never made a big deal about it. Believe it or not, I'm a private kind of guy. But we loved each other. We'd been together for two years and I was ready to take the next step."

She mouthed *marriage*.

"Yeah," he acknowledged. "But then my career came to a careening halt when I busted up my shoulder. It killed me that I couldn't do what I loved to do anymore. But what was worse, Shannon pretty much abandoned me. She hardly came to visit me when I was recuperating, and then she broke it off. The next thing I know…she's with Todd Alden, the NFL quarterback, and their pictures were splashed all over the news."

"That's pretty low," April said.

"That's how I found out Shannon was only using me to make her star rise."

"Must have hurt you badly."

His pride had him shrugging it off, but pain flashed in his eyes for a moment. "I'm over her now. Shannon wasn't right for me. Our lives are completely different, and at least we've managed to get past it. But I'll never allow anyone to make a fool out of me. That's not happening again.

"Back in Houston, the last thing I wanted to do that day was host the rodeo. But then I recognized you sitting in the stands and you smiled at me, and I felt ten times better. You reminded me of home, and in that moment, that's exactly what I needed."

"If it wasn't me, it would've been some other girl."

"Not true," he said adamantly. "I didn't expect to share my bed with a woman that night, but you were warm and bubbly and you made me laugh and forget things that were haunting me."

"I was a distraction."

He sighed and looked away, glancing out the rain-soaked window. "Want to know what I really thought?"

He paused, and April's heart began to pound. Was she ready to hear this? "Go on."

"I thought you were sweet and giving, a woman who wasn't starving herself to get a stick-thin body. I loved your curves and your confidence and your compassion. It was refreshing and…"

"And what?"

"Pretty damn hot, April." He glanced at her engagement ring again. "But in the morning, I had regrets. Not about you, but about me. I wasn't ready for any kind of involvement. It wasn't fair to you, I know, but just thinking about getting involved again so soon after I'd been burned wasn't happening. I should've told you that before taking you up to my hotel room. I should've been honest about my feelings. I knew you were the kind of woman who deserved that much from me. So I took off, vowing to call you and make amends."

"You never did."

"No. I should have, but I didn't. I'm sorry about it."

"So am I." She sighed.

"Now you know my deal with Shannon Wilkes. Enough said."

Well, yes. It explained a lot about his relationship with the movie star, but April still couldn't give him a pass on ditching her after a pretty incredible night of sex. Yes, he'd apologized already, but April wasn't ready to let him off the hook. He'd hurt her, and it had taken a long time to recover from that encounter, to get over her feelings of abandonment.

"You should've tried to reach me. To explain. I didn't leave that hotel room feeling very good about myself. You don't even want to know what I thought about you."

Risk had the good grace to squeeze his eyes shut. "Oh man, April, I deserve that. What can I say?"

She shrugged. "It's over and done with." And at least she'd now let her feelings be known. That was something. He wasn't going to let a woman make a fool out of him again? Well, she felt the same way: no man was ever going to play her for a fool and hurt her again, either.

That much she and Risk Boone had in common.

Thirty minutes later, April said, "I'm thirsty." They'd finished off what was left of the coffee in the thermos after their protein bar lunch. What sounded good to her now was a cold drink of water.

"The plumbing is working," Risk said.

"Amen to that. Our clothes are dry enough. Why don't we get dressed and go exploring? Might as well check the place out since we're stuck here. We'll explore the kitchen first."

"Fine by me. The fire's dying out anyway."

"There's dry wood outside in the woodshed," she commented. "I'll take the bedroom again to get dressed." She scooped up her warmed clothes from the hearth, anxious to get them back on. It was just too weird sitting in front of a fire, alone with Risk, knowing both of them were naked underneath.

Minutes later in her dry clothes, she went in search of Risk and found him fully dressed, checking out the kitchen facilities. The lodge's eatery had three sets of wide double doors that brought sunlight in on good days and kept the dining room cheerful.

"Well, we won't starve," Risk said. She liked the way his wet hair had dried, falling into his eyes. He'd shake his head and shift the pesky tendrils off his face. The move wasn't lost on her and she'd often catch herself staring at him.

"Uh, what?"

Risk raided the pantry. "There's a bag of potato chips and peanut butter in here. And we still have muffins and fruit from the basket."

"I guess that's luck, if we can say anything about this trip is lucky."

Risk turned on the faucet and let the water run for a while. "Just getting the cobwebs out of the pipes," he said. Then he rinsed out his thermos and filled it with water. "Have a drink," he said to her.

Accepting the thermos, she took a long, cool drink of water. When down to the bare essentials, there really wasn't anything better than water to sustain you. She gulped down the rest and handed the thermos back to Risk. He took his turn guzzling water. The thought of them sharing the thermos no longer seemed weird. It was almost as if they were on some sort of survival camping trip.

With Risk looking on, April took a few minutes to open all the cabinets. A couple of them were about ready to fall off their hinges. She opened drawers and found some off their tracks. All surface stuff. The kitchen was outdated, but the foundation was sturdy.

"The kitchen has a lot of potential. It's large and roomy, and that's a plus when cooking for many guests," she said, going into full Realtor mode.

Risk folded his arms across his middle. "But this entire room would have to be gutted. It needs a fresh start, and we're talking a major overhaul."

"But it would be your overhaul. You could do anything you wanted in here. You could go simple or sophisticated."

Risk's eyes narrowed on her. "Do you really like this place, or are you only trying to make a sale?"

"Both. I do love this lodge. I see the possibilities. And I think it's a good investment for your family's business,

Risk. I do. So, do you want to see the rest?" She pointed up toward the second story.

"Sure, it's not like there's too much else to do around here."

Showing the lodge in the midst of a storm was not the best way to entice a potential client. Risk was losing interest with each passing minute. Upstairs they found the roof leaking in three of the rooms and made quick work of finding bowls and vases to catch the water.

Twenty minutes later, they climbed down the staircase in the lobby. Low-lying embers did little to warm the room, and they both shivered. "You said there's a woodshed outside?" Risk asked.

"Yes," April said. "It's around the right side of the house."

"All right, fine. I'll go get us some firewood for tonight."

"Right now?"

"Better now while there's still some daylight than later tonight."

April bit her lip. The storm was fierce. It hadn't let up. "It's really coming down out there."

"It'll be fine. I'll be back in five minutes. While I'm doing that, why don't you fix us some dinner?"

She stared at him and shook her head. "Oh sure, when you get back, I'll have a five-course meal waiting for you."

He smiled. "I'd expect no less."

Risk put on his sheepskin coat and plopped his hat low on his forehead. He gave April a nod and grabbed the doorknob. Her expression seemed bleak; she was worried about him. "Be careful."

Her hair had dried into big blond curls that cascaded down her back in a style women paid big money for, but on her the curls were natural. He'd enjoyed watching them fall into place by the fire. Her usually bright blue eyes dimmed as she gave him a little wave.

"Always," he said, opening the door. A shot of wind blew into the room, pushing him back. He fought the force and stepped outside, pulling the door shut behind him.

Rain pummeled the ground as he made a run for the shed, his boots kicking up mud. The entire front yard was flooded, and he splashed his way to the right side of the house. He found the woodshed easily, and just like April had said, there was no lock. Gripping one of the double door handles, he pulled back hard, and the door creaked open. He stepped inside, and now protected somewhat from the storm, he glanced around the roomy shed. Roomy only because there was precious little wood left. Two bundles lay by the back wall, and he figured it was better than nothing. It should be enough to keep them warm for the night in the big drafty lodge.

He lifted the first bundle of firewood, piling a good amount in his arms. The wind blew the shed door shut, so he planted his boot against the door and kicked it open again. He made his way back to the lodge entrance and dropped the wood right by the front door. Taking a deep breath, he ventured out again to get the last of the firewood. Branches from the mesquite trees nearby all swayed to the right from the terrific gales, and he moved even faster now to get into the shed.

Once there, he bundled the last pile in his arms and made a run for it. He was nearly to the front of the lodge when something loud cracked behind him. He turned just in time to see a thick tree branch break from a mesquite tree and jettison his way. He ducked, but he wasn't fast enough.

The branch struck him in the head, and his knees buckled before everything went black.

April slathered peanut butter on the leftover muffins, set out the bag of potato chips and put two plump red apples out for dessert on the kitchen table. "There, how's that for a feast?" she muttered.

She felt at odds with the universe not having cell service. No weather reports to look up, no way to communicate with loved ones. Yet she wouldn't want anyone venturing out in this storm to come save them. She'd never seen it so bad. Shutters rattled, the wind blew unmercifully, the ground flooded.

She hated to admit defeat, but Risk hadn't seen much he liked in this old lodge. He was seeing it as a bad investment, while in her mind the place only needed surface repairs and some tender loving care. Which meant enduring the day and night together was all for naught. "Guess I'm not making this sale."

She stared out the window for a while, watching the never-ending downpour. Then she rearranged her scant excuse for dinner, trying to make it look like more than it was, before heading off to use the bathroom facilities. By the time she returned to the kitchen, five minutes had long passed. Yet Risk was still out there.

A moan sounded from the lobby entrance, a low groaning that could be the wind, yet her instincts said differently, and she raced to the front door. Bracing herself, she pulled it open.

And there stood Risk. Well, he was barely standing, his shoulders hunched, blood trickling from a gash on his head. "Risk! My God, what happened to you?"

He stared at her, looking totally bewildered, and slumped into her arms. She had just enough strength to catch him. Using her steam and some of his, she walked him inside. He wasn't talking, and she feared he was in shock. At that moment, she made a quick decision to get him into the master bedroom. He needed care, and that room was easier to heat and had a big comfy bed. "Stay with me, Risk. Hang on."

She took it slow, and they made their way through the lobby, down the hall to the master bedroom they'd raided just hours ago. He was drenched, his coat and pants a muddy mess. "Can you stand while I get off your wet clothes?"

He nodded, barely. She didn't have much time. She had to see to the gash on his head, but she couldn't let him sit in soaked clothes. She got his jacket off first, and then his shirt. "Okay, now let's get you down on the bed." He swayed, and she grabbed him the best she could to keep him from falling, then guided him onto the bed. She took his boots off and then worked at the zipper of his jeans and slid them off. He began to shiver, so she covered him quickly with a blanket, tucking him in tight and hoping he hadn't gone into shock.

"I'll be right back," she whispered.

She ran into the master bathroom, grabbed all of the towels and dashed back to Risk. Now he was out cold. With shaky hands she dabbed at the blood, clearing it away so she could see the extent of the injury. The gash didn't look too deep, but then she wasn't a nurse, so she really had no idea how serious this was. But a nice lump was forming underneath it. Something had hit him hard enough to knock him out.

As she continued to dab, he moaned. Then his eyes slowly opened. That had to be a good thing.

"Risk, can you hear me?" she asked in a loud voice.

He nodded, and then his eyes closed again.

Her heart pounded. She hated seeing anyone hurt, much less someone she cared about.

She cared about Risk?

Only in a Good-Samaritan way. He needed help, and she was it.

"Don't worry. You're going to be all right."

The one thing she did know was if he had a concussion, she couldn't let him sleep. She would have to watch over him for the rest of the day and night. She could do that. She had to.

The room was frigid. Even under the blankets, Risk was shivering. She needed to warm him up with a fire. She left him only for a second, recalling in the back of her mind she'd seen wood on the ground near the front door. After dashing there, she found a bundle he must've dropped near the lodge entrance. She hauled the fire logs inside and into the master bedroom along with another magazine she'd snatched up from the lobby for kindling.

"Are you awake?" she called loudly, tossing the logs into the hearth.

His eyes opened again. *Thank goodness.*

She'd never been a Girl Scout, but she managed to get the kindling lit and tease the logs enough to make a low-lying fire come to life.

She went back to Risk to check his wound. It had stopped bleeding, and gratitude filled her heart. He looked so out of it, so vulnerable, so entirely dumbfounded.

"You're not bleeding anymore, but I'm gonna wrap your head with this clean towel, just in case there's seepage. Let me know if it hurts."

She carefully folded the towel into a thin length and wrapped it around his head to cover the wound. "There. How are you feeling, Risk?"

Fire crackled, and a small blast of light shined on his face. "Who are you? And…why are you calling me Risk?"

Four

April stared at him. For one second she thought he was joking. But then good sense seeped in. He was in no shape to joke, not after the blow to his head… Even an Oscar winner couldn't pull off his total sense of bafflement. "W-what do you mean?"

"You…keep…calling me… Risk."

"Yes, that's your name. Risk Boone. Don't you remember?"

He seemed to search his mind, and the blank look on his face really worried her.

"No. I can't remember anything."

"You can't remember *anything*?" she repeated, swallowing hard.

He thought about it a few seconds more, appearing puzzled. "Not about myself, no."

Oh boy, if that were true then this situation just went from bad to worse. Could he really have…amnesia? The sharp knock to his head would've provoked it, but how long would his memory loss last? And what was she supposed to do about it?

"W-what happened to me?"

"You went out in the storm to get firewood. I think a branch broke off a tree and downed you."

He took that in, not seeming to recall it at all.

"What kind of name is Risk anyway?" he muttered.

Maybe if she talked to him about his life, it would stir a memory or two. "It's not really your name. Your real name is River Boone. And most people who don't know you very well think you got your name because you took a lot of risks on the rodeo circuit. It was sort of your brand. But the truth is your little brother, Lucas, couldn't say River very well when he was a baby. It always came out like *Risker*. The name stuck, and soon everyone was calling you Risk."

She'd learned that bit of trivia when she'd spent the night with him in Houston.

"Oh." None of what she'd said seemed to register with him and he frowned. "What's your name?"

"I'm… I'm April Adams."

"Should I know you?"

"Well…yes. But don't worry about that right now. Let me tell you about your family and maybe you'll recall something."

"You said I had a brother?"

"Yes, two brothers, actually. Mason and Lucas. You all live on Rising Springs Ranch in Boone Springs."

He shook his head slightly, obviously not recognizing the names.

"Your family founded the town a hundred years ago."

He closed his eyes. "I don't…"

"It'll come to you in time," she assured him, hoping that was truly the case.

"Tell me more." Even in his weakened state, he seemed desperate to find something he could relate to, something that might spur a memory.

"You were in the rodeo. Actually, you did really well as a bronc buster. But you hurt your shoulder after a toss from a horse named Justice and needed surgery," she said quietly. She ran her finger along the outline of the injury on his shoulder. "The scar is right here."

He peered deep into her eyes, searching for something. Touching him like that was a mistake, one she couldn't afford to make. Seeing him feeling weak, vulnerable and puzzled jostled something deep in her soft mushy heart.

"I, uh, I'll go get you some water. You need to drink."

She didn't know that for a fact, but the body always needed water. Then images of the storm popped into her head. Outside there was an obscene amount of water flooding the property.

"Don't go," he pleaded. The desperation in his voice made her freeze in place. "Stay here."

There was pain on his face and fear in his eyes. He didn't want to be alone, and she couldn't blame him. He didn't know who he was. He didn't know what had happened to him. To have your mind cleared of all your personal memories had to be unbelievably difficult. "I, uh, okay," she said. "I'll stay."

April watched over him, telling him about how bad the storm was and how they'd made a run for it to the lodge for safety. But he was drifting in and out despite how hard she tried to keep him engaged. As the fire burned low, the room got increasingly colder, and she finally relented and climbed under the covers to keep warm.

He turned toward her.

"It's important you stay awake a little while longer," she whispered, touching her fingers to his cheek. "Please, Risk."

He caught the glimmer of her diamond ring in the last of the firelight and grabbed her hand. Forcing his attention there, his voice lightened and a warm glow entered his eyes. It was the most life she'd seen out of him since she'd found him outside the lodge. "April, we're engaged?"

She was in bed with him, tending to his wounds. Anyone might assume that, but as she opened her mouth to deny it, his lips pressed into the palm of her hand, and the sweetness of the warm kiss he placed there crushed her denial. She should have pulled her hand away and climbed out of the bed, but the brightness on his face, the relief in his eyes, stopped her. It was as if he'd discovered something about himself, his connection to her, and it was hard to destroy his hope. "Risk."

"I like the way you say my name." He smiled.

"It's important that you stay awake tonight. In case of a concussion. You've taken a hard hit to the head."

"Tell me about it. It's pounding."

She jerked to attention. "How can I help?"

"Stay here and talk to me."

"I will."

"Good," he said, closing his eyes.

"But you have to stay awake."

He fought to open his eyes. "Then tell me more about my life, about us."

Oh boy, this wasn't what she'd expected, but what choice did she have? Was it so terrible for him to believe they were engaged for a short time, to give him peace of mind? She'd tell him the truth later, once he was feeling better. Right now, she had to keep him from dozing off.

She began slowly, giving him glimpses of his life as she knew it. She told him they'd met in high school but didn't get together until later in life—all true statements. She skimmed over facts, and thankfully he didn't ask questions but simply listened. Then she steered her one-sided conversation to his brothers and the ranch they lived on. She mentioned that Boone Springs had an annual Founder's Day party every year in town, honoring his ancestors and all the prominent people who'd contributed to the town. That big day was coming up soon, and all three of the brothers would be in attendance.

She knew a lot about the townsfolk, and so she kept a steady stream of information going, trying not to overload him with details but painting him a picture of Boone Springs.

"Does any of this sound familiar?" she asked, though she already knew the answer. She'd kept a watchful eye on Risk as she spoke, and there wasn't one sign, one spark of recognition registering on his face. So when he gave his head a tiny shake, she wasn't surprised.

"Let me check your wound," she said and rose up on the bed. She slid awkwardly across his body to garner a better look. She unwrapped the makeshift bandage, noting the lump on his head hadn't gone down. "Are you feeling any better?" she asked.

"My head still hurts a bit, but the rest of me is doing just fine."

She was inches from his face, and as she glanced at him, a small smile curved his lips and she caught his meaning loud and clear. When she'd first seen him injured, strong feelings had rushed forth. She'd cared for him, worried over him. He wasn't a stranger, but a man she might've loved if circumstances had been different. She hated what he'd done to her years ago, but she surely didn't want to see him injured again.

Risk had amnesia, she told herself, but that didn't stop her body from reacting to him, from tingling from head to toe, from turning her firm resolve into soft putty. With him smiling at her, his body granite hard, her defenses were down. And when he took her arms and stroked them up and down, drawing her closer, she didn't protest. She didn't back away.

And then his lips were on hers, gently, tenderly, kissing her as if he was experimenting to see if he remembered something. He was so gentle, so deliberate, and every second was better than the next. His feathery kisses drew her in, every nerve ending awakened to the sweet pressure of his lips.

She needed to keep him awake and engaged...well— she had the engaged part down. As in, he thought they were. Now was her chance to stop him. To own up to the truth, to tell him it had all been a lie to prevent this very thing. Yet the words were not coming. How could they, when Risk was kissing her like this? Each kiss brought her a new kind of thrill. She'd never met a man like Risk before; she'd never felt this way about anyone else. Wouldn't Jenna Mae just die to find out her engagement ring plot had backfired?

"You're amazing," he murmured between kisses.

"Do you remember anything now?" she whispered.

"No, but I do know one thing. This feels right."

He laid another amazing kiss on her with his masterful lips. "Risk, maybe we shouldn't," she said softly between his kisses.

"My head is feeling better and better by the minute. Didn't you say I needed to stay awake?" He kissed her throat and nipped up to her waiting mouth. She was torn, confused, feeling helpless as the truth wouldn't come.

"Well, yes, but...you don't remember me."

"You've been caring and worried and well... I think I do know you. Somehow, I feel you with me. I see how compassionate you are," he said, taking her head in his hands. His eyes were bright and intense and goodness, he looked like Risk again, even with the bandage around his head.

"And I'm certainly responding to you." He planted a beautiful kiss on her mouth and then paused. "Unless we haven't done this before? Have we? Tell me we have?"

"I, uh, yes," she whispered. "We've done this before."

"I need you, April. I need the connection."

She absorbed those words, and they touched down deep in her soul. She'd never reacted to any man the way she'd reacted to him. This Risk was sincere, genuine and sweet. This Risk was in need of more than sex, but intimacy, a bridge to his past. And today, she was it.

But could she discount her past with him? She'd been hurt by his actions, and he hadn't really made much of an effort to apologize to her. Her brain was telling her no, but her body was tingling all over and her big open heart was saying *yes, yes, yes.*

Only this time, she'd go in with caution, knowing not to have grand expectations. Could she be that woman who lived for this one night? Could she continue with the facade for just a little while longer? All the while knowing she would have to own up to the truth tomorrow?

She answered the question as her mouth pressed to his and she tasted him once again.

He touched her face, brushing a few curls from her cheek. "You're sweet and beautiful, April. I'm glad you're here with me."

"I'm glad I'm here with you, too," she said softly.

He kissed the words right out of her mouth. "No more talk."

"Is it hurting your head?"

"My head is not what's aching, sweetheart." His arms roped around her shoulders and he brought his lips down to touch hers in yet another kiss. April was at a loss to stop, and in the back of her mind she knew this would definitely keep him awake. He was definitely perked up now.

He might not know who he was, but he hadn't lost his finesse, and his near-naked rock-hard body was keeping her very warm. He stroked her arms and helped her remove her clothes. Then he began kissing the nape of her neck.

In the dimly lit room, he pulled the covers back a bit, exposing her body. There was admiration on his face, and deep desire. She was totally captivated by that look, by the reverent way his hands came to caress her breasts, as if in awe. She sighed at his intimate touch, her body trembling, her skin craving more from him. She was needy and ravenous and so taken by the attention he bestowed on her.

If he found her too curvy or lacking in any way, she didn't see it in his expression. She was at peace with her size and loved that he seemed to like her body just fine as well. He caressed her until tiny throaty sounds rose up from her throat, and then he moved lower on her torso and spread his fingers wide as he ran them down toward the apex of her thighs.

"Oh," she moaned once he stroked her center, and he smothered her cry with a deep lusty kiss.

Some time later, April lay beside Risk on the bed, her head on his chest. His arm was around her shoulders. "My head feels much better," he murmured.

April was glad about that, but she had to face facts: she was going to have to ruin all this bliss come morning, by owning up to her lies. She sighed and wished she'd never agreed to Jenna's plot in the first place.

"That's a good sign. I thought for sure you'd have a headache."

Outside the rain continued to fall, but with a little less force than before, and she wondered if the roads would clear or cell service would be restored soon. She doubted it would happen anytime soon. It was too risky for anyone to come out in such a torrential storm. The only saving grace was that Risk said he was feeling better.

"Well, I'd be lying if I said there wasn't a dull ache going on inside my head, but it's nothing I can't handle. Everything's a bit fuzzy." A growl rumbled from his stomach, and his eyes rounded in surprise. "Whoa," he said. "Guess I'm hungry. When's the last time we ate?"

"It's been a while. We didn't expect to get stranded in the storm, so what we have on hand is limited. But it's edible, and you should eat."

He nodded.

April rolled out of bed as discreetly as she could and quickly threw on her clothes. "You'll be okay here, right? I'll get us the food."

"I can go with you."

He made a move to get up, and she quickly put up her hand. "No, please. It'll only take me a minute. Don't try to get up just yet."

He looked at her, debating, and then lowered back down against the pillow. "Okay. Be careful."

She almost smiled at that. He was telling her to be careful when he was the one who'd gotten injured. Yet it was sweet of him to be concerned.

He thinks you're his fiancée.

She dashed out the door and made her way to the kitchen. There on the table was the five-course meal she'd promised to conjure up in the form of muffins with peanut butter, apples and potato chips. She filled the thermos with water and then grabbed the food. As she made her way through the lobby, she picked up Risk's duffel bag and headed back to the bedroom.

She found him sitting up on the bed, staring out the window. "Dinner is served," she said, dropping his duffel and coming to sit on the bed beside him.

He looked at the food. "You really know how to impress a guy," he teased.

"I'm a master at making lemonade out of lemons."

"I can see that."

She handed him the thermos. "You must be thirsty."

"I am. Thanks." He put the thermos to his lips and took several gulps, then handed it to her.

She sipped from the thermos. "At least water is one thing we have in abundance."

Risk pointed toward the window. "Gross understatement, sweetheart." Then he plucked up a muffin and shoved half of it in his mouth. Chewing, he said, "These are pretty good."

"Your aunt Lottie made them. She's living on the ranch for the time being."

"Yes, you told me a little about her. So tell me more about you."

What could she say? That she had a fantasy crush on him and had for a long time, even though he'd done her wrong? That seeing him injured and vulnerable had stirred up her feelings for him again in a big way? That looking into his beautiful eyes made her do foolish things? Like pretending to be his fiancée. Like making love with him. "I was a chubby young girl and have struggled with my weight all of my life."

He shook his head as if he couldn't believe it. "You're… perfect, April. Just the way you are." He brushed his lips over hers tenderly, his assurance a balm to her soul.

"Thank you. I feel good about myself now, but I didn't always feel that way."

"Well, you should. Tell me more about you and your agency. How did you get into real estate?"

April told him more about her life, about her years in Willow County, about how her mother remarried and how she came to buy Bueller's antique store. She ended her personal history and shrugged. "Having my own agency is a dream of mine."

"It's weird—even though I don't remember, I feel like I know you. There's something pulling me toward you."

"You mean aside from the fact that we're stranded here in a pretty romantic setting."

He grinned and those hidden dimples popped out. "I like the way you think, April. But yeah, it's more than that."

He grew quiet then, and she figured he was sorting things out in his head, or at least trying to. They spent time munching on muffins and chips and sharing both apples as the night wore on. "If you're still hungry, there's more chips and peanut butter."

"No, but what I am feeling is damn helpless." He swung his legs out from beneath the blanket. Before she could utter a word, Risk rose from the bed. He swayed a little but then righted his balance. She found herself staring at the back half of a buck-naked Risk.

Her mouth went dry watching the last of the embers cast light on his muscled form. "Are you okay?" she asked him.

"I think so. Feels good to get on my feet again."

He reached for the clothes she'd laid by the fire earlier and, with his back to her, gingerly put them on. She sighed in relief that he hadn't keeled over and that he wasn't naked anymore.

"This room is getting colder by the minute. Is there more wood?" he asked.

"Yes, but it's outside."

"How far?"

"By the front door. I only brought in what I could carry."

"I'll go get it."

"Risk, that's how you got hurt, going after firewood."

"The storm's letting up, and you said it yourself, it's only by the front door."

"Fine, but I'm going with you this time."

He walked over to her and put out his hand. "I'm good with that. Let's go."

After retrieving the last of the wood, Risk had restarted the fire in the master bedroom and now they were bathed in warmth once again. The small blaze was their only source of light tonight, since the lantern Risk had dropped outside when he was hit had probably been pulverized by the fierce winds. Once the fire died out, it would be dawn before they'd be able to see anything in the lodge.

But they'd made do with what they had and now both sat on the floor facing the hearth, letting the warmth seep into their bones. The rest of the lodge was freezing cold, but this room was like a sanctuary.

April rose. "I'll be back in a few minutes." She took some time to wash up and then soak a towel for Risk's head. When she came back, she spotted two foil-wrapped condoms that had magically appeared on the nightstand. Earlier Risk had been fiddling inside his duffel; he must've hit the jackpot, yet he hadn't said a word about it. They were just…there.

She didn't know how she felt about that. They hadn't actually had intercourse yet, but the night was long and they'd be sharing the bed. She knelt beside him and dabbed at his wound quietly as she mulled that over.

He grabbed her hand and ran his lips along her palm. "You take such good care of me," he whispered, gratitude in his voice. And then he lifted his head to look deep into her eyes. "You're amazing, April. You're the only real thing I know about myself." He pulled her close so that her leg brushed over his thighs and she sat straddling him. A groan rose from his throat and he cupped her head and covered her mouth with his. Teasing her mouth open, he thrust his tongue against hers in kiss after kiss. It was tender and sweet and hot all at the same time. She could kiss him all night long and never tire of it. Risk didn't hold back; he didn't temper or pace himself, and he certainly didn't seem unsure when it came to this.

It scared her a little that he'd put so much faith in her. That he'd accepted that she was his fiancée so easily, that she was the one thing he could count on in his world without memories. She'd wanted to tell him the truth, but his assumptions had been the only brightness he'd had. And resisting him at that moment hadn't been an option for her. Tomorrow would be soon enough, she told herself.

Suddenly, he stopped kissing her. "April?" She opened her eyes to the firelight dancing in his. "The fire's gonna die down soon, and there'll be a chill in the air. Maybe we should get into bed now."

She swallowed past her misgivings. She wanted this, wanted to be held and loved by Risk tonight. Unlike the last time, she knew nothing would come of it. "That's a good idea," she whispered.

Rising to his feet, he tugged her along, and they both climbed into the bed. He gave her the side closest to the fireplace.

His arms came around her to gather her up close, and with her back to his chest, she finally relaxed. She liked being held by Risk, liked the safety he presented, the warmth of his body against hers. Today had involved a crazy set of circumstances: the storm, racing to the cottage, Risk losing his memory. Now that they were in bed together, a sense of peace stole over her, which was crazy, because they were low on food and had no idea what the morning would bring.

Cocooned by his strong body, she fell into the cadence of his breathing. She felt one with him and absorbed that feeling with each beat of her heart. But minutes later, when she thought he might have fallen asleep, his lips pressed against the nape of her neck and everything relaxed in her body suddenly jolted alive. She gave her approval with a sigh that Risk picked up on immediately. His hand came to the top of her rib cage, and his fingertips teased the underside of her breast. She ached for his touch, for him to continue his pursuit, and he didn't disappoint.

Effortlessly, Risk helped her off with her sweater and unfastened her bra. Then his hands were on her, and it was thrilling having him caress her in such a reverent manner, as if she were solid gold. Her body heated to a beautiful flame that Risk stoked with kiss after kiss. And then he turned her to face him and brought his mouth to her breast, moistening it, bringing the tip to a pebbled peak.

She was eager to touch him as well, and as she fumbled with the buttons on his shirt, he helped her lift it over his head. Then her palms flattened on his powerful chest and she kissed her way up his torso, her lips on his hot skin. And then their mouths melded again, the kiss fiery and frenzied, and they both groaned, rocked by the impact. They were equal partners: when he gave, she took, and when she gave, he took.

"I found protection, sweetheart," he murmured between kisses.

"Thank goodness," she whispered softly.

Seconds later their clothes were off and Risk was sheathed. She was ready for him, her body dewy and welcoming.

His lips came down to crush a kiss to her mouth at the same time he moved inside her. Sensations rocked her, her body recalling the feel of him, the fullness and total thrill. "Are you good?" he asked before thrusting again.

"So good."

He shifted, and his body covered hers. She kept pace, each thrust exciting her more and more.

Risk took complete control, and she followed him, her body in sync with his, her heart nearly bursting from her chest, her breathing hard and fast. He seemed to know what she needed, when she needed it, and soon she found herself melting, her body giving way, her world going up in flames.

"Risk," she cried out.

And then she splintered, shattered. Her entire body combusted, and Risk was there to catch her as she floated down. His kiss held promise, and she was ready for him, ready to give back all he'd given to her. It didn't take long for Risk to follow, his face a mask of pleasure as he made that one last final thrust. And it was an amazingly wonderful thing.

In the early morning, Risk rose and dressed quietly, then placed a soft kiss on April's forehead as she slept. He might not know anything about himself, but he did know he was damn lucky to have found a woman like April to love. She was caring and fun and beautiful with those long curly locks and bright blue eyes. She'd been extremely attentive to him and tried her best to encourage him, even though his mind was like a blank chalkboard ready to have the memories filled in. At least he had April to chalk in some things, and that had been a big help. He'd connected with her on many levels, but their time in bed was off-the-charts good.

While he didn't want to disturb her sleep, he was curious about the lodge and wanted to explore a bit. Without

a sound, he made his way out the door and down the hallway to the lobby area. There he checked out the floors and
walls, looking for any permanent storm damage, and then
checked out the big triple-wide bay windows. Outside, the
rain was down to a drizzle, which was encouraging.

"Risk?"

He turned to find April in the doorway, her arms folded
across her sweater. "April, you're cold. Come here," he said.
"I'll keep you warm."

She walked over, and he folded her into his arms.

"I woke up and you were gone. I didn't know if you were
feeling okay or not," she said.

"Don't worry about me, sweetheart. I've got a hard head.
Empty, but hard. I didn't want to disturb your sleep."

"You mean like you did last night?"

He laughed. Round two had been just as inspiring as
the first time. Neither of them had gotten a lot of sleep,
April doing her best to keep him awake. In the morning,
she'd finally fallen asleep, and he might have dozed some,
too. He was pretty sure he didn't have a concussion. Being
with April was the best balm to his soul. She was his connection to his real life, not the one he'd had for less than
twenty-four hours. "Hey, I didn't hear any complaints at
the time."

She smiled. "No, no complaints."

He hugged her tight.

"So why'd you get up so early?" she asked.

"I got curious about the lodge. I mean, that's why we
came here, right? You're my Realtor, and we need to check
it out and see if it's a worthy investment."

"Yes, that's right."

"So, you want to do that?"

"Sure. Let's do it."

He took April's hand, and they finished up in the lobby,

noting that a few of the rocks in the fireplace were loose. But the floors were in good enough shape, just needed a little TLC, and the windows were well insulated.

The kitchen was another matter. "The tiles are chipped so the counters would have to replaced and updated." He opened a few cabinets and checked inside. "A few of these are coming off the hinges, but the actual structure is sturdy. They'd need a little refurbishing—maybe a face-lift," he said. He looked at April. "Do the appliances work?"

"They do. For the most part." April made a face. "You don't think the kitchen needs to be gutted?"

"It's salvageable. There's a certain charm about this big kitchen. I think it could work."

"Really?" April smiled. "I'm glad you think so."

They walked into the dining area next to the kitchen. "This room seems solid," he said, looking around.

"And on a nice day, those windows bring in lots of light—you can see Canyon Lake from here," she said. "It's really a beautiful view."

"I bet."

"And we already know the master bedroom is good to go."

"Yeah, we do know that."

"I'm afraid the second floor isn't in as good shape. I mean, it is, but some of the rooms sprouted leaks from the storm."

As they climbed the stairs, she filled him in on the history of the rooms, the brother and sister team who couldn't quite get their act together. It didn't make any sense to him, but April seemed optimistic about the place. Her passion only endeared him to her more. This was important to her, and he didn't want to quell her enthusiasm.

"I know the roof needs repair," she said, "but if you decided to replace it, there's room for negotiation with the owner."

A sense of déjà vu took place in his head. It seemed as if he'd had this conversation before. It was only a flash, a snatch of a memory, or maybe he was just imagining it.

Still…it was encouraging. "You know something, I like this lodge. I see potential in it."

"I'm glad you think so." April beamed from ear to ear, and then a grumble rose from her stomach and filled the quiet room. "Whoa. Excuse me."

"Hey, I'm hungry, too. What do we have left?"

"Not much. Potato chips and peanut butter."

"You mean…breakfast?"

"Yes," she said, chuckling. "Breakfast. Washed down with a big gulp of water."

"Can't think of anything better."

She batted her eyes, and it was so adorable, he planted a kiss right smack on her mouth, the first real kiss of the morning. If he had his say, it wouldn't be the last.

Minutes later in the kitchen, he watched as April gently dipped chips into the peanut butter and set them out on the table as if it was a gourmet meal. He liked her style and her lack of panic in a situation that might've brought another person to tears. She'd taken control, mending him, trying to keep him from freaking out. Which, he wasn't gonna lie, was a battle. Not knowing anything about himself, his family and his past life was daunting. April filled the voids, but she didn't overload him with facts he'd have trouble processing.

With her by his side, he was sure he'd make it through any rough patches.

She set the thermos down between them, and together they munched on potato chips and sipped water. "Looks like the storm is letting up."

"Hopefully another one isn't on its tail. Maybe I should try to get to the car and see how bad it is."

"You mean maybe *we* should get to the car and see how bad it is."

"We?" He began shaking his head. "No, April. You said it's a mile to the car. And if another storm is coming, you shouldn't be out in it."

"If I'd gone with you for the firewood, maybe you wouldn't have gotten injured."

"Or maybe we both would've been. At least right now, one of us has their memory."

"The truth is, I don't want to be left alone in the lodge," April said, and Risk narrowed his eyes at her. She was nibbling on her lip, her eyelashes fluttering. Was she being honest? Was she really afraid?

"Okay, we'll stick together," he said finally.

A genuine look of relief washed over her face. Risk had made the right decision, but there were unknowns out there, and he would protect her like his life depended on it.

Early this morning, April had vowed to tell Risk the truth about their relationship. She should've done it the first thing, but then she'd found him exploring the lodge, and she'd gone along with it, losing her nerve. It wasn't an easy thing to admit, that they really weren't engaged *at all*, but she found him so charming and irresistible, she'd slept with him multiple times. How could she explain that away? And then how would she have explained the engagement ring on her finger? She didn't know what harm the truth would do to his recovery. Right now, she was the only bridge to his real life.

Yesterday, she'd been more concerned about his safety, seeing to his wound and taking that puzzled and fearful look off his face. Sharing a bed with Risk Boone to ward off the cold had been necessary, and he'd told her numerous times how much it meant to him that she was there with him.

But it was wrong to let him go on believing something that wasn't real.

Wrong to pretend they had a future.

If only it were true, because she was falling for him again.

And wasn't that a stupid thing?

She needed to tell him the truth. Today.

"You're not ready?" he asked, tossing his arms through the sleeves of his sheepskin jacket. "You need shoes and a coat, sweetheart. The rain's stopped. It's a good time to go."

"Oh, uh, I'll be ready in two minutes. And Risk?"

"Hmm?"

"When we get back, I need to speak to you about something."

"Fine. If we can't get the car started or find a way out of here, we'll have nothing but time to talk."

A few minutes later, they closed the door behind them and ventured out in the soggy murk that used to be the road leading up to the lodge. The air was fresh and cool, and it felt good to be outside after nearly twenty-four hours of confinement. Risk had a firm grasp on her hand, and the connection kept a steady surge of warmth flowing between them.

They sloshed slowly, taking cautious steps, fighting through strong breezes that rustled the trees and blew her hair in every direction. Her foot hit a dip in the road, and she stumbled, struggling for balance, but Risk was right there pulling her up before she fell. "Careful," he said, drawing her close. He bent his head and gave her a tender kiss on the lips. "Are you okay?"

She nodded, staring at his mouth, wishing for things that were impossible. "Yes, I'm fine. Thanks for the save."

"Any time," he said, his dark eyes gleaming.

This man, this Risk, was appealing and kind and…

Suddenly, a sound from above had both of them looking skyward—a *whop, whop, whopping* as a helicopter came into view. It flew directly over them, and as they lifted their gazes to the chopper, April recognized the Rising Springs Ranch logo immediately. "Risk, it's your family's helicopter. Looks like we've been rescued."

Five

Risk refused a gurney, but the Boone County Hospital staff who'd been waiting for him by the helipad insisted on putting him in a wheelchair. He grabbed for April's hand and she walked alongside him as he was wheeled to the back entrance of the hospital. Lucas Boone, who'd piloted the helicopter and flown them to safety along with Mason, walked a few steps behind their brother's wheelchair.

Cameras clicked away, and reporters eager for the scoop shouted questions. April recognized many of them. It surprised her to see them there, but then she'd almost forgotten how important the Boones were in this town. News of a Boone missing in a storm, even for one night, was sure to make headlines.

"Hey, Risk, how does this compare to the fall you took from Justice?"

"What happened to your head?"

April squeezed his hand, and he looked up at her, baffled.

"Can you make a comment, Mr. Boone? Give us something?" one of them asked.

Risk put up his free hand. "Hold up a minute, if you

could," he said, turning to the nurse pushing him. The nurse looked none too happy as she brought the wheel-chair to a halt.

Risk looked into the faces of the reporters. "I can't an-swer those questions. I don't remember. But I will say my fiancée took really good care of me when I got injured. April's been by my side the entire time, and we're both very fortunate we made it through okay."

"What do you mean, you don't remember? Do you have amnesia?" a reporter shouted.

"Are you saying you're engaged?" another reporter ques-tioned.

Half a dozen more inquiries were shouted at both of them.

April froze as all eyes landed on her. She didn't have to see the look on Mason and Lucas's faces—they were behind her—to know they were in total shock about their brother's announcement. In less than a beat, cameras pointed her way and questions were hurled at her. She kept a stoic face, but inside her head was aching. Risk had just announced to all of Boone Springs that he had amne-sia and that he was engaged to be married. A photographer bent down real low and snapped a photo of the diamond ring on her left finger.

By then, half a dozen hospital employees circled them, blocking the reporters from entering the building, and a doctor stepped up. "That's all for today. We won't know the extent of Mr. Boone's injury until we examine him. I know Mr. Boone would want you to respect his privacy."

"Does he have amnesia?"

"As I said, we won't know until we have a chance to give him a thorough exam."

Minutes later, Risk was brought into an emergency ex-amining room. Lottie Sue Brown was waiting for him. His aunt Lottie was an icon around town, and even though April had never met her formally, she recognized her immediately from seeing her at local events.

Mason put a hand on Risk's shoulder, and Aunt Lottie bent to kiss his cheek. "You had us worried sick. We're all glad you were found safe."

Risk gazed at April, clearly baffled.

April whispered near his ear. "This is your aunt Lottie."

They'd been warned about his amnesia by a quick text from Mason giving them the information as April relayed it to him in the chopper. But Risk's total lack of recognition still seemed to come as a surprise to his family.

And needless to say, Mason and Lucas were eyeing her with extreme caution and curiosity after Risk's bold announcement that she was his fiancée.

Two ER doctors entered the room along with another nurse. "Please, I know you're worried about Mr. Boone, but we're going to ask you all to step outside now. We need to give him a thorough examination."

"Doctor, please let us know if you have any questions at all," Mason said.

"Of course." The doctor gestured toward the door.

Mason, Luke and Lottie filed out, while Risk held on to April's hand very tightly. She made a move to leave, and reluctantly, he released her fingers one by one. "I'll be just outside," she assured him.

He gave her a half smile as she exited the room.

As soon as she stepped into the waiting room, Mason, Luke and Lottie were waiting for her with wary looks on their faces.

Her stomach knotted into a tiny ball. She was in deep, almost wishing she was back at the lodge, away from the family, away from the media circus that would be her life unless she cleared things up.

Lottie was the first to speak. "Are you feeling all right, April?"

"Y-yes, thanks for asking. Other than feeling a little tired, I'm fine." She was drained, and not only because she and Risk had spent countless hours together, making love, keeping warm, staying awake out of fear of a concussion. The entire ordeal had been emotionally draining. How was she going to explain away the facts of the past twenty-four hours?

"Risk sang your praises," Lottie said. "You've taken good care of him."

"I tried my best." Her cheeks burned now.

"And is it a figment of Risk's imagination that you two are engaged?"

Once again, all eyes went to the ring on her finger. "Not exactly."

"What does that mean?" Mason asked, clearly puzzled.

Luke ran his hand across his forehead. "I'd like to know, too."

April closed the waiting room door and sat down. The rest of them took a seat, and she steadied her breath and garnered her courage. "We're not really engaged, but Risk thinks we are," she said, gauging their reaction. Her statement only puzzled them more. "You see, before Risk lost his memory, he thought I was engaged. I wanted him to think that for reasons I won't go into now. But then when I found he had a head injury and had lost his memory, I feared he had a concussion. I knew I had to keep him awake while I tended to his wound. I knew he couldn't fall asleep. He was weak, his brain foggy. But when he saw the ring on my finger and instantly assumed we were engaged, his whole demeanor changed and brightness entered his eyes. He saw me as a bridge to his life. I should've denied it then,

I know that, but he seemed to really need the connection. And in the moment, he was relieved and happy."

While the brothers stayed silent, Lottie spoke up. "It must've been frightening for you. Being all alone in that deserted lodge with an injured man and a storm raging outside."

"It was, but thanks to the care package you made up, we had food to sustain us."

Lottie smiled warmly. "The boys think I baby them."

"It's a good thing you're so thoughtful," April said. Her shoulders slumped. All of a sudden, the adrenaline she'd been running on took a nose dive, and exhaustion set in.

"You said before he lost his memory, you told Risk you were engaged. I take it that's not true?" Mason asked.

April blushed.

"Mason, I think April needs to rest right now. She's clearly been through enough."

"No, no," April said. "I want to explain. I need to tell Risk the truth, too, but—"

"Maybe now's not a good time," Lottie said. "I think they'll be running a lot of tests on him, and he'll be too tired after all this."

"I agree. But I want to hear what you have to say," Luke said.

He'd been their savior, the man who'd rescued them from the lodge. She owed the Boones the truth, and she wanted to clear her conscience. She hated the pretense, all of it. Now, acid spilled into her belly as she began. "If I tell you now, will you promise to let me be the one to explain it to Risk once the doctor gives the okay?"

All three of them nodded.

"But only if you're up to it, April." Lottie really was a very nice person.

"I'm up to it. I just don't want to lose my nerve. You see," she began, choosing her words carefully, "Risk and I have some history together. We met shortly after his breakup with Shannon. And, well, it didn't end well with us, either, but there was an attraction between us, so my friend concocted this silly idea for me to pretend to be engaged while doing business with Risk. As an…insurance policy, if you know what I mean." She narrowed her gaze on the three of them, hoping they'd understand.

Again, they nodded.

"That's about it." Without going into details. "I wanted to keep things purely professional with Risk."

"Which didn't happen, I take it," Mason said, one brow arching.

"Shush," Lottie said. "That's between your brother and April."

She felt her face flame. She was not about to respond to Mason's question. This was all so very hard to admit, but at least she'd gotten it out without faltering. "For what it's worth, I'm sorry about all of this."

"It's not all your fault," Lucas said.

"You couldn't predict the storm would do so much damage," Lottie added.

"You helped my brother when he needed it most," Mason said, his mouth twisting a bit. "We'll always be grateful for that."

Though they said the right things, she got the feeling the Boone brothers were not thrilled about her lying to their brother.

"Yes, that's right," Lottie said. "You took good care of Risk, and now it's time you take good care of you. April, it's going to be a long night. Why don't you go home and get some sleep?"

"Shouldn't I stay and wait for Risk? He's a bit disoriented."

"We'll tell him you really needed your rest. He'll understand. I'll keep you posted, I promise. Mason has your number. Our car will take you home now, if you'd like?"

"That's very nice of you."

Lottie wrapped her arms around her shoulders in a much-needed hug. Lottie was astute, and April appreciated the kindness she bestowed on her after all that had happened. "You've been through enough today. Let me walk you out."

Mason and Luke nodded their goodbyes to her. Lottie stayed by her side, making sure April got into the limo, telling the driver to see her safely home.

And once April reached her home, she called Jenna Mae. "Thank God, you're home, Jenna. I really need to talk to you."

"Are you kidding? It's all over social media already. I'm listening. Tell me everything" was Jenna's reply.

April pushed the Off button on her cell phone after her long conversation with Jenna. Her friend always knew what to say, how to make sense out of things that really didn't make much sense. She loved both Jenna Mae and Clovie like sisters and didn't know what she'd do without them.

She took a bath, got into her coziest pajamas, made hot cocoa, which she hadn't touched yet, and tried to push the Off button in her head. "Damn."

It wasn't working. The past twenty-four hours kept replaying over and over again in her mind. April couldn't pretend to be engaged to just anybody. No, she had to pick a nationwide rodeo and television celebrity. News of Risk Boone's sudden engagement was all over the internet, and there was no going back. She could only imagine the newspaper headlines in the morning.

Her cell phone vibrated on the coffee table, and she

nearly jumped out of her skin. *He* was calling. Risk. The guy she'd lied to over and over again.

She reached for her phone, her hand shaking. "Hello."

"April, it's me."

"R-Risk, I didn't expect to hear from you tonight. How are you?"

"I'll be better once I get out of here. I've been poked enough for one day, and I'll have more of the same tomorrow. They're checking me out down to my toenails, but I wanted to make sure you're doing well. I...miss you."

April bit down on her lip. "I know, and I'm sorry I left the hospital. Your aunt insisted that I get some rest."

"She was right. You've been through a lot, too."

"How's your head? Are you in any pain?"

He sighed. "I'm doing okay. There's some slight swelling on the brain still. The doc says if I have a good day tomorrow and all the other tests are normal, I'll be going home the following day. Seems weird calling it *home* when I don't remember the ranch or my family."

"But maybe seeing it and being surrounded by your loved ones will spur your recollection."

"That's what the doctors are saying. The only memories I have are of you and me at the lodge." His voice took on a deep rasp. "I wouldn't trade those for anything."

"Yeah."

"You'll come by tomorrow, right?"

"Y-yes, I'll come by." She'd stop by the hospital for a quick visit, but she wouldn't confess to him until he got a clean bill of health from the doctors. Until that time, she'd just have to go along with the ruse.

She wasn't looking forward to revealing the unholy truth to him. Yet she wanted to be there for him because he needed her, and wasn't that just crazy? He still thought they were engaged, and *that* Risk, the sexy, sweet man she'd known after his injury, called to her. *That* Risk was a nice guy, and her soft spot for him had grown into a crater full of marshmallows. "I'll see you tomorrow, Risk. Sleep well."

"You, too," he said. "Good night."

She hung up and stared at the phone.

It wasn't going to be easy hurting him. And what effect would learning the truth have on his recovery?

The next day, April walked into Risk's hospital room holding a vase of colorful flowers. He was lying in the bed, his head against the pillow, his eyes closed. She was about to walk out of the room to let him rest when suddenly his eyes popped open.

"Hi," he said quietly, a smile on his face.

"Risk, I'm sorry. I didn't mean to disturb you."

"You didn't. You're the best thing that's happened to me today. I've been waiting for you. Come closer," he said, gesturing for her to sit near him on the bed.

"Uh, first let me put these down." She set the vase on the table beside his bed and stood there, not sure what to do next.

"The flowers are nice, thanks. You look beautiful today."

She wore a short jean jacket over a blue floral dress. It was nothing terribly special, but she'd dressed up a bit for this visit. "Thank you."

He reached for her hand, and she stared at him a moment before locking fingers with him. He gave a little tug, and she was propelled forward, her knees touching the bedrail. "It's good to see you, April."

"It's good to see you, too. Still…nothing?"

"No, but seeing you makes it all seem okay." He stared at her lips, his eyes twinkling. "I think I need a kiss from my fiancée."

April blinked. She'd expected this, but it rang so false

right now. She bent her head and gave him the tiniest kiss on the mouth. He wouldn't have expected anything less than that, and she wasn't going to give him any more. Just as she was backing away, the sound of heels tapping the floor had her swiveling around. And she came face to face with auburn-haired, green-eyed, perfect-size-two, classically beautiful Shannon Wilkes.

April couldn't believe her eyes. She stared at the woman for a whole five seconds before words could form. But it didn't matter. The woman wearing high-heeled boots, skintight black leggings and a sleek sage-and-black belted tunic gave April a dismissive glance as she made her way over to Risk's bed.

A keen sense of déjà vu set in—the overweight girl of her youth felt invisible again.

"Risk, I came as soon as I heard. I'm so sorry about your injury. After how good you were to me when Mama passed last week, I had to come see you."

Risk shifted his attention to April, his expression blank. April was still stunned that she was in the same room with Shannon Wilkes, breaker of Risk's heart, among other things. And then it all became clear as she started putting two and two together. So, it was Shannon's mother who'd meant a lot to Risk. It was Shannon's mother who'd died. He'd gone to see Shannon when her mother was dying and had stayed for the funeral.

"I'm sorry to hear about your mother," Risk said. "But do I know you?"

"Of course you know me."

"Sorry, but I don't remember you."

Shannon's demeanor changed, her lips forming into a pout. "I'd heard about your amnesia on the news, but I wasn't sure if it was true. I didn't think you'd...you'd forget me."

As if no one in their right mind could ever forget such a super-duper star. The devil in April thought that was one good thing to come from Risk's amnesia: he'd forgotten the pain this woman had caused him.

"Sorry, but it's true. I don't remember you."

Shannon batted her eyes and turned to her, baffled. "You must be April."

"Yes."

"Shannon," she said, and then turned back to Risk. "I thought maybe if we talked a bit, privately, you might remember something about our past."

Risk turned to April, gesturing for her to come closer, and she went to his side. He reached for her hand and squeezed it. "I don't think it'll work. I mean, if my own fiancée can't jar my memory, I don't think you'll be able to." He entwined their fingers and kissed the back side of her hand. Shannon took it all in, her eyes flashing for a second.

There was loud commotion on the street, and April glanced out the third-floor window. "News vans are pulling up."

"Sorry," Shannon said on a shrug. "I tried to be inconspicuous and didn't tell a soul I was coming to see Risk."

Inconspicuous? With that face? In that outfit? She had to know that her coming to Boone Springs would create a media frenzy. It appeared she hadn't tried too hard to conceal her identity. She had one of the most recognizable faces on the planet right now. Sure, her recent love life had tanked almost as badly as her last movie, but she still had fans across many continents, and the camera loved her.

"I traveled a long way to see you, Risk."

"Are you famous or something?"

A wry chuckle escaped April's mouth.

"Yes, or something. But I came because we're friends now. You were so sweet to my mom, and you helped me so much during that time. And, well, you said if I ever needed anything, to come see you. Then I heard about your injury and, well, here I am."

Risk gave her another blank stare.

"Congratulations on your...on your engagement," she said, smiling at him. Then she turned to April. "To both of you."

"Thank you," April managed to say.

"It's funny, though. The entire time Risk was in Atlanta, he never spoke of being engaged."

Heat rose up April's neck. The woman was staring at her, and it was all April could do to keep her expression steady.

"I'm sorry, I don't have an answer for you," Risk said.

April kept her mouth clamped shut.

Two nurses walked in, one holding the biggest bouquet of exquisite red and white roses, both completely awestruck seeing Shannon Wilkes in person. The nurse set the vase on the table next to April's vase, and the overflow of roses completely drowned out her smaller bouquet. "Those are from me, Risk." Shannon smiled his way.

"Thank you," he said, uncertainty in his voice.

"Sorry to interrupt," one of the nurses said, her voice full of reverence. "But Mr. Boone is scheduled for more scans and tests this afternoon. We're going to have to ask you both to leave."

"Of course." April jumped to attention fast. She wanted out of this conversation. "I'll be going."

She pulled her hobo bag over her shoulder. Risk's gaze snapped to hers, regret in his eyes. It was clear he wanted a longer visit with her. She walked over to him and gave him a peck on the cheek.

Shannon seemed to home in on their interaction. "I'm staying at the Baron and planning on a long visit." She walked over to Risk and gave his hand a squeeze, gazing deep into his eyes. "You may not remember it, Risk, but you told me after Mama died to get away to clear my head, find out what I truly want in life. You invited me to your Founder's Day celebration, and I thought I'd have an extended stay in Boone Springs."

She had to be kidding. With the media surrounding her at every turn, peace and solitude would be the last thing she'd find in this town. Maybe Shannon was after more than a short respite.

Maybe she was after her hunky ex-boyfriend Risk Boone.

Six

Just after noon the next day, flanked by Mason on his left and Lucas on his right, Risk was taken in a wheelchair to the back entrance of the hospital. He'd gotten a clean bill of health: no concussion, no more swelling on the brain, no dizzy spells. They'd ruled out any health risks, and his tests had all come out normal. Yet he didn't feel normal, not when chunks of his memory had vanished. He was living in a vacuum; people knew him, but he couldn't remember them.

Shannon Wilkes was obviously a woman with a presence. She commanded attention with her style and manner. She had charisma, but he couldn't recall a thing about her.

"There'll be some reporters out there, so be prepared," Luke said. "You don't have to talk to them. Just get into the car and we'll do the rest."

"Am I really all that?"

"Yeah," both his brothers said simultaneously. "And your ex showing up here yesterday didn't help. Wherever Shannon goes, the paparazzi follow."

"You were nationwide news a couple of years ago, and now you're back in the news," Mason said.

Risk shook his head. "I don't get it."

"It's the life you led before you came back to work at Boone Inc."

"April told me some about my life on the rodeo circuit."

At the mention of her name, Mason and Lucas gave each other nervous glances.

"What'd I say?" he asked.

"Nothing," Mason was quick to respond. "April's coming by the house later on."

"Good, can't wait to see her."

This time the other two men stared straight ahead, zipping their lips. He wondered what was going on. Was this as weird for them as it was for him?

Risk wished April was here. She'd make this transition easier for him. But his neurologist had said not to overdo it on his first day, just to have family accompany him home. The doctor had already gone over the rules. Even though he was being released from the hospital, he still needed to take things slowly. Rest was important and so was seeing familiar things. And his fiancée was the most familiar thing he knew.

"Okay, it's showtime," Mason said as they approached the double glass doors. Half a dozen reporters were waiting, along with photographers lifting up their cameras. "Are you ready?"

Risk nodded and stood up. "Yeah, I'm ready."

The automatic doors opened, and Risk braved the onslaught of photos snapped and questions hurled at him while Mason and Luke ran interference, ushering him into the limo safe and sound.

"Go," Mason said, and the driver took off.

They managed to get out of the parking lot without incident, and as they made their way out of town, all of them relaxed. "Man, I don't know how you did this all the time when you were dating Shannon," Mason said.

"It's hard to believe I dated her."

"You did, for two years."

He shook his head, not recalling her at all.

"It's old news now. Don't worry about it," Luke said. "Hey, Aunt Lottie just texted me. She's making you your favorite lunch, Risk."

Risk scoured his memory, but nothing came to mind. "And what would that be?"

"Oh, sorry," his younger brother added. "Hickory-smoked steak sandwich with swiss cheese and crispy onions."

"Being that we were on a diet of peanut butter and potato chips at the lodge, that sounds damn good. I hope April comes in time to have lunch with me."

Mason slid a glance toward Luke when they thought Risk wasn't paying attention, but he picked up on it again. The secret looks were beginning to rub him wrong. What on earth was going on, aside from the obvious? "You gonna tell me why you're eyeballing each other every time I mention April's name?"

"We're not," Luke said innocently.

Mason shook his head like he was clueless, too, though Risk wasn't entirely convinced. He didn't know his brothers, so he wouldn't pursue it at the moment. Instead, he spent the rest of the time looking out the window, taking in the scenery, trying to conjure up a memory of the terrain, landmarks, anything at all that might spark a memory.

Nothing did.

April put her head in her hands as Jenna drove them through the gates at Rising Springs Ranch. It wouldn't be long now until she'd have to face Risk.

"Hey, April, you're going to be okay. It's the right thing to do."

She glanced up and turned to her friend. "I know. I've been rehearsing in my head what to say to him. I only hope I can get it all out before he kicks me out of the house."

"He wouldn't do that."

"I wouldn't be so sure of that."

"I'll wait for you, then. Or better yet, I'll go in and explain my part in all this."

"No, don't be silly, Jenna. This is all on me. I can do it. Listen, thanks for driving me. I really needed the lift."

"My pleasure. Besides, you left your car here."

"I meant the other kind of lift, too. You've been very supportive, and I appreciate that. You're the best."

"You'd do the same for me."

April smiled at her. They knew each other so well.

Jenna pulled the car to a stop in front of the house, and April leaned over and gave her friend a big squeeze. "Thanks for everything."

"You're welcome. Will you call me when you get back home?"

"Sure."

"Okay, go. Be brave. You can do this."

She nodded and exited the car, waving goodbye to her friend as she approached the front door.

The housekeeper answered on the first knock and ushered her into the big dining room. She stood on the threshold, feeling like an outsider. Mason, his fiancée Drea, Luke and Lottie were all sitting at the table poring over papers. She'd gone to grade school with Drea, and they were still casual acquaintances. April heard someone mention Founder's Day before all heads turned her way. "Hello, April," Lottie said. "Please come in."

She entered the formal dining that looked more like a

Founder's Day war room. "Hello, everyone. I'm here to see Risk."

"Yes, about that," Lottie said, rising from her chair. "Let me give you an up-to-date report." Lottie took her elbow and gently guided her to the foyer by the staircase. "Risk is resting in his room. He's anxious to see you."

Her stomach squeezed into a knot.

"I spoke with his doctor this morning, and he's in pretty good shape, thank goodness," Lottie said. "And I know you have to tell him the truth, but April, please do it in the gentlest way you know how. He's probably going to be upset. You're all he's been talking about lately. But he'll be able to handle it. Risk is tough, and I think the truth is always better than prolonging the lies."

"Yes, I agree. So I take it he still doesn't remember anything?"

"No, I'm afraid not."

"Okay, I'll do my best."

"His room is up the stairs, last one on the right. Would you like me to show you to it?"

"No, thank you, I'll find it."

"Okay," she said, giving her a sympathetic smile. "I'll leave you to it."

Lottie began to turn away. "Lottie? Can I ask you a question?"

The woman didn't hesitate as she faced her. "Of course."

"Why are you being so kind to me? I mean, I'm grateful that you are, but I wouldn't think I'm your favorite person right now, and you've been very understanding."

Once again, Lottie smiled, and her eyes twinkled. "Maybe because I've been in your shoes a few times in my life. We all make mistakes. We all make incorrect assumptions. Lord, we wouldn't be human if we didn't. And

I see the way you and Risk look at each other. Mistake or not, I think there's a possibility of you."

With that, Lottie excused herself, and April took a moment to let that sink in.

There's a possibility of you.

No, there wasn't. April wouldn't even give that a moment of credence. She would try to straighten out this mess and then walk away from Risk and the sale of the lodge.

She climbed the stairs slowly, going over her rehearsed lines in her head, and then walked down the hallway and knocked on the last door to her right.

The door was yanked open, and there Risk stood, dressed in jeans and a blue chambray shirt, his dark hair slicked away from his face. Not even the stubble on his jaw or the small square bandage on his head could detract from how remarkably healthy he appeared. It wasn't what she was expecting.

"April, sweetheart. Come in."

Two strong arms came around her to encircle her body and nearly crush her to him. His lips brushed over hers several times, the sexy, delicious taste of him speeding up her heartbeats, making her yearn for more, almost making her forget her mission here.

Almost.

"Risk," she said, setting her palms on his chest. "We need to talk." Her command came out breathy and soft. Not at all how she'd intended.

"Talk," he said, "is overrated." He picked up her hand and kissed it, and then his mouth came down on hers again and again, kissing her so passionately her lips swelled. Then he pulled back. "But you're right. We do need to talk." He led her over to his bed, which looked as if it hadn't been slept in, and they both sat down. The bed faced a fireplace with a giant television screen over it. Shelves filled with

Risk's rodeo trophies, champion buckles and awards lined one entire wall, and big manly pieces of furniture filled the large room.

"First of all, how are you feeling?" He continued to hold her hand.

"Me? I'm fine, really, but you're the injured one. How are you doing?"

"I still don't remember my family. Or this place."

"You…don't?"

"No, but I feel so much better now that you're here."

"That's what I wanted to talk to you about."

April rose from the bed and walked around to the footboard. Putting distance between them was essential to making her confession.

"Sweetheart, is something wrong?" There was alarm in his voice.

"No. I mean, yes. I have something to tell you. But first I want you to know that none of what I did was meant to hurt you. I, uh, haven't been exactly honest with you."

Geesh, this was harder than she'd imagined. He was looking at her like the fate of the world rested on her shoulders.

"This doesn't sound good." His voice lowered to a rasp, and the joy on his face faded.

"I can assure you, it all started out innocently."

"What started out innocently?"

"Well, not that innocently. When we first hooked up in Houston two years ago—"

"Hooked up?"

"Yes, we met there quite by coincidence, and we were together for one night. You see, you were heartbroken over Shannon Wilkes leaving you high and dry, and, well, I thought we might've had something, whereas you didn't. I spent the past two years not liking you very much. I know none of this is making too much sense. But when you came to me about buying the lodge, my friend thought it would be better to pretend I had a fiancé to keep things strictly professional between you and me, so that our past didn't interfere with our business relationship. That was working out well. Until you lost your memory."

Risk bounded off the bed and approached her. "I don't understand." His voice, a heartbroken rasp, churned her stomach. This was harder than she'd thought. "Are you saying we're not engaged?"

"Y-yes, that's what I'm saying."

"We were in the bedroom at the lodge."

"Yes, and you saw the ring on my finger and assumed we were engaged." She backed up a step.

"Are you saying you had sex with me when you were engaged to some other guy?"

"No, no, no. I wasn't engaged to anyone. It was all a… lie."

"And you didn't correct me about your phony ring?"

She shook her head over and over. "No… I didn't."

"You mean, you were in bed with me the entire night, letting me believe we were engaged? The things we did to each other, the way our bodies fit, the little cries you made, all of that was fake?"

"No, not fake. It was real. At least in the moment it was. Oh, I don't know." Tears welled in her eyes. "It's all so jumbled up in my mind right now."

Lines formed around Risk's eyes as he narrowed his focus on her. "So that night in the parking lot when we kissed, I wasn't imagining it. You were drawn to me. It was crazy good, but afterward you stuck the ring in my face and I couldn't get over how I'd mistaken your signals. Now I get it."

"I'm sorry, really sorry about that, too."

Risk's nostrils flared; his eyes were two hard black stones. If he was facing down a wild feisty bronco, he couldn't have looked fiercer. "You lied to me over and over."

"I'm sorry. I didn't mean for this to happen. I don't want to upset you now. Risk, try to understand. Try to calm down."

And then it hit her. "Wait a minute." She searched his angry face, saw the fury in his eyes. Her heart pounded hard as realization blackened her mood even more. "How do you remember what happened in the parking lot? That was before you got hit on the head."

Risk blinked. His cover was totally blown.

"You got your memory back, didn't you?"

He glared at her.

"You did. When?"

"Hell, all I had to do was walk into my bedroom today and see those damn trophies up on the shelf. It all came rushing back to lucky me. Everything. I remember it all."

"I don't believe this. You let me go on and on. I was trying to explain and apologize to you. And you let me do it. You wanted to see me squirm when all I wanted was to tell you the truth." April was blindsided. Just minutes ago, Risk had welcomed her into his arms and had kissed and caressed her. It had all been a game. A mean-spirited game to get back at her.

"Woman, you wouldn't know the truth if it hit *you* in the head. You've lied to me since the day I walked into the Farmhouse Grill."

"It wasn't like that."

"I know exactly what it was like. Remember, I was there. I wasn't some foolhardy man getting sucked into buying a lodge that was clearly falling apart. Yet, once I got hit on the head, you did your very best to seduce me into changing my mixed-up mind."

"What! You can't possibly believe that!"

"Oh, sweetheart, you don't want to know what I really think about you."

April's blood raced through her veins. She counted to three to keep from spitting vile curses at him. What Risk was accusing her of was dead wrong. "Listen to me. I did what I had to do to keep you alive. I didn't know the extent of your injury. I'm no nurse but—"

"But you sure as hell have a great bedside manner."

"Shut up, Risk."

He laughed right in her face. "Oh, that's rich. You act like you're the injured party when all I got from you was a pack of lies, tied in a neat little bow."

"What you did when I first got here today was a lousy trick," she said.

"And what you did to me wasn't? How on earth do you justify that?" He came to within inches of her face, so close that she smelled his musky scent, saw the dark anguish in his eyes. "April, you led me to believe I loved you. That we had a future together, and your sorcery under the sheets convinced me. Actions speak louder than words, and woman, you have the best moves in town."

Her cheeks blistered hot. "I don't have to listen to this. I'm leaving."

She brushed past him, but his hand came out instantly and he held her firmly on the upper arm. She looked over her shoulder at him.

"Not so fast."

"Let go of me."

He unclamped his hand. "Fine, but you're not leaving until we get something straight."

She sighed. She'd heard enough from him today. "What is it?"

"You made a fool out of me. And now the whole world

believes we're engaged. It's all over the newspapers and internet. There's no way to explain it away. With Founder's Day coming up and all that goes into that, I can't bring this farce out in the open now. It would completely overshadow an event that is important to my family. Shannon being here just complicates my life even more. It's a reminder to all how she dumped me two years ago. So, sweetheart, you're going to pretend to be my fiancée until after Founder's Day. And there's no way you're going to refuse."

She hoisted her chin. "I most certainly can refuse. I'm not doing that."

"You owe me this." He came nose to nose with her. "After all the lies you told. Which I still don't exactly get. But now we're in this together."

"No."

"Yes."

"No."

He sighed. "This can go badly for both of us. What do you think will happen to the Adams Agency when the truth comes out that you lied, pretended we were engaged and seduced me to get that lodge sold?"

"That's not how it happened and you know it."

"I'm not sure what I believe."

"You wouldn't do that," she said, not entirely certain what a vengeful Risk would do.

"I wouldn't have to. People would make their own assumptions. And honey, I'm not exactly thrilled about looking like a fool, first with Shannon and then you. The headlines would crush all the goodwill my family has worked so hard to achieve this year."

April thought about it a long moment. "What are you proposing?" She frowned. It was a lousy pun.

"That we pretend to be engaged until the hoopla dies

down after Founder's Day. That's ten days away. Then, later on, we'll quietly break up. It's the only solution."

"And my agency?"

"No one will know the truth. You have my word."

"I don't like it."

"I don't like it, either, but we don't have a choice."

"What do I get out of it?"

"Your agency wouldn't get dragged into all this. Isn't that enough?"

"No, I want something else from you, and it's a deal breaker."

"Hell, I'm afraid to ask."

"I want one more chance with the lodge. I want you to see it the way I envision it. I need your promise you'll consider it objectively, without bad weather and other things getting in the way. And then we have a deal."

Risk's eyes sharpened on her as he thought about it. She held her breath, hoping he'd come around.

"Done," he said finally. "I'll take a look at it one more time."

"Fine." April let out the breath she'd been holding. She wasn't thrilled with any of this, but she couldn't chance bad publicity for her agency, and if she could get an objective and fair opinion about the lodge from Risk, that's all she could ask. Then she thought about Mason, Luke and Lottie. "I've confessed to your aunt and brothers about the engagement, but what else should we say to them?"

"My family has to know the entire truth. I won't lie to them. I regained my memory just a couple of hours ago, and they don't know yet. We're going to tell them... together."

"Oh boy."

"What about you? Who knows about your fake fiancée scheme?"

"My two best friends. They'll keep the secret."

"Are you sure?"

"Yep, they're as loyal as they come. But how do we explain our quick engagement?" So far, she and Risk had been insulated from questions, but they were bound to come at a relentless pace once they made public appearances.

"We've been quietly dating for a few months and fell for each other quickly. That's all anyone needs to know. That part won't be hard. What will be hard is pretending to the outside world we actually like each other."

"Yeah, maybe I should get some acting tips from Shannon Wilkes."

When Risk frowned, April felt a momentary triumph. She'd cling to that, because she feared other victories would be hard coming.

Risk would see to that.

In the evening, Aunt Lottie poured Risk and herself steaming cups of coffee and offered up a batch of peanut butter cookies she'd baked just for him. He didn't miss the irony that he'd lived on peanut butter and potato chips during his time at the lodge, and it almost put a smile on his face. *Almost.*

The house was quiet now. After sharing the good news with the family that his memory had returned, his brothers had hung around most of the day but had taken off right after dinner. It was relaxing sitting here with his aunt, digesting the events of the day without a commotion.

"Too bad April couldn't stay for dinner." Aunt Lottie brought her cup to the table and sat down facing him.

"I think she's planning to avoid me as much as possible until this farce is over. She couldn't wait to get out of here today."

"Yet she agreed to your plan." Lottie sipped her coffee.

Risk grabbed two big cookies from the platter and set them on his plate. "She had to."

"Why? Did you pressure her?"

He chomped down on his cookie, chewing as he thought about the question. "A little. She got us into this mess. Now she's gonna have to be by my side until after Founder's Day. But only when absolutely necessary."

"It is messy, isn't it? Granted, I don't agree with her tactics, but she did take good care of you when you were injured, and for that we're all grateful."

He took a sip of coffee—the brew went down nice and smooth, unlike his aunt's comment. "You think I'm ungrateful?"

"You tell me. Are you?"

Risk was too steaming mad at April to admit she'd been instrumental in helping him when he'd been hurt. "No, not about that. But I can't get past why she found it necessary to lie to me, over and over, or why she concocted a story about her being engaged in the first place. I don't get it."

"Don't you?" Aunt Lottie's eyes twinkled a bit, and she smiled before taking another sip of coffee. "I think you can guess why she did it."

Risk wasn't going there. He couldn't possibly discuss having sex with April with his aunt. He couldn't tell her about their night in Houston and how he'd behaved afterward. Plus, that was then and this was now. And *now* he was pissed at April for making a fool out of him.

The sound of approaching footsteps and someone clearing his throat had them both turning toward the kitchen doorway. There stood Drew MacDonald, looking a bit sheepish, holding a bouquet of fresh yellow roses and a gold box of candy. "I hope I'm not interrupting. I wanted to pay you a visit, Risk. Heard about your accident."

"Hey, Drew, nice to see you. Come in and have a seat. You're not interrupting anything."

"Thanks." He walked over to Lottie first and handed her the flowers. "These are for you, Lottie. For baking me those delicious cranberry muffins the other day."

"For me? Why, they're beautiful." There was surprise in Lottie's eyes. "I, uh, assumed they were for Risk."

"Nope, Risk gets these." He handed over the gold box. "Mason told me they were your favorite."

Risk took a second to open the box and gaze at the dozen dark chocolate truffles in gold wrappers. "Yep, these are my favorite. Thanks, Drew."

"No thanks necessary. I'm glad you got your memory back. That must've been strange."

"You have no idea. Aunt Lottie, does Drew know how your muffins saved the day for us when we were stranded at the lodge?"

"I'm not sure he does," his aunt said, admiring the flowers, touching the petals. It was about time Drew made some headway with his aunt. They never seemed to be on the same page, but maybe now that Lottie was sticking around for more than a millisecond, the two would finally find common ground.

"She did. She packed a basket of muffins, protein bars and fruit for the trip to the lodge, and that food sustained us overnight. Aunt Lottie has good instincts."

Drew smiled at her. "I suppose she does."

Risk's cell phone rang. He took one look at the screen and then rose from his seat. "Drew, excuse me. I've got to get this."

"Sure, no problem. Go right ahead."

Drew watched Risk walk out of the kitchen, leaving him alone with Lottie. She immediately rose and walked over to a kitchen cabinet. "I'll just put these in water."

She opened the cabinet door and, standing on tiptoes, reached for a frosted glass vase.

"Here, let me help you get that." He came close to Lottie, his hip brushing her side as he retrieved the vase and set it down on the counter. He was as close as he'd ever been to her, and his heart began to race.

"Thank you," she said, gazing up at him. "These are very pretty, but they weren't necessary."

"You deserve them," he said, lifting a hand to her face. His fingers brushed her soft cheek. "I think I overreacted before and, well, I don't want a misunderstanding coming between us. We've been friends too long."

"I, uh, agree. But it was my fault for doubting you. When you lifted that bottle, I shouldn't have assumed you were drinking again. I jumped to the wrong conclusion, and I'm so sorry about that."

Ever since his wife, Maria, had died, he'd been battling alcoholism, nearly ruining every relationship he'd had. But he was clean and sober three years now, vowing to never go back and trying to make amends. Lottie's lack of faith in him had hurt his pride and blistered his heart.

"I've already accepted your apology. That happened a few months back and, well, I'm over it. Fact is, I miss seeing you."

"I've missed you, too, Drew."

"You have?"

She nodded, her eyes gleaming bright in invitation.

Drew bundled up his courage. "I've wanted to do this for a long time." He touched her cheek once again, bent his head and brushed his lips over hers. Lottie's mouth was soft and delicate. It'd been years since he'd kissed a woman. He was grateful she didn't pull away and call him a bumbling fool. When he finally did end the kiss, her eyes were still closed, and a sweet smile surfaced on her face, giving his heart a lift.

"Lottie?"

"Hmm, yes?"

"It's okay that I kissed you?"

She searched his eyes now and spoke ever so softly. "Oh, I think so, yes."

Something amazing filled him up now, and he wished he'd had the courage to pursue Lottie years ago. "Then I have a question for you."

"What is it?" she asked, her pretty eyes curious.

"Would you allow me to escort you to the Founder's Day party?"

"Oh yes. I'd like that."

Risk entered the room again, and they pulled apart immediately. Lottie grabbed the vase and filled it with water at the sink. Drew ran a hand through his hair. He was keyed into a dozen different emotions at the moment.

Risk didn't acknowledge he'd seen or heard anything, yet Drew still had a tough time looking Lottie's nephew in the eyes. And he supposed Lottie felt the same way.

But damn, the kiss had been good, so well worth the wait.

On Friday afternoon, April sat at her office desk making headway with her plans to stage the lodge for Risk's viewing next week. She'd contacted Mr. Hall and explained to him that the lodge needed a quick face-lift to spark interest. April planned on using many of her own home accessories to liven up the place. Since her return to town, her engagement to Risk Boone had stirred up revitalized interest in Canyon Lake Lodge. She'd gotten calls and answered questions about the lodge from a few potential buyers, and she'd made the owner aware of that. Luckily, Mr. Hall was a reasonable man, and he'd agreed to making some minor renovations.

She happened to glance up at the front door at the exact moment Shannon Wilkes walked into her office. April dropped her pen and gave Clovie a quick glance. Her assistant's eyes widened, and she rose from her desk. Shannon was the last person April had expected to see walking through the office door. Then three news vans pulled up on the street, and April quickly rose from her seat, brushing past Shannon to walk over to the door and lock it.

"I'm sorry about that," Shannon said, smiling. Her auburn hair was tied up in a tight ponytail that highlighted her perfect bone structure and pretty face. "I can't go anywhere lately." She put out her hand. "Hello, April."

April forced a smile and took her hand. "Hello."

Shannon glanced over at starstruck Clovie.

"Shannon, I'd like you to meet Clovie. She's my right-hand woman here at the agency."

"Nice to meet you," her assistant said.

"Same here," Shannon said graciously, and then turned to speak to April. "Do you have a few minutes? I promise it won't take long."

"Well, I am sort of busy."

"Please." Shannon kept smiling at her, not flinching, not backing down. April had to admit she was curious about what Shannon would want with her.

She glanced at her watch. "Okay, sure. I have a few minutes until my appointment." An appointment that consisted of going to the hardware store to pick out paint colors for the lodge's mini renovation. But Shannon didn't need to know that. "Why don't you have a seat at my desk over there?"

She pointed to the chair, and Shannon eagerly sat. "Thanks."

April took her seat behind her desk, stacking up her

notes and putting them out of view. "What can I do for you?"

"Well, first, how are you feeling after your ordeal?"

"I'm...great. No complaints. Thanks for asking."

"Aren't you thrilled Risk got his memory back?"

"Yes, thrilled." April gave a mental eye roll.

"I stopped by the ranch to see him yesterday, and he was back to his old self. I couldn't believe he didn't remember me at the hospital."

"No, well, that's what happens with temporary amnesia."

"So, we got to talking about this adorable little farm-house I was on the verge of buying when Risk and I were together. We wanted a place to have some privacy, you know, when I'd come visit him here in Boone Springs. He did tell you about this, didn't he?"

All this was news to April. Of course, she wasn't the resident Realtor back then, but Shannon was leading up to something, and April wasn't getting a good feeling about this.

"Well, I, uh, we haven't spoken about this, no." She hadn't spoken to Risk since he broke the news to his family about their pretend engagement. She'd felt so awful that day that she'd gone home and binged on an entire bag of chocolate chip cookies. Which had only made her stomach ache even more.

"I drove past the place yesterday, and it's still so quaint and charming. I was hoping to find out if the home owner is interested in selling?"

"Do you have the address? I have potential listings for several charming little farmhouses on the outskirts of town."

Shannon dug into her cherry-red Ferragamo handbag and came up with the address. "Here you go."

April took a look at the address and checked her register. "No, that house isn't listed, so I'm assuming it's not for sale. That sale did take place some time ago. Sorry I can't help you."

"Oh, that's a shame. I was really in love with that place, you know, as a getaway. It's peaceful there."

"But is it for you?" April blurted. After Founder's Day she wouldn't care where Shannon took up residence, but she didn't want to have to deal with her now. And of all places a starlet might want to live, she couldn't believe Boone Springs would be high on the list.

"That's what I'm hoping to find out. Would you mind checking with the people living there, to see if they're interested in selling? I'd give them a more than fair offer along with a bonus if they are. Maybe you and I could drive out there and talk to them."

It was the last thing April wanted to do.

"Ah no, I can't do that any time soon, but I will give them a call and get back to you. Is that fair enough?"

"I suppose it'll have to be."

"Oh, and Shannon, is it always like this with you?" She pointed to the reporters milling around the street waiting for her to exit.

"Some days are worse than others. And coming here to see you, Risk's new fiancée, might have something to do with it."

"You think?"

Shannon smiled.

April hated to believe the worst of people, but maybe Shannon's appearance in Boone Springs had more to do with her needing headlines and getting back in the public eye than anything else. Her last two movies had tanked at the box office. And presently she was unattached.

Shannon studied her a minute. "Thanks for your help today. I hope to hear from you soon."

"No problem, I'll call you. You're at the Baron, right?"

"Yes, I'm staying there. And don't get me wrong, the food at the hotel is fine, but I'm getting so darn tired of it. I was trying to remember the name of the Mexican restaurant Risk adores. They make his favorite meal there. Oh gosh, you must know the name of the place." Shannon gave her a pointed look.

"I, uh, you know, I'm forgetting the name of the place, too."

"Really? Gosh, Risk used to crave their food all the time."

April had no clue. There was so much she didn't know about her pretend fiancé. She rose from her seat. "Sorry to rush you, but I'm going to be late for my appointment if I don't get going. Let me walk you out."

Shannon rose, and they made their way to the front door. As soon as April opened it, cameras flashed and reporters started in with their questions. She backed away quickly and closed the door as Shannon met with her paparazzi.

April could only imagine tomorrow's headlines: "Risk Boone's Women, Then and Now."

Seven

April opened her apartment door on the second knock and faced Risk, standing there holding a bag of food from the Gourmet Vaquero. "You brought dinner?"

"I'm hungry, and when you called today, I got to craving these empanadas. Besides, I was followed by the press, so it looks good that I'm here, delivering my fiancée her dinner. Play along." He bent his head and kissed her boldly on the lips. Shock stole over her, and he murmured, "Guess you haven't taken any acting lessons yet. Better work on that. We're being watched."

She wasn't so sure they were—she didn't see anyone out there—but Risk wouldn't have kissed her otherwise. He'd made it clear what he thought of her.

She wrapped her arms around his neck, breathing in his scent, remembering a time when she thought it was sexy. She kissed him back, putting a good deal of pent-up emotion into the melding of their lips. For anyone watching from afar or snapping pictures, it must have looked like blazing passion instead of acute displeasure.

When the kiss ended, her heart was racing. Risk was staring at her as the seconds ticked by.

"Come inside," she said, so she could stop pretending she loved him—or liked him, for that matter. Yet her lips tingled and heat began rising up her throat.

He stepped into her apartment, and she immediately closed the door.

Risk ignored her sigh of frustration and scanned her place, approval gleaming in his eyes. April had a flair for design and color. She liked to think she had unique style in decorating. The front rooms in her apartment were furnished with varying pieces of contemporary furniture that lent a modern tone while still being warm and inviting. Risk was nodding his head as he took in the living-dining room. "Nice place."

"Thanks." She so wasn't going to give him a tour of the other rooms. "Listen, I only called you after Shannon left my office because I realized we don't know enough about each other to make this work."

"Yeah, you're right. It's not as if we could discuss this at a restaurant or anything. Besides, shouldn't a fiancé know what his girl's apartment looks like?"

That much was true. He'd never been here before.

"Okay, why don't you take a seat and get comfortable in the dining room. I'll get this meal on the table."

"I'll help," he said. "I don't expect you to wait on me, unless someone's watching." His lips twitched again and she wanted to swat at him with a dish towel.

"The little woman catering to her man. Risk, I honestly don't know how you survived in this century with thinking like that."

He shot her an innocent-little-boy look, as if anything about Risk could ever be innocent.

She grabbed the bag out of his hand and headed to the kitchen. "Let me take a look at these world-famous empanadas." He was steps behind, and when she put the bag on the counter and opened it, the most amazing aroma drifted up. Her stomach growled. "Wow, those do smell good." She pulled out half a dozen wrapped empanadas, along with a smaller bag of chips and salsa.

"Wait until you taste them." Risk was practically salivating.

"Okay, so empanadas are your go-to food. And that Tex-Mex restaurant is your favorite. That's a start," she said. "When Shannon showed up at the office today, I was sort of stumped by her questions."

April handed him plates and utensils while she picked out two beers from the fridge. "This okay? I also have wine or soda."

"Beer's fine."

"The thing is, I don't get Shannon. She claims she wants a little getaway here in Boone Springs. I'm looking into properties for her, but I can't see it."

"She's impulsive. I don't think she'll follow through. She has trouble doing that." Risk was thoughtful for a minute, and she wondered if he still harbored feelings for his ex. But it was none of her business anymore. All she had to do was get through this week, then she'd be free of this ruse.

Risk put the plates out in the dining room, and she set the food on a platter. She placed it on the table and then handed him a beer as they sat down. "I'm amazed that you're friends now after all she put you through."

Risk frowned. "It wasn't always like this. In the beginning, I was pretty devastated."

She knew. That's when she'd spent the night with him.

"Then my hurt turned into indifference, and I realized Shannon wasn't the woman for me after all. But her mama was a special lady, and seeing what Shannon went through these last few months made me sympathize with her. I mean, I lost both my parents at a young age, and it was extremely hard. We're on friendly terms now, but I wouldn't say we're good friends."

"She thinks you are. She made a special point of letting me know she came to visit you yesterday. She's absolutely thrilled you got your memory back."

"Look, all I'm interested in is getting through this thing, and then all of our lives can go back to normal."

Risk put the bottle of beer to his lips, and his throat worked as he took a swig. She found herself staring, remembering how things were with them at the lodge after he'd lost his memory. That Risk, any woman would want to be friends with, or more. She cleared her throat. "Let's eat and get down to the bare facts," she said.

Risk took a bite out of a beef empanada.

She grabbed one of the pastries filled with chicken and Mexican spices. "Oh wow," she murmured softly as the flavors erupted in her mouth. "These are delicious."

"Right?" Risk smiled, and his entire demeanor changed.

They spent quiet moments filling their bellies, the food tasting too good to interrupt with any discussion. When they were done with the empanadas, they began munching on tortilla chips.

"What's your favorite flavor of ice cream?" she asked.

"Butter pecan, but I don't refuse any flavor of ice cream. What's yours?"

"Chocolate chunk brownie. Drink of choice?"

"Bourbon straight up and beer." He lifted the bottle to his lips. "Yours?"

"Green tea."

He rolled his eyes. "Alcohol?"

"Margarita. Baseball, football or basketball?"

"All of the above. I watch them all. I played baseball in high school. You?"

"I ran track in college and play tennis once in a while when I find the time. I like to watch football, of course."

And after they left the food and sports category, they dived into their early childhoods. "What was yours like, Risk?"

"Mine? Pretty good. I mean I have two pain-in-the-neck brothers, but we all got along okay. We had a lot of fun on the ranch, even though Dad worked us hard. But after my folks died in that accident, we had some difficult years. Luckily, we had each other. My father wanted us to know the business from the ground up, and my brothers were fine with picking up where Dad left off. But I always knew there was something out there for me more exciting then raising cattle and making business deals. I think I was at my happiest riding rodeo. I loved the excitement and thrill. I loved challenging myself."

"And the danger?"

"It's not all that dangerous if you know what you're doing."

She stared into his eyes, not bringing up his career-ending injury.

But he must've read her mind. "I was off my game that night I got hurt. Things weren't great with Shannon. We'd had a fight the night before, and, well, I guess I was distracted." He finished his beer and set the bottle on the table softly. "What about you?"

"Me? Well, I didn't have a great childhood. My dad left the family when I was six. He just up and took off, leaving me and my mother to fend for ourselves. Mom tried her best to provide for us. She worked two jobs, and I was home alone a lot. I guess that's when I started overeating. Before I knew it, I was at an unhealthy weight, and I realize now, I used that weight as a form of protection. It's hard being hurt like that, you know?"

Risk listened and nodded, softness touching his eyes. "Does your mom live in Boone Springs still?"

She shook her head. "Mom remarried five years ago and lives on the East Coast now. She's been traveling Europe with her husband these past few months. He's a tech consultant and speaks four languages. My mom and I talk whenever we can. I think she's finally managed to put her heartache behind her and she's happy. That's all I wanted for her."

"What about you? Have you found what you're looking for?"

"Well, I'm living my dream, working in real estate, owning my own business."

"I meant about your love life?"

"Oh, I, uh…there've been a few men in my life."

"Anyone I should know about?"

She eyed him. "No one special, if that's what you mean."

"No one?"

She shrugged. Was it so hard to believe she'd never met a guy who made her heart sing? "I dated when I was in college, and that's where it ended. I never met anyone right… for me."

Why was she revealing all this to Risk? He only needed to know facts, not the emotions behind them, but once he opened up about Shannon, she felt a bit more comfortable speaking about her past. "Hey, how about we move on to music? What's on your Spotify right now? What do you like to see at the movies?"

They spent the next hour answering each other's questions, getting down to the basics. She took notes, and after they'd gone through a six-pack of beer, it was time to call it quits. She walked Risk to the door.

"I think this was a good idea," she said, feeling much more confident about her role as his fiancée now.

"Yeah," he said. "We managed to keep it civil."

"Yes. Good practice for when it's the real thing."

"Shoot. It almost slipped my mind. Our first test is coming sooner than I expected. We're invited to speak about Founder's Day at the elementary school tomorrow afternoon."

"We?"

"The principal asked for you to come specifically, and I accepted."

"You accepted? Really? You don't even know if I'm available."

"April, this week you're *always* available when it's necessary, and this is necessary. The principal thought you can speak about what living in Boone Springs has meant to you."

"But I'm not even prepared."

"They're grade-school kids. It won't be hard. Just wing it."

"Easy for you to say."

"Hey, a deal's a deal. And you agreed to all this."

He didn't need to remind her—she was well aware. "I was forced into this, remember? And next time, give me more than a half day's notice when I'm supposed to make an appearance."

"I'll email you the agenda of appearances ASAP."

"There's so many I need a list?" She wasn't happy about this.

He shrugged. "Thanks to our *engagement* and Shannon's visit to town, our dance card is filling up fast."

She walked him to the door. "You don't have to accept all of the invitations."

"I'm not, trust me. I'll pick you up tomorrow around ten."

She sighed. "I'll be at the office." Then she pointed a finger toward his chest. She didn't give a fig if the paparazzi were out there, stalking them. "And don't you even think about kissing me goodbye."

Risk's lips twitched, his eyes sharp and keenly aware. "I wouldn't dream of it."

With that, he walked out, and she gently closed the door before he could say good-night.

April stood next to Risk behind the podium in front of two hundred grade-school students sitting on the multi-purpose-room floor of Creek Point Elementary. Risk had them captivated with his stories about how the town of Boone Springs came to be. He spoke of his ancestors with pride and passion and then brought his young audience up to date on what each of his family members had done to keep Boone Springs thriving. He was good with the kids, inspiring, even, which totally surprised her.

"And now, I'll turn the microphone over to my fiancée, Miss April Adams. She wants to tell you something about what Boone Springs means to her." Risk gave her a charming, melt-your-heart smile, and she tried to smile graciously back at him. As if she liked him.

"Hello, children. I'm April, and I grew up in Boone Springs just like many of you. But when I was young, this school wasn't built yet. I went to Brookside Elementary. Back then we only needed one grade school in the community and now we have three, so you can see how much we've grown in just over twenty years."

Eight teachers stood at the back of the auditorium, their gazes glued to her. The children, too, seemed to be listening, but it was Risk's eyes on her that rattled her nerves. He seemed intent on her every word. She'd taken his advice and was winging it.

"So when I moved away to learn all I could about real

estate, my heart was always here in Boone Springs, where I grew up, where my family and friends were, and I worked very hard to come back here and open an office. *People* make Boone Springs special, people like you and your families. They work hard, too, and they give back to the community, by supporting the schools and libraries, by volunteering at the hospital and shelters, by helping their neighbors. Can you tell me what you can do to help the community, your neighbors and your families?"

Hands went up, and April called on a little boy in a red flannel shirt. "I can put my toys away when my mommy asks."

"That's very helpful." April grinned and nodded, then called on an older girl, whose gaze seemed to be fixated on her "fiancé."

"I want to be a doctor when I grow up."

"That's very helpful, too," April said. "There are all kinds of doctors. What kind would you like to be?"

The girl didn't hesitate. "The kind who helped Mr. Boone when he lost his memory."

The teachers all smiled, and Risk's lips twitched but he had the good grace not to chuckle, like some of the child's schoolmates were doing. "Yes, the doctors who helped my, uh, Mr. Boone, were quite competent, and we're very grateful." She turned to meet Risk's eyes and found softness there. He was a better actor than she was.

Once the assembly was over, Risk and April thanked Mr. Ritter for the opportunity to talk to the kids. But when the principal seemed in no rush to end the conversation, Risk took hold of April's hand and squeezed. "Sorry to rush off, Mr. Ritter, but we've got another appointment this afternoon."

"Of course," he said. "Thanks again. Both of you were great. The kids learned so much from your talk. And

Miss Adams, you did a wonderful job in engaging the students."

"She's an amazing woman," Risk replied and then began walking out of the auditorium, tugging her along.

Once in the parking lot and away from curious eyes, April let go of his hand. Risk opened the car door for her, and as they both took their seats, she turned to him. "I hope you weren't serious about us having another appointment this afternoon. It wasn't on the agenda."

He turned on the engine and buckled up. "I'm serious… about lunch. I'm starving."

"Well, you can eat. Just drop me off at my agency first."

He only smiled. "Sorry, can't do that. The place is around the corner from here."

"Risk, if I'm so horrible, why would you want to spend more time with me than necessary? Because I certainly think you—"

"April, I'm hungry, and it'll only take a few minutes to get the food and eat it. We don't even have to talk to each other."

She folded her arms across her middle. "Fine then."

Risk wasn't fooling; the Thai Temple was indeed just a few minutes away. He drove up to a take-out window and ordered two meals. They were cooked fresh, the scent of sizzling meats making her tummy grumble when Risk was handed the food in two white bags. "You like Thai?" he asked.

She nodded, though she hadn't tried this place. It was relatively new, she assumed, since this part of town, including Creek Point Elementary, had been recently developed.

He drove out of the drive-through heading in the opposite direction of her office. "Where are you going?"

"You'll see. There's a park on the edge of town. We're almost there."

It did no good arguing with Risk. He was determined to have his lunch on his terms, so she clamped her mouth shut as he turned into a dirt driveway and parked the car. He turned to her. "Walnut shrimp or glazed chicken?"

She stared at the two bags and took the walnut shrimp. "This one is fine."

He nodded, grabbed the other bag and got out of the car. He walked around to her side and pointed. "There's a table over there, looks out to the creek. That's where I'll be," he said, sauntering away. As an afterthought, he turned to look her square in the eyes. "You comin'?"

Then he headed over to a table set under a stand of trees. She stubbornly sat in the car and watched Risk take a seat at a wooden picnic table. She looked out at the annoyingly lovely view. The sun blazed over the ridge as waters from the recent storms rushed along. It was a far better place to have a meal than in the car. She hated that good sense won over her stubbornness. She opened the door, bag in hand, and walked over to the table.

Risk didn't say a word. He was busy eating and enjoying the view of the rocky bed and bubbling waters.

She opened her bag, stirred the shrimp, rice and veggies together, and began eating. The food was spicy and delicious, and she dug in with gusto.

Risk glanced at her. "You're a noisy eater."

"Am I disturbing your peace?"

"Always," he said. "As I recall, you're noisy about other things, too."

Heat rose up her neck. Was he deliberately taunting her and trying to humiliate her? She'd been hijacked into this lunch, but she didn't need to be insulted as well. She rose from her seat. "This wasn't a good idea."

"Hell, April. Why are you being so sensitive?"

"Because you're bringing up something I want to forget."

"You know darn well it wasn't meant as a put-down."

"I know no such thing." Because if it wasn't a put-down, then what was it? He had good memories of the night at the lodge? He liked the sounds she'd made while he was making love to her? None of it mattered; none of it was real. She hated the deception and didn't want to spend any more time with Risk than she had to. "I'm done here."

She marched off, heading toward his car. When she was halfway there, Risk sidled up next to her, took her hand and twirled her to face him. He came nose to nose with her and whispered, "Don't look now, but we were followed."

"What? Where?"

He touched her cheek with the flat of his palm. "Over by the side of the road. They're taking pictures."

"Oh. Who are they?"

"Reporters, no doubt. It looks like we're fighting."

"We are."

"Not anymore," he said softly, bringing his head down, touching his lips to hers. The kiss startled her, but he held her tight around the waist, keeping her in his embrace. Her pulse jumped, and her body shivered. "April," he murmured, "this is important to both of us."

Of course, this was the deal they'd made. "Right."

She put her arms around his neck and fell into the role of fiancée, kissing him back, kissing him as if he was her whole world. Let them take all the pictures they needed to. This charade would be over soon and she'd be able to go on with her life.

Risk made a good show of it, kissing her longer than she expected, and when he finally broke off the kiss, he was as breathless as she was. They'd always had chemistry, and she wouldn't give it any real credence that his eyes nearly smoked like hot coals. It was all for show.

"I think we've convinced them," she whispered, her lips tingling.

"Yep," he said, his gaze roaming over her face. "Good job."

Good job? She'd laid her best kisses on him.

It had been an extraordinary job, at the very least.

Eight

The next day April and Jenna drove down the highway heading back from Willow Springs, a sapphire-blue ball gown hanging in a garment bag from a hook in the back seat. "Jenna, I can't thank you enough for taking the morning off from the salon to shop with me."

"You're welcome. You're going to look great at the big Founder's Day dinner."

"Thank you. How about we go to lunch? My treat this time. Where do you want to go? I'll take you anywhere *except* the Farmhouse Grill."

Jenna's eyes rounded, her mouth dropped open and as their eyes met, both of them burst out laughing. "Okay, how about Italian then?"

"Sounds delish."

A short time later, they entered Italia Ristorante, and April immediately wanted to make a dash for it. "Oh man. Do you see what I see?"

Shannon was sitting with Risk in a corner booth with a handful of reporters and cameramen hovering nearby. She was all in black, from the bomber jacket and sequined top to her jeans and knee-high boots. Her ruby-red lips matched her fingernails, and the whole package screamed *well put together*. April would look silly in clothes like that, but on Shannon, it worked.

She'd had no idea Risk was having lunch here, apparently with Shannon.

"Is it too late to run?" Jenna asked.

"I'm afraid so…we've been spotted."

A cameraman rushed over and snapped their picture, and a reporter stuck a microphone close to her face. "Are you here to have lunch with Shannon and your fiancé? Did you know he was dining with Shannon Wilkes today?"

Risk glanced her way, and she caught his quick frown before he transformed it into a charming smile. He rose from his seat and made his way over. "Sweetheart," he said, brushing his lips over hers as he wrapped his arm around her waist. Her ears burned from all the attention, and the kiss to ward off the suspicious press simply pissed her off. "It's so good to see you," he said. "Hello, Jenna."

"Hello," Jenna answered.

Risk made sure to keep his attention on April, his dark eyes soft on her. He'd had practice being the focus of attention. She wasn't as smooth or polished, and a gnawing ache began to grow in her belly. She'd seen the look on Shannon's face when she had Risk all to herself, well…all to herself and her adoring press.

"I ran into Shannon here today, and she sat down and joined me for a few minutes while I wait for my meeting with the mayor," he explained as photos were being snapped.

"Were you checking up on your fiancé, Miss Adams?" a reporter asked.

She smiled at the reporter, then gave Risk an adoring look. "Risk and I happen to love this restaurant and each other. My friend and I came by to pick up something to eat.

It's an added bonus that I get to see him for a few minutes during the day."

By now, all eyes in the restaurant were on them. She couldn't blame anyone. It was a juicy story—Risk appearing to be caught with his ex by his present fiancée.

Optics were important. She was sure the headlines in the morning would inflame more than flatter.

Antonio, the owner of the restaurant, came over and apologized for the disturbance. Then he tactfully told the paparazzi they were bothering his customers and they would be effectively tossed out if they didn't leave quietly.

Shannon sauntered over, standing directly beside Risk, close enough to rub shoulders. To his credit he moved slightly away, but Shannon wasn't to be ignored. "Hello again, April."

"Hello, Shannon. I'd like you to meet my dear friend Jenna. Jenna, this is Shannon Wilkes."

The women nodded in greeting.

"I hope you don't mind me sitting with Risk for a while. We bumped into each other quite by accident." She smiled, her eyes lighting on Risk. "We were killing time, reminiscing. Lord knows, we have stories that could fill up a whole book. Don't we, Risk?" She gave him a classic Shannon Wilkes smile.

"We were talking about Shannon's mom," he explained. "She was a great baker."

"They say the way to a man's heart is through his stomach. And Mom always made Risk his favorite desserts."

"You mean she baked caramel peach pie?" April asked.

"Why, yes, she did. And butter cookies with—"

"Fresh-crushed walnuts on top."

Shannon's smug expression faltered a bit. "Yes, yes, that's right."

Risk darted his gaze April's way, their eyes meeting ever

so briefly, before he granted Shannon a smile. Apparently their life-story-in-an-hour training session had paid off. "I always appreciated Mary's baking for me."

"She loved you very much," Shannon said softly.

"She was a special lady."

Risk's phone buzzed. "Sorry, I have to take this. It's from Mayor Addison," he said, stepping away from the three of them.

Shannon eyed April. "Do you have any news for me about the house?" Her voice was sugary sweet, yet calculation entered her sage eyes.

"Oh, uh, yes, I do. That's one of the things I was going to do this afternoon, call you. I'm afraid the Russo family isn't interested in your offer."

Shannon's gaze moved to where Risk was standing in the back of the restaurant, speaking into his phone. "Offer them twenty thousand more."

April gulped, and Jenna stared at Shannon like she'd lost her mind. The original offer, along with this added bonus, was outrageously generous. Shannon really wanted this place. "I can certainly do that, but why, uh, does it have to be that particular farmhouse? I have several listings that are equally as nice."

Shannon's eyes sparkled as a faraway expression stole over her face. "It's personal."

She got it. It was personal between her and Risk.

"I'll see what I can do."

Risk returned to join them, looking none too happy. "The mayor had to cancel our meeting. How about I take all three of you out to lunch today?"

"I'm in," Shannon announced immediately.

Risk gave April a pointed look, as if he'd strangle her if she refused.

"You know what? I have to get back to the salon, so

thanks anyway," Jenna said. "But don't hesitate to stay, April. Have a good lunch, everyone!"

Jenna, the rat, abandoned her. Some friend she turned out to be. Weren't besties supposed to stick together? Now, she was stuck having lunch with Risk and his very flirty, very flamboyant ex-love, Shannon Wilkes.

The next night Risk stood outside April's apartment door. She wasn't going to like this, but he had no choice, so he knocked hard and hoped she would answer. It'd be easier to explain in person why he had to add to their list of appearances. He'd argue his case face-to-face rather than try to reason with her over the phone. He'd tried calling her today, and they'd gotten disconnected. Or she'd hung up on him. He wasn't sure which.

He knocked a second time and heard her call out, "Who is it?"

"It's Risk. I need to speak with you."

"What are you doing here?"

"Let me in and I'll explain."

"Hold on a sec. I just got out of the tub."

Visions of her naked body, all wet and round and beautiful, filled his head. She had curves in all the right places, and all too often lately he caught himself thinking about the two nights of mind-blowing sex he'd had with her. He wished he didn't remember. He wasn't as immune to her as he let on. Pretending to be her fiancé meant caresses and kisses that weren't all that benign, that stirred his blood and racked his body.

He wasn't forgetting her lies or how she'd made a fool out of him. That was the one thing keeping him in check.

The door opened, and there she stood, wearing some sort of silky kimono robe wrapped tightly at her waist. Her hair was up in a messy bun, and her face was washed clean of makeup. Makeup she didn't need, not with those big blue eyes and rosy lips. The subtle scent of fresh flowers immediately perfumed the air around her. They stared at each other a moment.

"Risk? Why are you here?" she asked.

"Please let me in. It'll look weird if you don't." He played the fake fiancée card and slid a glance around the building grounds, pretty darn sure he hadn't been followed tonight.

She opened the door wider, making room for him to come in, a frown on her face. Okay, maybe he should've called first and warned her he'd be coming over. But that meant risking she wouldn't hear him out.

The moment he stepped inside, he immediately noticed the starkness of the place. Things seemed different than the first time he'd been here. All the touches that made this apartment warm and homey seemed to be gone.

"Where were you today when we got disconnected?" he asked, trying to sound casual.

She sighed. "At the lodge."

"I tried you several times. Couldn't get through."

"I've been overseeing some work. The cell service out there is temperamental."

He nodded and glanced around again. "Why does this place look so different?"

"Let's just say I've been doing some…spring-cleaning."

"In the winter?"

"Well, it'll be spring in a few months." She folded her arms across her middle. "Risk, I'm tired. I've had a busy day. What do you need from me?"

"Why don't we sit down? You look like you could use a drink…to relax. How about we open a bottle of wine?" Her lips parted in feigned outrage, and he grinned. April was getting to be a pretty good actress, but tonight he wasn't buying it. His suggestion brought temptation to her eyes.

"Why don't you tell me why you want to ply me with alcohol?"

"You mean, aside from the obvious reason?"

"Which is?"

"You look hot in that getup."

She grabbed her robe at the lapels and pulled it tighter around her, her face flaming a bit. "This from the guy who can't stand me."

"I never said that." Well, not those exact words, but he had reamed her out pretty badly when he'd gotten his memory back. Still, he had blood in his veins, and it surprised him how attracted he was to her, even after all she'd done. "You're a beautiful woman, April," he said quietly. "It'd be hard not to notice."

She slumped onto the sofa, and he took a seat at the opposite end.

"Why are you buttering me up?" Suspicion darkened her eyes.

He chose not to answer.

"Speak."

He laughed. "You know, you're a worthy contender, April."

"I'll take that as a compliment. Go on."

He sighed, ready for the stuffing to hit the fan. "Okay, I know we agreed on an agenda, but some things have come up recently, and we need to make adjustments. Believe me, I wouldn't ask if it wasn't important. You see, since the mayor had to cancel our appointment, he called to invite both of us to dinner at his home tomorrow night. His wife would like to meet you. Apparently she went to school with your mother."

"No."

"April, be reasonable."

"I'm not going to dinner at the mayor's house and pretending...pretending we're in love. That's too intimate a setting for me. Sorry. Just tell him I've got the flu, was bitten by a rabid dog, broke my ankle. I don't care what excuse you make. I'm behind on my work, and I can only take so much at a time."

He rubbed the back of his neck and sighed. "All right, that was a long shot," he said, giving in. "I'll make an excuse for you. *None* of the ones you suggested, but I'll come up with something."

"Good." Her nod brought his gaze up to her messy bun, bopping up and down. He liked her look tonight: cute and sexy. Even though she had a perpetual frown on her face, or maybe because of it, he was drawn to her. "But this next item on the agenda I hope you'll consider. It's for our aunt Lottie. With Founder's Day coming up in just five days, she probably thinks we've forgotten her sixty-second birthday. She's rarely at Rising Springs on her birthday, so Drea had this idea to give her a surprise party day after tomorrow. It's family and a few close friends. Naturally, you should attend."

"But I barely know her."

"She's a good woman, April. And to the world, you're my fiancée."

"I know she's a good woman. She's treated me like family, which I find very sweet."

"I really think she'd like you to join us. You'll be with my family mostly, so very little pretending."

"That's a plus," she said all too quickly. "Will Shannon be attending?"

"Shannon?" That question came out of left field. "No, she's not invited. Why?"

April gave her shoulder a shrug. "Sometimes I think she's onto us. Whenever I see her or talk to her over the phone, she seems to be…testing me."

"How so?"

"Well, for instance she's been interested in buying the Russo property, and today I had to call her about it. Somehow she always finds a way to bring the subject back to you. She asks pointed questions and, well, it makes me uncomfortable. And then there's photos of us—you and me, or Shannon and me, or you and Shannon—plastered all over the news. It's a bit much."

"Did you say the Russo property?" *Holy crap.* Risk almost came out of his seat. What was Shannon up to? "That farmhouse on the edge of town?"

"Yes, she said she has personal reasons for wanting the place. And I think it has to do with you."

He had history with Shannon on that piece of property. Before it sold to the Russos, it had been a rental property, and Shannon had stayed there on her first visit to his hometown. The first time they'd made love in Boone Springs, it had been there. "You'd be right, April."

That's all he was going to say on the matter. They'd been so hot and heavy in those days, Shannon thought it best to stay somewhere off the ranch so they could have privacy day and night. Those days had been memorable, but now things were different.

"I see."

"I'm not restarting anything with Shannon." He had to make that clear to April, since they were in this together.

"You two looked pretty cozy sitting at the restaurant the other day."

"That was innocent. She walked in and spotted me at the table and came over to say hello. There was nothing illicit about it. It wasn't planned."

"There's been love triangle speculation all over the internet. This isn't easy for me."

"I get that, but that's why you should come to my aunt's birthday celebration. To dismiss the rumors. The more we look like a real engaged couple, the less speculation there'll be."

"Do you agree to see the lodge the very next day? It'll be ready to be viewed by then."

"The lodge?" He'd barely given it a thought. He'd been focused on keeping up his pretend-fiancé role and dealing with Founder's Day.

"Risk, you do remember our deal, don't you?"

He had to admire her gumption. She was a go-getter. "If I say yes, then you'll come to the celebration?"

She thought about it, making him sweat for a few lingering moments, and then her smile turned her eyes a soft baby blue and wiped the perpetual frown off her face.

"Yes," she said finally, "I'll come."

Late the next afternoon, after a full day of overseeing the workmen at the lodge and putting her final touches on staging the rooms, April sat down at a café table at Katie's Kupcakes three blocks from her office. She and Katie had both grown up in Boone Springs, and today they'd shared a few cordial words before she'd ordered a decadent brownie cupcake with a vanilla almond latte. She was exhausted, so feeling guilty about her indulgence wasn't even a remote consideration.

She'd worked her butt off this week, and she deserved a treat.

She sipped her delicious drink and then bit into her cupcake. "Oh wow," she groaned. Two bites later, she spotted Lottie Brown walking into the bakery. She had a smile on her face and looked well put together in a rose-colored blouse tucked into a belted denim skirt with pretty studded boots to finish off the look. Lottie had style and grace. April liked how she didn't let her age bring polyester into her life.

Lottie spotted her immediately and walked over. "Hi, April." She glanced at her partially eaten cupcake. "Seems like you and I had similar cravings today."

"Did we?"

"I'm here for Katie's chocolate explosion cupcake."

"Would you care to join me?" April's manners had her asking, but she wasn't entirely sure that was all it was. Lottie was someone she wouldn't mind getting to know better.

"I'd love to." Lottie took a seat, and within a minute Katie came over to take her order.

"Katie, it's good to see you. You haven't been out to the ranch in a while."

"No, I've been busy. You know, with the bakery and my work at the horse rescue, I hardly know what day it is anymore."

"Mason and Drea's wedding is coming up, too."

"I'm looking forward to it. I've got to get my act together and plan Drea's bachelorette party, too."

"I'm sure you'll do a great job," Lottie said.

"I hope so. This is my first time...as maid of honor," she said, then bit her lip.

April knew something about Katie's strained relationship with the Boones. Five years ago, Lucas had broken off his engagement to Katie's sister right before the wedding. Katie was to be Shelly's maid of honor. Her sister had been stunned and devastated, which put Katie in a tough spot. She and Lucas had been friends. Not so much anymore.

Katie took Lottie's order and walked off. Lottie turned to her. "April, it's good to see you. Tell me, how's my nephew treating you?"

It was such an unexpected question, she paused a second. "Risk? Oh, just f-fine."

"Glad to hear it. You two are both good people. I wouldn't want either of you being hurt again."

"That's very kind of you to say. I'm sure…we'll part ways without any fireworks."

Lottie raised her brows and then changed the subject, much to April's relief. As they conversed, April found she had a good deal in common with Lottie, from the kind of music and books they liked to their sense of style and design.

Half an hour later, April walked out of the bakery with Lottie. "I'm glad we bumped into each other," April said.

"Me, too." Lottie sighed and stared into her eyes. "If I can say something… I sorta wish you and my nephew were the real thing. I see you together, and it just feels right. I hate to say it, but I knew going in that Risk and Shannon weren't going to work. But I'm just Risk's favorite aunt. What do I know?" She rolled her eyes, as if mocking herself.

April laughed, not at all insulted by Lottie's earnest opinion. Of course, she didn't agree with her. She and Risk would never work. "Sorry to disappoint you, but I don't think we'll—"

"Oh no! Would you look at that!"

Lottie took off running, following a blond sheepdog trotting into the middle of the street. "Here, boy, here, boy," she called out, trying to coax him to safety. But the dog kept moving. "Get out of the street! Go, go."

Lottie didn't see the car rounding the corner. "Lottie!"

April ran as fast as her legs would carry her. She heard the screech of tires, saw the car swerving right before she shoved Lottie out of the way. April went down, her knees scraping the blacktop as she fell, the smell of burning rubber reaching her nostrils, the heat of the car's engine blasting in her face.

She opened her eyes and stared at the big blue sky, and then Lottie appeared in her line of vision. "Dear Lord, April. Are you okay? Did you hit your head?"

"No, no. I'm fine. I think." She did a mental scan of her

body. She hadn't hit her head when she went down. And she hadn't been hit; she fell while pushing Lottie out of the way of the car. It was a stumble and luckily only her knees were bruised under her skirt, though she was pretty sure her whole body would be sore as hell tomorrow, because that's how it worked. Fall today, ache tomorrow.

"You saved me and put yourself in danger. You could have been hit by that car," Lottie said. "That was a very brave thing to do. Thank you. I don't know what to say." Tears welled up, and she wiped them away. "Do you think you can get up?"

"I think so."

Lottie took hold of April's hands and helped her up. She straightened, locking her bruised knees, her entire body shaking. She felt her knees burn now as a small amount of blood oozed out. "We should get you to a doctor," Lottie said.

By then, a crowd had formed, and the lanky young driver of the vehicle came over, a look of fright on his teenage face. The car had come to a careening halt only inches from where April had fallen. "I'm so sorry," he said. "I didn't see anyone when I made the turn."

"It's not your fault, young man," Lottie said. "I chased after a dog darting out into the street, and you did your best to avoid hitting anyone. If anything, you did a great job," Lottie assured him.

He nodded. "Miss, are you gonna be okay?" he asked April.

"Yes, I think I'll be fine. I'm just shaken up a bit."

"Should I call nine-one-one?" a voice from the small crowd asked.

"Oh no, please. I'm going to be fine." April looked out into the sea of people gathering.

Cell phones were pointed her way as onlookers snapped

pictures of her. She heard whispers. Some had recognized her as Risk Boone's fiancée.

"Let me take you to the doctor, at least," Lottie said gently, taking her by the arm and leading her to the sidewalk in front of Katie's Kupcakes.

"Lottie, I think I'll go home and clean up my bruises. It's nothing serious."

Katie ran over, handing her a washcloth. "Here you go. It's clean. I rinsed it with cold water. If you'd like to come inside the bakery, you can clean up in there, April."

"That's a good idea," Lottie said.

"No, that's not necessary, Katie. But thank you for the washcloth." The last thing she wanted to do was make a scene. Once news got out, which was sure to happen with all the photos that were being snapped, reporters would show up. Her body cried out for rest. It had been a busy, crazy day. She dabbed at her knees with the cloth. They were only bleeding slightly, and the washcloth really helped. "That feels better."

"Let me drive you home. I insist," Lottie said.

Lottie wanted to help, and April wouldn't deprive her. "Okay, thanks."

She walked arm in arm with Lottie Brown to her car parked a short distance down the street. Once April put on her seat belt, Lottie turned to her, her usually jovial face sober and concerned. "Are you sure you don't need a doctor?"

"I'm sure."

"How about I take you to Rising Springs, where we can take care of your bruises and let you rest."

"I wouldn't think of it, Lottie."

"You are Risk's fiancée."

"For the rest of the week only." After their conversation about Risk being right for her, April had to remind Lottie their engagement had a very short shelf life. She and Risk had no future.

Lottie pursed her lips, admitting defeat. "Okay, to your apartment then. Point the way."

April gave her directions, and Lottie drove carefully, going ever so slowly. That's when April realized Lottie had been shaken up, too. As Lottie parked in front of April's apartment complex, she asked, "Lottie, I didn't hurt you with that shove, did I?"

"Considering I might've been flattened like a pancake if you hadn't come to my rescue, I'm doing great. Don't even think about it." Lottie took April's hand and gave it a squeeze. "I can't thank you enough." Then Lottie reached over and gave April a big, squishy, loving, mama bear hug.

She relished the feel of the older woman's arms around her. She hadn't been hugged like this in a long time, and it made her miss her own mother, who was in Spain at the moment. Lottie lent her comfort and showed her gratitude, which was what she needed right now. Once the embrace ended, April smiled at the older woman. "Thanks for the ride."

"Can I walk you to your door?"

"That's sweet, but not necessary. I'll be fine. I just need to rest."

"Okay then. Be sure to call if you need anything."

"I promise I will. Goodbye, Lottie."

April got out of the car, her knees still burning, but she waved to Lottie and watched her drive off before she turned to enter her apartment complex. She really needed to cleanse her wounds and collapse on her bed.

"April!"

Hearing the fast pace of footsteps behind her, she squeezed her eyes shut.

Oh no.

It was Risk.

Nine

"April," Risk called again.

What was he doing here? He was supposed to be having dinner with the mayor. She stopped walking and turned, bumping into his chest. He'd been right behind her. "Oh."

He reached for her, holding her arms still. "I heard what happened," he said softly.

"Already?" She knew what they said about small towns, but this was crazy.

"Katie called me. I was in town, at the office. Are you okay?"

Genuine concern entered his eyes as he scanned her body up and down. "You're bleeding."

She looked down. A few tiny droplets of blood trailed down her legs.

Before she could react, Risk scooped her up in his arms and began carrying her to her apartment. She clung to his neck, a bit shocked by his bold move. And a little bit turned on. It was a white-knight sort of thing for a man to do, one that many women secretly fantasized about. "I can walk, Risk. You don't need to carry me."

"Yes, I do. You were limping."

"I was not limping."

"I say you were."

"That's because you—" Then it hit her, and she lowered her voice. "Oh, I get it. You think someone's watching us, taking pictures."

He snapped his eyes to hers, his face twisting into a scowl. "Yep, you got it. That's why I'm carrying you."

She clamped her mouth shut, uneasy at the tone of Risk's voice, the look on his face. Something was off, and suddenly she wasn't sure about anything. Maybe it was fatigue, but being in Risk's arms again, soaking up his strength, breathing in his musky scent didn't feel all so terrible.

"Give me your key," he said as they reached her front door. She snatched her key from her purse and he unlocked the door.

"You don't need to baby me," she said softly, noticing his jaw twitch.

"Don't I?" He brought her into the apartment and laid her down on the sofa. "Stay still, April. Don't move. I'm gonna take care of your knees."

"Risk, you don't…"

But he was already walking down her hallway. She heard him scavenging around her bathroom, and after a few moments he was back with a handful of medical supplies, a look of determination on his face.

He sat at the foot of the sofa and gently pushed up the hem of her dress. His fingers brushing her thighs sent hot waves zipping up and down her legs.

"Let me know if it hurts," he said, fully intent on his task. He began applying a soapy cloth to her knees and the thin trail of blood running down her legs. He wiped her knees dry and lathered the wounds with antibiotic cream. "What you did today," he began, then cleared his throat, "was a foolish thing."

Her eyes flashed to his.

"You could've been killed."

He sounded sincere. "I didn't think so. I just reacted, calculating I could get to Lottie before the car mowed her down."

Risk bandaged both knees. It wasn't a pretty sight, but she did feel better not having open wounds. "You saved my aunt's life, April."

"Maybe."

"Not maybe. I saw the video."

"There's a video? My God." How on earth did that happen so quickly?

"It's the world we live in today. Someone on the scene sent it to the *Tribune*, and they immediately called for my reaction."

"And you rushed right over here?"

He nodded.

"What about your dinner with the mayor and his wife?"

"What better reason to cancel than my fiancée getting injured in an accident? He wouldn't expect any less from me."

"Because it wouldn't look right." Of course. That had to be it. "Sorry, I know that dinner was important to you."

"It's just business, April. It's not as important as—"

"I'm surprised you didn't want to see your aunt," she interrupted, stopping Risk from saying anything she didn't want to hear. She couldn't start believing he actually cared about her, actually worried about her well-being.

"Katie assured me Aunt Lottie is fine. I'll talk to her in a little while."

"Well, thank you for patching me up. My mom would say we're even Steven."

"How so?"

"I took care of you when you lost your memory, and you just repaid the favor."

He ran his hand down his face, staring at her for a moment. "April."

"You really don't have to stay. I'm fine now." And he'd done his fake-fiancé duty by rushing over here to check on her.

He set his jaw, stubbornly. She'd seen that determined look before. "You must be thirsty," he said, ignoring her comment. "Let me get you some water."

"Water? A glass of wine would be more like it," she blurted. As long as he was going to stay, she might as well have a real drink. She deserved one after the day she'd had.

"Got it." He rose, and she watched him make his way into her kitchen. She heard cabinets being opened and glasses clinking. He popped his head out of the doorway. "Red or white?"

"Red, please."

He smiled, a killer smile giving her silly nerves a workout. There was something different about him tonight. He was being…nice.

Because he felt he owed her something for saving Lottie.

By the time he returned with two goblets of wine, April was sitting up. He handed her a glass. "Thank you." He sat and met her eyes again. "You tired?"

"I was. It's been a crazy day, but now I think I'm a bit too antsy to sleep."

"There's a great movie on right now."

"Which one?"

"A Day in the Life."

It was one of her top-ten favorites. They'd discussed this just a few days ago. "A girlie movie. I'm up for that."

"Me, too."

The wineglass halted midway to her lips. "You're going to watch it, too?"

He shrugged. "For a little while, until I finish my wine. If that's okay?"

"Oh, um. Yeah, for a little while. You'll be in charge of the remote."

Risk already had it in his hand. He turned on the TV and began channel surfing. "Ah, here it is."

April relaxed into the cushions of the sofa, the wine taking the edge off. She eyed Risk, who was also settling in. He appeared at ease. They'd never done this before…just be. Like a regular couple.

She couldn't stop the warm exciting thrill traveling the length of her body.

Was it the wine? Or was it Risk?

Whatever it was, she liked the way she was feeling right now.

The next afternoon April and Clovie had just finished a quick lunch at the diner and were walking the two short blocks back to the office when Clovie nudged her arm. "Don't look across the street," she said quietly. "And keep walking, unless you want to be photographed again."

April put her head down and did as her friend said. "Why, what's happening?"

"Looks like Shannon and…uh, your fiancé are together outside the bank. Shannon's speaking to a bunch of reporters swarming them."

April slid a glance that way and saw for herself. She had no idea what was going on. Risk was like a magnet to the woman. She seemed to seek him out, finding ways to insinuate herself into his life. It hadn't bothered April before, and it shouldn't bother her now, but Risk had been so kind to her last night. She didn't remember him leaving, but she'd woken up on her sofa around midnight, tucked cozily into the one blanket throw she hadn't brought to the lodge.

The TV was off, the door was locked. And this morning, she'd found his note.

Hope you slept tight.
Take care of those pretty knees—
we have dancing to do.
I'll pick you up at 6 p.m.
Risk

The note was a welcome sight and had put her in a good mood this morning despite being sore and achy. She'd almost called Risk to thank him for taking care of her. But he was with Shannon now, out in public, and April wanted no part of it. She had enough going on in her life. She'd been asked to do a local radio show, a segment on her heroism saving Lottie Brown, which she politely turned down. And there were photos of the whole thing and articles written on the internet and in the *Tribune*.

The only positive coming out of this was that the Adams Agency was getting a load of good publicity, and that never hurt. But she wasn't sure if that one positive could overcome all the negatives.

Their engagement was a big fat fraud.

And her fake fiancé was busy spending the afternoon with his ex-girlfriend.

Risk straightened his collar and brushed lint from his stitched dark gray sports jacket as he stood outside April's door, ready to knock. After dealing with Shannon for most of the afternoon, he was looking forward to a night out with April. He wouldn't say his fake fiancée was low maintenance after all the trouble she'd caused, but she sure as hell was a lot easier to deal with than his superstar ex.

He knocked, and it took her a while to answer the door.

But when she did, it was well worth the wait. "Wow." He liked her in red, and this dress fit her to a tee, accentuating the curves he found so damn appealing. Her hair was down, the curly tendrils framing her face. "You look gorgeous, April."

"Thank you," she said. "It's not too much? I have no idea where we're going, but your note mentioned dancing?"

He took his hat off and ran his hand through his hair. "You got my note. Good. Yes, dancing if you're up to it. The family rented out Aunt Lottie's favorite restaurant for the evening—not one our family owns, for a change. The Garden House."

"I've heard about it. All good things." April opened the door wider and let him inside the apartment. She went about picking up a black clutch and sweater from the sofa arm.

"How are your knees?" Her dress was covering them, which he assumed was a deliberate move on her part.

She frowned. "They're not pretty."

"Let me take a look."

She flinched, her eyes opening wide.

"I have a vested interest, since I was your Florence Nightingale last night."

"Not by choice."

She tested him time and again, and he could easily lose patience, but he held himself in check. "April, please."

She gave him a look as if to say this was above his pay grade as her fake fiancée, but he didn't care. His uncanny concern sort of baffled him, too, but he was determined to see how she was healing. They stared at each other a few seconds, and finally she shrugged.

"Oh, okay. It was nice of you to help me last night," she admitted, though it sounded like she had to force the words out of her mouth. She lifted the hem of her dress a few inches and showed him her injuries.

To gain a better view, he bent and cupped the back of her right leg, which was a big mistake. She was soft there and firm all at the same time. Touching her flesh sent a pang of desire shooting down to his groin. It was instantaneous, and crazy. She'd been on his mind lately. He couldn't help wondering if he'd misjudged her. Wondering if she'd been caught up in something bigger than the both of them. He glimpsed her left knee and then took a hard swallow. "They, uh, they look much better."

"You think so?"

He rose and met her gaze, taking in the warm blue glow in her eyes. "Yeah…you're healing fine."

"Thanks, Dr. Boone."

They both chuckled, easing the tension in the room, but then her gaze landed on him again and she laid one hand on his chest, to keep him near or to keep her distance—he wasn't sure. Whatever it was, heat rushed to his chest where her palm rested. "Risk, I saw you today…with Shannon. I suppose I'll read all about it in tomorrow's newspaper."

Risk looked away, mentally cursing. He'd been the one harping on April to keep up this pretend engagement while Shannon seemed intent on derailing it. "It isn't what you think."

"I don't know what to think, but you're the one who needs the world to believe we're engaged. And you keep showing up with your ex. It puts me in a bad position."

"I know, I know." He blew out a breath and shook his head. "Shannon wanted to make a sizable donation to the Boone Foundation. It's a charity my parents started when Mason was born, and all proceeds go to underprivileged children in Boone County. She asked me to meet her at the bank, and as we were walking out together, reporters were there for the story, most likely summoned by her. I should've expected it, since this was always Shannon's MO.

Doing a good thing is a trade-off for the positive publicity she gets."

"Is that all it was?"

"That and lunch at the Farmhouse."

April blinked. "You had lunch with her again? After all the warnings you've given me about being careful. I'm sorry, Risk, but that wasn't—"

"You're not jealous, are you?" Risk's chest swelled at the thought of her being jealous, and that confused the hell out of him. Both Shannon and April had played him. So why in hell was he humming inside? And looking at April differently tonight?

"I am not jealous," she said defiantly, her face turning a shade of pink, "so let the air out of that balloon, Risk."

He smiled. She *was* jealous.

"I'm…concerned. But if you don't mind blowing your cover, then it's on you. I'm holding up my end of the bargain."

"Right, okay. Got it. Are you ready? We can't be late for Aunt Lottie's surprise party."

"I'm as ready as I'll ever be." She rolled her eyes adorably, and Risk had to rein in his emotions. He was starting to like April Adams again. He couldn't seem to help it.

She headed for the front door. "Let the show begin."

Risk only smiled at that and took her hand as he led her to his car.

Risk didn't think the surprise party for Aunt Lottie could go any smoother. Her dear friend Wanda, who lived in Willow County, had brought her to the Garden House, and as soon as she'd walked into the restaurant, the roomful of twenty-five of Aunt Lottie's good friends and family members shouted, "Surprise!"

Aunt Lottie jerked back, tears welling in her eyes as she

looked around at all the people who mattered in her life. She seemed genuinely surprised. "I wasn't expecting this," she declared to everyone.

"Tell me you didn't think we'd forget your birthday?" Drea stepped up and hugged Lottie. "This time, we wanted to surprise you."

"Well, you certainly did."

Mason put his arm around Aunt Lottie's shoulder and kissed her cheek. "My fiancée gets all the credit for this. You know she's an expert at planning parties."

"Drea is the best," Lottie said, love entering her eyes. "And this place is just right. Thank you all for coming."

Mason and Drea looked good together. Risk's older brother was totally in love, and he'd never been happier in his life.

Risk glanced at April standing beside him, and a sharp pang hit him in the gut. He'd vowed not to get involved with her again, and he was trying to stick to that, but it was getting harder these days. After her deception, at first they hadn't liked each other, but that was hardly true anymore. He was beginning to like her too much, not only because she'd sacrificed herself for his aunt's safety, but because she was hardworking, dedicated, *sweet*.

Sweet? Oh man, he wanted April.

Their eyes met now, hers brilliant blue and sparkling with life. He liked her curly hair bounding past her shoulders, her lush ruby-red lips matching the hot dress she wore.

April was no longer persona non grata in his family. She was a superhero, and that worked on his conscience. He'd called her a lot of horrible things in the past, hated how she'd played him for a fool, but he hadn't exactly been perfect, either. The first time they'd been together, he'd walked out on her, and she'd deserved more than that.

She smiled at him, and his heart did a little flip. Somehow, he didn't think it was a phony smile meant to please onlookers. This smile was real, meant for him.

He took her hand and smiled back at her, then led her over to Aunt Lottie and kissed the older woman's cheek. "Happy birthday. What are you, thirty-nine again?"

Lottie placed her palm on the side of his face. "I'll never tell. And neither will you, if you know what's good for you."

The three of them laughed. "This is such a wonderful surprise," she continued. "I thought I was having a quiet dinner with Wanda. And now, you and all my favorite people are here to help me celebrate." She turned toward April, taking her hand, her eyes soft and sincere. "I'm so touched that you're here, April. It means a lot to me."

"I wouldn't have missed it."

She nodded, glancing from April to him, a sweet smile on her face. "You both look wonderful tonight. A real handsome couple."

Then Lottie was whisked away by Drea and her father. Drew was being a bit of a sourpuss tonight. He seemed to be going through the motions for the family's sake but he'd been grumbling a lot about Lottie nearly getting herself killed running after that dog.

Those two always seemed at odds.

Formally dressed waiters came around with trays of appetizers. Risk and April took a few and walked around the restaurant. April was fascinated by the lush gardens groomed to perfection inside the dining rooms. Palms and greenery along with flowering plants and vertical gardens of ivy, moss and trailing vines made up the perimeter of the room. A five-piece band stood at the ready on a small stage in front of a dance floor.

"Hmm, this is so good," she said taking a bite out of a miniature beef Wellington. "The pastry is so light."

He'd already swallowed down two. "Sure is."

He liked that April enjoyed food and wasn't shy about it. He'd been on dates with women who'd eat nothing but salad. In Texas, that wasn't a meal—it was barely a side dish—and April seemed to feel that way, too. "Not as good as peanut butter and cranberry muffins, though."

She glanced at him. Uh-oh, was that also a memory she didn't want to rehash?

"No," she said, her voice breathless. "Nothing's better than our survival food."

"Yeah, about that. I've never thanked you for taking good care of me when I was injured."

"I know."

He'd been too angry when he'd found out about her lies that he'd ignored the care she'd given him. Care that he hadn't wanted to acknowledge until recently.

"I'm thanking you now, and I mean it, April." He spoke straight from his heart this time.

"I believe you do."

"Seems you've saved two members of my family this month."

"Is that why you're being nice to me?"

"It's not just that." He paused for a second and then gave her the honest truth. "Maybe you're easy to be nice to."

"Maybe, huh?"

The lights dimmed, a spotlight finding the band as they started playing, and all Risk could think about was holding April in his arms. He put out his hand. "Dance with me?"

She looked around as others were heading to the dance floor, including Aunt Lottie with his brother Luke. "It'll make Aunt Lottie happy," he added.

"Well in that case, for the birthday girl," April said, taking his hand.

Fortunately, the band played a slow love song. As they reached the dance floor, Risk drew April into his arms, her sweet scent wafting to him. She moved fluidly with him, her body limber and easy to lead. They touched often, her breasts brushing his chest, and he had trouble staying focused on the music. His heart beat hard; his body was revved up. She laid her head on his shoulder, her silky blond locks teasing his nostrils.

"April," he whispered, lowering his hands onto the small of her back and drawing her closer. She was too much of a temptation for him, too close for his sanity. His instincts taking over now, he bent his head and claimed her lips in a soft kiss.

She opened her eyes and looked up at him. "Are there reporters here?"

"I don't think so."

"Is it for the others, then?"

He shook his head. "What others? I only see you."

She smiled and so did he, and then he pressed his lips to hers again.

After the song ended, he pulled back to gaze into her eyes. The dewy, soft way she was looking at him stirred him up inside.

Luke walked up to them, interrupting their moment. "Mind if I cut in, Risker?"

Hell, yeah, he minded. His brother had to choose this moment to break in? It was bad timing, but it was also Aunt Lottie's night and he wasn't going to cause a scene, though he hated letting April go. He gave his brother a warning look and then relented. "Sure enough, Luke boy."

Luke grinned at that. "We'll never live down our nicknames," he said to April.

"I think they're great. Does Mason have one?" she asked Luke.

"Nah, he wouldn't have it. If we called him Masey, he'd get his drawers in a knot. He's just plain Mason."

"Got it."

The music began again and Luke took April into his arms, leaving Risk to walk off the dance floor. He took a place at the back of the room, watching April smile at Luke as he danced her around the parquet floor.

Mason walked up and stood beside Risk. "Here you go," he said, handing him a bourbon on the rocks. They stood quietly for a while, sipping the liquor, Risk's gaze focused on April.

"You know, you've got it bad," Mason said.

He sipped his drink. "Do I?"

"Man, Aunt Lottie nearly applauded when you kissed April right there on the dance floor."

"She likes April."

"So do you. A whole lot."

"Maybe."

"There's no maybes about it. You care for her. Either that or you ate some bad food, bro. You're turning green watching her with Luke."

His stomach squeezed tight. Was he ready for this? For opening up his heart again?

"Just saying, after this fake stuff is over, she's bound to move on. Maybe find another guy. Are you ready to face that?"

Picturing April with another man tied him up inside. "Is your sermon over?"

"Yep, all over. I think I got my point across."

Mason walked away smiling. He found Drea, the woman he was to marry soon, and gave her a giant kiss. Mason was in seventh heaven, totally committed to the woman he loved.

Risk had never been more envious of anyone in his life.

Her hand locked with Risk's, April walked dreamily to her apartment door. She'd had fun tonight, enjoying Lottie's birthday surprise and how the woman's face lit up as her loved ones gathered to celebrate her birthday. At the end of the evening, after a delicious dinner and dancing, Lottie had given a little speech, mentioning April's selflessness and heart, and had proposed a toast in her honor. Lottie had been sensitive enough not to put April in the spotlight, or drag out her thanks, but rather kept it light and cheerful.

Now, as the night came to an end, April was filled with a warm, wistful glow inside. "Thank you for a lovely evening," she said to Risk, laying her head against her door. "It was a beautiful night." Risk had been attentive, thoughtful, the perfect date.

"I'm glad." The huskiness in his voice, the deep penetrating look in his eyes, gave her heart a rattle. "I had a nice time, too," he said, running his index finger down her cheek. The slight touch sizzled on her skin and brought her gaze to his. "I liked holding you, dancing with you, kissing you," he whispered.

"You did?"

"Oh yeah." Then his hand was in her hair, playing with the curls.

She stared at his lips, firm and full and appealing. She set her palm on his jaw, loving the feel of his stubble under her fingertips. "Risk, this isn't for show, is it?"

He paused a second, thoughtful. "Feels pretty damn real to me." And then his mouth was on hers, taking away all doubt, all questions. He kissed her until she was breathless, her mouth ravaged, her body beginning to burn.

"Invite me in," he said between kisses.

"G-good idea."

As soon as the door was closed behind them, Risk pulled her sweater down her arms, taking it off and flinging it on the floor. Their lips melded together in another searing kiss. Breathing was hard, thinking impossible.

It was real this time. It felt right. "Bedroom," she murmured.

"Oh yeah." He whipped off his jacket and lifted her up, his arms strong and powerful underneath her as he carried her to the bed.

As he lowered her down, her feet hit the floor gently. Moonlight poured into the window, illuminating the hungry look in his eyes, the promise in his expression.

He touched her face, kissed her mouth and then whispered in her ear, "You're amazing, April."

Destiny seemed to keep bringing them together. The third time had to be the charm, because she certainly felt charmed tonight. She also felt a whole lot of things she didn't want to name.

Risk kissed her throat, trailing his lips farther down to nibble on her shoulders. His hands came around her back, and with sure, steady fingers he unzipped her dress. Cool air hit her for a second, until Risk's hands were on her again, warming her skin as he rubbed her back, his fingertips soothing her flesh.

She grabbed at his shirt and unbuttoned it, ready to get her hands on his granite chest. As she laid her palms there, raw heat seeped out, and a deep, appreciative groan rose from his throat.

"I love when you touch me," he whispered, right before his lips covered hers again.

"I love touching you," she whispered back.

Another groan escaped his throat, and then they were reaching for each other, removing clothes in a frenzy, his boots, her heels, his shirt, her dress. When April was down to her lacy black bra and panties, Risk stood back, admiring her. "You're perfect," he said, cupping her full breasts, kissing each one. Then he trailed his hands to the curve of her waist. "Just right here, too," he said, her skin heating under his palms. He caressed her hips, and her skin prickled under his touch. "These hips are sexy," he said. "Did you know that?"

She shook her head. She'd come to grips with her body and was no longer ashamed of her size, but no one had ever made her feel like this—like she was perfect and undeniably sexy—the way Risk was doing now.

He wrapped his hands around her hips to flatten his palms on her butt. Bringing her closer, he knelt down in front of her and removed her panties. Then he took her into his mouth, tightening his hold on her and using his tongue to make her wild. She whimpered as he stroked her over and over, the sensations hot and electric like tiny bolts of lightning. Out of her mind with pleasure, she clasped Risk's shoulders and hung on. And then she felt a pull, an internal magnet that took hold and wouldn't let go.

She moaned and Risk was there, keeping pace, bringing her higher and higher. When she finally broke apart, a shudder of pleasure racked her body. Trembling, she moaned and Risk rose then, bringing his mouth to hers, kissing her gently until her body calmed.

Then he lowered her onto her bed, took off his pants and joined her.

She wanted more of him, in the worst way. She brushed her mouth over his, relishing his firm lips, feeling his muscles tightening up, his body growing hard. There was a difference in him tonight, a look of fearless giving in his deep-set dark eyes she hadn't seen before. She wasn't imagining it—it *was* real this time.

And when their bodies merged, a sensual joining that made him close his eyes and grunt in pleasure, April gave him every bit of herself, leaving nothing back, kissing, caressing and loving him with a fierceness that came straight from her heart.

It was almost too powerful, too beautiful, too…much.

She came apart first, her body in glorious tatters once again. Her breaths came hard and fast and then Risk covered her mouth, kissed her again as he moved inside her. He held her arms above her head, covering her body, their skin pressed together, hot and sweaty.

"Oh man, sweetheart," he muttered through gritted teeth as he towered above her.

And found his way home.

April opened her eyes, her body easing into the morning. She felt languid and delicious waking up after an amazing night with Risk. She rolled over on her side, ready to cuddle, but he wasn't there. His warm rock-hard body she'd loved during the night was gone. She was hit with a momentary flash of déjà vu.

She rose from the bed, touching her feet to the floor, looking around for a note or some sign of him. All of his clothes were gone, too. Her joy immediately evaporated. That horrible feeling of abandonment seeped in again. She hated the feeling, hated thinking she wasn't worthy and feeling unlovable.

This wouldn't be the first time Risk had left her.

Damn you, Risk.

"Good mornin'. I see Sleeping Beauty has finally woken up." Risk strode into the bedroom, charming her with a smile. He walked right over to her and gave her a quick kiss on the lips. His appearance, that one kiss, woke her out of her misgivings. Risk was hardly a prince, but he was here. He hadn't deserted her again, and her relief overwhelmed her.

"Good morning back at ya."

Risk had showered; his hair was still damp and pushed

away from his face. He smelled of her lavender soap and was wearing the clothes from last night.

"I, uh, guess I overslept."

"You deserved to. I kept you up late last night," he rasped.

"Yes, I remember." It would be hard to forget all the sensations she'd felt last night.

"April, you're good for me," he said, taking her into his arms. He held her tight, kissing the side of her cheek, gently rocking her back and forth.

God, she felt safe and cared for in his arms, and it worried her a bit. She still didn't fully trust him; if she did, she wouldn't have thought the worst this morning when she'd woken up to an empty bed.

"I hope you don't mind, I used your shower."

"Oh no. Not at all. Sorry I slept so late."

"I'm only glad you didn't wake up and think I ran out on you," he said.

When she didn't answer, he added, "Or did you?"

"I, uh, didn't have time to think. I was just getting up when you walked in." It was only partly a lie.

Risk gave her a nod.

"Well, if you still want to get an early start, we'd better get moving. I've got to stop by the office for a change of clothes."

Early start? Oh, right. She'd been so keyed into Risk, she almost forgot. "Yes, let me make us a quick breakfast, get dressed and then we'll drive out to the lodge."

"I've got breakfast covered," he said. "That's if you don't mind hard-boiled eggs, toast and juice?"

Her mouth dropped open. "You did all that?"

"It's hardly a culinary marvel, but yeah. I cooked."

She smiled. "Okay, then. Let's try out your meal, Chef Boone."

He took her hand and led her to the kitchen. But before they returned to the lodge, she had to get something off her chest first, something he'd accused her of doing that still ate away at her to this day.

She looked him square in the eye, determined to get her point across. "Just for the record, Risk, I'm asking you to keep what happened between us last night and your thoughts about the lodge separate. One has nothing to do with the other. Our deal was for you to give me your honest, objective opinion. That's all I'm asking."

Risk squeezed her hand. "I will. I promise."

She nodded. "Thank you. It matters to me that you know that. We both made mistakes, and hopefully we can put that behind us now."

"Yeah, I like the sound of that."

Ten

The lodge looked fabulous. The grounds were groomed, and a new coat of paint gave curb appeal a whole new meaning. April was proud of the mini renovations done to the property. But she wasn't the one who had to like it. Risk was. She gauged his reaction as he exited the car and opened the door for her.

He scanned the grounds with a thoughtful eye. "This place looks different in the daylight."

"It does," she agreed. "There's more to do out here, of course, but take a look around and see the potential. We can discuss anything you'd like."

She led him around back and showed him the view of Canyon Lake. It was a brisk but beautiful day, sunlight caressing the blue waters off in the distance. Just outside the dining area, café tables were set on the decking overlooking the lake, perfect for a morning breakfast and lunch, or a sunset dinner during the summer months.

"Canyon Lake is great for boating and fishing, and the area directly in front of us is designated for swimming. There's a slide that drops you ten feet out into the water. It's in bad shape but wouldn't cost much to replace," she said.

Risk was quiet, taking it all in. And then as they walked back around, he spent some time looking over the stables before he stopped at the woodshed and looked at the trees nearby. "One of those suckers nailed me," he said.

"I know. I never should've let you go get the wood."

"You had no choice," he said, puffing out his chest. "I wasn't going to let both of us freeze to death. Come on. Let's go inside."

April held her breath. She was super nervous about him seeing her vision for the place. As they entered the lobby area, Risk took a long look around, his gaze staying on the pieces she'd brought from her apartment. Furniture had been moved around. There were pictures on the walls.

"I see your influence here, April. You made the lodge homey, yet modern. Sort of like your own place."

"You noticed."

"Yeah. I never saw this place with sunlight streaming in."

"It's cheerful, isn't it? I had the wood beams conditioned."

Risk looked up and nodded. "Okay."

He walked around, testing the banister leading to the second story. He viewed the photos on the wall more closely and then gazed at the round rock fireplace that was the focal point of the room.

He made his way to the kitchen, and April's nerves squeezed tight. "We did some minor renovations here."

"You had the cabinets painted. They look good," he said. "And the appliances?"

"All in working order."

"The tiles are still chipped."

"The new owner can have his choice of new countertops."

He gave a quick nod. "What else do you have to show me?"

"The dining room and the master suite, down here. And then the upstairs."

She could tell Risk was impressed at how the dining room looked straight out onto Canyon Lake. The tables had vases full of flowers, and a few were set with dishes and cutlery. "You can almost see the guests dining here, enjoying the lake view."

Again, Risk only nodded.

When they walked into the master suite, Risk studied it thoroughly, glancing at the champagne and crystal flutes she'd had Clovie set on the dresser. It was too personal, too intimate, and she wished she hadn't taken that extra step when staging the room.

"Your vision," Risk whispered.

"It's just a suggestion on how...or rather... This is a special room," she said finally.

Risk looked at her and smiled. "I think so, too."

He took her hand and tugged her along. "Show me more."

They climbed the stairs. "How's the roof holding up?" he asked.

"We made minor repairs, but it will eventually need a new one. I can't do much about that."

As they reached the top of the stairs, she showed him each room, one by one, unable to keep the pride from her voice. "I really loved figuring out how to fix these rooms."

"You did this?" he asked.

"Well, I didn't physically paint them or remove pieces that didn't work. I gave the workmen those tasks. But I did make sure each room flowed, yet was unique as well. And I ordered all the new bedding."

"This is incredible, April."

"You really like it?"

He nodded. "You said you could transform the rooms, and you did it."

"Thank you." Her heart swelled from Risk's praise.

"Is there anything else you want to show me?"

"No, I think we've seen everything."

"So the business part of our day is over?"

"Y-yes, I suppose."

"Good, because I've been dying to do this all day." He tugged her into his arms, his hands wrapping smoothly around her waist as he lowered his mouth over hers and touched her lips. She felt his intensity even as he struggled to keep things tender and light. But with Risk, there didn't seem to be a middle ground. He was too passionate a guy to hold back, and it was a big, big turn-on knowing he was so attracted to her.

She roped her arms around his neck and fell into the kiss. Parting her lips, she invited him in, and he swept through her mouth, causing heat to build and little sounds to emerge from deep in her throat. She could get lost in him and she warned herself to slow down, to not fall for him again. But she was scared silly it was too late.

When he ended the kiss first, both surprise and relief swamped her. He backed off, frowning as he glanced at his watch. "Shoot. We've got a long drive back to town, and I have an appointment at four today. If we don't stop now, we may never get out of here."

"You mean I would be stuck in here with you all day?" She batted her eyelashes.

"Yeah," he said, scrubbing his jaw and eyeing her. "On second thought, screw the appointment. Where were we?" He made a move toward her, and she immediately backed off.

"Not so fast, Romeo. I have work waiting for me, too."

"How about a late dinner then?"

"Sounds...perfect."

* * *

The next morning, April sat at her desk, going over the books quietly, disappointed she hadn't seen Risk last night. He'd sent her a text apologizing for his meeting going longer than he'd anticipated. The apology went a long way in making her feel better about her relationship with him, whatever that was.

Yet she was worried that Risk wasn't overly impressed with the lodge. She'd done all she could possibly do to make the place appealing. He'd been pretty quiet about it, praising her work but not really committing to the sale in any way. The little devil in her head thought he was stringing her along, but she refused to believe it.

Ten minutes later, she wasn't so sure of anything when Shannon Wilkes walked into the agency, a big satisfied grin on her face. "Hello, April. Hope it's okay that I'm here?"

April craned her neck to check outside the front window. "Did you bring your entourage?" Meaning, did she alert the press she was coming here?

"Gosh, I hope not. I have good news to share with you."

The best news would be she was leaving town. "What's that?"

"I went to see the Russos and made another offer on the house."

"You did what?" April wanted to jump out of her seat.

"I offered Tony Russo more money, and he said he couldn't afford *not* to take it. Anyway, looks like you and I are going to be neighbors."

"Shannon, you can't do that."

"Why not? It's not as if you had his listing or anything. He's agreed to sell me his house, and of course, I'll let you do the transaction. An easy commission for you."

"That's not how it's usually done."

"Yes, but we'll make it work, won't we?" Shannon flipped her long auburn hair to one side and gave her a sugary smile.

She had nerve. Barging into April's life like this, plotting to steal away her fiancé, fake as he was. "I'm gonna have to think about it, Shannon."

"Don't think too long. You need this sale. Last night when I spoke with Risk, he didn't sound like he was going to buy the lodge for the company. He made it seem—"

"You spoke with him last night?" When he was too busy to call her, too busy to have dinner with her? And he'd confided in Shannon about the lodge when he hadn't given April the courtesy of his answer.

"Yes, yes, I did. I'm in negotiations for a new project, and I needed Risk's advice."

"What does Risk know about making movies?" she asked casually while her stomach knotted up.

"Not much, but he knows me. He's the one who said I should slow down, take time for myself. He's been a good friend since my mama passed."

She could almost feel sorry for Shannon. Almost.

April glanced at her watch. "Shannon, I'm afraid I have an appointment with a potential client. Maybe we can speak about this later." Much later.

Shannon gave her a smug smile. "Of course. I'll be going. But please don't wait too long. I'm anxious to become Boone Springs' newest resident."

April forced a smile and watched the superstar leave, striding down the street like a princess.

While April felt anything but.

Ten minutes later, April stood at the reception desk at Boone Inc. "I'm April Adams. I'm here to see my fiancé, Risk Boone," she told the receptionist.

The woman came right to attention. "Of course, Miss Adams. Let me check if he's available." She picked up the phone.

"I'm available anytime for my fiancée," Risk said, striding out of a conference room. He had a big smile on his face. "April, sweetheart," he said, ready to kiss her. She gave him her cheek, and he eyed her before giving her a peck.

"Mr. Boone, I was just going to check if your meeting was over."

"Thanks, Dorothy. We just finished up and I spotted this beautiful lady waiting for me."

Again, he smiled at April, but she couldn't return the gesture. His brows furrowed, and he looked puzzled by her appearance here and her cold greeting. Good. She wasn't going to hide her head in the sand anymore. It was about time she stood up for herself.

"Is there someplace we can talk?"

"Sure, sweetheart," he said, lowering his hand to her back. "Dorothy, no calls, please."

"Of course, Mr. Boone."

He guided her down the hall to his office. It was a sprawling ground-floor room with a wet bar, a massive desk and a suede sofa. There were photos of the Boone family when they were younger, black-and-white photos of his ancestors and awards and company logos on the wall. A bronze bust of his great-great-grandfather Tobias Boone occupied a stand in the corner of the room. She'd seen photos of that bust in various Boone holdings around town.

The austere room didn't seem to suit Risk, or at least that was the impression she got.

"This is a nice surprise," he said, taking her hands and tugging her into his arms. He kissed her lightly on the lips, and she immediately pulled away.

He frowned. "April, what's going on?"

"I got a *nice* surprise this morning, too. Shannon stopped by the office. Did you tell her you weren't going to buy the lodge for the company?"

"What?"

"You heard me." She gave him the point of her chin.

"I'm not sure I did."

"Did you tell Shannon you had no intention of buying the property?"

He blinked several times, unable to mask his irritation. "Hell, no. I wouldn't confide in her about that. All I said to her was that I've got a lot on my mind lately with Founder's Day tomorrow and all. I can't make a decision without discussing it with my brothers. It's none of her business, and I told her that, too, as gently as I could."

April's temper cooled a bit. "So, you haven't made a decision yet?"

He shook his head, his eyes softening on her. "No. And when I do, you'll be the first to know. You're gonna have to trust me, April."

That was just it. She didn't know if she could truly trust him. Even though Shannon stretched the truth as far as it would go, April had believed her instead of giving Risk the benefit of the doubt. Despite his claims to the contrary, Risk might still have feelings for Shannon. Just a little while ago, she would've said the two deserved each other, but now she was torn, her emotions all mixed up.

Risk gazed deep into her eyes. "And for the record, I missed you like crazy last night."

Her heart melted a little bit. She'd missed him, too.

But somehow those words wouldn't come.

The next afternoon, April, Clovie and Jenna stood on the sidelines of the Boone Springs High School football field, where hundreds of families had gathered for the Founder's Day festivities. Carnival games were set up in each end zone, everything from ping-pong toss to balloon darts.

Risk, Mason and Luke all took turns at a podium set up on the fifty-yard line, urging everyone to enjoy the day.

Sizzling-hot grills were filled with burgers and chicken and ribs from vendors who'd donated to the celebration. People lined up for soft-serve ice cream and cupcakes provided by Katie's Kupcakes. There was a sense of community and pride everywhere you looked.

April watched Risk and his brothers interact with the kids running relay races. Every once in a while, he'd look her way, and their eyes would meet. There was no doubt she had strong feelings for him, but she was taking it slowly. Their official charade would be over tonight after the Founder's Day Gala and so far Risk hadn't mentioned ending their relationship or continuing with it. Both notions made her queasy.

"C'mon, April. Let's grab some junk food before your fiancé whisks you away," Clovie said.

"He won't. He knows I want to spend time with you guys today."

"That's right, you two have a hot date tonight."

"Yeah, and I can't wait for you to get all blinged up," Jenna said. "Once Risk sees you in that gorgeous dress, it'll be like, *Shannon who*?"

"Shh." April lowered her voice, looking around. "You never know who's listening."

Clovie rolled her eyes. "At least Shannon's not here. This isn't her thing, I presume."

"I wouldn't think so." April was glad about that. One less bullet to dodge, since there were plenty of journalists here today reporting on the hundred-year-old town and the Boone legacy.

"So what'll it be, girls?" Jenna asked. "Ice cream, cup-cakes or caramel apples?"

"Ice cream," April said, and the others agreed.

As they walked across the field to the ice cream stand, Risk sidled up next to her, keeping stride. "How's it going, ladies?"

He spoke to all of them, but April felt his presence surround her, his overwhelming appeal kicking her in the gut. He seemed carefree, letting loose, his smile a thousand megawatts strong. He wore his jeans well, and a white T-shirt hugged his chest and biceps. His hair was wild from racing with the kids, dark strands falling into his eyes. He was breathtaking. Masculine. Sexy.

"We're having fun," Clovie said.

"We're going for ice cream and then maybe a cupcake," Jenna said. "You know, health food."

Risk chuckled, white teeth flashing in contrast with his tan skin. Even Jenna, who had not been Risk's biggest fan, was affected, judging by her friend's big smile. "That's what the day is all about."

Then he turned to her. "April, can I steal you for a few seconds?"

Her friends nodded. "We'll meet up with you in a few. I'll get your favorite," Clovie said, and April held back as her friends got in line for ice cream.

"Hi," he said, putting his hands in his back pockets. He looked like rodeo Risk now, disheveled and, well, comfortable.

"Hi."

He smiled, and she smiled back, her heart racing a hundred miles an hour.

"I, uh, just wanted to let you know, I'll pick you up at seven tonight."

"Okay. Are you excited? It's a big deal for your family and all."

His lips twitched. "Fact is, I'm looking forward to being with you, April." The sincerity in his voice nearly did her in.

"M-me, too."

"Oh yeah?" Then he leaned in and planted a delicious kiss on her mouth. One she wouldn't shy away from, one she'd been craving. As much as she wanted to spend time with her friends, she missed him. For the first time since this charade had started, she didn't mind him showing her affection in public. He dazzled her with that kiss. After he walked off, she watched him until he vanished into the crowd.

"Wow," Clovie said, handing her a chocolate chunk brownie ice cream cone as she and Jenna returned. "You are in freakin' love with him, April."

"Totally," Jenna said. "I mean, I get it. He is pretty dreamy."

April sighed and took a bite of her ice cream.

Her favorite flavor didn't taste nearly as good as Risk had, but then, chocolate chunk brownie ice cream would never disappoint her. And she had to remember that.

That evening, April walked into the Baron Hotel ballroom on Risk's arm, wearing a floor-length sapphire-blue gown. The dress was simple and elegant, showcasing her curves. She was a little self-conscious at how low the folds of material draped in the back, but Jenna had convinced her this was the perfect dress for her, and the shade made her sky-blue eyes really pop. She'd also tamed her curls a bit, giving her more of a sophisticated look.

Risk, in an ink-black tux and newly grown beard, gave new meaning to dangerous and gorgeous.

Luke, Mason, Drea, Lottie and Drew were already at

the long head table. His family greeted them with smiles and hugs, and the warmth in their eyes hit home. They welcomed her as if she was really part of the family. Her stomach twisted up tight; she was on shaky ground. She had no idea what would happen after tonight. This was her last official duty as Risk's fake fiancée.

She put her sequined clutch down and looked around the ballroom filled with a hundred and fifty of the most prominent people in Boone Springs: landowners, ranchers, bankers and businessmen and women. They were all here because Tobias Boone had a vision. He'd developed that vision into a town that had grown and prospered. Now the Boones were not merely wealthy, but a source of inspiration to the folks who lived here.

"Mr. Boone, can we have a few photos of you with your new fiancée?" a reporter asked. Gosh, didn't they have enough already? April had been photographed more these past ten days than she had in her entire lifetime.

"Sure," Risk said, snaking his arm around her back, the heat of his hand sizzling her bare skin. April plastered on a smile and posed for the camera. Others in the room took out their cell phones and began snapping pictures of them, too.

The orchestra on stage began playing, the tunes light and easy.

"I think that's enough for now," Risk told the journalist. "It's time for a dance with this beautiful lady." Risk led her onto the dance floor. "How are you holding up?" he asked, whispering in her ear.

"About as well as can be expected."

He smiled and swung her into his arms. "It'll all be over soon."

April didn't know how to take that exactly, so she kept quiet as Risk whisked her around the dance floor, his hands firm and possessive on her back. "Have I told you how much I like you in this dress?"

"Only three times."

"The night's not over yet." He grinned, bringing her closer, pressing a little kiss to her forehead. Risk could be charming and funny and nice, and tonight he was all three.

Thirty minutes later, as dinner was being served and all the guests were seated, there was a commotion at the front doors of the ballroom. April couldn't see what was happening, but she heard Lottie sigh loudly. "Oh no."

Then a sea of paparazzi parted, and Shannon Wilkes appeared, making a grand entrance, reporters following behind her like trained puppy dogs. April could see her clearly now.

Shannon looked stunning.

She wore a slinky black off-the-shoulder gown with horizontal slits running up and down the sides of the dress, showing off creamy skin and her incredible figure. Her auburn hair was in an updo that defined chic and fabulous, a delicate tiara on top of her head catching chandelier light. Her smile dazzled as she made her way to her seat at the front of the room. Five men rose quickly, each vying to pull out her chair.

April turned her head to catch Risk's reaction. He stared at Shannon, taking a big swallow, and when the superstar spotted him, she acknowledged him with a coy smile and a little wave.

Risk gave her a nod then sipped his wine, and April got a sick feeling in the pit of her stomach.

"I don't know why you invited her," his aunt Lottie mumbled.

Risk rubbed the side of his face. "It's no big deal, Aunt Lottie."

For whom? April wanted to ask. His family surely didn't want her here. And he had to know how awkward this would be for her, having her fiancé's ex showing up on such an important day. She feared Shannon was Risk's Achilles' heel. He had trouble saying no to the woman.

"I couldn't uninvite her," he told April.

"I…guess not." Besides, April wasn't his real fiancée, so what did it matter? "And like you said, it'll all be over tonight," she said quietly.

Risk snapped his eyes to her, and she stared back at him. She was simply repeating the words he'd spoken to her earlier.

"April." Risk took her hand, and his tender touch caressed her heart. "Let's talk about this later. Right now, I'd love us to simply enjoy the evening."

There was a plea in his voice and a sincere look in his eyes. What could she do? It was his family's big night, and they were in the spotlight now. "I'm all for enjoying the evening."

He smiled and squeezed her hand. "Me, too."

After dinner, Risk took the podium welcoming everyone and thanking them for honoring Tobias Boone and the other Boones who'd come after him. He praised his ancestors, speaking a little about each one individually, and then turned his focus to the folks in the room who'd made contributions to the town by way of enterprise and service. It was a dynamic and often emotional speech that brought applause and tears and laughter.

Risk looked over toward his family table. "And now, I'd like to invite my entire family up here for a toast."

Luke took Aunt Lottie's arm and escorted her to the podium, while April hung back. But Drea approached her. "This means you, too, April."

April met Drea's eyes, silently communicating her resistance, but Drea wasn't having any of it. "The Boone fiancées are invited. If I go, you go." She smiled.

April had no choice. All eyes were on the family, so she rose from her seat. Risk met her halfway, taking her hand and bringing her to stand beside him. The entire family raised their flutes of champagne, and Risk asked the rest of the guests to join in.

"To our ancestors, our friends and neighbors, and especially our loved ones, here's to another hundred years of prosperity for Boone Springs."

Risk touched his glass to hers, and their eyes met. His were gleaming with pride. Risk had it all. He seemed genuinely happy, and that happiness rubbed off on her. She was living in the moment with Risk, not knowing what was going on inside his head, where this would lead, but he'd been right. They should enjoy the evening, and as the orchestra began playing, she went willingly into his arms.

It felt so right, so wonderful having Risk guide her along the dance floor. "It was a beautiful speech, Risk." She was touched by his sincerity, his gratitude to the townsfolk, his strong sense of family.

"Not too mushy?"

"No, it was spoken from the heart."

"Thank you." She laid her head against his shoulder and snuggled in, her body fitting with his perfectly. She liked dancing with him this way, as if there were no one else in the room. These past few days she'd felt a shift in their relationship, a deep mutual desire, but even more, they seemed to really like each other. Considering they'd run the gamut of emotions from hatred and resentment to fury and heartache, that was saying something.

Three dances later, she was floating on cloud nine, Risk sneaking in brief kisses as they flowed to the music. Then

he sighed, regret dulling his dark eyes. "I should probably mingle with the guests," he said grudgingly. "Will
you join me?"

She hated to break the connection. She hated to share
him with anyone, but he had a job to do tonight, and she
understood that. "In a few minutes, after I use the ladies'
room."

"Okay, I'll see you soon." As she moved away, he held
on to her hand, his fingers brushing over hers until the contact was finally broken and they stared into each other's
eyes. It was poignant and real.

And then photographers were there, catching their special moment. Risk didn't blink—he didn't seem fazed by
the cameras. Had he known they were there, waiting to
snap pictures? Was that the reason he'd been so attentive
to her?

April made her way into the hallway and ran into Lottie and Drew. They didn't look too happy with each other.
"Excuse me," she said politely.

"April, you're just the one to settle this." Drew gestured
for her to come closer, and she took some tentative steps
toward them.

"Please tell Lottie what a fool thing she did by chasing
after that dog. She could've been killed right there on the
street. And she put you in danger."

April looked at Lottie's face, which was hot with color.
"I'm sorry about that," she told April.

"I'm fine, really, Lottie. No harm done." She didn't want
to get in the middle of this, but Drew was blocking the way
and Lottie seemed upset.

Drew sighed. "I held my tongue at your birthday celebration, but I can't keep it in any longer. When are you
going to start acting your age, Lottie?"

"And when are you going to stop acting older than yours? I swear, Drew, sometimes you're no fun."

"I'm no fun because I don't want to see you get crushed on the street? What in hell were you thinking, woman?"

"Don't you dare cuss at me, Drew."

Drew's veins popped out of his neck. "Good Lord, Lottie, I wasn't cussing at you, just the stupid things you do."

Tears welled in Lottie's eyes. "Now I'm stupid."

Drew looked at April, completely at a loss. He tossed up his arms. "I give up."

With that, he turned around and walked off, leaving the two of them in the hallway.

"Stubborn man," Lottie muttered then broke down in tears.

April wrapped her arm around Lottie's shoulder and walked her to the ladies' room. "He's acting that way because he cares about you."

April grabbed tissues from the restroom countertop and sat Lottie down on a settee. "Here you go." She handed her a tissue then sat beside her. Luckily, they had the room to themselves.

Lottie dabbed at her tears, catching her breath quickly. "Sorry, I usually don't break down like that, but that man frustrates me. He's trying to change who I am."

"I know it seems that way, but remember he's a widower. He's already lost a wife, and I don't think he wants to lose you, Lottie. Maybe that's why he's reacting that way."

"We've always butted heads. Ever since we were young."

"I'd heard that. Lottie, I really think his intentions were good. I'm pretty sure he wasn't cussing at you, and I know, just by the way Drew looks at you, he doesn't think you're at all stupid."

Lottie's eyes warmed a bit, but a bittersweet expression

stole over her face. "Sometimes…sometimes it's just too hard. Sometimes being with someone you care about is harder than not being with them."

April saw the wisdom in that, but she hated to see Lottie and Drew miss their chance at love.

Eleven

Risk and his brothers took turns dropping by the tables, shaking hands, making small talk. He'd spoken to Shannon briefly. After her big entrance into the ballroom, things seemed to settle down with her. The paparazzi were dismissed, and the Boone security team made sure they were off the premises.

As he made his way toward the head table via the dance floor, he searched the room, looking for signs of April. Where in hell was she? It seemed like she'd been gone a long time.

Music started playing after a short break, and someone grabbed his arm from behind. He smiled. "April, where—" But as he pivoted on the empty dance floor, he stared into Shannon's big green eyes.

"Risk, I'd love one dance with you before I leave the party." Risk hesitated, finding several guests watching them. "I'm sure April wouldn't mind one dance."

There was a plea in her voice, hopeful expectation on her face. He couldn't refuse her without looking like a heel. "I, uh, sure thing."

Risk kept her at arm's length as they danced to a slow

tune. As soon as he looked out and saw cell phone cameras flash, he knew this was a bad idea. How had things gotten so damn complicated? He had an ex and a fake fiancée keeping him on his toes tonight.

"This reminds me of old times," Shannon said, her eyes gleaming. "Remember when we went to Barbados and we danced on the beach most of the night?"

"Yeah, I remember."

"We had good times," she said, inching a bit closer.

They did, before their relationship started to crumble. Shannon had a selective memory at times, and Risk hadn't forgotten the hurt and pain of their breakup.

"That was a long time ago."

"Not that long ago, Risk." Then she gripped her stomach and scowled. "Oh no. This is not good."

They came to a stop in the middle of the crowded dance floor. "What's not good?"

"My stomach's been acting up lately. With Mama's death and all, I haven't been—" Her lips tightened, and color drained from her face. "Risk, I'm not feeling well."

"Shannon, do you want to sit down?"

She shook her head and squeezed her eyes shut. "No. I'd better go up to my room."

"I can call a doctor for you," he said, feeling her body waver. He gripped her arm to hold her upright.

"No, I think I need to lie down. I'll just go up to my suite. Thanks anyway." She gave him a small forced smile, her hand still on her stomach. "Have a good rest of the evening."

She turned from him and bumped into a woman on the dance floor, the jolt knocking Shannon off balance. Risk saw her going down and grabbed her upper arms before she fell. The woman, whom Risk recognized as the principal of Boone Springs High School, apologized immediately.

"I'm so sorry. I didn't see you there, Miss Wilkes." Jodie Bridgewater's eyes filled with concern.

"It wasn't your fault, don't feel sorry. I'm uh, oh wow. My head's spinning now."

Risk held her steady. "I'll walk you to your room, Shannon."

"Not necessary," she said. "You don't need to leave your party."

"Oh, I think he should," the principal suggested, and her dance partner nodded in agreement.

Risk sighed. "You're in no shape to walk up to your room by yourself, Shannon."

She looked at him then and nodded. "Okay, maybe you're right."

Risk took her arm and slowly led her out of the ballroom. As they approached the grand staircase leading to the second floor, he stopped. "Stairs or elevator?" he asked. The elevator was located farther away around the back end of the lobby.

"I think I can manage the stairs, Risk, with you beside me."

So they climbed the stairs, Shannon leaning against him until they reached her suite. She opened the door, and Risk put his hands in his pockets. "Well, I guess this is good-night, Shannon. I hope you feel better. But if you don't, call a doctor."

"Oh, Risk. Please come in for a minute. There's something I want to tell you."

He hesitated, glancing up and down the hallway.

"It's important," she added.

He inhaled a sharp breath. "Only for a minute. I really should get back." To April. He wanted more time with her tonight. He wanted…a lot of things with April.

He stepped inside, and Shannon closed the door behind them. "Don't you want to lie down?" he asked.

"Uh, yes, a little later. Come sit with me a second." She took a seat on the sofa in the living room of the suite and waited for him.

He sat in a chair and eyed Shannon carefully. What was she up to? "How are you feeling now?"

"Better now that you're here." She smiled, and color rose in her cheeks.

"Shannon, what's going on?"

"I'm buying a place here in Boone Springs. I've, uh, made a deal with Tony Russo. He's agreed to sell me his house…our little farmhouse, Risk."

He stood up, his ears burning. "Shannon, what in the world?"

"Just listen, Risk. Mama told me time and time again, I was a fool to let you go. It took me a while, but I see that now. We belong together." She had no trouble rising from the sofa and walking straight over to him. "I miss you, Risk."

"Is that what this is all about?"

"I see you with April, and it's obvious she's not right for you. There's something up with you two, and I haven't quite figured it out yet. But I know she won't make you happy. I know when a guy is truly in love, he tells the whole world, but when you came to visit Mama before she died and then after her death, you didn't say a word about April or your engagement. That got me to thinking—"

"Shannon, you're not really sick, are you?"

She nibbled on her lip, giving him an innocent look, one he used to think was adorable. She shook her head.

"Well, you're a better actress than I thought. And for the record, April is an amazing woman. She's my fiancée, and we're completely right for each other. I love her… very much."

As soon as he said the words, it dawned on him he wasn't

lying or making excuses. He really did love April. And as soon as he could, he wanted to make this fake engagement real. His feelings for her were so powerful he could hardly believe it. As much as he hated the way Shannon had lured him up here, he couldn't be angry, because now he knew exactly what he wanted.

"You can't possibly love her the way you loved me."

"Shannon," he said gently. "What we had is over. It has been for a long time. Face it and move on with your wonderful, fabulous life. I mean that."

"But, Risk, you—"

"Good night, Shannon."

Risk left her room, anxious to find the woman he loved.

April stood with Lottie at the back corner of the ballroom. They'd had a good talk in the ladies' room, yet Lottie wasn't quite ready to mingle again. She needed a few more minutes, and April didn't mind staying with her. April had helped console her after her big blowup with Drew; not that she was an expert on men, but she was a good listener and Lottie seemed to appreciate it.

From where she stood, April scanned the room looking for Risk. She missed him and couldn't wait to resume their evening. As soon as she spotted him on the dance floor, she gasped, and her heart instantly plummeted. Risk held Shannon in his arms as they danced to a love song. The two of them were a striking pair: Shannon a princess, tiara and all, and Risk looking like a roguish prince. It sure hadn't taken Risk long to replace her as his dance partner. She looked away, her pulse racing, dread entering the pit of her stomach. These awful sensations weren't new—they were the same old feelings of not being enough, of being abandoned. She was tired of allowing people to let her down. She wanted no part of it anymore.

When she regained the courage to look again, Risk and Shannon were walking out of the big ballroom double doors arm in arm. "Excuse me a second, Lottie," she said.

She strode out of the ballroom just in time to catch Risk climbing the grand staircase with Shannon, her head leaning on Risk's broad shoulders. April's whole body shook as she watched him reach the top of the staircase and head down a hallway leading to the suites.

She'd seen enough. Risk was involved with Shannon. She was still in his life, which left April with nothing more than the clock ticking away on a fake engagement.

It took her a second to realize Lottie had come up beside her. "It may not be as bad as it looks."

"It looks pretty bad, Lottie." Tears welled in April's eyes, which made her even more angry, more hurt. She didn't want to cry over Risk. Ever. Again.

"It's time for me to end this charade once and for all." Her bravado concealed the pain that was beginning to burn its way through her body. Goodness, what a fool she'd been. But it was better being a fool than a rat.

Which was what Risk Boone was being to her right now.

An hour later, Risk pounded on her door for the third time. She knew it was Risk because he was calling her name and knocking loud enough to wake the dead.

"April. Open the door. I need to talk to you."

She held a washcloth to her face, cooling her eyes that burned from the tears she'd promised herself she wouldn't shed. But as soon as she'd gotten home and undressed, her tears had flowed like an open faucet. "Please just go away, Risk."

"No. I'm not going away. Not until you hear me out. I mean it, April. I'm stubborn enough to wait all night."

She yanked the door open and faced him. Risk seemed surprised, and then relief shone in his eyes. "Thank you."

"Say what you need to say, Risk."

"You're not letting me in?"

"No." She pulled her robe tight and folded her arms around her body.

He sighed deeply. "Okay, fine. Aunt Lottie said you were very upset tonight."

"Obviously."

"Why?"

"No way, Risk. I'm not answering your questions."

He rubbed at his jaw. "If this is about Shannon, I can explain."

She rolled her eyes. "It's not about Shannon. It's about me. And what I want in life. And how I deserve to be treated."

"Okay, look, I admit I've made mistakes. And I'm sorry about that."

"It doesn't matter anymore, Risk. We're done. I owned up to my part of the bargain. You can do whatever you want now, with whomever you want. The charade is over. Thank God."

He stared at her a long time. "You don't mean that. April, what we have—"

"Is nothing." She put up her left hand and showed him her bare finger. "I've already given Jenna back the ring." She wiggled her fingers. "See, nothing there."

"You won't even hear me out?" He gritted his teeth.

"You know, your aunt said something profound tonight. And it hit home. She said sometimes being with someone you care about is harder than not being with them. Sometimes it's just too hard. That makes a lot of sense when it comes to the two of us. Let it go, Risk. Let *me* go," she pleaded.

His jaw twitched. "Is that what you really want?"

She nodded, unable to voice the words.

Risk closed his eyes briefly, and when he reopened them, moisture pooled there. "Okay."

She was touched by the tears in his eyes, but she held firm. The two of them were not meant to be. They'd tried and failed too many times. "Goodbye, Risk."

"'Bye, April," he said quietly.

April shut the door on him, and immediately a new stream of tears began to flow down her cheeks.

Risk sat in his office, going over figures from the latest Boone acquisition. The figures weren't adding up. He'd been at it for two hours. This job wasn't for him. It never had been, and it was time he owned up to that. He wasn't a nine-to-fiver like his brothers. They poured their hearts into the business. But it never had held that kind of appeal for him.

He pushed away from his desk, giving up. He wasn't going to get any work done today anyway. It'd been three days since he'd spoken to April, three days of not hearing her voice, not seeing her sweet smile, not looking into her crystal-blue eyes.

April wouldn't take his calls, wouldn't answer his texts. She was shutting him out, and it was taking its toll on him. He couldn't concentrate on work; he was having trouble sleeping.

Deep in thought, he didn't hear Mason walk into his office. "Man, you look like hell."

He didn't have a comeback for his brother. "I know."

"April?"

He nodded. "She won't talk to me. I don't know what to do."

"You love her?"

He nodded. "More than anything."

"Have you told her?"

He shook his head. "She hasn't given me the chance. I doubt she'd believe me now. I don't think she has much faith in me."

"I think she does, or wants to. According to Aunt Lottie, April's looking about like you these days."

"Miserable?"

He nodded. "Miserable."

"Yeah?" He hurt inside thinking of April feeling bad, but that little shred of hope put a smile on his face.

His brother put a hand on his shoulder. "You're not gonna let that girl go, are you?"

"I don't want to. I can hardly think straight without her. But I can't barge in on her and demand that she love me back."

"Maybe you don't have to. Maybe you can find a way for her to come to you. That's what I did with Drea, and it worked. Remember? She was leaving town and I had to think fast on my feet. I couldn't bear the thought of her leaving Boone Springs and me."

"Drew helped you with that."

"He led her to me and believe me, she wasn't happy about it. I hijacked her to get her to hear me out. It took some convincing on my part, but it was well worth it."

Risk scratched his head. "I don't know. How am I supposed to make April come to me? She won't answer my calls."

"Think outside the box, Risk. You're a smart guy—you'll come up with something."

April rushed into her office at half past ten, her body achy, her head fuzzy. "Clovie, I'm so sorry I'm late. Thanks for holding down the fort. You're the best."

Clovie gave her a sympathetic smile. "It's no problem. Didn't get any sleep again last night?"

She shook her head. "I think I finally dozed off at five this morning."

"Your internal clock is out of whack."

"It's like I have jet lag." She shook her head to clear out the fuzz.

"More like you have Risk lag."

April sighed. "I don't want to talk about him, Clovie." Every time she thought about Risk, her stomach would ache, her head would hurt. He'd been good about letting her go that night, but ever since then, he'd called her five times a day, texting her just as often. Yesterday, all of that stopped after Risk called Clovie, giving her the news that he wasn't interested in the lodge after all. He didn't think it was a good fit for the family business. He'd wanted to speak to April in person, but she hadn't been ready for that.

So the deal was dead.

Had Risk finally given up on her? She should be glad he wasn't calling her, wasn't making her doubt her decision about him, because a big part of her was still devastated at the way things had ended with him.

"Right, no Risk," Clovie said. "But I do have good news for you. I just got off the phone with a couple, a Mr. and Mrs. Rivers, who are very interested in Canyon Lake Lodge. They're from Willow County, and they heard about the lodge from news reports and taking the virtual tour on our website. They'd like to view the property. I checked your calendar and made an appointment for tomorrow morning at eleven. Is that okay?"

"Is that okay? That's the best news I've had in days. If they're serious about it, I can call Mr. Hall and ask him for an extension on the listing."

"I thought it would make you happy. I mean, it's not a

done deal, but the clients seemed excited about the lodge. And I know how badly we need this sale."

"It's great. Maybe we should get there earlier and check on things."

"We? Y-you want me to go with you?" Clovie rubbed her forehead.

"I'd like it if you'd come." The truth was, she'd need moral support, seeing that lodge again after what had happened between her and Risk. But Clovie didn't look too well all of a sudden. "What's wrong, Clovie?"

"I'm, uh, nothing much. Just have a little headache, and my throat feels a little dry."

"Oh no. I'm sorry. Your head is probably hurting from putting up with my moods lately, listening to me complain about everything."

"That's what friends are for, April. We only want what's best for each other, and I don't mind listening if it makes you feel better."

"Thanks, hon. That means a lot."

The next morning, April drove down the highway leading to Canyon Lake Lodge all by herself. Poor Clovie had called in sick, waking up with a sore throat and a monstrous cold. There was no way April would allow her to come. She missed Clovie's company, but she'd put on her big-girl panties this morning and bucked up.

Reaching the lodge fifteen minutes early would give her time to take one last look around before the potential clients arrived. This sale was big, and she needed it, but it didn't stop her from remembering all that had happened here. The joy and the heartache. But the sun shined bright today, the skies were clear, and it was a perfect day to paint a picture for her clients.

She sucked in a big breath and got out of her car. Ceramic pots filled with her favorite flowers, pink stargazer lilies, decorated the front porch. Dozens of flowers in every state of bloom brought new life to the entrance of the house. Where had they come from? Had the new clients brought them by? A gift from the landscapers?

The door creaked open, and she jumped back, shocked that someone else was on the grounds. She hadn't seen any other cars. Her heart began to race. The door opened wider, and she faced a man with deep-set dark eyes and a stubbly beard that made him look one hundred percent dangerous, yet he was wearing a charming smile.

"Risk, what the heck are you doing here?"

Risk winced at her tone. She didn't care; he'd scared her to death.

"April," he breathed out, looking her over from head to toe. "Man, I've missed you."

She couldn't let the sound of his voice, the tender look in his eyes, persuade her. "Risk, I have no idea why you're here, but you have to leave. I have clients coming any minute now."

She glanced down the long road, and when she turned back to him, he arched a brow, his dark gaze penetrating hers.

"I mean it, Risk, you have to go."

He kept his eyes trained on hers.

"Oh." She felt dread in the pit of her stomach. And something clicked in her head. She put two and two together. Mr. and Mrs. *Rivers*. As in River Boone, Risk's real name. What a dirty trick. She'd been set up. "There are no clients coming, are there?"

Again, he gave her a tender look and shook his head slowly.

"Clovie?" She couldn't believe her friend had set her up.

Where was her loyalty? "Wait until I get back to the office. I'm going to ream her out for this."

"It's not Clovie's fault. I talked her into this. She only wants what's best for you."

April gave her head a shake. "In that case, you want me to ream you out instead?"

"It'd be better than the silent treatment you've given me."

"It was well deserved." The sight of Risk here, despite his tactics, confused her. Dressed in dark jeans, a black Western snap-down shirt and dark boots, he seemed to fit here at the lodge. He wasn't a corporate suit but a man of the land. Gosh, he looked amazing, if not tired around the eyes. Was he having trouble sleeping, too?

Her resolve starting to melt, she sighed and talked herself out of any warm feelings for Risk.

She couldn't do this again. She couldn't let her feelings for him persuade her to change her mind. How many times would Risk burn her?

"I'm going," she said. She turned her back on him and began walking to her car.

"I thought you really needed this sale," Risk called out.

She stopped and pivoted around. "I got your message, Risk. You're not going to buy the lodge. Enough said."

He climbed down the steps and strode over to her. "What if I said that's not entirely true?"

His eyes were glowing now, the dark rims light and bright. "I don't understand."

"I didn't, either, April. Not until a few days ago. There's been something missing in my life, something that I couldn't put my finger on. And it took losing you to see clearly, to see what was staring me right in the face."

"What's that?" she asked quietly, mesmerized by the soft ray of hope in his eyes.

"This lodge is my calling. I have always loved a challenge, always sought something that I could accomplish that really excited me. I'm not buying the lodge for the company, I'm buying it for myself, April. It's a private venture. I want to run this place, open it up to fishing, boating and horseback riding. I want to make it a destination for the adventurous guest. I know horses, so I can do trail rides and teach roping and riding as well. I'll be sinking my own money into this."

"Really, this is what you want?" she said, nibbling on her lip.

"Yes, it's what I want. But I want something else even more. You, April. I can't imagine living my life without you in it." He took her hand, capturing her attention with the warmth in his eyes. "You're what's also been missing in my life, sweetheart."

"Because I'm a challenge?"

He laughed. "Because I love you with all of my heart. I've never loved this strong before. I've never been so sure of anything. We belong together."

April was floored. She was all set to walk away from Risk, to try to pick up the pieces of her life and move on, but that was never what she'd really wanted.

What she'd wanted for the longest time was the man standing in front of her. Not the celebrity, not the wealthy rancher, but the man behind all that. The kind, sweet man she knew him to be, deep down. "What about Shannon?" she had to ask.

"I pretty much told her to go home, that there was nothing for her in Boone Springs. We are over and have been for a long time, April. That's what I told her the night of the Founder's Day party. She's not going to buy the farmhouse. I went to see Tony Russo and learned the only reason he'd agreed to sell to her was because he'd recently lost his job."

"I didn't know that. I didn't know any of this, Risk."

"I offered Tony a job. Their family will be okay now."

April's eyes teared up. "That was sweet of you."

"Excuse me, did I hear you say I'm sweet?"

"I did," she said, lifting her hand to caress his stubbly cheek. "I love you, too, Risk."

He moved her hand to his mouth and kissed her palm. "I love you, April. You're the perfect girl for me. I swear, I'll never let you down." He tugged her into the lodge, and she stared at the most beautiful array of pink stargazer lilies she'd ever seen. They decorated every nook and cranny, every table, and adorned the steps leading up the staircase.

"It's beautiful, Risk. You remembered my favorite flowers."

"Of course. I pay attention when it comes to you." And then he grinned. "And our fake-fiancée list really helped."

She laughed as he guided her to the master suite. When they got there, she gazed at the embers burning in the fireplace, the silver bucket of champagne and two crystal flutes set out on a tray on the bed. This was a special place to her. She couldn't believe she was here with him and he was professing his love to her.

She turned to Risk with tears in her eyes.

"Don't cry, sweetheart."

He cradled her in his arms, his shoulders big and broad and safe.

And then he pulled away and knelt on bended knee.

Her hands went to her mouth, her gaze on the black velvet box Risk was opening. Inside was a shining square-cut diamond ring mounted on a pedestal of smaller diamonds.

"April," he began, "you've worn an engagement ring before, but it was all pretend. And the more time I spent with you, the more our fake engagement began to feel real. It scared me at first, because I was always the guy who wasn't going to get serious with a woman again. But then something changed, something shifted, and I realized that my fake fiancée was the love of my life. Maybe we've done this a little backward, but there's nothing backward about the way I feel about you. I'm crazy about you, and I promise to love you forever and ever. Will you do me the honor of becoming my wife?"

April's legs wobbled as she bent on both knees to meet him on the floor. "Yes, Risk. I'll be your wife, your partner and whatever else comes along."

She cupped his face and kissed him then, giving him her whole heart, no longer holding back, no longer worried about being hurt by him.

She trusted him.

And it was wonderfully liberating to finally admit her feelings, knowing they were returned.

When the kiss ended, Risk took her hand and placed the stunning ring on her finger. It sealed their love, and her heart soared.

"Thank you, April."

"For what, my love?"

"For helping me find my real place in life."

"The lodge?"

He shook his head and kissed her lips. "Loving you."

* * * * *

COMING SOON!

We really hope you enjoyed reading this book. If you're looking for more romance, be sure to head to the shops when new books are available on

Thursday 5th September

To see which titles are coming soon, please visit

millsandboon.co.uk/nextmonth

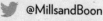

MILLS & BOON

HEROES

At Your Service

Experience all the excitement of a gripping thriller, with an intense romance at its heart. Resourceful, true-to-life women and strong, fearless men face danger and desire - a killer combination!

MILLS & BOON
MEDICAL
Pulse-Racing Passion

Set your pulse racing with dedicated, delectable doctors in the high-pressure world of medicine, where emotions run high and passion, comfort and love are the best medicine.

MILLS & BOON

HISTORICAL

Awaken the romance of the past

Escape with historical heroes from time gone by. Whether your passion is for wicked Regency Rakes, muscled Viking warriors or rugged Highlanders, indulge your fantasies and awaken the romance of the past.

JOIN US ON SOCIAL MEDIA!

Stay up to date with our latest releases, author
news and gossip, special offers and discounts, and
all the behind-the-scenes action
from Mills & Boon...

 millsandboon

 millsandboonuk

 millsandboon

It might just be true love...